£1-
I2

# The Mysterious Burnchester Hall

The Mysterious Burnchester Hall is the first part
of an evolving story

# The Mysterious Burnchester Hall

Dominic Miéville

DM
Productions

Published by DM PRODUCTIONS
PO Box 218 IP22 1QY United Kingdom

Copyright © 2003 Dominic Miéville

First printed October 2003
Second impression January 2004

The right of Dominic Miéville to be recognised as the author
of this work has been asserted in accordance with the Copyright, Designs and
Patents Act 1988

British Library Cataloguing in Publication Data
A Catalogue record of this book is available from
The British Library

ISBN 0 953 6161 2 6
ISBN 0 953 6161 3 4 (Adult cover version)

Cover illustration and typesetting by Luke Florio
Set in Palatino

Printed in Great Britain by
The St Edmundsbury Press Limited
Bury St Edmunds, Suffolk IP33 3TU

For Pamela and Sophie

not forgetting
Rosie, Milo, Barney, Casper, Jake and Ru

# I

It was only the third day of the holidays and Tyro was bored. It wasn't that she liked school, just that, well, parents asked you to do things. All she wanted was to sleep late, watch TV and, if the weather was fine, walk Rompy, the dog. Even now she was planning how to avoid going shopping with her mum, Abby.

"You've got lots to do," said Abby at breakfast. "Clean out the rabbit hutch, clean your room, tidy your desk, write that thank you letter, practise the piano, do some work even. We're not going shopping until you've done something useful," she added, "and certainly there will be no friends."

Tyro didn't answer. Though she didn't like her mother's sort of shopping she loved to shop for herself, and now at the age of eleven and two thirds she preferred to go off (even under her mum's guidance) with her best friend Jess and spend (rather dream of spending) money. But with no friends (and no money), the threat of going to the shop to buy dog food made her dream even of reading. Some books were alright, but she only believed a little bit in magic. Tyro had been given some homework over the summer holidays. She didn't like reading much. Why was it that the books they gave you at school to read were always so boring! Her report hadn't been that bad. It hadn't been that good either. In fact she felt rather ordinary. Others sensed her energy and insight.

"But Mum, it's the holidays," said Tyro, swallowing a piece of toast, "I think I'll go and tidy my room."

Abby looked up, surprised.

"I have to go to the shops before work. Are you going to come?"

"OK," said Tyro as she left the room.

"And by the way, the washing-up doesn't do itself!" Abby added. Tyro, who was a bit spoilt, being an only child, turned back and put the milk back in the fridge.

Tyro loved her mother very much, of course, but they were always arguing. Her mother was often very stressed. She had little help in the home which was far too big for them. She worked in the local hospital as a senior nurse which was enough to give anyone a breakdown. Her husband Jack had died in a tragic accident some years ago. The house had been theirs ("A dream home to bring up children in the countryside," he had said) and, for the sake of Tyro, Abby had decided to keep the old house on, so that Tyro could have some 'stability' until she was older. Abby half knew that the home was slightly magical, though she would never have admitted that to herself as a practical person. It was also a bit spooky. It was called the Old Hall and was next to the Church of All Saints.

As she climbed the stairs, Tyro was thinking how she could get out and see Jess. She wanted adventure. She wanted something to be able to talk about at school next term. Anything to stop the holidays getting boring.

Six whole weeks and she was getting edgy! Not a good start.

She would have her cousin Penny coming to stay in three weeks time, and they would be going to France (if they had the money) for a week but that was years away. Not having any brothers or sisters made things worse.

She entered her room, looked out of her window onto the garden below and put on some music. She sat down at her desk and opened her diary. She picked up a pen and began to write.

"Dear Diary, help me. I love my mum and I love my home, but I'm bored. What can I do?"

She looked at the cat, Biscuit, on the bed. The cat had been called Jacob, but one day he had eaten all the biscuits he could lay his claws on and then fell asleep for six hours. Abby and Tyro thought he was dead. But when, after considerable bouts of snoring, he raised his left paw and said "more please", they decided to change his name.

The diary didn't answer. She would phone Jess, then take Rompy for a walk. She crept out of the room and down the back stairs. It was useful having a secret way into and out of the house.

Abby was putting her coat on in her usual panic. She worried all the time, perhaps because she was artistic. About money, about her job (which she loved and hated at the same time), above all about Tyro, who she adored. What was God up to taking away Tyro's father like that? What could she do to make her life easier and give her daughter more time? She would *have* to sell the house, but she wanted to do her best to keep it on. Something else held her back. She tried to console herself by saying how lucky she was - so many people had much harder lives.

"Tyro!" she shouted up the stairs. "I'm going now. Are you coming, or not?"

As there was no answer, Abby walked out of the front door and got into the car.

As the car rolled along the weed-filled drive, Abby was beginning to sing to the radio, when suddenly a figure jumped out of the bushes to her right, led by a muddy Rompy with a tail wagging!

"So there you are! Hop in and we'll buy something nice."

"Mum" seemed to have forgotten the homework, the tidying of the room. So the car moved on, all three of them feeling better - Rompy loved to ride in it. They could see Bill by the far hedge and gave him a wave. He waved back. Thank heavens

3

for Bill, Abby thought. What would she do without him?

"What about ringing Jess?" said her mum, reading Tyro's mind (that was another problem). "She can help you with your reading too."

"I have, Mum" said Tyro. While she had been walking Rompy, she had had an idea. It was something to do with the way that Rompy had followed that scent. Wandering along in the long grass he had suddenly got agitated and stuck his nose hard to the ground. With a sudden growl he'd pounced. Tyro too was going to have a wonderful summer after all. She was going to follow her nose. She may not be very clever, but if she followed her nose, something was bound to happen. She had an idea. Just like Rompy had followed that scent. Instead of concentrating on the shopping, Tyro seemed preoccupied. The names of her friends were rolling around in her head. Who should she choose? Jess of course. Julia? Not Julia, she had been horrid to her at the end of last term, even though she lived nearby. Rick?

As they were about to leave, the crunch of a bicycle was heard on the drive.

"Jess!" said Abby, winding down the window, "we were just talking about you. Why don't you two stay here while I quickly go and get some things?"

"Hi!" said Jess, shyly.

Tyro gave her mum a hug and a kiss, and jumped out of the car.

"See you later, girls. Be good!"

"Jess!" screamed Tyro, running over to her as if she hadn't seen her for a month.

Jess was slightly taller than Tyro, with light brown hair. She was a few months younger. They had been friends since they were three. She lived in small house in the next village.

"Thanks, Mrs Wander," said the polite Jess before parking the bicycle under the porch.

"Bill's about if you need anything," added Abby as the car

pulled away, "or call me Tyro, or your mum, Jess. I'll see you both later. There's food in the fridge, if you're hungry."

Abby drove out of the drive. She felt sad and grateful at the same time. She wished she could be at home more to see her daughter grow up, especially in the holidays, which were, after all, supposed to be magical times. She wished she could cook them both a proper lunch. But they had a big garden in which they could roam and the air was fresh. And Bill was there to keep an eye on them. Bill was reliable, kind, discreet. He lived in the village and did odd jobs for Abby. He looked after the house and Tyro when she was out at work. He had felt it a duty ever since Jack had died. He had liked Jack and the family and felt attached to the house.

"What do you think?" asked Tyro excitedly, even before Jess had had a chance to sit on the bed in her room. "It came to me in a slow flash, as I was walking Rompy this morning."

"Who's ever heard of a slow flash? As for running away *to* school! Nobody's ever thought of running away *to* school," said Jess perceptively. "There are lots of books about unhappy children running away *from* school. But running away *to* school. I've got to say, Tyro, you're crazy!" she added, detecting Tyro's disappointment. She didn't want to tell her that going back to school in the holidays wasn't her idea of fun.

"It's not exactly running away, is it Jess? It's not very far. We can take the bikes and be back by the evening! Besides, I'd like to find out a little bit more about Mrs Limpet, after what happened last term. We could sneak into her room and sniff around."

"I thought holidays were about forgetting school. Besides, it's one thing to be driven every day during term. Another to cycle without a map," said Jess infuriatingly. "We might get lost."

Jess was a worrier, which is probably why she liked reading so much. But she knew that Tyro was a doer, which is also why they got on so well. So before Tyro could disagree, she added,

"We'll take Rompy. He'll go crazy! I'm sure he'll find rats creeping from under the kitchen floorboards!"

"It's a brilliant day! Let's go then!" said Tyro.

Tyro was surprised by Jess's sudden change of tone but didn't say anything. Jess, who was very clever, liked to analyse things and didn't often get very enthusiastic about anything.

"We'll have to ask Rick, of course," added Jess.

"We can call in on him on our way," said Tyro, taking charge again. She still thought that boys mostly messed things up, or got things wrong, but in Rick's case she was happy. He was OK. He lived with his miserable Aunt Patrolia, and she felt sorry for him. You couldn't go wrong with Rick. He was very loyal, though he might want to invite Tom. Already Tyro's plans were going sideways. But she couldn't control everything. So she shrugged her shoulders. She certainly wasn't going to comment on the fact that Jess fancied Rick! Not yet anyway. She didn't want a row on day three.

"Let's get going! Rompy!" shouted Tyro at the top of her voice. And then, with the voice of her mother ringing in her ears, she added, "after we've, er....tidied my room, and made a picnic."

*

It wasn't long before both the girls were on their bikes on the drive. On the back of one of them was what looked like a hamper. Bill was standing by the two girls. Rompy was sitting expectantly. If *they* were going to have an adventure, what was *he* going to have!

"You're got a lovely day for a ride," said Bill. "But keep off the main roads."

Though this was rural Suffolk, and the nearest main road was at least five miles away, that didn't always stop people from driving like mad animals.

"We will," said Tyro. "We'll be back by tea-time. We're only going for a picnic by the stream. Rompy! He's so excited. See you later, Bill!"

"Take care, girls. Bye!"

Tyro didn't like to lie but didn't want anyone to know where they were really going. Adults didn't always understand.

The girls rode off. Rompy, having given Bill a lick of the hand, was by the gate. He was happy to go on and hunt by himself but he thought he would go through the motions of letting them know that they were his masters! Rompy, like most dogs, knew how to handle his superiors! He had in fact been well trained, by Bill, and knew exactly when to sit and when to behave. But it was summer, and there was nothing wrong with a bit of enthusiasm. And there were rabbits to chase. And pheasants, and rats.

Jess went first, Tyro following with the hamper. As the girls went out of the gate Bill got back to finish the bit of weeding that he had started. Bill had never had the opportunities that these girls had, but he never felt envious. He loved his work. It gave him more satisfaction that anything he had done in the past. He hadn't always been a gardener. A few years ago, he had had an accident. He still had a slight limp.

Out on the road, the two girls rode side by side.

"Supposing Rick's out?"

"He won't be. He never goes away. The only problem will be getting him permission. You know what his aunt's like. I'll leave you to do the talking. You're the brainbox!"

Tyro said it affectionately. Jess's cheeks reddened.

Rompy was soon way ahead, running along the grass verge, his wagging tail visible and then gone. As they approached him, he would reappear, sit in military fashion and then, after the girls had passed, run on ahead of them again, in an endless game of lead, follow, lead. He was used to this as Tyro loved cycling. It was his way of keeping in touch, but doing his own thing.

They passed the farmhouse where Mr Granger, the local

7

farmer, lived - on the left and shortly after a few straggling houses on the edge of the village. It was in one of these that Bill lived.

Tyro was emptying her mind and letting the wind flow through her hair. Jess was still a bit anxious about going back to school. But soon her mind emptied too.

"What do you think, Jess?" asked Tyro.

"Weird," said Jess. "People would think we were mad if they knew where we were going. Do you think it will be OK? Supposing Gruff is there!"

"Of course it will. Everything will still be open and we can say we've got to get some books from the library. Besides, it'll be different. Like somewhere else."

Jess looked meaningfully at Tyro, trying not to lose her balance.

"OK. *You* can say you've got to get some books, *I'll* say I've left my trainers in the changing rooms and that I need them for choir practice. Chill out!"

Tyro was now beginning to relive school. She was having doubts.

"What about Mrs Limpet?"

Tyro had forgotten about Mrs Limpet.

"You're right. Perhaps we should go back," said Tyro, thinking of Mrs Limpet, the biology teacher. She and Mrs Limpet just didn't get on. Which was stupid as she liked biology.

Jess was wondering what Tyro meant by the school being like somewhere else. How could school be anything but a place smelling of dead cabbage, and stale disinfectant?

Fortunately their attention was suddenly taken by the sight of a huge tractor ahead of them as they were approaching a junction. The tractor was in the middle of the road, and so big that it nearly covered it. The tractor was standing still. A man was looking into the engine. It was Luke, one of Mr Granger's sons.

8

"What's up?" asked Tyro, as they pulled up.

"The engine's playing up a bit. He'll go in a minute," said Luke, continuing to peer into the engine.

"Can we go and get help or something?" asked Tyro.

"No problem! We'll be fine," said Luke, looking up. "Temporally-mental is Herbert. Doesn't like these late starts. Prefers to get out at dawn to get the job done."

Tyro and Jess were quite happy just watching for a moment. Rompy was nowhere to be seen. Jess looked at Tyro in amazement and mouthed the word "Herbert?", but not quite quietly enough.

"They've all got names," added Luke casually. "The tractors that is. We find they work better that way, though of course it does make them more human, more temporally-mental."

He gave the girls a big wink and got back in the cab. The engine fired up first time.

"Don't you mean temperamental?" asked Jess.

"Oh no," answered Luke, "that's quite different. He's not that human. I expect he wants his breakfast, though," added Luke. "See you."

With a huge roar the tractor rolled ahead and turned left. For a moment it looked more like a prehistoric animal snorting smoke.

"Who was that?"

"Old Mr Granger's son, Luke," said Tyro, as though nothing more need be said. "He's cool."

Jess was going to add that he was a bit strange but she decided against it, as she knew what Tyro's response would be.

"I'm beginning to be a bit hungry myself," said Tyro, thinking of the tuna sandwiches in the hamper.

"Let's wait till later. Till we're sitting at Mrs Limpet's desk!" said Jess.

She pulled out a bar of chocolate and broke some off, giving half to Tyro. Then she took a big bite.

They seemed to have forgotten their doubts.

The sun was shining, the air was warm, the church tower of St Rimpulent shone brightly through the leaves on the trees as they approached Greenfield, the next village. They could hear the purr of Herbert going along the road somewhere over there. They could see plumes of smoke above the hedge. The holidays were going to be good after all.

"Oh no! Rompy! Where's Rompy?"

Tyro looked all around. Rompy was nowhere to be seen.

"Calm down, Tyro!" said Jess. "He's always disappearing and coming back again." It was Jess's turn to do the reassuring.

"There he is!"

Rompy was doing some kind of dance in and out of a tuft of long grass, sometimes visible, sometimes not.

Suddenly, a rabbit shot out from behind him and raced across the road into the hedge opposite. Rompy continued to dance.

"I bet anything Rick's not there," Jess said. "I've got this feeling."

"He will be. He always is. It's his aunt we have to contend with, remember!"

Jess was right. When they got to Rick's house, a small cottage in the village of Greenfield, they parked their bikes against a hedge between the village shop and his aunt's house. The cottage was rather old and thatched.

Even Rompy had decided that Aunt Patrolia wasn't worth annoying. Last time he had managed to make the smooth lawn (her husband, Uncle John, kept it like a billiard table, under Aunt Patrolia's instructions) into a bombsite. If only that mole hadn't made one, just one molehill, and if only he hadn't decided to excavate. It hadn't been the size of Vesuvius but Aunt Patrolia's reaction was.

They could hear Aunt Patrolia's voice before they had reached the gate.

"Where is he then?" she was shouting.

John Grumble, Rick's uncle, was trying to calm his wife.

"I only asked him to get some bread," he was saying. "For his, er.... our, breakfast."

"But why didn't you ask me? I could have given him a list. You know he does my shopping on a Thursday morning! And what are you doing here?" Aunt Patrolia glared over her husband's shoulders.

"Hello girls," Uncle John said kindly, turning.

"We wondered if Rick was here, and if he could come with us for a picnic," Jess said slightly nervously. "Mrs Grumble," she added, as a polite afterthought.

"Don't you say good morning? What's happened to manners? He's not here, and he can't go out. He's got things to do. And don't let that dog of yours onto my lawn!"

Tyro had wisely put Rompy on the lead, and tied him to the gate. Rompy was doing his best to look like a well trained gun-dog, wishing that he could fetch Aunt Patrolia, and not any old pheasant. Uncle John was probably thinking the same, thought Rompy, by the way he was looking at his wife.

"We thought, as it was the holidays, it would be nice for Rick to come," added Jess.

"Holidays! More time to help me!" stormed Aunt Patrolia, leaving the girls and Uncle John together on the lawn.

"Don't worry girls, I'll tell him when he gets in - and he can come and join you. Patrolia is angry with me for not telling him to do all the shopping. She's always angry. Where are you going to be?"

"Er....well, we were going to be by the river, but we're not sure. Don't worry Mr Grumble," said Tyro, "we'll see him soon anyway. Perhaps he can come over tomorrow."

"And please tell Mrs Grumble that we'd be happy to do her shopping for her, anytime," added Jess, before Mr Grumble could answer.

She couldn't bear the thought of Rick having to suffer this every time the shopping needed to be done, even if she did sound a bit ingratiating.

Tyro tried not to stare at her but smiled as they turned to go.

"See you another time," said Mr Grumble, "and...." Mr Grumble was about to add something, but stopped short.

Rompy's tail began to wag, just a little, though it was only his head that could be seen through the gate.

"Yes, Mr Grumble?" said Tyro encouragingly.

"Nothing, er...," added Mr Grumble, "just wanted to wish you a good picnic. I used to picnic once....what summers are for. You'd better get going," he said.

Tyro stared at Jess. "We can't," she whispered, "not this time."

As they were riding out of the village, Jess turned to Tyro.

"I'd want to run away, if I were Rick, wouldn't you?"

"Yes," said Tyro.

Rompy trotted alongside the girls as they rode out of the village. Soon the sun began to shine again, and the summer air could be felt once more.

The road wound round to the left and then went into a slight dip where it crossed the river. This is where they were supposed to be having their picnic. The river ran eastwards to the sea.

Tyro suddenly stopped.

"What are you doing?" shouted Jess, as she swerved, before coming to a halt.

"Wait there!"

Tyro jumped off the bike and ran to the bridge. She looked about until she found a stick. She went to the edge of the bridge and looked down. Then she threw the stick far out into the river. The stick, looking more like a floating eel, sank and then resurfaced before beginning, very slowly, to come back towards Tyro with the current.

Jess had by now got off and found a stick of her own. She also threw it in. Even Rompy had got into the spirit and was searching for a stick in the undergrowth.

Jess and Tyro ran to the other side of the bridge and

watched, as the first stick came into view, followed in a little by Jess's.

"Why didn't we throw them in together?" asked Jess more in surprise than anger. "Look, mine's catching up!"

"Only an experiment, Jess... it's not Pooh Sticks. I just wanted to try something. You'll see. We're too old for Pooh Sticks."

"Don't tell me you're going to follow it to the sea," said Jess.

"No, just to the school," said Tyro.

Jess had forgotten that the river weaved its way along the edge of the school playing fields, further down river, though she was sure the sticks would have passed long before they got there. Of course they were too old to play Pooh Sticks. She was sorry she had mentioned it.

They got back on their bikes and rode on. Up the hill and with the wood on one side. A cow field on their left.

A very funny feeling came over them as they reached the top. The reality of coming back to school in the holidays was dawning on them. It seemed a crazy thing to do, something they had better keep quiet about. Tyro was beginning to think it was a bad idea, and would almost rather have been tidying her room. Jess was doing her best not to show her feelings at all.

The familiar signs that Tyro passed in Abby's car, during term - the villages they passed through; the old farm that seemed to be falling, through  disuse, into the pond by the roadside; the horse-field, from which horses crossed the road, holding up the traffic; the old gipsy man who lived in a caravan at the top of a small ridge by the road, with chickens living on his roof - made her think about the homework she had not done, and the arguments she had had with enemy Julia, and the sports clothes she had left behind, and the detention she had been given by Mrs Limpet. Jess was calmer, as few of these things ever happened to her. Nevertheless she too felt a little nervous. She preferred to keep school and holidays separate. Being a good pupil was not a reason for wanting to come back in the summer holidays.

Before either of them could finish their thoughts, let alone share them, they had come over the hill and taken the first small turning to the left.

There below them, in the still, broad valley of the river Dean, stood the school, Burnchester Hall, in all its splendour. A huge Elizabethan hall surrounded by buildings, teaching block, refectory, art room, the Headmaster's garden, changing rooms, the groundsman's cottage, sports fields. All of them came into view.

With the sun shining on the tall Elizabethan chimneys, it looked like a dream school. It was still some way off, but they could freewheel down the hill now, which they did, sticking their legs out in front of them as they went. The two girls rode side by side, the hamper just holding on.

Soon they came to the edge of the wood that ran on the other side of the road that led to the main entrance.

Soon they were cycling up to the front gates. They were too curious, too excited, too confused to notice that this time Rompy was nowhere to be seen.

They stood in front of the school gates, which were open invitingly.

# 2

Burnchester Hall had a chequered history. It had only become a school 51 years ago. It had been built by Sir Cheesepeake Lumsden, a courtier in the Elizabethan era (reputed to be a friend of Shakespeare), whose family had come from Warwickshire. Sir Cheesepeake had been given the land as a gift from the Queen, for services rendered to the crown. He had moved there with his family in 1597. He had three sons and two daughters, by the charming daughter of a local farmer, Rosemary Templedean, whose family had been responsible for the building of many of the finest churches in East Anglia, and were also sponsors of several religious houses. Descendants of the family had lived in the house until just before the Second World War. The last remaining daughter of the line had married unwisely, and the debts that her husband had accrued made the sale of the house a necessity, as their fortunes had crashed in the great depression of the 1930s.

The Hall remained empty for some years during which time its demolition was deemed possible. But the advent of the war gave it a new lease of life, when it was bought by the Ministry of Defence. Its extensive grounds, isolation, and history, made it ideal for a secret training camp for spies who were sent on covert missions into France, during the German occupation. Although many of the people who trained there had come from outside, many people who worked there were local, and they had been sworn to secrecy. This had meant that the rumours grew even more than under the Cheesepeakes. Regulars to the Burnchester Arms, the local pub, were even cagier than normal when any visitors arrived for a drink. They were not averse to helping the rumour mill along a little either. In this way the borderland between fact and fiction was even more blurred than usual.

The first Sir Cheesepeake was a lover of books and had made one important stipulation in his will. On no account should the library which he had acquired be sold. It should only be removed from the house in the event - Heaven forbid - of it being absolutely necessary for its survival. It should also be available to anybody who should ask, as long as they could show they were genuine. Sir Cheesepeake was reputed to have one of the most interesting libraries in the country, as he was not only an avid acquirer of books of all kinds and in several languages, but was himself a learned man, with a love of the unusual, of esoteric things. There were persistent rumours that the house contained secrets that had never been found, hidden rooms and tunnels, but also of something less tangible, like the source of great power. But nothing had been confirmed, and though the rumours had been a great source of inspiration, and most teachers had done their best to quash them, for the sake of the parents and the students of the school, these rumours only increased the sense of mystery. Occasionally stories got into the local press, but got no further, when a wall of silence would fall across further enquiry. Some hidden agreement meant that they would always be denied. But the stories only added to Burnchester's reputation. Especially as the family's past was not without tragedy.

After the war, the MOD sold the main buildings, and a generous benefaction by local families who had lost sons and daughters in action led to the foundation of the school. The foundation specified that the school should be open to pupils of all abilities and backgrounds, and all denominations, and where possible from other countries.

Tyro and Jess had been at the school since the age of five.

They paused at the gates and got off their bikes.

"Let's hide the bikes in the woods, here," said Tyro. "Better not to advertise ourselves."

They put their bikes behind a tree a few metres away from the road and lay them on the ground.

"We won't be long anyway, will we?" asked Jess. "Are you sure it'll be OK?"

"Of course it will! It's our school, isn't it?"

"In the term it is, but I don't know about the holidays. And Rompy?" added Jess.

"He'll turn up. He knows the school like the back of his hand. Mum brings him for regular walks here when she comes to pick me up."

With this Tyro and Jess crossed the road towards the gates.

Something told them it would be wiser to take a side entrance.

It was just, well....they weren't really allowed in the school after school during term time, or at weekends, never mind the holidays, and despite their holiday mood, they didn't want to bump into any of the teachers who might be straggling - though they thought it unlikely. Especially, they didn't want to run into Mr Gruff, the caretaker. So they walked a few metres along the road and found a small gate. This they entered and found themselves walking hurriedly along a yew avenue towards a side-building, which was one of the teaching blocks.

As they approached the building, the yew avenue ended where the drive that ran in front of the school crossed it. Now they could see the whole stretch of Burnchester Hall up close, from left to right, imposingly above them. The main Hall itself, where the Headmaster's office was, and the common-room and the library (Jess was wondering if it would be open), lay to the left. Here were also the cellars.

Then the refectory, the site of many food-throwing competitions. Rick, amongst others, was adept at hurling mashed potato across the dining room from a low level spoon beneath the edge of the table, and looking innocent when it landed accidentally on a teacher's plate! The kitchens were below. On the storey above were some private rooms, which they thought belonged to Mr and Mrs Rummage, the Headmaster and his wife, and then a dormitory area, for the boarders, who regarded themselves as rather select. There were other dorms on the third floor.

The main Hall was mounted with tall chimneys and decorated in old criss-crossed red brick. In front was a drive that led from the road, and immaculately manicured lawns.

The Church of St Mary Magdalen (which acted as the school chapel) stood hidden behind a line of lime trees and another line of yews interwoven into a hedge. Gravestones emerged from the grass here and there. Mostly they were well preserved, though one or two were a little broken. There was a rookery in the tall pines above. Over the south porch was a rare and beautifully carved figure - what is known as a 'green man', an image from pre-Christian times.

"Doesn't it feel strange," said Tyro.

"Wait till we get inside!" thought Jess aloud. "Spooky without anyone here. It's sort of different. As though we've come to another place."

"Come on, let's go to our classroom and then go to Mrs Limpet's room."

A passageway joined the old hall to the teaching block. They crossed the open path, not a person in sight, the sun shining high above them.

"Just think, "said Tyro, "most of our friends are on holiday abroad, or swimming by the sea, or stuck at home while we are, can you believe it, back at school!"

"And what about Rick, and Julia, and..."

"Come on!"

As they ran excitedly along the corridor to their classroom, they peered into other rooms as they went. Theirs was number 7R.

The science block opposite stood alone, as if it was watching them through the passageway windows. It was here that Mrs Limpet's room was.

Beyond were the changing rooms, teachers' houses, tennis courts, swimming pool, and the sports field. Below in the distance the river meandered gently towards the sea. Here the pupils could row, in primitive boats, occasionally on summer days. There was the old disused boathouse, which was out of bounds.

The classroom door was open, so Tyro and Jess went in. They stood and stared a moment then ran to their desks, next to each other on the back row. On the wall were pictures, notices and posters. At the front of the room beside the blackboard was a shelf of books. They sat down and looked at the blackboard.

"You be Mrs Rachel!" said Tyro. Mrs Rachel was their form teacher. She was both kind and strict at the same time. She taught Maths.

Jess went to the front of the class, taking off her glasses in a mock-serious manner, and turned round, looking only occasionally at Tyro, and the rest of the imagined pupils.

"Today we are going to have a test. A Mammoth test."

Groans from Tyro.

With this she turned to the blackboard and took a piece of chalk, and began to draw an enormous Mammoth, with huge white tusks and long hair. It looked sideways as if it was about to strike. It looked very Siberian. She even added a bit of ice to make it real.

"But, Miss...," came the ventriloquist voice of Tyro who was in fits.

"Stop whining, Jane!" said Jess trying not to laugh. "You had plenty of warning and should all be prepared. Now get out your books!"

Tyro gave a rattle of the desk tops and did a few other effects, including a "But Miss...." though this time in a deeper voice.

"Not you too, David! David, you hand out the papers."

"But, Miss, it's my turn!" said Tyro, now in a high-pitched tone.

"No it isn't, Julia! Sit down, Julia, and stop interrupting!" shouted Jess, thoroughly enjoying herself. "Everyone be quiet. The Mammoth is watching."

Tyro gave Jess a thumbs-up. Then Tyro of the deeper voice came to the front of the class, trying to look like an unkempt boy, and held out a hand. Jess handed her a set of papers and turned to the blackboard.

"There should be exactly enough papers to go round. And where's Rick?"

"Late again!" came the softly spoken voice of a cowering pupil known as Lotty.

Tyro was in hysterics, while Jess was putting back her glasses, and beginning to return to her desk.

Suddenly they heard footsteps. There was a knock at the door. It was a slow and regular knock.

Both nearly jumped out of their skin.

"Oh, no!" said Jess, "It's a ghost. The Ghost!"

"Quick, under the desk," said Tyro. Tyro was not one to be frightened but she knew the value of self-preservation.

"Don't be silly," said Jess, regaining her calm. "Whoever it is must know we're here otherwise they wouldn't have knocked."

"What's our excuse?" whispered Tyro.

"Er.... holiday reading books - forgot!" said Jess.

There was another knock. Both girls stared at the door.

Jess put on her most powerful voice.

"Enter...." she said folding her arms.

The door opened slowly. Hearts began to thump. A hand appeared high up the door. A foot, another hand, and gradually a boy came in. A boy with a round, alive face, slightly freckled, of medium build, wearing old trousers and a jumper. He was rather muddy.

"Rick!" screamed Jess, "What are you doing here? You nearly

gave us a heart attack!"

The answer followed on a piece of string. Rompy, covered in mud, came through the door as proud as punch, tail wagging.

"Sorry about that. Been shopping," said Rick, holding up a sagging plastic bag, "and then found Rompy running in through the front gates. I knew he wouldn't be alone, so I came looking for you. What are you doing here?"

"Paying the school a visit. We called at your house, but you'd gone!" she said. "Your aunt wasn't pleased to see us!"

"Makes a change. Still, having to go shopping has its advantages." He pulled out a large bar of chocolate.

"Brilliant!" said Tyro.

"I'm glad you've found Rompy. But why is he muddy?" asked Jess.

Rick was evasive. "Had to follow him into a ditch," he said. "Managed to brush most of it off, though. Gruff's about and I don't want to leave any signs that we've been here. That dog of his will find anything!"

Jess thought that Rick's attempt to clean his clothes was terrible, but said nothing.

"Come on, let's go. We're going to Mrs Limpet's room."

"What's so special about Mrs Limpet? She's an old cow!" said Rick.

"Rick!" said Jess, pretending to be shocked.

"I want to find a way of getting my own back at her for what she did to me last term," said Tyro. "She went right over the top!"

"You *were* giving a running commentary all through the lesson," said Jess. "Rumour has it she's also going through a divorce," she added, trying to be supportive but fair.

"Who'd marry her?" said Rick.

"The devil, I should think. Locking me in her cupboard for an hour in the dark. Never been so scared!" said Tyro.

"You said she gave you a detention!" said Jess, now feeling slightly guilty.

"Not something to boast about, is it? Besides, I didn't say what sort of detention, Jess....come on, let's go."

"You should at least have told Mrs Rachel," said Jess.

"I know, but first I wanted to find out more. I've got a feeling about that woman. I don't think Mrs Rachel would have believed me anyway."

"Can't blame you," said Rick. "If I told my aunt that I'd been shut in a cupboard, she'd probably have written a thank you letter and told her to throw away the key! Come on Rompy. Go!"

Rick and Rompy were old friends.

As they moved it was Rick's turn to sound serious. He turned to the girls.

"We mustn't be seen by Gruff," he said in a low mysterious voice. "He doesn't allow anyone near the school - day pupils that is - out of school hours during term. Think what he'd be like if he caught us in the holidays. Thank Heaven he goes on holiday tomorrow."

"How do you know?" asked Jess.

"Because I've got a reason to be here too. But I can't tell you now. We've got to get out of sight. We may have to forget that picnic."

Jess looked at Tyro, who raised her eyebrows, as if to say, "What *is* he on about?"

"What have you found this time, Rick?" asked Jess.

"Not another helmet?" added Tyro.

Rick had a reputation for finding things, mostly rubbish in the undergrowth, which he would pretend was of great importance. Whenever he did a project for school - which was not often - instead of writing anything he would bring in examples of his subject on an old tray borrowed from the kitchens. For example, for a project on energy he brought in an old battery, a piece of (burnt) coal, and a pair of sweaty running shoes. Rick went red. The girls looked at each other again, and said nothing.

"I can't tell you," said Rick.

The three of them left the class. Rick first, Rompy pulling hard on the string that Rick had tied to him, then Tyro and Jess. They each looked both ways down the corridor, then hurried out of the building and crossed the yard to the science block. As they approached the door, they heard a low whistle. Rick listened. The whistle came a second time.

"What is *that*?" asked Tyro.

"The ghost of St Mary Magdalen going for a stroll," said Jess, getting into the spirit of adventure.

"Ghosts don't appear in brilliant sunshine. Come on, we've got to hurry," said Rick. They began to run.

They could now hear footsteps. A heavy clomp, clomp, getting louder.

Rick, Tyro and Jess reached the science block door. It was shut.

"Quick, round the back!" said Rick.

In moments, Mr Gruff appeared from around the teaching block, proudly led by Titan, his dog.

Mr Gruff always wore an immaculately polished pair of army boots. He was rather thick set, with a head attached to his body without a neck. He had curly dark hair, and wore a creased shirt and tie, overalls and a jacket. He carried a stick with which to beat Titan.

Gruff was never in a good mood.

Gruff came to a halt. Titan had caught a scent. He pulled hard on his lead and began to bark.

"What now, you devil? Not another rat! Bloody rats!"

Gruff gave a swish of his stick, but Titan didn't take any notice and pulled harder, nose to the ground. His tail wagged furiously.

Three pairs of eyes watched from a first floor window.

"All you ever think about, you lazy beast! Why don't you catch one, instead of barking? There'll be no supper tonight until you do! Go on, get after it! Get in there, yer devil!"

With that, Gruff released Titan, who ran forward sniffing hard.

He seemed momentarily confused.

Then he barked again and ran towards the teaching block door and tried to push it open, with his paw.

"No rats in there," said Gruff. "Checked an hour ago, didn't we, you idiot!"

With that Gruff got hold of Titan's lead and yanked him away from the door, and began walking towards the main building.

There was a huge sigh from the first floor.

"That's better! Chocolate has its uses! I left a bit on the ground which confused Titan. Here, have another bit."

Rick took three slabs and gave a piece to Tyro and Jess.

"Now for Mrs Limpet's chamber of horrors," said Tyro gorging the chocolate. "This is turning out better than I expected. Will Gruff come back though?"

"If he does we'll have some warning," added Rick.

"What do you mean?" asked Jess.

"Didn't you hear that whistle?"

Again Jess and Tyro looked at each other. This time they sighed.

"Yeah" they said together. "Don't tell us. You've got a smell sensor out in the yard, checking for nasty pongs?"

Mr Gruff's reputation wasn't only for his attitude.

"Or a petty dictator detector?" said Jess.

"No," said a voice.

It was Tom, Rick's best friend. He was unpopular with most girls in the class, including Tyro and Jess. He came across as awkward and weird, but as Rick was so popular he was accepted, if grudgingly. He was very strange, and often away. In fact nobody seemed to know much about him.

"Hi, Tom!" said Rick. "You were brilliant. Has he gone?"

"Yes," said Tom.

He was looking at Tyro and Jess a little suspiciously as if to say, "What are they doing here?"

"Found him - " looking at Rompy, "- in the school grounds and was led to these two," said Rick.

The girls began to make for the door.

"I'm going out again. Must keep an eye on Gruff."

With that Tom ran back down the stairs, passing Tyro and Jess who were already halfway down. They were on their way to Mrs Limpet's room. They had run to the first floor to hide in Mr Flabberty's room. Fortunately, the back entrance to the block had been open. Some of the rubbish from last term had still to be collected and the bins were outside smelling foul. Tom ran past the girls without stopping.

"Why don't you ever say anything?" said Tyro angrily, without expecting a reply.

"Leave Tom alone! He's better than you think. Than any of you think," Rick said.

"Not that I can see!" said Tyro.

Tyro and Jess went into a classroom marked 'Mrs Limpet - Head of Science', and beneath that 'KEEP OUT! Experiments with chemicals are dangerous and can cause serious illness, even death.' Someone had drawn blood dripping from the word death. Beneath that someone else, judging by the handwriting, had written in pencil, so as not to be seen, 'Like it or Limp it. We know which we'd rather.'

"Pathetic!" said Tyro.

"That was Rick," said Jess, pointing to the writing, but not agreeing. "How come the door's open?"

The two girls paused at the front of the lab and looked in. The work surfaces that surrounded the room were immaculate now. A cold, clinical place, like an operating theatre waiting for a patient. Jess pointed to the back of the classroom.

"Wow!" said Tyro, now quite cautious.

At the back of the class was a door which led to a store-room for chemicals and animals, those that were waiting to be brought out for experiment, and had already been sacrificed. It was the room in which Tyro had been kept, during her detention. It was very slightly ajar. From it came a sound.

"Someone's in there!" whispered Tyro.

"Must be the cleaner!" said Jess.

"Mrs Limpet doesn't let anyone in there, ever!" said Tyro.

The noise from the back room had stopped.

"We'd better get out of here," said Jess.

Then there was a sharp, subdued, but high-pitched scream, and the backroom door was thrown open. Mrs Limpet, a tall, thin, nervous woman with grey hair and dark eyes, came out clutching her hand which was dripping with blood. A rat was dangling from it, its jaws fixed firmly in her hand. But it was Mrs Limpet's face which was extraordinary. It was completely without feeling. A cold unreal face, as frozen as the cold northern seas in a dark winter storm. She looked like a walking corpse.

Mrs Limpet went to her desk and pulled open a drawer. She took out a knife, and, with a look of cold anger in her eyes, she cut through the neck of the rat until its body fell to the floor. The rat's blood sprayed everywhere. She placed the knife on the desk and yanked the rat's jaws open, and let the head fall to the ground. Mrs Limpet seemed content. She raised her head slightly, and caught sight of the two girls. For a split second Mrs Limpet's cold stare fixed on Tyro. She smiled with the same delight with which she had sliced off the rat's head.

"Come in, girls," she said, in a hollow voice.

The rat's body went through its final spasms and became still.

For a moment, Tyro stood, trying not to stare at the face of the teacher that she hated so much. She wanted to scream and to run at her and punch her. But Jess held her arm tight.

"Let's get out of here!" said Jess.

Tyro pulled and pulled. Jess held firm, like a terrier.

Mrs Limpet continued to smile, and stared at Tyro's eyes.

"Take her! There will be another time."

Then she got up and turned towards the back room door, licking the blood from her hand.

Jess managed to pull Tyro away, and the two girls turned. It was not like either of them to run from trouble, but they now ran furiously out of the room. They caught Rick's arm as he came towards them and dragged him out. Rompy followed, thinking it was a game, chasing them, and growling.

"What's happen...." Rick began.

As they crossed the yard, Rick began to pull back.

"Hang on. What's going on? If we're not careful we'll be seen by Gruff."

"Forget Gruff! We've just seen the evil Limpet, rat-killer! I'll explain later," said Tyro, catching her breath.

Jess looked behind her anxiously.

"She won't come now," Tyro added. "It's me she's after."

"She didn't look in a fit state to follow us," said Jess, "I think we should get out of here - back to the bikes, quick!"

"What are you talking about?" said Rick angrily.

"We'll tell you later," said Tyro.

The holiday adventure was turning into a nightmare.

They were now heading towards the main drive which led back up to the wood where their bikes were. About a hundred metres ahead from behind the main gates came Titan, followed by Gruff.

Before Titan even saw the children, they were running towards the main building.

The door was open. Soon they were inside the old familiar wood-panelled interior of the Hall. They turned back to look through a window.

A car had come through the drive and Gruff was bending his head towards the driver.

"Everything alright, Mr Gruff?"

"Everything under control, Mr Rummage. Quiet as the grave, Sir," he added with a kick at Titan.

"It's Rumbags!" screamed Tyro, "I don't believe it!"

"Whose silly idea was it to come back to school in the holidays?" said Rick. "What's *he* doing here?"

"Never mind what he's doing here," said Jess, "he's coming this way!"

The car came down the drive and halted in front of the main door. Gruff was now marching off towards the playing fields.

Mr Rummage got out and came towards the school.

"Where now?" came a whispered voice. The three of them quickly ran up the stairs.

Mr Rummage entered the hall and walked towards his office. He was a tall man with a strong, kind face. The sort that you could trust and respect. He took out a key and entered.

Within moments he came out, walked over to the staircase and went up. At the top he turned to the right and pushed open the first door.

He entered the library and walked over the carpeted floor to the back of the room, where there was another door. Normally when he entered this room he felt a kind of peace come over him, though on this occasion he was in a hurry.

From behind him, from somewhere in the recesses of the main room, came a noise.

Mr Rummage turned the key in the lock. He heard it again. It sounded like the whimper of a dog. He was used to the noises of the old Hall, but this was different. "Can't be!" he thought. He shrugged his shoulders, went through the door and closed it behind him.

"What's in there?" whispered Tyro.

"Never seen it open before," said Rick, who, like Tyro, was not a great reader. "Old books, and other documents, according to rumour," he added. "About the past. I'm going to have a look."

Rick ran over to the door. He looked through the keyhole. Tyro and Jess had now come up to him. Each looked through in turn.

"He's coming out," said Tyro, "quick!"

The three of them ran back to the desk and bent low, Tyro covering Rompy with her jumper.

Mr Rummage came out of the door and locked it. He was carrying some papers under his arm.

He paused and listened. Then walked straight out of the library door.

"What a mess you nearly got us into!" said Rick.

"He's got a right to be here!" said Jess.

"Trust you!" said Rick.

"Shut up!" said Tyro.

Mr Rummage left the library. As the door began to shut, Tyro thought that he was going to lock it, but thankfully he didn't.

After a few moments, they hurried towards the door. From the top of the landing they could see Mr Rummage's back go into his study again.

Without a word the three children crept down the stairs, Rompy now with a sock tied round his nose, as a sort of muzzle. Rick, then Tyro, then Jess.

At the bottom of the stairs, they turned to the right and made for a door that led to the front of the Hall, the front that looked out over the river.

Once they were out in the warm air, they breathed a sigh of relief. Tyro now led them to the line of yews in the garden in front of the school and they hid behind one of them to catch their breath.

"We'll leave now, but we'll have to come back," said Tyro.

"Of course," said Rick. He said it as if he knew something.

"We can have our picnic by the river after all," said Jess. "And you can tell us what you're really doing here, Rick."

"No way!" Rick said.

With that they followed the line of yews that joined a row of lime trees.

When they reached the gate they looked behind them, and hurriedly crossed the road to the wood where the girls had left their bikes.

From the trees, they saw Mr Rummage's car come up the drive and turn left at the top. Tyro felt sure that he had seen them in the trees in front of him. Still, they were not in school.

Rick had left his bike close by. The three of them got on, and taking a quick look at the wide open gates, made their way the back route towards Greenfield, relieved, excited, if confused. What was Mrs Limpet doing there? Acting so strangely. What was Mr Rummage doing in the library? Rompy ran on ahead, as if nothing had happened. In Tyro's case she was also haunted by the sight of the teacher she hated so much staring at her, as if from another world.

# 3

Tyro, Jess and Rick rode as fast they they could down the hill that led to the river. This followed the boundary of the school grounds. At the bottom, they crossed the bridge at a point where the road veered to the left and followed the river for a few hundred metres. At this point the school boundary continued back up the hill to a small copse at the top - a magnificent place to look back on Burnchester Hall, this time the other side of the river, especially in summer. It was to this spot, called Folly Hill, that the children had to run on their cross-country runs, even in the darkest winter, and where, unbeknown to the sports teacher Mr Bellevue, several stragglers would take a short cut across the meadow (which was hidden by a hedge), to join the track back up towards the changing rooms. Amidst the trees of the copse stood the ruins of a folly, where they could also hide from the icy easterlies that so often blow in all the way from Siberia on cold winter days. Now it was the haven of a few summer birds which liked to roost on the top of the old stone, where an occasional pair of robins would build a nest. A careful look at the stone walls revealed not just the names of pupils who had decided to celebrate their love for posterity (Dave 4 Jane, Mandy loves John) but the deeper and perhaps darker etchings of other figures from secret history, not least those whose names will never be known to the world at large. Men and women who had lived and worked at Burnchester for months before being flown by night behind enemy lines, into unknown territory, alone and often prematurely silenced. A few came back, and died in obscurity, unknown heroes beneath the stars.

"We can't stop here, we're still in bounds," said Tyro suspecting that Mr Gruff was still on patrol.

The three of them rode on. Their initial plan had been to have their picnic near the bridge, somewhere on the school grounds. But, without speaking, they decided to ride on, knowing that they could not stop so close to the school after the morning's encounters. These were still running around in Tyro's mind, though the hurry and the fresh warm summer air weakened the images a little.

They followed the road until they reached a junction to the left. The road ran on ahead - this led to the Burnchester Arms. Here they turned, and crossed the river again. This road led back towards Greenfield by a 'wild country' route, and eventually to Tyro's home. It was little more than a narrow tarmacked track, with the occasional passing place, forged out of the ground by a succession of meeting vehicles, mostly tractors against cars, having to negotiate these ancient side roads, once a little less than drove roads, at impossible odds.

At the top of this second hill, from which they could see the folly, they could see below them another of their favourite places - a place they had been coming to since early childhood. From a field gate, a meadow led down again to the river. This was normally a cow field, but there were none there now.

By the water's edge was a small concrete shelter, covered in old ivy. It had small narrow vertical gaps in it and a ground level entrance that led downwards on a few concrete steps. This was another relic of the war, though it was not obviously in a position of vantage, except that a hundred metres further on, beneath a large willow tree, was what could have been some kind of landing stage, now nothing more than a muddy verge, half-sunken by the feet of drinking cattle, held up from the moving water by aging boards which had prevented it from complete collapse. They called it Shelter Field.

"Let's stop here," said Tyro. "We need to be able to see around us."

The three of them pulled up to a halt on the brow of the hill and threw their bikes against the verge. Rompy ran up behind (this time he had kept close to them, no doubt because he could smell lunch). They did not expect to meet anybody except perhaps local farm vehicles which used it more at this time of year. Harvest would soon be upon them, when the fields of golden barley and wheat would be taken in, as the first step of high summer. Jess took the hamper from Tyro's bike, and joined Tyro who was looking below. It was from this same place that agents would listen for planes arriving at a nearby field. Rick walked towards a fallen tree along the hedge.

"That's better," said Tyro, pausing for breath and turning to Jess. "Let's eat." She hid whatever fears she might have had.

"I'm starving," said Jess, as she placed the hamper on the ground.

"Great idea, wasn't it?" said Tyro.

"You're crazy!" said Jess opening out the pack of sandwiches onto the paper roll. "I'm scared."

"What of?" asked Tyro. "Not that blood-thirsty animal-killer of a teacher. I'll get my own back on her yet. I knew she was up to something."

"What?" asked Jess.

"That's for us to find out, isn't it?" she added, almost as a challenge. "We'll have to go back."

To Tyro's surprise, Jess didn't answer her. Instead she concentrated on sharing out the sandwiches in equal portions.

"Aren't *you* scared?" asked Jess.

Tyro looked out across the valley, as if she was trying to look for something. She was thinking. She saw Rick, who had reached the tree.

"What do we tell Rick?" asked Jess.

"Everything," Tyro continued, sitting down. "Except for the rat." She did not quite know why she wanted to hide this from Rick. "I don't think he should know all the details. Just that we saw Mrs Limpet. I wonder what happened to those sticks? I bet they're down there somewhere, either drifting along or caught in the weeds," she added. Rick had dragged a couple of large fallen branches up to them and lay them out like a bench overlooking the valley.

"A pound a perch!" said Rick, who was as happy on the grass.

"Cheek! For that you don't earn a sandwich," said Jess, looking at Rick approvingly. Rick looked up, and tried not to smile. He wasn't used to compliments of any sort, and wasn't sure how to respond.

"I'll have to go soon. Can't keep making excuses for being late with her shopping. She wants me to cut the grass, weed the flower beds and mend the fence. She'll kill me! The....! Thanks, er....Jess."

Jess enjoyed handing round the food. It was something to do with her cleverness that she also enjoyed serving, though she wasn't very practical. Somehow, making other people happy gave her more pleasure than anything else - even reading. This was a side that Tyro admired but also hated, that 'too-good-to-be-true' aspect that always won over parents. It made you sick.

For a few minutes they all sat quietly, munching, each with their own thoughts about the morning. The warm sun made up for the cold interior of the near-empty school, and the sound of turtle doves purring, for that is what it was, added to the sense that they had now re-entered the summer mood again. Far ahead beyond the folly were fields of corn. Over the river, another field, this time of grass, beside an ancient wood. And beyond that the sky. Just summer sun, and the calm that always comes before bad weather. For the moment they forgot their experiences, and close encounters with Gruff, Mrs Limpet, and Mr Rummage. They were feeling elated, if guilty. The girls because Mrs Limpet had seen them, Rick because he felt sure Mr Rummage had caught sight of all of them as he had driven off. Mr Rummage felt protective towards Rick, because of his aunt and uncle, but Rick was disruptive, and there had been several times over the past year that he had wished not to have had him in the school. Mr Rummage had never expelled a pupil. It was sometimes hard. For Jess there was also the matter of what Rick had really been doing there. Perhaps this was why Tyro wanted to be cagey. Rompy, of course, suffered none of these doubts. He had caught his breath and the smell of tuna, which he loved. He was sitting with his tail wagging furiously. As long as there was food and someone to look after him - from time to time - and the freedom to roam, he didn't care.

As they ate, they could see to the left below them, Shelter Field. Over the valley ahead, Folly Ridge, and to their right, at some distance, they could see the school grounds and that part of the river that flowed through them, though the main building was hidden from view. For a moment Tyro had thought she saw figures on the hill by the Folly. But when she asked the others, they said they couldn't see anything. Must be ghosts from the past, she thought. It was almost as if something was being blotted from their memory.

"Who made these terrible sarnies?" said Rick. "Brilliant!" he added, catching Jess and Tyro's glare.

The field where they had stopped ran on for a hundred metres or so before descending rapidly out of view.

"You don't think anyone's going to find us here?" asked Jess.

"No," said Tyro. "Who cares anyway? We're nowhere near the school. Besides, nobody ever comes up this road."

Tyro spoke with confidence again now she was full.

"I've got to go. Thanks," said Rick, suddenly.

He got up and started to walk towards his bike.

"Rick," said Tyro. "We have to get together and talk about this morning."

"What's there to say?" said Rick, picking up his bike and getting on.

"Rick! You were going to tell us why you were at school. Why the secrecy?"

"Oh! That!" said Rick. "Digging," he added.

"For what?" asked Jess.

For a moment Rick said nothing. Tyro said nothing, but then said, "Thanks for helping us out. For finding Rompy. We wouldn't have got away without being seen, but for you, Gruff might have killed us."

Rick was on his bike.

"Treasure!" Rick said. "The key to secret knowledge!"

"Don't believe you, Rick!" said Jess.

"See you," he replied. "Call me and we'll meet up in a few days."

With that Rick rode off, Rompy following behind, barking him along for a few metres.

Rick wasn't at all sure that he wanted to meet up that soon, he had work to do of his own, even though it was Jess who asked. But they might be useful. He thought of Tom, and hoped that he was alright. It didn't surprise him that the girls hadn't mentioned him. To them he was an inconvenience. To him, he was like a brother. A reliable one at that. He was preparing himself for the onslaught that was sure to come his way. Aunt Patrolia wouldn't take kindly to a picnic, never having had one in her life. One of these days he wasn't going to bother. But he was so inured against Aunt Patrolia's ravings that he soon forgot her. Uncle John, he was OK. He would understand. One day.

After they had eaten the remains of crumbled biscuits, Tyro and Jess raced down to Shelter Field and looked into the water. Rompy didn't do any looking. He raced in and chased a young duck that was hiding under the bank. Tyro was looking at a small group of fish who were idling near the water's edge. She felt sure there would be a pike nearby.

The two of them then climbed on top of the shelter, just as two agents might have done, into what had been one of their favourite hideouts. Had been, that is, until they had turned eleven, and they got too old for hideouts. All thought about the morning had now gone.

They both looked dreamily in front of them, imagining this a large river, with traffic, boats of all sizes carrying people on their many errands, as if it had been in the centre of a large town. Somewhere in the back of their minds came a line from that boring play that they had read extracts from last term, what was it now? The Merchant of Something. Venice. This was hardly Venice, this quiet, unknown, ordinary part of the East Anglian landscape. It was the Dean.

"Are you going to try for the school play next term, Tyro?" asked Jess, picking up on her train of thought.

"It depends," she said. "If it's Mr Baxter, yes."

"It's always Mr Baxter, in the senior school."

"Yes, then."

Mr Baxter was their English teacher. He was popular throughout the school, except with some of the other teachers who were too old-fashioned to understand him. He walked around the school carrying a mask, and would stop to say, to a colleague, "How far is called to the Burnchester Arms?" To which they would mostly say. "OK, see you there at five-thirty." It wasn't just Mrs Limpet who didn't like him, but old Mr Rafferty, who was out of touch and taught Latin and Greek, which, a bit like himself, had been resurrected in recent times. Mr Rafferty was popular, but in a different way. And of course Mr Gruff. He just obstructed in every way he could when it came to the school play. This made the annual productions even more of an achievement. The plays were reviewed in the local press. Mr Baxter threw himself into these with great energy, every year, which is why he needed to go away for the whole of the summer, to recover. Nobody knew where to. It was a mystery why he had not left years ago for a career on the stage or to one of the grander schools in London, even to one of the ancient universities from where he had come. A few of the parents didn't understand his style. But none of this mattered. He respected his fellow colleagues, and got good results. He sometimes joined classes with the art teacher, Ms Peverell. She had long dark hair, and wore stylish clothes, making riches out of the least expensive things. She designed the sets, and helped with the rehearsals. It wasn't only that she looked like a friendly witch with penetrating eyes.

Tyro caught sight of something in the reeds by the near bank.

"Jess..." she began, and jumped down.

She was at the water's edge.

Jess was looking at Tyro looking down.

"What now?" said Jess.

"You're not going to believe this. Our sticks. Our two sticks!"

Tyro bent down and picked up two sticks out of the clear water. They were indeed the two sticks that they had thrown in the water only a couple of hours earlier.

Jess had come down to join her.

"I think you're right," said Jess, who was now looking at them carefully.

"That proves it," said Tyro.

"Proves what?" asked Jess.

"That water flows in a certain direction and that if you throw sticks into it, they can only go one way. Like picking up a scent. Isn't that right, Rompy? Oh Heavens! Rompy!"

Rompy was showering them both with water.

During this shower, Tyro gave Jess a stick and together they threw them back into the river, far enough out to get caught in the flow. Slowly they began to drift out of sight.

They watched the sticks as they flowed past the edge of the ancient forest that bordered the river further on.

"Wish them luck," Tyro suddenly said.

"Tyro?" said Jess in an exasperated tone. "*Sticks?*"

"They remind me of two friends, you and me! Come on, let's go," said Tyro. "We at least can have a talk about the day. Even if Rick won't. But I think we should get home first. Unless you want to go to yours?"

"I don't mind where," said Jess, "We also need to tell someone what we saw today. I know your mum would listen."

"She'd also get into a panic."

"What do you think Mrs Limpet was up to?"

"I don't know. I'm not sure I really want to."

Normally they would have had a swim a little downstream in a natural pool in the next field - but they decided against it. Tyro would swim anywhere, anytime. On the frequent occasions they got to the cold North Sea she raced in, even in winter, much to the consternation of Abby, who didn't really like water much. Tyro had never forgotten a teacher (she felt sure it was Mr Baxter) telling the class that the best way to prevent a cold in winter was to roll in the snow. Just like the best way, perhaps, to avoid getting a disease was to be given a very slight infection. Mrs Limpet came into mind.

Jess enjoyed swimming too, but with better judgement - when it was sweltering hot.

As they turned to go and began to walk back up the hill, towards the road where their bikes lay, they both stopped in their tracks.

From somewhere nearby, came a call. Like the hoot of an owl. This time it was low.

It didn't take much to bring their nervousness to the surface. They both jumped.

"From the wood!" said Tyro.

"I don't think so," began Jess. "More like from the shelter."

"The shelter hasn't been used for years."

"Maybe that's why owls live there."

"If it was an owl. I bet the shelter is haunted."

Tyro said this half in jest. But it was enough to get them both started again.

"Let's have a look," said Tyro.

"Careful. You might see Mrs Limpet holding a dead rat!"

"Jess! That's not like you. That's mean!"

"Sorry," said Jess. Jess was so often the gentle diplomat, but just occasionally showed another side to her character, though normally not to Tyro. She didn't like herself a bit for it. She made the mistake of trying to backtrack.

"I'll go. Stay back, have that swim."

"Legs might get entangled in weeds, according to Mrs Rachel."

School rules forbade any swimming in the river, ever. There was a school pool. Many years ago, it was rumoured, someone had drowned not far from the spot where they now stood. Perhaps it was the call of the drowned child.

Tyro went to the old concrete shelter, covered in ivy. She pulled back the ivy and peered into the dim interior but could see little. She went round to the front and bent down through the low entrance, and looked carefully. The floor was strewn with leaves on a hard muddy base. The odd decaying sweet packet could be seen amongst them.

"No owl here," she said. "One or two pellets, though. Must be feeding in here."

Then, turning round, she lifted her arms and raised her shoulders and hunched her back and squinted her eyes, and ran towards Jess, with a screech! She had wound herself and Jess up so much, that the only course for Jess was to run. This she did, racing up the hill shouting, "I'm not staying to check!" holding out her arms whilst making owl-like noises.

Tyro ran after her, laughing and swooping down on her. She hadn't been sure where the sound had come from, but it sounded as if it had come from underground. But not from inside the old shelter. Owls were nocturnal anyway.

"Let's get out of here!"

In moments, the two girls were back on their bikes and riding along the back road in the direction of Greenfield.

Tyro and Jess were now riding side by side again. The river was some way off, school hidden behind at least two low hills and woodland. They were back in the no-man's land of country lanes, to an outsider rather dully repetitive and lifeless, but subtly differing from each other and beautifully tranquil.

They rode past Greenfield, the church tower to their left, past houses and farms, which made them feel more relaxed. They heard Rick facing the music of his aunt in no uncertain terms as they approached the road towards Tyro's home. Greenfield was the crossing-point from unknown territory to home territory, and no amount of trips to school would ever shake that feeling.

Rompy was ahead of them, panting. He too looked tired.

"I'm exhausted," said Jess. "Let's stop a minute."

With that she pulled up to the verge and got off her bike. She began to push it. Tyro did likewise and walked along beside her. Rompy came up to them wagging his tail, with his tongue hanging out.

"OK, Rompy," said Tyro, "up you come."

Big and muddy though Rompy was, Tyro put him in the basket on the front of her bike, and sat him in it. Rompy could look in front of him as they walked along. From time to time he would lurch forward at a passing fly or stand up to grab at that butterfly which came too close. Then the bike would wobble and Tyro would give him a little shove to sit down.

They came to a T-junction, and turned left. This led to the house. From the right a tractor raced around the corner and nearly knocked into them.

Tyro fell over onto the bike. Rompy jumped out barking. Jess turned round to look straight up at the face of Luke who ran to help Tyro.

"Where do you think you're going?" he said, "Up you get.

Are you OK? Good. I'll give you a lift. The General wouldn't have hurt you. Got a nose for people."

It was true he had been going too fast, but there was no way the General would have bumped into them.

In moments all of them were in the trailer behind, Tyro and Jess, the bikes and Rompy. Luke revved up and the General departed. He swung into the entrance to Tyro's house. Although there was no name on the rather dilapidated gate, everyone knew the Old Hall.

Bill was working the beds at the front and looked up as the girls jumped out. Luke took the bikes out of the back of the trailer.

"Need a hand, Luke? Had a puncture or something?" asked Bill.

"No thanks," said Luke, "just giving them a lift. Got to go. The General wants to get on with it. Herbert's afternoon off and he doesn't get as much work in as he'd like."

Luke winked. Bill said nothing. It was Luke who was temporarily-mental, Bill thought.

"Thanks Bill," said Tyro.

Bill smiled. "Good picnic, girls?"

"Er....brilliant, thanks, Bill. Great!" said Tyro. Bill wasn't convinced.

By the time Abby returned from work the girls were listening to music. They ran down to see her, and helped her with her shopping.

"What's up?" she asked. "Unlike you, Tyro, to put yourself out. Something the matter?"

"No, Mrs Wander," said Jess, "it's just that we've got something to tell you."

"Give me a few minutes and I'm all ears. But have you done what I asked you, Tyro?"

To her total amazement, she had. Something was up.

Tyro of course had downplayed everything. She had not wanted to tell her mother in the first place, partly because she didn't think it was very important, partly because she didn't want any adult to know, especially because she knew what her mother's reaction would be. It was Jess who had persuaded her, in fact virtually forced her by saying that if she didn't she would tell her mother who would tell Abby anyway. "It's normal for a biology teacher to kill rats," Tyro had said. Finally she agreed to let Abby into the secret, expecting her mother to be angry.

She was. But not at Mrs Limpet. At Tyro and Jess. "No going back. Banned. School - out of bounds for the rest of the holidays. Plenty of countryside, things to do in the garden, friends to see. But school. No. Finito. End of story! What on earth made you go back there in the first place?" she asked.

The opposite of course was going to prove true.

Not long afterwards Jess rode home, in the clear early evening daylight, having refused a lift from Abby. She would not have let her go alone any later, and was always a little anxious about allowing any of Tyro's friends, let alone Tyro herself, cycle home alone, but Jess came over so frequently, especially in the holidays, normally when she was at work, with her mother's blessing, that she felt less unhappy than she would otherwise have been. And she always made sure that she carried with her a mobile phone, her own if necessary, and insisted that she call when she got back. They all knew exactly how long it should take, and within a few moments of her arrival she would quickly call, just to say, "All OK, thanks." It was both a precaution and a necessity. The peace of the countryside could no longer be as guaranteed as it could when she had been a child. Jess phoned, Tyro answered, Abby had a quick word with her mother, Clare, and Abby and Tyro settled in for the evening, of which there still several hours of sunlight.

First they had tea, a sort of tea with supper. Tyro was able to tell her mother in more detail of the events of the day, and of meeting Rick and Tom.

"Do I know Tom?" Abby had asked. "Of course, the Whistler. Nice boy, if a little distant."

"Er, no Mum, not nice boy - creep. We tolerate him because he's a friend of Rick's."

Tyro was a little calmer and less defensive of the facts, and less protective of herself and Jess. Mother became a confidante and a trusted ally in perhaps a way that no other person ever could or ever should. Particularly as her father was no longer alive. Even so, she left out one or two details, as her allegiance had now swung more fully to her friends, and she knew how her mother would fuss. She didn't tell her mother that the rat had sunk its teeth into Mrs Limpet's fingers, or that she had sliced its head off. Nor the details of Mrs Limpet's stare. This had been the worst of it. It was as if she couldn't be quite sure if it was her imagination. For these reasons alone, perhaps, but also because of her innate belief in the integrity of her daughter's teachers (children often got things out of proportion, didn't they?), Abby ended up taking the view that a teacher had been seen in her classroom in the school holidays and that she had been slightly surprised and annoyed to see the girls there, unannounced and without permission. As for Mr Gruff, he was doing a difficult job as well as he could, and there was no reason at all for Mr Rummage not to be in the school, especially the library, given his interest in old books. Certainly she noted what the girls had said, but thought no more of it. And they were not going back.

No more of it then, anyway. Abby also knew that her daughter had the gift of insight, as well as energy, and that this was not always welcome to either of them. She often saw what others didn't see, sometimes in a confused way, and her opinions should never be entirely dismissed. So a very slight lingering doubt remained in her mind. She determined to remain alert.

They spent much of the rest of the evening in the garden. Bill stayed late, and all three of them got one of the flower-beds looking tidy again. The weeds, which were doing such a good job of suffocating the various flowers, were now relegated to the top of the compost heap.

A light breeze refreshed the still air as the sun began to set. When Tyro was in bed, Abby told her that her uncle (Abby's brother Dennis) was coming to stay for a week or so in a day or two - "to get out of London". This would make home more of a home again. The house thrived with having people in it. It was a sign that the holiday was really about to begin. Dennis was quite a bit younger. He became more like a brother than an uncle, for Tyro, during his visits. Tyro was thrilled.

# 4

Sometime during Tyro's supper with Abby, other events, not unconnected to this story, were unfolding. We switch our eye, for a while there, to be with them.

The Burnchester Arms is the kind of pub that you could not find by looking, by 'cold search'. It needs to be discovered in a haphazard way, to be come upon in the process of exploring, as you turn the corner in an exasperated mood. Giving directions doesn't always work, as it is as likely to lead you to the wrong place. It is one of the few remaining pubs in East Anglia which does not pay homage to the eccentricities of the marketing barons, or to the brewery despots. That is to say, it keeps itself to itself and doesn't generate its own propaganda by offering anything more than good beer, a few carefully selected wines, and good, home-made cooking, on certain days only. The chef, an apt description as he is a long resident Frenchman, M. Le Petit, with a twisted moustache, is a little erratic. That he should be found in such a place would have been something of a surprise only a generation or so ago, when the clientele would mostly have been of local stock (meaning very varied - a mixed lot) if not persuasion, and the sight of this generous-faced if unpredictable monsieur the subject of amusement in the vein of acceptance. He manages to make the weekend menu regular but at other times, his calendar, like his character, seems to be lunar rather than

Gregorian. It also means that the food follows the seasons: game as the shooting season (or poaching activity) allows and vegetables as the seasons and weather determine. The milk still comes from a local cow, from a herd that also keeps itself to itself and seems to ignore every virus that flies hither and thither, with such tormenting devastation, elsewhere in the country. The Burnchester Arms advertises nowhere, it doesn't have special features or facilities. The only once disquieting feature, to some of the local inhabitants, might have been that M. Le Petit was a Catholic. For though the local people were tolerant in principle, they were, like others, rather less tolerant in practice, whatever the local priest, the Reverend John Sandals, might have done in an attempt to treat everyone with equal enthusiasm. Things are of course different now!

The Arms stands beside the river, downstream from Burnchester Hall, a mile or so from the place where Tyro, Jess and Rick had stopped after their secret visit to the school. Tyro and Jess had visited the pub on many occasions, normally in the company of Tyro's uncle, Dennis.

The Arms has existed, rather like the Hall itself, for hundreds of years. It has been an inn for at least four hundred, and before, that, possibly a farmstead belonging to one of the local renaissance magnates, possibly the Templedeans, nobody quite knows. Rumour has it that Shakespeare's father had visited it. If his son's love of life is anything to go by, no doubt the father enjoyed a drink there as well. Built from wattle and daub originally, supported by beams with a thatched roof, it has been extended and adapted bit by bit over the centuries, perhaps like our nation itself. During the Second World War it played a support role to the training camp at the Hall, by offering relief in conviviality. It also acted as a magnet for strangers who might, even then, have passed that way, especially for those who showed any interest in the Hall itself. The fact that it adjoined the river, ultimately with access to the sea, allowed for covert comings and goings, despite its open-eyed charm. All those directly connected with it had been sworn to secrecy, like the present landlord, Mr Gatherin, a man of untold depths, and equal weight. Like a colossus he stands behind the bar, unbowed by age, watching the tide of people come and go, the fashionable and unfashionable alike, the teachers from the Hall, the other professionals, the technocrats and self-employed workers from home, local farmers and the variously mobile.

The Burnchester Arms is a place where you would go for a quiet drink, and to catch up on local news and gossip, should the landlord allow it (for he, unlike his chef, is strict), particularly towards the end of the week, when things begin to hot up, relatively speaking. Perhaps ten people as opposed to the habitual four would come in, and on Saturdays numbers grow significantly, filling the warm interior with people from the surrounding villages, and further. The pub thus serves the community, and beyond.

Besides being on the river, the Arms has the special charm of being only approachable on foot, cars needing to be left at the top of the slight rise, above the pub.

Mr Gatherin, the landlord, welcomes everyone, but is intimate with no-one. He has to be judge and jury on the occasions of disputes between customers, and has the difficult task of reminding them when it is closing time. He rules the bar with great authority, and if not always charm, with enough warmth to make the genuine welcome, but deter the few who he could sense had other agendas. Years of experience have given him a well-trained eye, and he could generally judge his customers, not so much from first glance, but from the first time they ordered a drink, when they encountered his penetrating but friendly eye, which always contained humour, mostly against himself, beneath the mask of control.

Tonight there are few people at the bar. It is early evening. It is midweek.

Mr Gruff, the caretaker at Burnchester Hall, is feeling satisfied. This is a rare feat for a man who rarely smiles. He has checked and rechecked every building in Burnchester Hall, every lock, every window, all the emergency exits. He and his dog Titan have done several rounds and confirmed that everything is secure. Titan had whined from time to time, but Titan often did. Sometimes, before the summer holidays Mr Rummage would inform Mr Gruff that there would be various works to be done over the summer break: walls to be painted; redecorating of classrooms done; the management of gardens and the preparation of pitches for the autumn. But this time none of it is needed. Any new works would now be delayed until next year, when, on account of the 600th anniversary of the building of the Hall, special preparations were being made. The teachers have now gone, including Mrs Limpet, who has just left, delayed because of her 'experiments' ('sorcery' is the word Mr Gruff preferred). Mr Rummage, the headmaster, and his wife Jenny, come and go, mainly only to their flat and the library. Other than that the school is quiet and tranquil as are the graves of St Mary Magdalen. Mr Gruff can safely say that the school is perfectly at peace. For the first time in many years he feels justified in letting his hair down. He is preparing for a holiday.

Mr Gruff had planned to go to his sister's house in Margate. He had once known love but had been jilted many years ago, so badly, as he saw it, that he resolved never to go through that pain again. He had found solace and pride in doing his job well, if not with popularity. Respect came first in his book, popularity a poor second. The children liked him, at a distance, though they were afraid of him close to. Sometimes he was abrasive, and it was this that led to his bad reputation in the children's eyes. His job was to keep the fabric of the school going, and look after their security. Not to be mates, or friends with the children, who would only move on. It was perhaps the moving on that would have brought a tear to his eye, had he let it. Order and routine were matched only by his love of facts. It didn't do to have an imagination, so many dark corners held fantastical things at Burnchester Hall, and an old military man like Mr Gruff, with a head like a football and eyes like a referee (they had a nervous blink), only liked to deal with things he knew.

Everything is arranged. His luggage is packed, his ticket bought, his sister Lorna will meet him at the station. Titan will accompany him.

Mr Gruff has put on a tie for his walk down to the the Burnchester Arms, along the river's edge, and plans to come back for an early night. Nothing could be more pleasurable than to walk across the school playing fields to the river, swallows filling the air and the cuckoo still, just, calling, for the half hour or so it takes to reach the pub. He can feel the splendour of it all, the privilege that he had not had as a child, but feels part of now, as he strides along to the stile that separates the school field from the path. This is not public, but it has long been recognised by the local farmer - Mr Granger - that it is a natural right for those working at the school to be allowed access across his land to reach the road and the later path to the pub.

Mr Gruff can see the Folly on the hill ahead of him - the same that Tyro, Jess and Rick had passed by a few hours earlier - crouching beneath tall trees. Having seen action himself, he feels proud of the symbol, but wouldn't dwell on the memories, carved in stone as they had also been on his own sad heart. The sun catches the top, where the flint stones shine. He turns to look back at the Hall, majestic, if a little alien. He is master of it in his own way. He is in charge of this huge anatomy of age, but knows little of its darker purpose.

He has his phone with him which is switched on. Mr Rummage can contact him directly, if he needs to.

On he strides, only the distant purr of a tractor over the field. Now on the other side of the river, which is a little deeper here, the tall trees brilliantly lit on this ancient piece of woodland. The green speckles of light enriched by an extravagant ground cover. Dense patches of undergrowth near the edge, the haunt of turtle doves, which purr too. Strange as it may seem, he has never crossed the bridge further up, and explored the woods. He has had enough to look after at the Hall. But he admires them. He is perhaps a man of open country, less happy in the shadows, where the light plays tricks and the vegetation is more complex. He has watched the deer leave and enter the wood many times, especially at dawn and dusk, to go mainly to feed on the fields and in the ditches away from the school, and on Mr Strangelblood's land. There are badgers here too. Somewhere inside, as far as he can recall, are the ruins, remains rather, of an iron-age fort, (some say it had been a priory) higher up the hill, towards the edge of the wood. There had been Roman pottery, but this had been lost under the vegetation. He doesn't read much, but likes to pride himself on knowing about the school and the local area, in case he has to take parents round. He knows that the school had been host to spies during the war, and he knew some of the ancient tales, but he does not want to know all. Knowledge is dangerous. Enough is it that he has been given the responsibility of looking after it. He does not wish to know the secrets. He tolerates the children, but they are secondary to his main task as the keeper of keys.

\*

Mr Rummage had left his flat, after going to the library, also on the same day that Tyro, Jess and Rick had made their escape, to pick up his wife, Jenny, from the station at Pickering, one of the small local market towns nearby. She had returned that afternoon, after going for a brief shopping excursion in the town of Sleepsake.

They were to pick up their children, Julia and Simon, who were learning tennis. Sport had always played a part in the lives of the family. "Good health is dependent on the balance of mind and body," Jenny said. Everyone sighed. For the past day and a half, Mr Rummage had been engaged in minor matters relating to  the school, and preparing for a short trip over to Cambridge, where he had some important business. He was to leave Jenny and the children at a friend's house near Wyemarket and go on for a day, before returning to pick them up to start them on their annual summer holiday, on an island off the coast of Scotland. They would not be returning to the school for two weeks.

On the afternoon in question, he and Jenny had got into their car and set off. Their children were with them, Julia, eleven and two thirds and Simon, nine. They were both at the school, a privilege, some would say, of being the daughter and son of the Headmaster, though not a great success from anyone else's point of view. Having your own children under your charge always led to an element of implied favouritism, which meant that you sometimes played it down, and in fact ignored them more than you would have done in another regime. Teachers felt obliged to treat them differently, even only marginally, though they would have protested against the slightest suggestion of it. Parents, especially those with children in the same class as Julia or Simon, would subtly try to exploit the connection for their children's, or more particularly, their own, ends. Jenny is a music and drama teacher in a school nearby ("I couldn't possibly teach at Burnchester" she had once told him). This was one of the best ways of reducing some of the hints of favouritism, or the influence of her husband. She was respected for 'supporting' another school, and for being a professional as well as a mother, an attitude that infuriated her. From her perspective, being a mother meant that you were likely to be a better professional. Anyone who knew her recognised her complete lack of any social climbing, scheming or politicking, sometimes to her husband's dismay.

Julia was in the same class as Tyro and Jess. She didn't get on with Tyro at all, and Jess was a sparring partner. Only she and Jess devoured books so avariciously.

Mr Rummage had spent many years as a physicist in a research station outside his old university, but had always wanted to teach. So, after nine years working on particle physics, he decided to change direction, and gave up his ambitions in space research. He trained as a teacher, and taught for several years in local schools before being appointed as Headmaster at Burnchester. At first his appointment was unpopular (internal candidates were always a favourite) but he managed to turn the majority of the governors, and certainly staff, around. He was deeply committed to the children, regarding the responsibility under his care as a gift. He felt himself a keeper of the past and the future. Children were both. Nothing gave him greater satisfaction than running rings around parents who quibbled about this or that action, as they knew that he was often considerably their superior intellectually, and had no time whatsoever for the pretensions that accompanied the understandable ambitions that some parents had for their offsprings' development. He worked hard to achieve the best he could for each and every one of them, making sure that he did what he could to help them into their future careers. He believed that all children were more gifted than was often recognised. There were 'failures' of course, and he struggled with these. To some extent one of these was Rick.

One of his weaknesses was that he tried sometimes to do too much (he still maintained academic and scientific connections), and achieved less than he hoped. This was an insurmountable fact, the result of the choices he had set himself.

Another reason for his being chosen as Headmaster was that

Mr Rummage had long been interested in books. He loved history. He knew Burnchester's past, and some of its secrets, others of which he was still in the process of unravelling. He knew that the darkest secrets of all were yet to be revealed. Those who had appointed him, themselves living in the shadows, knew that he could be trusted to keep them.

It would not have been a surprise to learn that not only was he well acquainted with the school's role in training spies, but that he himself had been asked at his old university if he would become one. But this secret was his alone, though Jenny, no less discreet or intelligent, would not have been surprised, as she had been asked herself.

Mr Rummage had phoned Mr Gruff on the evening of his departure towards the Burnchester Arms, to wish him a pleasant holiday and to check that everything was OK. Mr Gruff was his usual self - brusque - which satisfied Mr Rummage. It was with a light heart that he left Jenny and the children near Wyemarket. He drove into Cambridge by the back route that he had known so well as a student. He drove to a small flat in central Cambridge, and parked the car.

He walked up the steps, and rang the bell. The door opened. The face that greeted him was not a face at all. It was a mask.

"For these are actions that a man might play. Welcome Horatio!" said the mask. And Mr Rummage went in.

*

By the time he reached the Burnchester Arms, Mr Gruff was feeling on top of the world. The walk did him good. He was thirsty and feeling almost sociable. The sun was still high, and there was warmth in the air.

As a man of some importance in the community of the school, he felt no less important here, so he straightened his tie and went in.

There, in front of him, was a sight to behold. The light of the western sun cast shadows over the tables by the fireplace, which held flowers, rather than embers, for the summer. Ahead of Mr Gruff, Mr Gatherin was perched on a seat behind the bar, in conversation with two men whose backs were turned. On Mr Gruff's entry however, they turned in his direction. One of the men Mr Gruff recognised, but could not place. It was in fact Dennis Wander, Abby's brother. He had a habit of stopping off for a drink before going on to his sister's house. He was a day early and would surprise her. He was a fairly frequent visitor and was well known to Mr Gatherin, though he was a little brash and confident, and came from London. This was a minus, though compensated for by the cash that (in his case) went with it. He had light reddish hair and the eyes of a giant. He talked purposefully, and with animation, regaling them with stories. When necessary, or when it suited him, he could be as receptive as the grave and could draw from people those confidences they wished they had not revealed, probably because of the warmth he had generated. He was a man of the world, beneath a simple exterior.

Mr Gatherin got up, as Mr Gruff entered.

"Abandoning your duties, Mr Gruff?" said Mr Gatherin. "What will it be?"

"Not at all, Doug," said Mr Gruff, "duties done, all in order. Pint please, landlord. And these gentlemen?"

Mr Gruff was not a man of words, but he hoped the tie would make up for it. Nor was he normally a man to offer drinks to people he didn't know well, indeed even to those he did.

"Gentlemen?" he repeated.

"A pint please," said Dennis, clearly at ease, talking as if he had been playing tennis. "Most kind of you, Mr Gruff."

Outside there was the sound of children playing in the beer garden, which consisted of a wooden table with two benches set close to the river.

The wooden bar stretched half the length of the room. Around two sides were two long benches, both empty. In front of the fireplace, to the side of the entrance door, were two round tables, with chairs around them. At one of these was a group of students, clearly not all English, laughing loudly, and dressed in theatrical clothes.

They were as oblivious of their surroundings as Dennis appeared to be.

Only Dennis noticed a man reading quietly in the far corner of the bar. He sensed a cold face, as cold as he had ever seen.

"And yours, Mr Pinchet?" said Mr Gruff turning to the other man beside Dennis, as Mr Gatherin brought him his drink.

"Don't mind if I do, Mr Gruff," said the man. This was Geoffrey Pinchet, the local gamekeeper and a very regular visitor to the Arms. He was not quite to be trusted.

"Pint please, Doug," said Mr Pinchet. "Good of you, Mr Gruff. Things must be looking up."

Mr Gruff straightened his tie.

"And you, Mr Gatherin?" asked Mr Gruff to his own surprise and the even greater surprise of the publican. "I am," he looked at his watch, "very nearly on holiday."

"Alright, Mr Gruff. I'll join you. But that doesn't mean we stay open late," said Mr Gatherin, going to the back of the bar to fill the glasses from a wooden barrel.

"Soon be litres, Doug," said Mr Pinchet, attempting to wind him up.

"Not in my bloody lifetime - not that it makes much difference."

The words flowed with great precision from Doug's unusually animated face as he returned with the drinks. As a man of seventy, he crossed the few feet to the bar like an agile turtle, carrying as much weight around his girth and probably as much sensitivity beneath his well developed shell.

"Cheers, Mr Gruff!"

The room seemed to echo "Cheers".

"Cheers!" said Mr Pinchet.

"Your good health," added Mr Gatherin.

"Here's to you all!" said Mr Gruff, beginning to enjoy himself. He was pleased that he could still generate some kindness, his life was in fact lonelier than he realised. At this he looked at Titan and gave him a friendly kick.

"Leaving the place on its own, I hear," began Mr Pinchet, in quieter tones. "Still, you deserve a holiday. I hope you've got someone to keep an eye on the place while you're away?"

The students' revelry had become a little more subdued. The man in the far corner was listening.

Mr Gatherin leaned over. "Drama students, staying over at the College, Motley Fall."

"Thought it closed for the summer," said Dennis.

"No. Special workshops in the summer. Brings in the cash."

The students in question were now in quiet conversation.

"Of course," said Mr Gruff, joking, "couldn't leave the place unattended. I believe they've asked you to watch over it, haven't they, Mr Pinchet?"

Nobody was convinced by this, but Mr Pinchet liked being flattered.

"I don't mind checking it over for vermin," he said with slow emphasis, "from time to time. Mr Strangelblood wouldn't want me away. I've got enough on my hands, with summer visitors taking liberty walks in my woods and disturbing things. Bloody nuisance having old ruins on the place, never mind the game."

Dennis looked up, as if he couldn't help thinking of some of the present company, but said nothing.

"Still, I expect you can kill at 600 metres, Mr Pinchet, should you need to?" said the landlord, bringing back memories of earlier times.

This astute observation was disturbed by rapturous applause. The group of students had all turned round and were clapping.

The reason was obvious enough. A very large if no longer youthful gentleman, wearing a beret and a coloured apron, and rolling towards them like a marionette, was carrying, shoulder high, a large plate, on top of which were arrayed all the accoutrements of a meal. He was beaming with unusual vigour as he leant down on the table, a space having been created for him by the student nearest the door.

"Et voilà!" the man declared with a flourish, "ze steak and kidney pie, à la Française! Specially prepared for our guests. And in keeping with my tradition, az a foreign guest myself, I have taken the liberty of trying a little to check it is OK. It is," he added after a little reflection. "Ummm. Even si I zay so myself! Bon appetit!"

He continued with a further flourish garnished with deep mystery, rolling his eyes to the heavens, and with a quick glance over to Mr Gatherin at the bar. Mr Gatherin of course noticed nothing.

It was an interesting habit of Mr Le Petit (meaning Mr Small, in view of his enormous size) that he would always try his clients' food first, not on the basis that it might be poisoned and that he therefore should be the first to 'go' in the event of such a tragedy, but because he could not consider parting with one of his own creations, for that is what they were, without ensuring its integrity first. Another interpretation might have been that he liked his food too much. He had even been known, as a result of this generous exercise in self-denial, to take the food back with a swift and very voluble condemnation, such as "Rubbish! Take it away!" at which point he would, and come back some time later with a second and always successful second attempt. The client (they were never customers) might have been in a hurry, or not. He (or she) might even have found the flavour most satisfactory in the first place and not in need of further enrichment, but this was never considered. If M. Le Petit (also known as M. Le Grand) was unhappy, everybody else would be too. This is the downside of being a great artist. Temperamental but always sincere. Mr Gatherin indulged this extravagant behaviour by assuring the client that they were lucky to get a meal at all, and would they like another drink in the meantime. An act of generosity that always seemed to work, and covered the cost of the additional electricity needed for the remake.

The students looked down in amazement. Then, within moments, there was a general rattling of plates and tinkling of cutlery as they began in earnest to do justice to ze pie. Such is the triumph of substance over presentation, for it was, truly, home cooking at its best, with a little garnish it must be admitted, and garlic.

During this magnificence, Dennis, Mr Gruff and Mr Pinchet had continued their conversation quietly, with the occasional smile in acknowledgement of the infectious energy at the table. This even induced Mr Pinchet to buy a round, though Dennis was a little cautious before accepting. Something else was on his mind, and he had to get back to Abby's home.

The unknown visitor reading in the corner of the bar, had got up and slipped out. He wore a long cloak.

Dennis pretended not to notice at first, not wanting to upset Mr Pinchet and his generosity, nor wanting to break the pre-holiday mood that had now more fully infected Mr Gruff as he was smiling broadly (his tie loosened), while Titan was dreaming. However, he was anxious to follow, and prepared to leave.

"Mr Gatherin," said Dennis with gentle firmness, "Mr Gruff is in need of a refill. Not for me, but I'm sure Mr Pinchet will also have one and please take one for yourself. A quiet word if I may."

Mr Dennis was renowned for quiet words, and they never aroused suspicion, for which reason Mr Pinchet nodded as he took the first pull of smoke into his lungs, a bit like a fish drowning out of water, so much did he enjoy it, and in acknowledgement of the fact that quiet words were undoubtedly the best form of communication. Mr Gruff put his glass down amiably with a, "Thank you, I won't say no. One for the road. Have to leave."

He drew in his breath proudly and lent forward and added, "First holiday in eleven years. Lots to do. One last drink and then off. Off," he said, gently kicking Titan.

Mr Gatherin slid a couple of paces along the bar and bent his ear across it. He spoke in a quiet voice to Dennis. Mr Pinchet, only caught the last part.

"Never seen him before in my life. Just one drink."

Dennis thanked him and his drinking companions and exited with a nod to the students, who raised their forks.

Outside, Dennis reacted very quickly. He ran up the path to the car park, and checked over the cars. His own rather beaten up estate, what he presumed was Mr Pinchet's old short-wheel-based Land Rover, and a van containing twelve seats and maps of East Anglia. On the side was written Motley Fall. Mr Gatherin's old pick-up stood apart, in its own clearly regular space.

Dennis ran on up the track towards the road and looked both left and right. Nothing. A deer by the entrance to the wood in the distance. An empty road the other way. The sun was still visible at this point across the river valley as he looked back. There was enough light to have seen anybody had they been walking in the open along the river bank.

For a moment he stood and watched. He could not recall the sound of a car, nor could he recall having seen any other in the car park on his arrival, though he was not sure whether he had arrived before or after the man, so subtly had he come and gone.

"Damn!" he said to himself. He hated imprecision, especially when he needed his powers.

He ran back to the car park and got in. He took out a pair of binoculars from the glove compartment, put them on the seat beside him, switched on the engine, backed out up the rough drive, and went left. By following the road for a mile or so he would come to the road which passed the place where Tyro and Jess had had their picnic. From there he would see, even in this light, anyone who might be walking along the river, and the wider landscape. He continued on to the junction at the bottom of the valley, close to the river.

After a short drive, he backed the car into a field entrance, hiding it between two tall hedges. He got out and walked to the field edge, Shelter Field, and hid. He took out his binoculars and waited. He knew something was wrong.

*

By the time Mr Gruff has reached the Shelter Field, he is in a happy mood. He has let Titan free. He has begun to sing.

"Oh, what a beautiful evening! Oh, what a beautiful day!" The sounds of night are not quite upon him and would not cast judgement. Dennis, having waited for some time, is alerted by the voice that heralds the man, still hidden behind the hedge close to the river bank. "This is it," he thought, now completely awake. The stranger is here. Now he will find out what he is up to.

Think of his disappointment, not to say amazement, when he sees the amiable Gruff strolling along like a top above the grass. Titan is too far below to have picked up Dennis's scent, and downwind, though he seems suddenly to have caught another and begun to race along the path towards the school.

Dennis watches them go into the school field where he loses sight of them. He walks back up to his car. Whoever the strange man is, he hasn't come that way, unless he has inhuman powers.

He has done what he could. Perhaps he had been exaggerating. He thinks of Abby and Tyro. He even thinks of Rompy. With these homespun images he climbs back into his car and pulls away. As he does so, a beautiful owl crosses his path, and flies towards the river valley.

As he watches, the owl glides silently to the edge of the oncoming mist. In the back of his mind he can sense a growing shadow.

Mr Gruff is now well onto the school playing fields. Over the river, the dark Folly lies at rest beneath the trees. Above to his right, the vast spread of the Hall is now shrouded in darkness. At once his mood changes. The thought of the school, vast empty and alone, strikes him as never before. How can he go away? He isn't frightened but he can imagine the empty space, like everlasting death, unprotected, silent and waiting. Should he not, even now, stay, to look after the place? There had been rumours.

The sudden muffled sound of his phone. A voice calling for help. Come quickly. Where? By the river. The old boathouse. Should he go? Titan has run ahead and can not be seen in the enveloping night. He wishes he could go home. He even wishes he could catch a night train and join his sister, immediately. But he cannot refuse. He cannot refuse the voice that calls to him. He is, after all, still on duty. Against his better judgement, and slightly disorientated by alcohol, he makes his way down to the river.

The old boathouse. The lapping water. The water's edge. He finds the boathouse door open. The door that had been kept locked, year in, year out. He enters. There at his feet lies Titan, unconscious or dead. His eyes cannot stop blinking. Ahead of him the head of a man staring out of the night.

Mr Gruff tries to call out. The man's hands grab his throat and drag him down. All he can hear as he falls and loses consciousness are the words, "Welcome to your nightmare, Mr Keeper of Keys."

# 5

Mr Rummage had spent a lively if difficult evening with his colleagues, one of whom was Mr Baxter, the English teacher from the school, though you would not have recognised him. Slight changes in his face, brought about by lensless glasses, changed hair shape, subtle shading without giving the impression of being make-up, a moustache, and slightly greying hair, gave him a more academic middle-aged feel. Here he was Professor Southgate, of the Cambridge Institute.

Two others had been present. Jeremy Vale, a researcher from London, and Jane Fellows, a historian based at the Courtly Institute. The evening had gone on late, their business had been dealt with sufficiently, though it raised as many questions as it answered, and they had decided to meet again in the summer on Mr Rummage's return from the Highlands.

For his part, Mr Baxter had employed three masks, with equal vigour, the three of them now sitting in his small study as he looked out at the back garden of this neat, centrally located Regency terrace. These he called The Three Muses, though they had nothing in common with the real thing. Nothing gave him more pleasure than to give his masks full vent, and then to leave them aside and allow his own creative and varied nature reign.

Mr Baxter believed in the power of the imagination, perhaps above all others, as the source of greatest wisdom. He enjoyed teaching. He learned much from his students, and from some of his colleagues at Burnchester Hall, but also loved not to teach. He was always learning. One day perhaps people would find what he had to say was interesting enough to read in a book, but for the moment these things remained scattered in note form and in his mind alone. He could hear the voice of his father saying to him as a child as he returned from school, "And what did you learn today?" His father had continued saying this right up to his death, at the age of sixty-seven, two years previously. Every day, even during his final days, he would look lovingly at Peter, his son, and ask "What have you learned today?" though gradually he became weaker, and the words more distant. When he died, Peter felt sure, as his eyes finally closed, that he had said, for he was with him, with his last breath, "What have I learned?" He wondered whether his father had felt a sense of failure to achieve what he had hoped, and was capable of, so much had he given his son.

Mr Baxter, though gregarious, was as happy to work quietly in the evenings alone. And yet he missed something in his life, and it was this deep yearning - the unknown quest - that led him on, in a direction or for a purpose that had not yet been revealed to him. He sensed that Ms Peverell had seen this in him, and they had become close friends. It was also this that had led him, by a roundabout route, to become acquainted with the three others who had gathered at his flat the previous evening. He used the flat in Cambridge on occasional week-ends away from Burnchester, but mostly during the holidays.

Mr Rummage had stayed in Mr Baxter's spare room and had left early that morning. Jeremy Vale and Jane Fellows had driven back to London very late.

Mr Baxter was in the process of unravelling his disguise whilst enjoying a black coffee, without sugar. He would call Ms Peverell shortly. He needed her advice, her flair. Then he would set off for the fast train to London, to fly to Toulouse, in southern France. She would join him. He would soon lose all his disguise and return to the character with whom he felt most at ease. His disguise was both a ritual and a necessity. Different places required different habits; different habits, different features. Life could become a play, as long as you knew which was which, and knew how to manage both. Mr Baxter was a keeper of secrets.

That same morning Mr Rummage met with Jenny and the two children, Julia and Simon, in Wyemarket where they had stayed. After a brief chat with their friends, they made their excuses and started on the laborious journey to 'The North', as it was so inspiringly described on the sign on the A1 M, that haulage firms' alter ego, the crawlers' paradise. Mr Rummage did not enjoy driving, and Jenny did, so after a brief lunch at one of those motorway restaurants - the kind you slip into or miss with equal ease - it might have been a Smiling Banger or a Jolly Spud, he would soon forget, though the children preferred the Smiling Banger, as free gifts appeared on the waitress' tray with their meal, especially on holidays. Even Julia, with a growing sense that she was not a child, was tempted into returning for some moments to that happier time and indulge her long-since abandoned interest in plastic toys that don't work, and which have no character at all. This is probably why she liked books, at least there you could make much more than you could from the toys, and out of nothing. At the same time she was hard-headed and could retreat out of dreams as quickly as enter into them. In this respect she was unlike Tyro.

The car was packed full of everything imaginable, from a tent, to an inflatable dinghy with one oar (the second would have to be improvised), to dried milk, books and every conceivable item of clothing to cater for any weather, which was always more reliable than the experts predicted, which meant that most of the anoraks and leggings would probably not get used. Even so, the packing was half the fun, as Jenny had told the children in her attempt to get them involved. This seemed to work, partly on account also of the holiday money which had appeared at the same time, though generally the children didn't get much.

Simon loved the whole process, and especially bargaining with Julia as to which side of the car each should have, and who should sit behind whom. If Tyro had known these curious facts perhaps she would have liked Julia more. For Julia, despite her strong personality, protected her brother whilst also patronising him, and allowed him mostly these freedoms, in exchange, for - well, nothing, just what she called love.

With Jenny at the wheel, Mr Rummage wound back the seat and watched the clouds out of the window. Simon was playing 'I spy' with Julia, who was also trying to read a book. Jenny was trying to concentrate on the lorry ahead, which seemed intractably wedded to the middle lane - it was one of those two-wagon jobs from the continent - and she didn't have the power to overtake. There was a more coherent reason. She had always felt that driving North meant going uphill, and that needed special energy. Coming home was, she imagined, downhill all the way, which explained why they always came back more quickly than it took to get there. Jenny could compose while driving. Something to do with the rhythms and pauses within a given framework and time scale. She could have done without the fumes. She preferred trains and even more she preferred running water, or the sea.

Mr Rummage's mind began to wander. Although they were now on holiday, it always took time to let go of what was on his mind. School politics were never-ending. Who might replace the biology teacher who was looking increasing vulnerable? Mrs Limpet, a great servant and a good teacher in her time, now needed protection and was, as he saw it, losing it. He had had to step in on several occasions, but had not yet found the cause of her behaviour, the most recent example being the cruel detention of Tyro (which he had heard about). Her own troubled life could not justify or allow for a deterioration in her performance, or behaviour. He had seen her erupt on more than one occasion, and felt sorry for those students who were on the receiving end. He tried to cover for this, and had confronted her about it. She had been aggressive. She said she didn't know what he was talking about. Then she broke down and cried. Then he felt sorry for her, because he knew that she had an inkling of trouble, as her tears revealed, though she could not fully admit it to herself. So the floodgates might have opened, though by holding them shut, the catastrophe was likely to be greater, when it came. He felt that something outside his control, and certainly hers, had emerged in recent months. Something more troubling than he had yet defined. It was as though, from the mists of the river, a dark cloud was beginning to stalk the school, infect the place, and Mrs Limpet had caught the first wave of the virus. He was sure it was not only of her making. Tyro's mother had been very understanding.

Then there were parents! They were his greatest difficulty. From the highest to the lowest, each had their own agenda. Understandably, perhaps, but there was an increasing tendency to ignore teacher professionalism. He appreciated parent in-put, but only as one element in the bigger picture. Yet it was his job to explain. He wished that he had understood less well the connection between parents and children. How many children's difficulties could not be traced to their parents? How many parents failed to make this connection in the fullest degree? He was a parent too.

The car purred like a dreaming cat.

Children's results; maintenance; managing the school's 'reputation'. Leave aside the interferences of government, poor policies and initiatives. League tables indeed! Since when was education like football. Looming up next year was the 600th anniversary of the building of Burnchester Hall, which was to double as the fiftieth anniversary of the school (though it was the fifty-second).

Then there were family matters. Julia was doing well. She had a slight tendency to tantrums. Perhaps this compensated for his desire to appear balanced. Perhaps it was the expression of a strong character at a certain stage. In this she was not unlike Jenny, whose tantrums were mostly inner and highly evident in her music and in the plays she chose to stage.

Simon was doing OK. He was, every teacher told him, 'average' - what a terrible label! Mr Rummage had tried to decree that no teacher should ever put 'average' on any student report without finding some area in which he or she could excel. This was wishful thinking, others kept telling him, but he would not let go of this ideal, and it often turned up trumps. Most if not all children did have special abilities or qualities even if it required time, and digging. Yes, digging. Gold didn't often lie on the surface, any more than true wealth was normally immediately visible. Teachers were occasionally the problem. They had neither the time nor sometimes the insight to see beyond the chaos of the fraught academic year. But then, they were human too and often highly stressed. And yet teachers had been children once. So what happened?

Simon would be OK. He was popular and, yes, average. Perhaps that was the best protection.

Above all there was the feeling that something was in the air, some half-formed infection, in the first stages of conception. But what? It was only a feeling.

Jenny had put on one of her tapes. This was a combination of flute and bass. He appreciated her taste (generally), but there was a time and a place. Here she was, playing the two instruments, the pure tones of the flute able to describe distant cadences, while the dark triumph of the bass filled the background like the trees on an olive grove. But...the image of the virus would not go away. Mrs Limpet had left that afternoon with a bandaged hand. What, he wondered, were the three children doing at the school (for he had caught a glimpse of them out of the corner of his subtle eye)? Should he have investigated, or let sleeping dogs lie? He had almost thought "die".

"This is so boring, Mum," said Julia.

Jenny gave her a stare in the central mirror. "When you can play better, I'll take your word for it!"

Parents were a pain!

The clouds were thicker now. Simon was playing Julia at car scrabble.

Then she added, as if from nowhere, "Does anybody read this stuff these days? I mean it's so boring!"

"What is it this time?" said her mother turning up the volume on one of her favourite passages, where the flute and the bass, as she saw it, became one.

"Shakespeare. We've got to read this bit from Hamlet, or whatever it's called, for next term. There's no way Ophelia is believable."

Mum muttered, "Perhaps you're right. But then," turning the volume down again, she added, "it's not quite like that, Julia, is it. It's not really supposed to be real."

"What do you think, Dad?"

"Let him be. He's asleep."

Why did parents always have to be not available when you wanted them most?

The weather had changed. The wind was now pushing the car from the west, suggesting heavy rain from the Pennines.

Mr Rummage was indeed asleep. He was in another world. The events of last night began to take over, the clouds now seemed to be a large table surrounded by people, playing cards with each other's destiny. Were they the Gods of Olympus, and bloated like dead sheep? Perhaps the sheep had caught the virus too.

Something else was troubling him. To do with the school, with last night. Perhaps he shouldn't have gone away. Would the school be safe? He dreamt of Burnchester Hall, locked up in silence, keeper of secrets from the infernal hosts. Something was knocking at the door. Where was the keeper of the keys?

\*

Mr Rummage had spent the previous afternoon and early part of the evening with Mr Baxter before the others had arrived. He and Mr Baxter followed a routine. At first Mr Baxter had been friendly and polite. He had placed the mask of Diplomacy in the mask-holder beside his chair. During this time they discussed a few school matters. Then he replaced it with the mask of Anger, a red-faced dragon, beside him. Then he smiled, but with a smile of vicious intent, as one might smile and 'be a villain', or 'look like the innocent flower but be the serpent under it'. Finally he placed the mask of Curiosity, at which his face became an innocent child's looking out on to the assembled.

"What do you think, John?" Mr Baxter had asked.

"I think your masks are getting better. I only hope that Jeremy Vale and Jane Fellows will remain convinced. We have no reason to doubt either of them. I like them both. And they are colleagues."

"We have to doubt somebody," was Peter Baxter's answer. "Otherwise we will not be prepared. Something is on the track of the secrets we have been asked to find, something or someone has given them a clue. Where else would they get their information, but from one of us? I want you to watch their reactions."

"It is widely recognised that Burnchester holds many secrets, even if the details are not all known. After all, we do not know them all ourselves, yet."

"That is why we must get there first. That is why our work is so important and why they, whoever they may be, the so-called Priory, should be defeated. Vigilance is better than sorrow that comes too late. If we are all reliable, so much the better. But our job is to be suspicious - even, sometimes, of ourselves."

"That is not something I am very happy to admit, Peter," added Mr Rummage whose sense of honour sometimes clouded his understanding of personal psychology.

By the early evening, in fact at exactly 6 o'clock, the bell rang and Professor Southgate went to the door of his flat. Two people came through to find John Rummage in a comfy chair reading a document. He got up at their entry, and shook hands with them both.

"I hope you had a pleasant journey," he said. "The trains to Cambridge are easier than travelling by car. And they're getting better. It's good to see you again."

"Professor Southgate's instructions are always exact," Jane Fellows had said, with a degree of evident satisfaction, as if it had suited her apparently breezy temperament.

Professor Southgate had taken their coats, and shortly came in with a tray of drinks.

Jane Fellows took a dry sherry. Jeremy Vale, a gin and tonic, apologising for having to have the bottle opened. John Rummage a Scotch, "in readiness for the Highlands. And I'm not driving tonight."

Professor Southgate had a fizzy water mixed with orange juice, and topped it up with ice.

"And how is the life of academe?" Jeremy Vale said. "Cheers," he added, as if forgetting his question.

Professor Southgate replied courteously.

"An unending process, first with asking the right questions, second with finding the right sources, and third with language. Nothing is ever clear. That is why we need something else, something beyond us, if yet ourselves. Reason has its limits too. Yet we seek the infinite. And the life of fine art?" he added to Jane Fellows.

"It is always slow when you think you are approaching a breakthrough. But I think you will find our results interesting. If not definitive," she said with precision. Then she smiled and

71

added, "perhaps nothing ever is, as we are dealing with illusions, except death?"

What made Jane Fellows digress cannot be known. The more striking fact was that she showed no sign of knowing quite what she had said.

"Oh, I don't think so," said Jeremy Vale. "As a historian yourself you will know that the past and the future are separated only by a thin but powerful umbilical chord. The past is everywhere. Death, if you like, stalks us from every direction. Isn't that why we are here? About the future I will say nothing, though it is everywhere too."

For a moment Jane Fellows was silent. Then she said, turning to Professor Southgate,

"We are here to prevent the spread of false knowledge on the back of the abuse of power. I don't see any masks, Professor?"

"You remember my little game!" replied the Professor, with a little caress of his moustache, and the glee of a child. "My little ploy for communicating with colleagues."

"How could I forget, Professor Southgate? Each of us has expertise. Yours is illusions."

"I thought it inappropriate for this evening's activities. Some masks of course are invisible. These," he continued, pointing to the three masks on the side-table, "are enjoying a rest. They are merely to direct ways of being."

He then took each mask in turn and performed a little silent drama, first stretching himself up to his full height, with a frown, arms open and hands displayed, adding a delicate, but serious smile. His hands played the role of appeaser, casting an air of tranquillity on the imagined audience. He mouthed his words calmly and with a consistency of tone that could only mean Diplomacy. Then he raged like a wild wind, gesticulating, striding about the room, moving his lips in short motions mixing volume, with pause, beating his fist, tearing his hair, stabbing his imagined opponents. Finally, after Anger, came Curiosity. Here he looked, without guile or intent, on the world, like a child gazing up at an ancient tree.

He sat down, slightly exhausted, but in control. He caught his breath and had a sip of drink. He looked at his colleagues with a blank if inwardly amused face, as if to say, "shall we get on with the business?"

During this time, John Rummage had watched Jane Fellows and Jeremy Vale. He had the impression that Jeremy Vale's responses were sympathetic and playful, those of an audience ready to be persuaded, and with an openness that bordered on a kind of love. As a research academic, he had long forgone the ambitions of power, and was reminded each day of the need to enjoy the moment, each moment, to the full. Jane Fellows, on the other hand, began with a quizzical look as if to say "not again" and tolerated her host only with forbearance. She only regretted that she had mentioned the masks. But when it came to Anger, she became inspired, as if she shared something of that rage, that surging destructive force, that could, if used properly, and controlled, cleanse and create, Phoenix-like, as from a spent fire. And if not, would lead to dark forces preying and exploiting the energy to drown the fragile peace of our world.

"Which is why we are here, I think," Professor Southgate said, with great sincerity. "To listen, to learn, and to go forward. We have a common destiny. I hope our work will help us to find what we seek, and, perhaps, shed a little light on the identity of our enemy. Please, John. Please begin the proceedings."

He ensured that everyone had a full glass, and was comfortable.

Mr Rummage was happy to start the proceedings on the understanding that when it came to his turn, he would ask Professor Southgate to take over.

The format would be simple. Each in turn would tell their story. Then they would discuss the situation which had brought them together. Then he would end with a summary and fix a further time to meet. He stressed one point. That the contents of the meeting would remain confidential to the four of them, unless it was agreed by all of them to disclose such information as they chose to a wider audience. There would only be one exception to this requirement. That circumstances forced them to do so.

He called on Jeremy Vale to start. Dr Vale was a humble man who did not like the limelight. He was an authority on the Christian Church. Besides an encyclopaedic knowledge of the mainstream faiths, he had a special interest in religious sects, including non-Christian. He had begun his work by learning of their development across the ages, and more recently in our own culture and society, and followed as much as he could of the most strange sects, which were becoming more prominent and more powerful in this era of increased secularism. Some of these were interesting, at best beneficial to their supporters, at worst, dangerous. He had a passing knowledge of what was happening in other religions. He had a special interest in groups that might threaten the stability of the Church as a whole and therefore, he believed, indirectly, the state. He was not so simple as to believe in the mutual exclusivity of each.

He was an ordained priest at an Independent Church in London, which had a troubled relationship with Rome, about whose history he was not always proud. But his contacts with Rome gave him access to special information, and structures of influence, the cross-over between so-called religion and political power.

Dr Vale felt caught between a wish to keep the old language and traditions which he strongly believed had formed some of the most positive qualities of our culture, from its central values to its art, with a recognition that change was demanding a repositioning of church structures and doctrines, if not the emergence of a completely new framework of religious symbolism.

He knew that out of the decline in institutionalised faith

there were both dangers and opportunities. He was most concerned with the dangers. Recent history showed how clearly atheism could lead to extreme intolerance, as could fundamentalism, yet he viewed with horror the vacuum created by the growing perception that the church was redundant.

His present role, he said, was to bring his 'colleagues' up to date about a group who were making dangerous claims about fundamental tenets of Christianity. These, presented in the wrong way, and in the wrong hands, could be used by extreme groups, seeking power for their own dubious ends. The dangers of extremism were clear. Intolerance spread fear, and led to the destructive abuse of power. One such group, known as the Priory, was active in small cells in Europe, and had recently become active in England. It was believed that they were now present in East Anglia. To what precise ends he was not sure. His sources had told him that their aim was to blackmail the Church hierarchies of England and of Rome with this information, in order to gain power, if not to destroy them.

He would not at this stage go into further details, but he believed that a certain document, with explosive power to do damage, might be hidden in the complex cavernous depths beneath the school. The fact that there was a school at all gave both protection but also exposed children and staff to particular dangers. Abduction, blackmail, perhaps worse. It was known to the present company that, as part of the training of spies, and as part of the efforts to challenge the power of evil that fascism had promoted, training had taken place in countering dark arts within the deep recesses of the tunnels, and that those still held very significant symbolic and actual power. That the Church of St Mary Magdalen was on the site of one of the most potent energy sources in Western Europe gave it a significance of which only few were aware.

The Priory were aware of the history and role that Burnchester had played during the Second World War, of the hidden chambers, and documents that were reputed to be contained within its walls. He explained that there was an active cell in the vicinity of Burnchester and that they should be vigilant. There were other groups, also active, perhaps under the guise of other names with their own sometimes dubious agendas. His colleagues should not rule out some interaction between them for mutual expediency's sake.

The Priory had shadowy connections with dark unknown powers that lie at the root of the struggle for supremacy in the world.

"What are you implying, Dr Vale?"

"I am implying that if the knowledge and power fall into these people's hands, people like the Priory, we may lose the battle, and goodness will be enveloped by darkness. Perhaps for ever. We have to stop them, we have to get there first, find the information that is lost. Before it is too late."

Following his speech, Dr Vale sat down. There was a brief pause, after which Mr Rummage thanked him for his words. He asked his colleagues to reserve questions till later.

"So that we can see the connections between us," he explained. "But if you wish a break, please take one now."

The sun outside the window had begun to set, the evening glow filling the room with light. Jane Fellows got up and left the room. Professor Southgate filled Dr Vale's glass, and offered another drink to Mr Rummage, who declined.

When Jane Fellows had returned, Mr Rummage asked her if she would mind following with her report.

Her tone was more business-like, as if time were running out. She began as follows:

"As you know, I was asked by the Board of Trustees of Burnchester Hall to consider the origins of a painting which had come to light by accident a few years ago. The painting had been found in an attic of a house frequented by the Reverend Sandals, vicar of St Mary Magdalen, the church at Burnchester, during a visit to one of his parishioners. It appeared to be medieval in origin, from the subject matter, but not much else was known about it at the time.

"Once it had been cleaned by experts attached to the Courtly Institute, it was clear that it could not be a fake. Gradually we have been able to piece together something of its history. It is almost certainly of late 13th century in origin though some would put it at a little later. It seems to have come from a priory near Thetford, by a circuitous route. It later came into the possession of the first Sir Cheesepeake. His grandfather had hidden it during the dissolution of the monasteries. This, it seems, was less out of a religious conviction, more from a belief in its beauty. As we know, the family were patrons of the arts for centuries, if with varying degrees of enthusiasm.

"The painter is still not known. He was probably English, of considerable skill. He almost certainly trained abroad, possibly in Italy or The Low countries. This we can deduce from the style. It is believed to be one of the most important, if not *the* most important painting from the medieval period, to have survived in this country. But this is not the only feature of considerable interest.

"Let me first consider the painting's subject. This is in many respects conventional. Its central image is of the Crucifixion. The panels on either side contain portraits of key figures in the early Christian Church. St John, St Peter, St James, St Mary Magdalen. Surrounding these is a smaller strip of added panelling showing scenes from Jesus's life, inspired by, but not an exact replica of, the Stations of the Cross. There are many interesting images and symbols. These are still being connected into the web of research, pictorial and historical, for the period and the area. Many are of course well known.

"As with many such paintings, its function was various. It was of course a icon of worship. It was also a record and an illustration. But further than that - and this is the main reason for our meeting here - it also contained coded messages for those who could interpret them. That is to say, images and symbols only recognisable by those with special knowledge. Some of these relate to the aristocratic orders of the families of the time, others are of a deeper, esoteric symbolism, understood by a very few."

"And these relate to the power that is being sought by groups who wish to threaten the Church?" Dr Vale asked.

"More than relate. They hint at the whereabouts of the knowledge that they need to obtain it. Let me explain. It is thought that this painting may have been inspired in part by a secret society connected with the Knights Templar, the powerful if secretive order who lost favour so suddenly in 1307. The Templars, you will remember, had access to secret knowledge, which gave them huge power over the Catholic Church. They regarded themselves as the keepers of these secrets, and the true line from which they were to be passed on. This will be of interest to Dr Vale. I have already discussed with him whether there are any connections, to his knowledge, to other paintings in the Templar tradition. I believe he thinks there may be. He only knows of one Templar building in the vicinity, but they travelled widely and had huge influence and resources. We do not know the name of this order connected to the Templars, though some have called it the Order of the Magdalene. It is likely to have been an inner circle, within the Templars themselves. Some have claimed that the Priory, the society thought to be active in our region, are connected to that group. I am not convinced. I suspect that they are giving that impression in order to confuse us, or in order to lay claim to the secrets that they seek."

Jane Fellows paused, took a sip of her drink. Professor Southgate was not alone in thinking how impressive she was. He even wondered....but no! It could not be! Jane Fellows looked around the room and continued.

"Of the symbols themselves, some remain obscure, others we are working on. One in particular we think could be of special importance. It may even hold the key. In particular, one that relates to one of the depictions of the surrounding panel.

"The panel concerned is below the image of Christ on the Cross, and the centurion, piercing Jesus's side with a spear. The blood flows, as you would expect, into a cup, which is believed by some to be the Holy Grail. Though the Grail is a central mystery in itself, and cannot be ignored, it is not this that sparked our curiosity. It is the head of the Spear which is interesting, and which concerns us.

"For the head of the Spear has broken off from the stem. Rather than being, as is normal, at the head on the stem, almost touching the body of Christ and smeared with His Holy Blood, it lies on the ground - or should lie on the ground - at the foot of the cross. I say should, because the panel representing the Spearhead itself is missing. But where it has broken the earth, with the royal stain, a tree has sprouted. A Tree growing from the Blood of Christ.

"To my knowledge, this image is unique. But there is more. Beneath the tree have fallen many fruit. At first we thought that the tree was a vine, and that the fruit would therefore be fruit of the vine, grapes. Another powerful and common symbol of Christian lineage. One common in Christian painting. But there were apples, oranges - yes, grapes, other berries, some as yet unidentified for certain.

"And beneath these, on the ground, is a further space. A blank space where there should be something. Not the natural space of a boundary or border. But a space which we think almost certainly contained an inscription, which we think may give a clue to the whereabouts of the Spearhead. This object, the Spearhead, and indeed the spear itself, is one of the most prized objects in Christian history, and its whereabouts a profoundly guarded secret - one of the greatest in the Church. It is also of vital importance. For, so the myth would have it (we do not doubt the power of myth and symbol), the person or group that possesses the Spearhead will have enormous power. As you know, it is known as the Spearhead of Destiny. Whoever holds the Spearhead will rule the world, for as long as they have it. If it is lost, power will pass to the new owner."

There was a pause. Jane Fellows continued.

"During the Second World War, enemy groups made special attempts to find this object, which can only be regarded as magical, as others have done from time to time throughout history. Burnchester Hall is thought to contain clues to the secret of its whereabouts - assuming it exists - which is why it has been the object of attention from all sorts of groups. It is also why Burnchester Hall was chosen as the centre for fighting the darkest enemy known to Western civilisation. This is confirmed by Dr Vale's account. We believe that the panel exists, somewhere in the grounds of Burnchester, and that the panel would give us a vital clue as to the whereabouts of the Spearhead."

"In addition," Mr Rummage added, "Burnchester holds great power of its own, older than Christianity. The site on which it is built is ancient, its chambers and stones capable of calling up energies beyond our understanding. The two combined make it especially powerful but also vulnerable."

Jane Fellows went on.

"We can imagine why it is so important to know where the panel is, indeed the Spearhead itself. There are even those who doubt that it is a Spearhead! We think it highly probable - and our intelligence sources confirm this - that the panel was deliberately taken out of the original for safe-keeping, and is now 'lost'. But there is no reason to believe that it should not be somewhere nearby. Perhaps in the church. You can imagine how easy it would be to hide it. You can imagine too, how important it might be for those who might want it for their own doubtful ends. If the other stories about the Hall are true, and I am sure Mr Rummage will be able to tell us, there have been those who have used this power for dark as well as light. And may do so again. It is essential that it does not fall into the wrong hands."

With that Jane Fellows looked about the room and at each of her colleagues in turn, and sat down. A cold gleam passed over her eyes.

As she reached the climax of her story, she seemed to have grown in stature. Like a priestess from another age, predating Christianity by many hundreds of years.

There were several minutes' pause. Professor Southgate was making notes. Mr Rummage was flicking through some papers, in readiness for his speech. Dr Vale stared into the night. Jane Fellows' eyes were fixed on Professor Southgate.

It was he who spoke. He had one question.

"Jane, thank you for an excellent review. You mentioned, in passing - almost as a joke I might say - that some people believe that the Spearhead may not be a Spearhead at all. What do these people believe that it might be?"

Jane Fellows remained in her seat and answered quietly, almost dismissively. "I do not know."

That she was lying, Professor Southgate could tell.

There were no more questions for the moment. Mr Rummage rose.

"Thank you, Jane, for your very clear description. Our silence, I think, only confirms the intensity of our response. In my case, though I am not surprised, I have had further confirmation of my fears. I have heard of the Spearhead of Destiny, as I shall shortly mention, but that its history is so clearly linked to Burnchester gives me further concern. In view of Dr Vale's interesting story, I can see that the dangers are mounting and that the urgency increases. I thought that we might have more time, but it seems that we may not.

"As you know, when I was appointed Headmaster of Burnchester School I also became responsible, under the guidance of the governing body, for the development and preservation  of our understanding of its history, and the cataloguing of part of the library. The library is unique. It may be of interest for you to know that I was required to have had extensive knowledge of both. One of the tasks of Headmasters since the founding of the school, only fifty years ago or so, has been to protect its secret history from unnecessary publicity or exposure, whilst giving access to those true seekers and academics, such as friends and colleagues here today, and developing our knowledge of its past. To some extent this has had to be done quietly, out of school, or in the holidays, a privilege that we are  lucky enough to have. In addition to the library, Dr Vale has confirmed the importance of the site - the whole site I mean, not just the site of the school or church - which is becoming increasingly known to certain sects. The activities of the school during the Second World War and more recently have gained new prominence in view of the instability in our world. Anything to do with intelligence and with the preservation of the state has gained a new emphasis. In the context of the changing world, as described by Dr Vale, where our religious institutions have been in decline - not always unjustified, some might argue - this becomes more potent. The Priory is only one group. There are other groups who might well be equally interested in the skills developed by our agents, as well as in the fragment and the Spearhead.

"I am also responsible for maintaining the letter and spirit of these requirements laid down by The Cheesepeake family.

"The library contains some of the most interesting documents available anywhere, pertaining to Alchemy, the ancient art of transforming base metal into gold. Though these are still in the process of being examined - for which I would like to thank Professor Southgate - it is clear that the information they contain may be unique. John Dee, the famous astrologer, was known to study here. It may not surprise you that we think that Shakespeare, a verbal alchemist, if you like, is believed to have visited the library in 1597. Newton is known to have visited. Some lesser-known figures, adepts in the art, are recorded in the books over the centuries. Some of this activity is to do with prediction, some with confronting the power of darkness, most potently in transforming darkness into light. Not just fighting fire with fire, but fighting it in order to extinguish its malevolence. To fight evil, it is sometimes necessary to use its techniques, but with greater conviction, for it is a terrible fight indeed.

"The Spearhead is important (or the belief in it) but so are other skills of the mind. In this process there developed a tradition of mental training, some of which could be used for religious purposes, even though the mainstream religions liked to keep quiet about it - and for the specific purpose of fighting a war, like the Second World War, in which not only were we threatened, but in which an evil so profound was afoot that it threatened the future of civilisation. As with all the great traditions of inner wisdom and learning, the process of improvement is long, is difficult, and finally, was once open only to a few. Today, however, more and more people, better educated than ever, have the possibility of contributing to good change. The task should in that sense be simpler. On the other hand so would it be easier to exploit this increased knowledge for perverse destructive ends.

"All the evidence shows that we are at a turning point in our history. What the outcomes will be we do not know. It is my job to help ensure that the direction we take is as good as we can make it. What better opportunity than to run a school, especially one linked to Burnchester and all it stands for?

"In selecting this group, and in bringing us together, I have deliberately chosen expertise that will give us a lead on events, and help us find the fragment, perhaps the Spearhead. Exploiting what we know to find what we would like to know, in order to protect, preserve and improve our futures. It will not surprise you to know that others, in the highest ranks of governments and the military, are also aware of, and in some cases part of that process. The Ministry of Defence has been most helpful in providing information about the Hall's activities, though it has been slow. Only now, as we have proved our worth, have they been open to share what is essential for us to have. Some of their secrets remain hidden of course. Perhaps we will learn these in due course, just as we may be able to help them. Partly this is because we have always to be on our guard against treachery. The determination of some to use the riches of Burnchester, and the area around, for negative reasons, must put us all on our guard.

"We know that battles are fought on many fronts. The most important, the most difficult but the most powerful is the battle for people's hearts and minds. And that means fighting for the truth. If we lose that battle, we lose everything."

"Souls, I think you mean," said Jane Fellows.

"That is not a word that I wished to use," said Mr Rummage. "But it may not be inappropriate. Our task is now to be alert to any danger that may appear on our horizons, be prepared for the intrusion of those whose interest in the Hall and its activities are suspect. I liken them to a virus, for their influence could catch hold and spread wildly. By developing our knowledge and our defences," and here Mr Rummage laid great emphasis, "without making things too obvious, or creating unnecessary stir.

"The task that we face is daunting to say the least because, when all is said and done, I also run a school, with children from all backgrounds and abilities and increasingly nationalities, whose futures are ours, and whose destiny cannot be separated from them. I must ensure that the school continues to function effortlessly. I will not allow anything to interrupt that. We have to protect their rights. Parents and pupils alike must know nothing. At least not yet. This may not be possible, but we must try. We must preserve their innocence for as long as it is feasible.

"I have begun to take steps about our security. We have a very good Keeper of The Keys in Mr Gruff. I do not expect any immediate developments during this holiday. But I cannot be certain and events have a habit of taking over, sometimes silently. I do expect us to be alert and to keep in touch, and to convene again in a month's time, or before, if events dictate. That is all."

With this Professor Southgate, who had taken over as chair of the meeting, thanked Mr Rummage and, after a brief pause, invited questions.

These were unsurprisingly brief, given the thoroughness of each person's account. Dr Vale was asked for the evidence of the existence of the Priory in East Anglia. To this he was only able to give a guarded response, but one that suggested that it should be taken seriously, as it hadn't yet become fully manifest. There were individuals who had been identified, he said, particularly near the coast. He was also asked to clarify the Priory's intentions. He would only say "information that would be destructive to Church and State." Then he added, "power." It was evident that the Spearhead of Destiny would be one major target, "though there were many groups who would wish that," he said.

"We have to get there first. Our work must continue with the greatest urgency," Mr Rummage added.

Jane Fellows was asked by Dr Vale whether she had any idea as to the whereabouts of the missing panel. She could only guess, she said, but in view of other factors, there was no reason to suppose that it could not be "within the grounds of the Hall".

She then asked Mr Rummage what security measures were in place to protect the fabric, contents, staff and students at Burnchester. He would not reply in detail, and only said that these were evolving, but as yet were still "low key, for reasons that I have explained. Though I am taking advice."

With this the questions and discussion ended. Not before, however, Jane Fellows engaged in a rather strange behaviour. She asked whether Professor Southgate was intending to speak. When he declined, politely, Jane Fellows asked why not. He said that he had nothing further to add to their discussions and that he personally had no more information to give them. This, despite the fact, Jane Fellows challenged, "that you have been working all year, mostly at weekends it is true, in the library at Burnchester?"

Was that a start in Professor Southgate's face? If so it was well concealed. When he said, "nothing to report", Jane Fellows went to the table and picked up one of the masks that lay there, the mask of Anger. She stood the point on which it rested on the table and faced its raging image outwards.

"I am not satisfied with that! I demand to know why then you are here! What exactly you can contribute or are contributing to these secret discussions which have required intense, painful work, sacrifices of our own?"

Mr Rummage tried to interrupt. Jane Fellows would not have it.

"I demand to know!" she said, standing to her full height, and looking at Professor Southgate. It was then the turn of Dr Vale to enter the discussion but she brushed him aside with "I am not talking to you!"

Professor Southgate looked at the mask, and smiled. He knew it too well. He looked at Jane Fellows and the smile disappeared. He got up and bowed to his two other colleagues. Then he faced Jane Fellows eye to eye. His look was more penetrating than she could have imagined and she tried to look away. It was not dissimilar to the stranger's in the Burnchester Arms. But she could not. He held her there for a moment, in a gaze of such power that even her anger mellowed. But she did not give in. Rather she threw her head back and laughed. She laughed and laughed and laughed, not the laugh from the belly as if at an amusing joke, but with a resonating hollow echo that seemed to come from some tormented depth, beyond her, and yet nearly within her grasp. Then, as suddenly, as if to deny what had happened, she began to chuckle. She had replaced the mask. She began to look her most feminine, even vulnerable, and sat down.

"My mistake," she said.

But Professor Southgate continued to look into her eyes, and saw nothing but cold dark energy beneath the growing smile, unfit for any worthy human soul.

"I will be brief," he said. "We are all tired and need to reflect. I shall not keep you much longer. There are journeys to be made. But since I have been asked I will mention one thing. As Jane Fellows says, I have indeed been working at the library at Burnchester. In fact, more than the library. Anywhere where the documents can help with the training that I have decided to do. If our agents could do it, then so could I. It is to do with the development of my mental faculties, not my technical skills. I have also been trying to learn the art of divination. In this I have had to focus mental power and try to direct it to towards a particular goal. I am learning, but it is not something that can be done overnight. It can take years."

"And of what use will it be?" asked Dr Vale.

"Time will tell. But if we are to fight evil, indeed any enemy, it is well to engage all our resources - and senses - because, in the end, as has been said, we must fight on all fronts. Not just in technology, knowledge and psychology, but also with the power that is ours within."

With that he paused and sat down. It was if a curtain had fallen. Professor Southgate took out a diary and asked everyone to give him a date for their next meeting, but here Mr Rummage intervened suggesting that he could make the arrangements by phone, as everyone was tired.

This was agreed. Professor Southgate got up and collected coats, as Dr Vale and Jane Fellows gathered their things.

"We travel together, I think?" asked Dr Vale.

Jane Fellows bowed.

She then proceeded out of the room, took her coat from the Professor, and shook his hand. She looked into his eyes, but found nothing but a tired academic. She shook the hands of Mr Rummage, thanked them both and began to leave.

But before doing so, she turned and said, to everyone,

"Remember the Spearhead of Destiny. Fight the enemy with all your resources. Goodnight."

When they had left, Mr Rummage said he was tired and wanted to get some sleep. Before doing so, Peter Baxter held his arm and asked if he had noticed anything. Any reactions?

Mr Rummage paused a moment and said,

"What exactly were her words when I said, "If we lose that battle - that is, the battle for hearts and minds - we lose everything?"

" 'Souls, I think, you mean.' "

"I thought so."

Was this the virus that so concerned him?

*

The purring car entered Mr Rummage's consciousness again, with the words of his daughter Julia, who had asked her mother when they were going to stop for tea.

"When your father has...." She was about to say "returned to the land of the living", but thought better of it, and simply said, "woken up. Now, in fact. Welcome back," she said, without a trace of jealousy.

"Brilliant," said Julia and Simon in a sort of wicked unison.

"Sounds a good idea to me," said Mr Rummage, stretching and beginning to think he too was truly on holiday as the hills emerged around about him, out of a rain-swept sky.

"Summer holidays. Hummph. And by the way, Julia, if Ophelia's unbelievable what about Hamlet?"

"Boring!" said Simon and Julia together. "We thought you were asleep!"

Jenny swung to the left into a slip road that seemed to appear out of nowhere and descend into nowhere, though the sign had said 'Services,' so she was prepared to believe it.

# 6

"But we've got to go at night!" Tyro said to Jess, as they walked Rompy in the field at the back of the house, on the day that the Rummages were travelling north.

"Our parents will kill us."

"Our parents won't know. There's nothing to fear. What can Mrs Limpet do to us? Mr Gruff is away on holiday, and Mr Rummage wouldn't mind - that much. Anyway, there's nothing to fear but fear itself - that's what my father used to tell me."

"That's great if you're not frightened," said Jess.

"I used to be afraid of the dark, Jess, when I was little. Then one day, when I was lying in bed, trying to go to sleep, I told my father, who had come to see if I was OK (I suppose) that there was something in the cupboard. He told me not to be so silly and go to sleep."

"So?"

"So then my father began to walk out of the room, thinking I was trying to go to sleep. I wasn't of course and he knew that I was worried. 'OK, I'll check,' he said turning back. 'But I don't know how anything can have got into the cupboard.' When he opened the cupboard door he stood back amazed. 'Good Heavens!' he said, 'You're right. There is something, rather someone, here.'

"By this time I was sitting up in bed and fumbling for the

light switch. He put his hand in the cupboard, much to my horror. 'Don't, Dad!' I said, but he continued. 'It's alright,' he said, 'I think you know who it is.' Slowly he drew back his hand. A foot appeared. Then a body, then a head. At this point I was smiling and holding out my arms. Calling. It was my teddy. I never felt afraid of the dark again."

Jess was silent for a moment then said, "But why do we have to go at night? And this is different. You were little then. You were afraid last time we went."

"Because we don't want anyone to know. I've thought about it. She's not going to harm us, is she? It's you who are afraid."

"A little," said Jess, not quite honestly.

"Then I'll go alone. With Rompy," Tyro said, turning away, and running ahead.

Jess wondered how she could persuade Tyro to listen. She didn't want to let Tyro down.

"What's the big deal?" she shouted, "about going back?"

Before Tyro could answer a call came from the direction of the house.

"Are you two coming or not?"

It was Dennis's voice. He appeared from the side of the house, looking for them.

"We want to get there before the crowds."

With that Tyro ran on, with Rompy racing ahead, and Jess taking up the rear.

"Five minutes," he said.

How often did Dennis feel what it must be like to have your father die at the age of eight? How often did he feel that he must be some kind of a protector to her? She was wild enough sometimes to need one. Her mother couldn't always cope alone, and he didn't think she would remarry. He knew how common it is for children to be brought up by only one parent, but that didn't make it any easier.

Within a few minutes everyone was in the car. The old estate car came into its own in the countryside, especially for trips to the sea. Rompy was in the back looking out of the rear window, sitting on top of the inflatable dinghy that they always took. A picnic basket and a wind shield and clothes and buckets and spades. Not for the children. For Dennis and Abby.

Abby was delighted to have her younger brother around, even if only for a few brief days. You didn't have to explain yourself to Dennis. He was the most open-minded person she knew. They got on, respected their differences, though they didn't often socialise together. In fact she didn't know very much of what he did. She didn't really mind, though she sometimes found his secrecy frustrating.

"It's not that I've got anything to hide," he had once told her, "it's just not my character to talk about myself."

The miles flew by. They even passed the sign to Burnchester. This prompted Dennis to ask jokingly whether the girls would like to spend the day at school. "You must be joking!" said Tyro. Abby had said nothing of Tyro's experiences, though she was planning to at some point. Dennis had not yet told Abby of his experiences a couple of evenings before. She was the worrier and there was no need to create something out of nothing. Besides, she often laughed at his 'fantasies', as she called them.

The two girls sat in the back. As they drove along - Dennis was driving - Tyro lent over to Jess and whispered a few words, though it would have been difficult to have been heard in the front anyway.

"Don't tell anyone," said Tyro a little more gently than before - she was prone to seem aggressive.

"About what?" said Jess.

"About what I said earlier."

"Oh, that!" said Jess. "Of course not."

It was now that Abby, in coded language, told him about the girls' adventure. He listened carefully, but said nothing. He was going to enjoy the seaside while he could, but he felt, as

Mr Rummage did, that the mist was beginning to creep over the landscape, and he needed a bit of fresh air to think.

Elderfield, Cribton, Boxford, and on towards Warblersbay, where they had come every year for as many years as they could remember. Abby and Dennis had come as children. At nearby Dunemoor they had walked the beach and collected human bones from sea-ravaged tombs that lay exposed in the sandy cliffs, where the sea had punished the shore. It was hard to imagine the huge priory that thrived there, let alone the large medieval town that had been once been so important and was now under the sea. What would be next?

It isn't just the sky that gives Warblersbay its uniqueness, but the sea. A turmoil of grey water crumbling over the stones, which echo as they fall amongst the waves. The still, picturesque calm that sometimes coats the beautiful sands at low tide, in summer. The fishermen at night, with curved rods lit in the dim light, waiting, or hoping, for a catch. The undulating dunes, knotted with marram. The jilted village houses, and the wooden beach huts, by the reeds. In one direction the clear pinnacle of Southwold lighthouse, in the other, beyond the huge sweep of beach and the sandy tree-topped cliffs, a huge white dome in an otherwise ancient landscape, with its own terrible lucidity.

At Warblersbay, Abby always pointed to the Church of St Michael & St John with its inner chapel, humbly attached to the outer ruin, like an embryonic shell. It was, she thought, as if a new religion was waiting to be born from the ruins of the old. It captured something of the contradiction between faded power and retained authority. The kernel remained, despite the decline of influence. In some ways it was better for it.

The Church could never be completely destroyed, could it? And what if it were? The sea would always beat the fragile shore. And yet...perhaps this was not such a bad thing. It allowed history to sift out from the layers of tired patronage an essence that could still carry with it the spirit to eternity.

Somewhere in the midst of decayed opulence the truth was still capable of being revealed. Now, in the ashes of its past, the wonder of newness might grow to regain its place in light. The lichen-encrusted flints showed nature's capacity to exploit man's fading monument to God.

At the beach, Tyro and Jess had a great time, in the falling waves, as the tide was coming in on the sharp easterly wind, providing the few wind-surfers with energy for their sails, and surf into which they could plunge. Yet even in summer, there was a hint of autumn in the wind, though the sky was clear.

Abby and Dennis walked along the beach, watching the girls. There were others on the sand, others in the water, but even in this holiday time, the numbers were as low as you could imagine for such a beach so accessible from London and the smaller country towns. Even on the hottest days, when the roads leading into the village showed signs saying 'Car Park Full', it was always possible to find a space, beyond the signs. Would there be new car parks, better roads, hotels? Eventually, perhaps. But for the moment, the faded elegance could be forgiven for believing its place was permanent and secure.

Remnants of sea defences still stood on parts of the dunes, memories of other wars, concrete slabs layered into the sand to prevent invasion, bunkers, and further south, Martello towers. The complex web of estuarine shallows along the coast, where the rivers weaved towards the sea, held broken defence systems and secret training grounds, still.

The pressures from new people, the subtle invasion of the East Anglian domain by the enthusiastic educated and less educated modern tribes, were part of a broader theme (it had happened throughout history), a more intrusive story. The same was happening elsewhere, across Europe, across the globe, where expansion drew to it people, and invigorated yet despoiled simultaneously, with ideas, with fresh interchange, and with rubbish. Could they ever be compatible? And how slight was this intrusion compared to the concretisation of ancient shores for the mass exploitation of sun for beer and eros. How trivial compared to the swelling millions, the tens of millions whose story had not yet been told, who knew little of these things, and were not able to care, for they had not even enough food to live, in some cases not even enough food to be born.

Abby and Dennis felt the power of the contradictory myth, the varied equations and shifting balance between light and dark. The privilege of discrimination. These things also came to others, who in different ways, and in different contexts, embodied these archetypal themes.

The sun shone, and the wind added edge. Those with their hands on all the ropes continued, more or less, to manage. To keep the illusion in orbit. To pay bills, and earn their keep, and trade and develop and persuade and deceive and do all the things (as well as delight) that are necessary to the ongoing development of the economy of our world into whose elliptic we have been unwittingly thrown. And the Moon, what of her? And the planets, and the solar system and the outer planets, and other solar systems and the galaxies that glow, somewhere in the waste, and bear silent witness to the tragedies of the consumptive power of darkness set against the redeeming power of even minimal light. Those other voices in the distant spheres, would, it is certain, one day, be heard.

"Let's have an ice cream!" said Abby, taking Dennis's arm, "and then we can watch the girls go crabbing."

Standing by the water's edge, Dennis carved the shape of a cornet out of the air, and then held it up to his mouth and took a huge, imagined, bite. Tyro and Jess were standing, the waves covering their shoulders.

"Ice cream!" he shouted.

"In a while!" Tyro shouted back against the wind, then dived into the water, getting her eyes salty. Rompy was beside her pushing furiously against the waves, holding the stick he had retrieved.

Dennis and Abby walked on. As they passed a young family on the sand, Dennis went up to the man and spoke to him. Over the brow of the hill, Abby stopped, and turned to look back.

"Where are they?" she said. "They must still be in the sea! I must go back."

There had always been a rule for children and the sea - never let them out of your sight. Time and again, Tyro and her friends had, with a few struggles and shoutings across the water, proved their capacity to be responsible. But that had always been when Abby was present. They were still young enough to be foolish. The sea was unfathomable, and could be terrifying.

Abby saw both girls were running towards them, a towel over Tyro's shoulders, Jess carrying hers. Stepping jaggedly over stones. A pause to pick up a shell. The sun on their backs. Beyond them, a short distance away, a small boat making its way to the river entrance.

"I was just coming back!" said Abby.

"What for?" asked Tyro.

"Come on," said Dennis, "last person to the ice cream van pays!"

The girls sprinted on, forgetting the stony ground beneath their feet.

As they ate their cornets, they went over to the river's edge leading to the harbour wall, where they could see the river traffic, an occasional yacht or small fishing vessel, motoring its way up to the harbour a few hundred metres inland. Dennis loved boats.

They sat down for a few minutes, feet dangling over the wall.

"Who's crabbing?" asked Tyro.

"I'll come," said Abby. "To watch anyway."

"Me," said Jess. "Though we'll have to develop a method. Crabs can only be caught if you understand their behaviour."

"Sure. Bacon on the end of a line," said Tyro. "Mum?"

"In the boot of the car. Here. I'll be with you in a minute."

She handed Tyro the keys. The girls sauntered off, Tyro trying to catch the melting ice cream that was dribbling down the side of her cone. Jess had already eaten hers, according to sound principles, not losing a drop and keeping her hands clean into the bargain!

Dennis was watching a boat going inland, under the protection of the harbour wall.

"Some boats can only go up river at high tide," he said.

Abby was looking towards the girls who were now a blur against the car beyond.

Dennis suddenly sounded alarmed. He stood up and raised his binoculars. He focused rapidly on the small boat, now moving towards the small harbour wall on the other side.

"I don't believe it! The stranger. The stranger from the Burnchester Arms, the man who disappeared. The one I told you about. He's on that boat!"

"Not that unusual, is it, Dennis?" said Abby. "We're here, and you were in that pub too. How about he left the pub in the usual manner - through the door?"

Put like that, Abby was right. But feeling came into it. There was something odd about it, and he was going to find out.

"I'll pick you up..."

"You don't need the car, Dennis," said Abby, "you can cross over there on the ferry."

Abby was a little impatient at Dennis's tendency to imagine things.

"Meet us at the crabbing bridge in an hour!"

Dennis was on his way, then turned and called,

"If I'm not back in an hour, meet you in the cafe. And should I not be there, go home and I'll call!"

One of these days, the joke would become a reality.

Crabbing was well under way when Abby reached the girls. Tyro stood on top of a thick post (which supported the bridge) and was bending down towards the water, looking in. In her hand she held a thin line, at the end of which was a nail with a piece of bacon attached to it. This complicated device was the means of catching the crabs. She was trying to place the bacon into the deepest part of the murky water, in the hope of finding the largest crab, though the tide kept moving it. Jess lay on her tummy on the bridge and was trying to direct the line with a stick. Behind her was a plastic bucket full on brackish water. On either side other children of every description, like the buckets, were doing their utmost to trap these playful creatures, who seemed to come and go with the tide, and enjoyed the feast of food offered to them, possibly knowing that they would be thrown back. Though some children (and a few older people) would take them home to a dubious end, their main enemy were the gulls who quartered the shore. Here the remains of the unlucky ones lay in various states of wreckage amidst the seaweed and stones. One bucket had crabs to the brim, from the ludicrous to the small. Jess wanted to pour them all back. Children, parents, friends, uncles, aunts, grandparents and humanity in general, stood on the thin wooden bridge over the muddy estuarine stream for this beguiling business. It was as if here, humans were the Gods.

"I've got one!" shouted Tyro, and then fell silent. "It's gone."

Abby watched, engrossed, and then joined them, squeezing in between Jess and a little dark-haired boy, covered in mud. He was less refined than some of the others, but had rather more crabs in his bucket. This drew Tyro to him. She was reminded of a younger Rick. What was he up to, she wondered? Something he shouldn't be, no doubt. She smiled.

The sun and the sea breeze had thoroughly dried the girls by now and they seemed to be enjoying themselves as much as if they had been eight. Abby too. Crabbing must be a great leveller, thought the bridge, who, like the crabs, carried people without discrimination from one shore to another, in all weathers, and without fuss. What an admirable example to others.

Rompy stood by the water's edge, watching. Occasionally he would bark and jump up, and run along a bit and then back, as if on patrol.

In no time Tyro, Jess and Abby had caught two crabs between them, though it had in fact been Jess, with a 'method', who had managed to catch the first and largest.

"Keep off, Mum!" was all that Tyro could say, Abby now almost one of them, as far as she was concerned, but not as far as Tyro was. Children, after all, don't always like adults being children, especially parents. Especially mothers.

After about an hour, Abby told the girls to start packing up. Tyro tried to make a fuss, but was in fact beginning to lose interest herself, especially as she was having less luck than Jess. This normally would have encouraged her to go on. Now she was beginning to think of other things. Burnchester Hall came into her mind. She knew it wasn't empty, not only because of Mrs Limpet. Like a being struggling to be born.

By the time they had reached the car, they were beginning to feel like another swim. But instead, Abby persuaded them to go to the cafe in the village to have tea. This was a family ritual. First they would walk around the village green (and go on the swings if no one was looking). This was a triangular slope which made you feel welcome, and very tall when you were at the top. Abby could remember the old tea room when they had been children. Then they would enter the shop, where the tea room is. Tyro was happy with this type of shopping, because her mind could wander over the strange things on sale, while dreaming of scones, jam and cream. It was the buying for practical reasons that drove her crazy, even when she had money, which was pretty rare. Jewellery, cards, clothes, home-made fudge, chinaware, local crafts, every gift imaginable. Paintings by local artists adorned the walls and stairs. Local books on shelves by the door. One entitled, 'Dunemoor, The City Beneath The Sea,' unusually, caught Tyro's eyes. Rompy would sit impatiently outside doing his best to persuade passers-by to give him a stroke. Someone would bring him a cake wrapped in a paper napkin, albeit rather late!

*

In the harbour Dennis was standing outside the Laughing Mariner. He had come over on the ferry, and walked inland towards the moorings where he had seen the boat stop. The boat was called the Neptune. There was no sign of the man. Everything looked normal. He went to the Harbourmaster's Office - a broken down shack with a tide sheet pinned onto an outside board - and spoke to the Harbourmaster, a tanned, bearded man and with wild hair, but with the smile of an orchid. Mr Greenshank was an old friend. In a casual manner that belied his interest Dennis asked about the boat, and "did he know anything of the owner?" Mr Greenshank was his usual open self - like the sea wind, there was not much that could be hidden there for long. He had known Dennis many years.

"Arrived a couple of days ago. Nice looking boat. He's done some work on it since she's been in. Comes and goes quite a lot, even at night, I'm told. He'll be at the bar now."

Dennis entered the Laughing Mariner, realising that he was already late for his family. A quick glance at the bar found the man drinking a pint of beer. A few other people were scattered at tables, some from the boats, holiday-makers. He knew one or two, but the way he raised his hand and looked ahead indicated that he didn't want to talk.

Dennis ordered a beer, and lent against the bar. The stranger continued to stand, seemingly unaware of Dennis's presence. As the drink arrived, and he handed over the money to the barman, Dennis said,

"Been out today, Brian? Fine weather to be on the water."

The barman, Mr Greenshank's son Brian, returned Dennis's

change, and lit a cigarette.

"Brewing weather," he said. "Won't last. Be rain by sunset, with this westerly."

"Don't say that, I'm on a day out with my family."

It was still sunny outside and the possibility of rain seemed far off.

"It'll be bucketing down by sunset! Pity those poor devils like me who are out in it," Brian said. Brian did some part-time fishing, mostly at dusk, to make ends meet, though the fish were fewer these days.

The stranger finished his drink and walked past Dennis who was holding his glass up to his face.

The stranger didn't stop, but Dennis caught sight of his face in the mirror at the back of the bar. It felt like an expressionless face, without any sign of humanity. A cold face, reflecting nothing but twisted energy, as if a ferocious power was waiting to be released. And then, in an extraordinary moment, only visible to Dennis, the image in the mirror disappeared, and left a blank.

Yet as he turned to see the real face, Dennis thought that his mask was capable even of warmth, beneath the cold exterior. Had Brian noticed this?

"Haven't I seen you before? In the Burnchester Arms?" Dennis asked.

The stranger paused, and held the door open, then turned enough to reveal a profile, and then again to face Dennis.

"Perhaps," he said, "perhaps not. I don't recall."

And with that he turned and went out. He was lying.

Dennis was momentarily confused. He had not wanted to say anything, yet had spoken without thought, with little courtesy. It was as if the man had, in some way, tried to prevent him from talking with him, yet he could not stop himself. A confused moment of will, where boundaries crossed. The man had left, and it would seem false to force a situation out of nothing. It was nothing at all that he could explain. He was probably wrong. And why should the man engage in conversation with a complete stranger? Not everybody was that open.

Nevertheless, Dennis hastened out and looked to the left and to the right.

The stranger had gone.

Dennis walked hurriedly to the Neptune without wanting to seem anxious and called out, in case he might have gone inside, not realising that his actions were becoming more suspicious. If the stranger was involved in something criminal, for which there was no evidence at all, he should not be trying to meddle in advance. His mood changed as quickly as it had started. But he did notice something that astonished him. Beside the name Neptune was a beautifully decorated sword. He had seen one like it before. Where? He tried to cast his mind into the pool of memories and images. He paused. Was it not the insignia of a secret society that went by the name of the Priory?

He walked back along the quay to the ferry, fired-up. He was right! He was going to find out what was going on. If it was the Priory, serious trouble was at hand. He had read the reports. He didn't care what others like Abby thought. He would make it his job, for the next few days, to find out as much as possible. At the very least, it would be challenging. It would also be dangerous. He couldn't dismiss the stranger's face from his mind. He must have imagined the empty mirror.

From a window close to the pub, the stranger was looking at him on his short journey by dinghy across the water. He showed no expression at all.

By the time Dennis reached the cafe, the wind had got up. And by the time he had collected the girls and Abby from the shop, making his peace by buying them each a small present, which made up for being late (Abby said), it was already threatening rain.

As they walked towards the car, he received a call on his

mobile. The voice at the other end crackled, but was just audible.

"Who?" Dennis shouted against the breeze. "Oh, Brian? Hi!"

Down the line Brian from the pub, tried, in his Suffolk lilt, to pronounce the stranger's name, as his father had registered it in the Harbourmaster's log. "Borlick, Mr Borlick." Dennis listened carefully and thanked him. He would have to do some research. He wondered what the real name was. The accent that he had heard had not been familiar. But it was a lead.

On the road, the first drops fell.

"Did you have a good time, Tyro? Jess?" asked Abby.

"Brilliant!" they said together.

"Did you catch any crabs?" asked Dennis. "Sorry I missed it. Sorrier I missed tea."

"Loads," said Tyro.

"How many?"

"Loads," she repeated.

"Two," said Jess and Tyro together.

"Was he there?" asked Abby, with renewed, if guilty, interest.

"Yes."

"Who?" asked Tyro, always liking to know anything about anyone.

"Just someone I've seen before. No one you know." he said.

"Sounds pretty dull then," said Tyro, who turned off as quickly as she had turned on.

"Quite the contrary. I think it's most interesting. Before very long I shall have to go to the Burnchester Arms again. It was there that I saw him. He looked trouble."

"That shouldn't be difficult to arrange. You promised the girls a meal there."

"How about tonight?"

Tyro was chatting to Jess. But she caught the word tonight.

"No, not tonight! We're too tired."

By the time they reached Boxford the rain was falling steadily.

The journey back was full of laughter, though soon, Tyro fell asleep. Jess remained awake.

"I expect you're looking forward to going home, aren't you, Jess?" asked Abby.

Jess was embarrassed.

"Mrs Wander, Abby I mean, didn't Tyro tell you?"

"You mean you're staying. Good. Yes, she did mention it, now I come to think of it."

Jess was relieved.

Abby looked at Dennis, as if to say, "a real family party," and smiled.

They passed the woods near to Burnchester. Dennis decided to make a detour, down to the Burnchester Arms and round by the school. He liked the countryside round there and he wanted to show Abby where he had watched Mr Gruff striding home.

As they drove back in front of the school's main gates Dennis looked across the lawn at Mr Gruff's house. There was his car.

"I thought he was on holiday," he said to Abby. "That's what he said in the pub. He was unusually cheerful."

"He doesn't need a car to go away with, does he? Could have got a lift."

"Suppose so," he added. "Still, a bit odd to leave the garage door open, isn't it?"

He drove on.

There, in a heap beside the road, was what looked like a crumpled shape. At first their hearts leapt into their mouths. Then they realised it was only a discarded cloak.

"Should be cleared up," said Dennis stopping the car and getting out. He picked it up and threw it in the back.

Rompy, who had his head out of the window, started whining.

# 7

Mr Gruff's sister Lorna had waited for her brother George at Margate station at the appointed time. She was feeling very pleased with herself. Knowing how particular George was, and how big Titan, she had done everything she could to prepare for the comfort of both.

To help the holiday mood, she had bought some cans of beer for him and some special treats for Titan. This was a sort of dried offal, wrapped in the shape of a bone. It smelled awful. She had bought a bottle of sherry for herself, not wanting to deprive her brother of a shared holiday toast. She'd made his room neat, and warm, and had put a fresh towel on his bed. She had put a shoe rack in the cupboard as he could not bear to leave them touching the ground, a fact that, had it been widely known, would not have done his image much credit. She had even invested in a Teasmade (that is to say the one she had been given for Christmas three years ago by Mr Gruff, out of the cupboard), so that he could have the luxury of waking at his leisure to his own cup of tea, and she would have the pleasure of not having to wake him up at the wrong time. Besides, the tea she made was always too weak. It was not that she enjoyed the possibility of a lie-in herself. Everything was spick and span.

But no George. The train had arrived on time, in good weather. This had made Lorna wear a pink hat. She knew how exact he was in his instructions, but nevertheless checked the times that he had sent her. They was very clear. She had them in front of her. 14.38, arrival at Margate Station. In brackets he had written *leaves Victoria at 13.05.* He had underlined the first two words. But he hadn't come on the 13.05 or arrived at 14.38, as he had said he would. She didn't really want to believe that he might have got it wrong. The next one would arrive at 15.38. She decided to wait. There was a small cafeteria on the station close by the ticket office - not the sort of place one would normally go - and had a cup of tea. The train rolled in, whistling as it did so. But, again, no George. Had she got the day wrong? He could not have missed two trains. Could he?

Now a little irritated, she would have to go home to check the date. So home she went, the few hundred metres to her terraced  house, where she had lived for 18 years. When Mr Boot, her late husband, had died, she decided to stay, preferring the ghosts she knew to those she hadn't yet met. On a board in the kitchen, the date read: '13th July, George. At last!' It was indeed the 13th.

This was when the doubts set in. Something must have happened. The car must have broken down. He had had an accident. She tried his number. How he hated being disturbed. But as there was no answer, she returned to the station to wait for one more train. It did not take long. There it was. But this didn't have a George on it either.

Lorna prided herself on not being a woman of moods. But now she passed from irritation, to disappointment, to anger. This was not like him. Not like him at all. She could hear her mother say, "You can always rely on George. Lorna is different. She has her qualities but being on time isn't one of them."

She asked the station manager (who took a bit of finding) what she should do. He naturally, suspected a crossed wire, a failure of communication - something which he had had some experience of at Southern Railways. Fortunately this was not a peak time, and he had just done a day's training in customer care. Had Madam tried Wyemarket Station (Mr Gruff's point of departure)? Had Madam tried her brother's home? His mobile? What about his work? We pride ourselves at Southern in putting the customer first. It wasn't just about getting the trains there (and back) on time, it was providing a total experience. It was indeed.

The Station Manager (who went by the name of Ray Stoker), admirable though his tone and sentiments were, forgot to mention that it was no longer possible to phone Wyemarket or any small station about such matters as to whether someone had or had not got on a particular train.

Madam left none the wiser and more confused. With these suggestions in mind, and the swarm of others that had begun to flood there, Lorna was beginning to panic. When she got home a second time she made a second call to George's home. She had lived for eighteen years in this house, with barely a visit from her brother. And now, having decided at last to make the effort, he had not come at all. The worst visions came to her. Was he dead? Perhaps he was lying in a ditch with his throat cut? Her practical side brought her back to an even keel. She was, after all, the manager of a dental practice (private) in the town.

*

George's phone rang and rang. He did not believe in answer machines. Lorna hadn't been given his mobile phone number, on the grounds that it was only for use at work. In desperation, she decided to try Mr Rummage, the Headmaster. She remembered the name, as George had so often spoken of him. George would be horrified, but she was desperate. She needed to know. She had to phone 'Directory Enquiries' who were polite, if a bit mechanical.

"Ummage? Sorry, Rummage," said the bland voice. "Initial? No initial. I'm not sure I'll be able to.... No need to raise your voice, Madam. Headmaster of, yes, near? I'll see what we can do." Instead of a recording, the operator read aloud. "The number for the Headmaster, Mr Rummage, Burnchester Hall, is....."

They even had his private number. She tried both. The first connected to a simple message saying that the school was closed for the summer holidays but thank you for calling. Term started again on the 4th September. When she tried the second number, she became a bit more nervous (even though, as manager of a dental practice (private) she was used to talking with top people). She was sure she would speak to Mr Rummage himself. If Dentists were anything to go by, Headmasters might be super-cool. That was it. To be a professional you needed telephone cool. She would have to go on a training course. She could see it now: 'How not to show any emotion (or feeling) in times of emergency.'

The phone rang for a long time. After many rings, the answerphone clicked in. It was a lady's voice. Mrs Rummage, thought Lorna.

"We are sorry that nobody is available to take your call, please try later. In an emergency phone....." The number was familiar enough. It was her brother's. She had reached a dead end.

There was only one thing to do. She would have to try the police.

Suffolk Police, in their pristine Headquarters, were a little impatient. The Duty Officer wasn't sure what Mrs Boot was talking about. "Your brother hasn't turned up at the station? Yes, Mrs Boot, we'll look into it", was the immediate response. If Mrs Boot hadn't mentioned Burnchester Hall, and the fact that Mr Gruff was caretaker there, he would certainly have abandoned the call to its proper fate. But he had heard of Burnchester Hall. That made it important.

She was transferred to PC Relish's office in Burnchester. It was rare for a small village to have a police station, but for historical reasons, connected to the Hall, it did so. It was also rare for quite big villages to have a police station, but this is not the main thrust of the story. PC Relish himself could not have been a better servant to his profession. Not only had he worked there all his life (his father had been in the Force too), but did so with the relish that went with his name. Born and raised in Burnchester, he knew everyone on his patch,  and beyond, and made it his business to know as much about anyone who visited, and many who did not.

PC Relish was not the kind of policeman of the old school who gave kids a whack over the head when they did something wrong (like steal apples), and occasionally when they did something right, but he was firm on discipline - he preferred a baton - making it his job to visit all the schools in his area to get to know all the young people in advance, "so that he knew a bit about them when they went astray." The advancement of more serious crime in recent times, of the occasional murder (not to date on his beat), of illegal goods being spirited away from the local docks, mostly in the direction of the big cities, trouble at discos, drugs, didn't faze him one bit. He rose to the challenge, only wishing he had more support to "get the bahstuds!" as he told his wife privately on more than one occasion, in his heavy Suffolk tones: "git 'm bahstuds!" By most standards his was a quiet patch, though the Church of St Mary Magdalen drew some unusual visitors. He enjoyed appearing a bit simple. Though he embraced technology, he sometimes preferred to ride a bicycle, as it got him closer to the ground.

He also used method. He watched, assimilated, analysed, unless of course he was confronted. Then he struck true and straight, and thought afterwards. Fortunately for both parties this didn't happen very often.

PC Relish was polite. "Yes, Mrs Boot, of course I know your brother, Mrs Boot. Mr Gruff, an excellent man. I'm sure it'll be alright but I'll go over to his house and check that everything is OK. Yes, he did mention something about a holiday. I'm sure there will be a simple explanation. Your number, Mrs Boot? I'll call you back as soon as I have any news." He took notes as he put the phone down. He always took notes.

Mrs Boot sat back and put the kettle on. She'd have another cup of tea.

PC Relish didn't waste a minute. He wasn't convinced that there was anything in it, but he would have to check even though he had other calls to make. He left his office (attached to his house) swiftly and went to the garage. He would take the bike. He got on and cycled away, down to the footpath that led to the river. There he would follow the river to the school and then make his way up to Mr Gruff's house. It would take longer by car.

PC Relish had two visits to make that day, but could certainly visit the school and get to his appointments in time for his tea. One was to the Reverend John Sandals, who had phoned him the previous evening on a matter of church security. "Not urgent, but if you could come tomorrow, that would be very much appreciated." God's agents had such a fine way of talking. The other was to the shopkeeper in the nearby village of Motley.

PC Relish arrived at Mr Gruff's little cottage on the western edge of the school grounds, overlooking a slight wooded decline. This decline led to a small tributary of the river Dean, in fact not much more than a ditch, which acted as an inefficient run-away, after heavy rains. The garden was surrounded by a low fence, but for the small drive entrance to the garage. The neat garden at the front was immaculately weeded. The beans were in full fruit, ready for a second harvest. Mr Gruff clearly had a gift with vegetables. Here and there were touches of care and humanity that wouldn't have been obviously consistent with Gruff's reputation. Everything seemed tranquil. The car was still parked in the drive. It was clearly rarely used, so pristine was it. It looked as if it might have been taken out in readiness for a journey, but he couldn't be sure. There were after all other ways to get to Wyemarket Station. A friend might have taken him, there were local taxis. Leaving the car out was no bad thing. Knowing Mr Gruff's hatred of being beholden to anybody, he would have guessed that he would wish to use his own car. On the other hand, leaving it at Wyemarket Station for a week wasn't ideal either.

PC Relish had a look over the vehicle. It was untouched. He tried the door, which was open. This was slightly surprising.

He then walked around the house, peering in at the downstairs window at the back, into what looked like a bedroom. The bed was made.

Coming round the front, he passed the two front room windows. There could not have been a better kept house. Certainly there was no sign of anything untoward. And yet, he had been taught never to trust appearances.

He walked up to the front door. Peering into the window at the side, he could see the kitchen. Everything seemed immaculate. But the feeling grew.

He tried the door, which was locked. This was a relief. It made PC Relish feel sure that Mr Gruff had left the house safely even if he had not yet reached his destination. For a moment, Mr Gruff's past came to mind, his arrival at the school.

PC Relish tried the sort of places where a key might be found. Under the mat, beneath the milk crate, at the back of the post-box, in the small garden shed. Here were several keys which PC Relish tried in turn. Each key was numbered. One, two, three, four, five, six. Mr Gruff's reputation for aggressive protection of the school clearly didn't extend to his own property. And he had Titan.

Where was Titan?

It was key number four that opened the door. Even though he was a policeman, and had had to enter every type of building under the sun, sometimes breaking down doors, he always felt he was trespassing, and was now on edge.

A quick search of the rooms didn't reveal much. There were no bags, no clothes lying about, nothing half-finished that might suggest being interrupted. Certainly no break-in. Shoes were in place, on racks. There was, however, in the waste-paper basket in the kitchen, a scrumpled up piece of paper. PC Relish picked it up and unravelled it. On it there was a list of tasks, 'THINGS TO DO ON MY RETURN', Mr Gruff had written in large writing. 'Science block back door - check/needs attention. Keys. Hinge on main gate - see to. Library locks. Key. Titan.' PC Relish put the piece of paper into his pocket. Why would Mr Gruff throw into the bin a list of things that he needed to do on his return? He might have thought it was unnecessary to keep, once he had memorised it. He might have thought that he didn't want anyone else to know what needed doing.

PC Relish studied the marks on the floor. Mud, not prints. Probably Mr Gruff's big boots.

He left and locked the door. He was running late. He would call Mrs Boot when he returned to his office. For although there was nothing obvious to report from his searches, the fact is that Mr Gruff was not at his home or at his sister's home. He had to be somewhere. He was convinced that there would be a simple explanation. There was also a nagging doubt in his mind. He needed to know more.

He put the key back in its place in the shed. It was then that he noticed that key number four and key number three had been switched round. They were in the wrong order. He hadn't noticed this when he first checked each key in turn. Had he switched them by mistake, or were they switched before? If they had not been in the order they should have been in, then someone else had been into the house. Mr Gruff would not have put keys in the wrong order. Still, he himself might have switched them by mistake, as he had tried each in turn. Could it have happened while he was there? There was mud. PC

111

Relish's doubts increased but he would not exaggerate.

Titan's kennel was surrounded by a small run with a high wire and stood at the side of the garden shed, against the outer fence.

PC Relish found it empty, but with the gate open. Titan must have gone with Mr Gruff or been left with someone to look after him. Dogs are allowed on trains. Perhaps Mrs Boot was a dog lover.

PC Relish was thinking what a useful dog Titan would be to him from time to time. He would ask Mr Gruff if he could borrow him on his occasional trips to football matches. His own rather ageing labrador wouldn't have touched a fly.

PC Relish made notes and got back on his bike. He decided to cycle round the main school building, leave by the main exit, and then back down to the road that led to the river.

The Hall was looking magnificent in the sun, though to PC Relish it was just another building. Buildings without people were not much good, he would say. Especially big buildings full of empty rooms. He knew the school well, from his visits to talk to the pupils. 'Regular Relish' he was known as by the pupils, on account of the visits, always on time. The science block back door was ajar, confirming Mr Gruff's note.

As he was cycling up the main drive, he looked across to the Church of St Mary Magdalen.

A figure was walking towards him. PC Relish saw the figure against the gravestones.

PC Relish stopped and lent his bike against one of the small trees dotted about on the lawn to his left.

"PC Relish!" came a familiar voice."What a piece of luck! I hope you were coming to see me!"

The Reverend John Sandals was a tall man and walked with purpose. He had long flowing hair, and a smile regularly arched across his youthful face.

"Afternoon, Your Reverence," PC Relish said.

"I hope it is not business that brings you here on such a

lovely day? Apart from mine that is."

"A minor matter, Your Reverence. Mr Gruff's sister is worried about Mr Gruff. He was due to arrive on the afternoon train and he hasn't turned up. Wanted me to check his home. As far as I can see, everything is in order."

"Perhaps she's got the day wrong?" said his Reverence.

"Car's there, but dog's gone. Lovely dog. House spick and span," was all PC Relish could add. He felt guilty that he had said too much already. It wasn't that he didn't trust the Reverend Sandals.

"Titan is a grand dog. We could do with more of his sort working in the cloth: could sniff out sinners a mile off. Do let me know if I can help, Mr Relish. Now, to business. I hope I'm not delaying you? But now that you are here...."

"I was on my way over to the rectory now, as a matter of fact."

"Most kind of you, Mr Relish. I appreciate it, especially as I know you are very busy at this time, as we all are. Follow me - if you would."

He sandalled off towards the south door of the church. PC Relish put up his bike and followed.

Reverend Sandals entered the church, stood momentarily at the centre of the aisle and bowed towards the cross in the distant sanctuary. This ritual was carried out with such simple conviction that nobody could doubt of its sincerity. He passed a small wood panel on the south wall. This was a list of church incumbents, starting from the thirteenth century. Curiously, he looked at it, and made the sign of the cross as he passed.

Behind the cross on the altar was the most astonishing painting. Apart from two candles which remained lit all day and all night, summer and winter ("to keep out bad spirits", was what the Reverend Sandals often wanted to explain to visitors, though this normally came out as "a symbol of the eternal message and spirit of Our Lord"), there was no artificial light. By candlelight its beauty and power was astonishing.

However, at this time, with the afternoon sun streaming through the south aisle windows, it seemed quite exquisite. At least there was no coin slot that would light up the painting for three minutes only.

The picture rested implacably, if ambiguously, against the back of the altar. Its clear but polished execution belied a subtlety of tone and colour, and design, disguising eternal truth in its partly conventional symbolism. A second look revealed mastery and always left the visitor defiantly transfixed by its miraculous humanity, as if its appeal lay beyond the scope of its present resting place and might belong to time itself.

PC Relish was not immune to its power, which added to the gnawing feeling inside him. He noticed, for the first time, the empty space at the base of the cross, on the surround, where the Spearhead should have been.

The Reverend Sandals walked down the aisle and turned left at the sanctuary entrance towards the organ. At the back on the north wall was a door. This led to the vestry. PC Relish followed Reverend Sandals into it. It was simply furnished. A small table and chair, a few hanging cloaks. The musty smell of trapped air, enriched by lost incantation. Mildewy looking notices had fallen from the bare wall onto the floor. Odd bits of incomplete church furniture. What might have passed for a set of files, on top of an old cabinet. A thick red velvet curtain covered the vestry door to the outside.

"Sit down, please Mr Relish."

"I'd prefer to stand, if that's alright with you, Your Reverence," said the PC, with due care. For a brief moment, PC Relish imagined his Reverence preaching from the pulpit.

"I won't keep you long. As I said the matter isn't urgent. But it may be more important than I first thought."

"Fire away, Sir," added the PC eagerly, taking out the notebook from his pocket.

"To put it briefly, somebody, or something, has been trying

to break into the church. The attempts are small, but the signs are visible. As if someone is just trying something out as a preliminary."

"Pre-what, Sir?" asked the PC.

"As a start, Mr Relish. It's as if they wanted to see how easy it would be without causing too much damage. In fact, almost invisibly. Look here."

The Reverend Sandals walked to the velvet curtain that hid the vestry exit. He pulled it back. He bent to the ground and felt a small gap beneath the wooden door.

"This gap is normally sealed. We never use the door. Partly for security, but more to keep the heat in. But somebody, or something, Lord be praised, has broken this seal. When we go outside, you will see what I mean."

"How did you find out, Your Reverence?" asked the PC, applying his mind.

"Papers started being blown off the table when I was working. We haven't had a draught for months, not since the door was sealed and the security measures were put in place with the return of the painting."

"State of the art, I believe, Your Reverence, so to speak."

There was a pause.

"I will take a look outside, Sir, if I may?"

"Before we do, there is another thing, perhaps more serious. Someone or something has been trying to climb the church tower."

"The tower?" said PC Relish in amazement.

"Yes, you will find evidence of nails being hammered into the flint walls. Climbing-irons I should say. They hadn't got far, only two so far have been put in place. So I don't suppose anybody has yet broken in - certainly nothing has been taken - but  somebody is trying, and I'd like your advice and help. As you know we have alarms direct to Wyemarket police station, which I believe may be redirected to your office. I wanted you to know. Especially with everyone being away. The painting draws all types and is vulnerable."

"You mentioned some*thing*, Your Reverence. Some*thing* might be trying to get in? Could you explain?"

"As a man of the Church, you will appreciate that I come into contact with both Good and...." - here there was pause - ...."the Other, Mr Relish. Sometimes the power of the Other tries to take over. We have constantly to be on guard. Call it a figure of speech, a tinge of imagination."

The Reverend Sandals crossed himself.

PC Relish looked at his notes and held his gaze there. He wanted the Reverend to continue his train of thought unhindered by eye contact. He held his gaze firmly on the page. The feeling would not go away.

"The point is, Mr Relish, that there is something else. The power which supplies the alarm system was temporarily suspended. It is now on again. But it was off yesterday evening for thirty minutes, at about 10 pm. Nobody has yet come up with an explanation. We only know because the disconnection caused the back-up to set the alarm, just as a real break-in would. So your headquarters were able to ring me and check with the security company. That is when I came round, and found everything was OK. But it was this added to the other incidents that made me concerned. That is why I called you, Mr Relish."

"I heard nothing in my office, Your Reverence," said PC Relish lifting his gaze.

"Perhaps you weren't in, Mr Relish."

"I can't for the moment suggest any further action, except that I will keep an eye on things."

"I'd be very grateful, Mr Relish. Meanwhile I won't keep you much longer, except to look at the evidence outside."

"Who has a key to the church?" asked PC Relish.

"Myself, of course. Mr Gruff, as caretaker. The church is also the school chapel, you understand. And Mrs McCleod, the church warden. She lives next door."

The Reverend John Sandals led the way back through the church, first locking the vestry door, then checking the alarm system on the south wall beyond the font, bowing before crossing the altar and exiting into the summer evening air.

This was refreshing after the air of the silent church.

The evidence outside was not straightforward. At the base of the exit door the lichen-covered stone had been slightly scarred. There had been some interference with the lock, but not a serious effort at breakage. There were foot depressions embedded in the grass, but insufficient to be definable prints. Nevertheless, these gave an indication of size, which at a guess was of the order of a tall man. There had been sufficient growth overnight to lift the grass a little, making it difficult to be exact. But the fact that the grass was long meant that with careful scrutiny, a track could be made out, leading to the back of the church, in the direction of the wood that led downhill towards Mr Gruff's house.

At the tower, the Reverend Sandals showed PC Relish the two climbing-irons in the flint exterior on the west side. PC Relish looked at these in bewilderment - the certainty that something had happened to Mr Gruff grew - though he tried to focus on what was in front of him.

On closer inspection, two things were immediately striking. The first, that the clips which had been embedded in the wall, onto which metal 'horizontals' could later be hooked, were barely visible, so well camouflaged were they in the dappled flint. Only when the sunlight had reflected on the metal had the Reverend Sandals seen them.

The second was that a considerable degree of force would have been necessary to drive them into the gaps between the flint, which would have required both a powerful implement and great skill, almost inhuman power, as no piece of wall stone had been chipped. Such activity would also have meant considerable noise. Not a problem if nobody was around, but a risk for anyone trying to avoid attracting attention. However, the most important question was why anyone should try to climb the church wall.

"Why do you think someone - or something - should want to climb the tower?" asked PC Relish.

"Probably as the best means of avoiding triggering the alarm," was the Reverend Sandals' suggestion.

PC Relish acknowledged that it was possible.

The Reverend Sandals then left PC Relish, saying that he had parish matters to attend over at the Old Hall. He had had a call from Mrs Wander about something connected with the church there.

"Let's hope it's positive," he said. "God's will. To try us," he added. "Thank you for coming. It may be nothing - kids' pranks. It may be a professional checking the security, disturbed in the act, with a view to returning. Whoever did these things may not realise that I know. It was only a piece of luck that I found the iron clips. The Lord's will no doubt. It may be nothing to worry about, but I think we should take precautions. At least the painting is safe."

"If you don't mind I'll have a little look around," said PC Relish.

"Of course."

"There are two things that come to mind immediately, Your Reverence."

His Reverence turned and looked at PC Relish.

"Who else have you told of these incidents?"

There was a momentary pause.

"Nobody. Nobody yet. I will have to tell Mr Rummage of course, and Mr Gruff, but as they are both away, I didn't want to make an unnecessary fuss."

"I'm sure that is wise," said PC Relish.

"I will of course tell my church wardens and the church council and my Bishop. As you know the Church of St Mary Magdalen is unusual. It is on an ancient site of considerable importance, as well as being connected so intimately with

Burnchester Hall. I needn't remind you of the painting."

"How important is the painting?" asked PC Relish innocently.

"It's unique, Mr Relish. It is the best preserved medieval painting in England, and its value cannot be estimated. It is also immensely interesting. Some say it has special power."

It was this rather than the value that struck a chord.

"It is also believed to hold a hidden message. At least it did, until a fragment of the painting was lost."

"Do we know where that fragment is, Your Reverence?"

"Not yet. But it may be close by."

With that the Reverend John Sandals departed. PC Relish was left momentarily looking up at the church. He had been longer than he had intended. He had another appointment. He should have called Mrs Boot. He decided to go back to the vestry exit, and follow the depressions in the long grass.

These, as he suspected, went into the wood. It was probable that they followed on towards the river, but he could not be sure. Would a kid be interested in such a prank? He did not think so.

He returned to his bicycle, puzzled and less confident than he had been before meeting the Reverend Sandals. He would return to his office, call Mrs Boot, make his report and go on to Motley shop. He should also call his boss at Wyemarket. The feeling was growing, gnawing at his heart.

He wished he knew where Titan was. He had a horrid feeling that Titan was dead.

# 8

Being too tired to go "that night" didn't faze Jess. She was reluctant to return at all to Burnchester Hall, let alone in the hours of darkness, which was completely crazy, and any delay might mean a complete postponement. The next day anything might happen, as it often did when you were with the Wanders.

When they came down to breakfast the next morning, Dennis announced that he and Abby would have a day doing routine jobs in the home and garden.

At some point Abby was due to have a brief meeting with the Reverend Sandals, about a church matter. Living in the house next to the church gave her some responsibilities, though she had mixed feelings about religion, as well as the Reverend. The least she could do, she felt, was occasionally help with flowers. A small matter about the fabric of the church had come to her attention which she wanted to pass on to the Reverend. The fact that Jack had been a churchgoer, albeit an intermittent one, increased her sense of needing to help.

Both girls were welcome to help, said Abby, taking over from Dennis, or "make yourselves scarce." But there would be no more cycle rides at least until the afternoon. The choice offered focused the girls' minds admirably. Supper at the Burnchester Arms had been put off till that evening. Jess was of course welcome to stay, Abby added, as she always was.

Jess got up, taking the toast rack meaningfully from its prime position on the breakfast table and carried it respectfully to the side cupboard.

Tyro picked up the hint - she was obviously after something - and managed to carry at least three things from the table (the cereal, two plates and three spoons - six things) as if to remind Jess that she was a model daughter.

The girls went contented up to Tyro's room to discuss matters and 'chill'. Tyro told her mother that she was going to write that thank you letter.

Jess plonked herself on Tyro's bed.

"I think I'll cycle home. I ought to go and help mum anyway. I can come back later."

"There's another reason not to have gone yesterday," said Tyro, ignoring her. "It's tonight, not yesterday, that there's the full moon."

Jess stared at Tyro. Tyro had not only not forgotten, she was inspired! She had that look!

A good meal at the Burnchester Arms would give them all the energy they needed to make their assault, Tyro explained. The language of a military campaign gave it a sense of daring.

Jess continued to stare in amazement. Tyro was like a dog with a bone. She would keep hold of an idea as long as she wanted to, and nothing was going to take it away, unless she decided to bury it herself.

This gave Jess the will to react strongly. No way was she going to visit Burnchester Hall at night. Night was bad enough in your own home. Holiday mood and excitement or not, there were limits. She was not going to be a sacrificial lamb to Tyro's madness.

That is what mild Jess thought. Outwardly she adopted a different approach. She had even temporarily forgotten that Tyro had ignored her!

"Tyro," she began softly, in her most charming tone, as if to say, "I am probably wrong but I'd like you to know how I feel anyway."

"Tyro," she went on. "I think we shouldn't go at night. I have a better idea. Before you interrupt, I'd like to say that I'll come with you, even though I don't really want to, but not at night. Never. I'm not doing it even if it means you going alone. Listen to me."

Tyro had begun to object but was being restrained by a very determined advocate. She decided to listen for a change.

"We're going to have a meal at the Burnchester Arms tonight, kindly arranged by your Uncle Dennis, to which I've been invited. I think by the way he's going to invite my mum and dad too. I don't know what time we would finish, but probably we wouldn't be back till quite late. But when we get back, then what? We wait until your mum has gone to bed and Dennis has gone to bed, and I have gone home with Mum and dad, or I stay here, and then sometime around midnight (at the earliest) go back to the school in the pitch black...alright, full moon-lit dark....on bikes, along country lanes that we don't know well, with no lights on our bikes, to be terrified out of our skins. Don't interrupt! If you don't agree, I'm sorry - I'm going to let you go alone. I'm going home now anyway, in case you weren't listening."

This must have been the longest speech that Jess had ever made, and it had made her flush. She was as passionate as she was determined. Tyro admired her for it.

There was a moment's silence.

Tyro decided to play a little.

"OK. I'm going to do my letter now. If you want to go, go. If you don't want to come tonight, that's fine, I'll go alone."

"Listen to me Tyro! Why don't we go back there this afternoon around tea-time, explore if we must - though I still think it's stupid. Then we go to the Arms. That way we get to do what you want, in daylight, and have a brilliant meal, afterwards. But no Rick. We can meet up with him another time."

Tyro could see that her best friend had struggled to get these words out, so unused was she to having her way. She could also see that she meant very well. The plan, moreover, was rather sensible.

She went over to Jess and gave her a hug.

"OK, Jess. I agree. It is a better idea. Maybe we can do the midnight wanders when we're older," she said. "Though I think it's better not to have lights, then you can be more invisible."

With that the two friends parted.

Jess went downstairs and saw Mrs Wander in the kitchen talking to the Reverend Sandals.

Out in the garden, the sun was out. Dennis and Bill were talking by an old bonfire deep in the field at the back of the house. Jess remembered the last time when she and Tyro had helped set it alight and the flames had burnt some of the leaves high up in the surrounding trees. She hated that. Trees were special. She believed they were magical if anything was. She could feel the pain of the burns now. She thought suddenly for no reason of St Joan of Arc. Burnt at the flames. She wondered what it was like to be burnt for your beliefs. She couldn't understand how anyone could light the torch. She shuddered.

Jess waved at Dennis and Bill. Rompy was beside them. They waved back. "Full moon," thought Jess. Anybody'd think the werewolves would be out. She loved Tyro, but felt proud of what she'd done. She didn't like the sound of her own anger. She also wished Rick could come, but trying to wrench him from Patrolia would only slow things up, if he was at home. She did wonder what he was up to though at the school. Something, she felt sure. She got on her bike and rode off, contented that the day was working out very well, especially that she would be spending more time with her own mum, which she enjoyed. She loved her dad too. So did Tyro. She felt sorry for Tyro.

Out on the road, Jess tried to work out why some people got angry easily and didn't really mind about it; others didn't get angry easily and cared very much when they did. Did it make one person better than another? Who would win? She knew the answer to that. She also wondered what it would be like to be without a dad. And then, thinking beyond her own world, if you had no home, no money, no food. She could not understand where God was supposed to be in all this, though she was happy to pray to him from time to time. She felt that not all those good people who believed could be entirely wrong, could they? And yet, perhaps they weren't entirely right either. "Believing where we cannot prove" rang in her ears. Proving where we cannot believe, she thought.

That's me. Isn't it? And then she looked up, and there, high in the sky, yes, she could even see it from her bike, was a skylark, singing.

Tyro had nearly finished her letter. "Love from Tyro" she wrote in huge letters at the bottom with a series of large kisses. Her aunt appreciated these things. This was her dad's sister, who she saw only occasionally, as she lived abroad. But she, Aunt Jane, was like a distant guardian to her, always remembered birthdays and Christmas and exams and, well, any occasion to comfort her with good news. She loved writing letters once she got going, especially to Aunt Jane. She folded up the letter and put it in the envelope. She sealed it and left it on the desk.

Her next task was her room. With considerable determination she faced her bed, which looked as though it had been hit by a bomb, clothes everywhere. Biscuit was asleep on top.

However, instead of starting with the bed, she got on her hands and knees and looked under it. Apart from the rings of dust and cat hairs that lived there pretty permanently, there was a wooden box. It was locked. She pulled it out and opened it with the key that hung from the lock on a piece of string.

It was writing the letter that had made her think of it. Her father often came to mind when she was writing to Aunt Jane.

The box was full of odds and ends from her childhood, special toys (including her bear), letters, keepsakes that were important to her. This was her secret box, into which nobody was allowed. Presents that her mum and dad had given her. Even a Valentine's card from her first boyfriend. Jules was in her class when she was eight, at Burnchester. They did a lot of things together, and she liked him. That year Jules had given her a card and signed it. He had gone very red when he learned that he was supposed to keep his name secret. She loved Jules, but he had gone away, the following year, somewhere to another country.

Among these things, memories of her father loomed large. There were three photos, one of her dad holding her as a baby, another, a shot of her father holding her outstretched arms as he was walking her along the beach. He was looking up smiling to camera. She was concentrating on the ground in front of her. Under the photo her father had written. "Tyro takes a few steps", to which had been added, by her mother she thought, "like father like daughter!" The exclamation mark said it all. A third was of her father reading a story to her, as she lay, in fact asleep, in his lap. In this very room. A few tears welled up in her animated face. Where was he now?

Tyro, like Jess, for all her brief years, was not alone in struggling with so-called God. If heaven didn't exist, how could God? Yet she talked to him sometimes, like a brother, who had let her down badly. She shouted at him, for taking her father away from her. She hated him much of the time. And yet, some lingering, unexplained desire made her seek his help, from time to time. Her father's faith added to this. But she felt he hadn't got the right reward for respect. So why should she bother? But still she cried, in the night, in her dreams, in the day when she was alone. Tears were beginning to well up, now.

"Dad," she called softly. She listened for a moment. Nothing could be heard but the very soft murmur of a cat, asleep on a crumpled duvet. One day he would answer.

Underneath the photos was a small rather broken cardboard box. Tyro took this out and opened it. She went very red, even to herself. Inside was a tiny bottle, on which was a label. This read: 'Magic Potion. To be used in acceptional sircomstances only.' She looked at the bottle and examined it carefully. There was also a small toy sword. She took both of these and put them on the bed. Then there was a key. This was the 'wishing key'.

All three things had been given to her by her father for when she went on 'expuditions' into the garden, when she was little. These never took her much further than the first line of trees at the back of the house along the far edge of the lawn. Occasionally to the ditch beyond. But they offered her full protection from every imaginable goblin, monster, dragon, witch, or whatever she might have met along the way. She never went without them. She always tried to take Biscuit with her as a companion, but Biscuit wasn't very reliable, and would somehow disappear for hours on end. She could hear her father say, as he sat at the end of her bed, making up one of his stories, "not to forget the bottle, the sword and the key. All of them are magic. You never know when you might need them. Treat them well."

In the stories of course the heroine had been someone else. But when she acted them out afterwards, in that line of trees at the back of the lawn, or in the house, she pretended to be that person, and so had to take these things with her. Otherwise it wouldn't have been real. The tears fell freely. Tears of remembrance.

Tyro was a little ashamed at what she was doing, now that she was eleven and two thirds. She would not have told anybody for all the tea in China, or India for that matter, but put the tiny bottle and the toy sword in her shoulder bag, and the key in her pocket. A sort of ritual, to protect her from Mrs Limpet. If she could slay that dragon (the image came to mind

- it had been a terrific fight, but good had prevailed in the end
- another phrase from her father's stories) Mrs Limpet would
be easy. She thought of Jess and her fear. Perhaps she herself
was more frightened than she had let on.

"Tyro!" came Abby's voice from the end of the corridor. "I'm
just going over to the church with the Reverend Sandals. Got
to sort out some flowers. Do you want to come?"

"Mum! Mum!" Tyro cried, in a broken voice, "Can you come
here a minute?"

"What is it, Tyro?" said Abby entering her room.

"Mum, it's just that, well...."

" 'Unlike you, Tyro, to hesitate. Act first think later, that's
you. What's up? What have you got there?" She saw the bag.

"Nothing, Mum."

Abby could see that she had been crying. So she sat her on
the bed and gave her a big hug. Tears poured down Tyro's
strong face. Abby regretted what she had just said.

"What's troubling you, darling?"

But Abby knew, and tried to hold back her own tears. Her
own anger only increased at moments like these. She felt even
more of a hypocrite going to the church and pretending to be
a believer.

"Mum," said Tyro in a low voice, "thanks." Then she added,
"Mum, you know we're going out for a meal tonight?"

"Well?"

"Would you mind if Jess and I met you there? I mean we
wanted to have a bike ride beforehand, and do some
exploring. We could, couldn't we?"

In the circumstances Abby couldn't refuse. In fact she
encouraged the idea. Build up an appetite she said. She didn't
mention Burnchester Hall.

"But take your phone and be careful. I'm not sure that
Dennis would approve. Tell me before you go."

"Thanks, Mum."

"And Tyro," she added. "I know how you feel. I feel a bit the same, you know. It will be alright, I promise you."

Tyro looked at her, not really sure if her mum believed it. She was angry at her mum sometimes, though she knew she shouldn't be. Then she raced downstairs leaving her mother feeling empty. The bed was still a mess. Biscuit was still sleeping. What was she going to do with her daughter? What could she do? From earliest childhood Tyro had had a strong head and a powerful will. Even her father hadn't been able to control her. She didn't have the strength to fight it. It was a will often allied to intuition and energy which was a pretty strong mix. But there were dangers.

Perhaps she could start by relaxing a little, or by becoming a little more consistent herself. How she wished she was not so alone. But this was selfish compared to the solitude of her child, and the solitude of others.

By about four o'clock in the afternoon, two girls were cycling down back lanes, on a fine summer's day. Their direction was an old Hall with a mysterious history. Their purpose, adventure. Tyro rode furiously, a bag on her shoulder, the wind blowing through her hair. The tears that she had shed had somehow given her strength, now forgotten in the bliss of action. She wore old jeans and a comfy top (their good clothes they had put in Dennis's car). Jess, in light trousers and pale top, didn't try to keep up, but managed to catch Tyro when she paused for breath, and sometimes glided past her, without her noticing until she was some way ahead. Tyro then caught up in a rush of excitement, then would stay at Jess's side. They would be careful, and knew instinctively what to look out for - so they thought - even though Rick would not be with them.

They could not have known, or anticipated, what would happen.

By the time they got to the school gates, Tyro and Jess were quite exhausted. They had hardly spoken on their way there, except once when Jess wanted to tell Tyro something. She had overheard Dennis on their way to the sea the day before. Something about following a stranger out of the pub at Warblersbay and thinking he might be a threat to the school. Jess had thought this impossible, which is why she hadn't mentioned it before now, though she did wonder why he had wanted to keep it secret. "Dennis is like that," Tyro had said. "Imagines things, then expects to find them happening."

Even so, the idea made Jess feel more anxious, though it only made Tyro cycle faster. Jess had seen what Tyro had not, that reality sometimes catches up with you when you least expect it.

At the school, they decided not to leave their bikes in the same spot as the previous visit, but at the entrance to the church, to the left of the main gates. This could be done without drawing attention to themselves, as the church was often open to visitors. Living next to a graveyard herself made Tyro quite relaxed about this, and Jess felt, in some odd way, a little bit more protected as a result. There was a certain tranquillity associated with the dead.

During the ride Tyro had made a plan. They would follow the track on foot to the back of the church, from where they would continue on past Mr Gruff's house, along the line of yews and back up round the far side of the school to the science building. That way they wouldn't have to be out in the open at all. From there they would make their way to the biology room, keeping a look out for old Gruff and Titan along the way. Tyro carried some biscuits with which to distract Titan in case of emergencies (or in case they got hungry which was more likely).

They hurried through the churchyard, feeling on top of the world. What they didn't know was that high on top of the tower a cloaked figure was watching them, a figure in black, with no visible face. The figure kept low, but a pair of eyes might be seen through one of the castellations, as it watched the children. It seemed like the spirit of a monk. Then the figure disappeared. A cold dark shadow seemed to follow it into the hollow of the tower. It seemed to have a red cross on its back.

As the two girls left the churchyard, Tyro caught sight of something on the path, next to a gravestone. At first it looked like a piece of plastic or a broken balloon. She paused and walked up to it. Then it took shape. It was an upside-down mask. Like a party mask. Tyro turned it over. The mask had the face of quite a young woman, with a stern expression. It looked very strange abandoned amidst the graves, and Tyro gave a gasp, as she studied it. It felt oddly familiar, almost not unexpected, though she didn't know why. But Jess was not so calm.

"Let's get out of here!" she said.

"It's only a party mask," said Tyro. "It's pretty realistic."

She pulled it over her face and stared through the eye sockets.

She moved her mouth and the mask moved too. Jess was amused, against her will.

"Come on, give it here," said Jess, keen to be rid of it. "I'll take it back to the bikes. You wait here. Must have been some kids playing, don't you think?"

Tyro didn't answer. Within a couple of minutes Jess had returned. What she wanted to say she could not say.

"Perhaps it's Mrs Limpet's," said Tyro, without knowing why.

"What makes you say that?" asked Jess.

"Just a thought. Silly really."

Once out of the churchyard, the girls followed the line of yews that passed Mr Gruff's house, where the car was neatly parked in the small drive.

They were in the garden at the front of the school, which runs parallel to the river below them at the bottom of the sports' field. They had noticed that Mr Rummage's car wasn't there, from which they had concluded that he was away. On they hastened.

Round the corner, past the swimming pool and the assembly hall, they approached the science block.

Tyro led, Jess very close behind. The building entrance was locked, but sure enough, the back entrance, as before, was open.

They both entered. The door creaked just a touch as they drew it to behind them.

They found Mrs Limpet's room locked, but knew that the keys were kept in a cupboard on the first floor. Tyro ran up to get them, returned and opened up.

Tyro entered the room, which smelled of ammonia, and again looked like an empty operating theatre. She sat very briefly at Mrs Limpet's desk, looking at Jess who had now entered, but stood by the door. Then she went on to the front of the class.

There on the floor was the patch of dried blood.

"I didn't imagine it!" Tyro exclaimed.

"Why should you imagine a thing like that?" Jess asked, irritated.

"You can imagine anything. Even demons."

"I don't think, for all her uptightness - and terrible treatment of you - Mrs Limpet is a demon. I feel slightly sorry for her, if you ask me!" Jess remonstrated.

But talk of demons made them both look at each other, a little anxiously, before they broke into a laugh. Yet the sight of the cupboard door beyond, where Tyro had been locked, and from which Mrs Limpet had come the last time, made them pause. This time a creeping feeling arose, as if from the blood on the floor, and like the blood could not be easily ignored, or even washed away.

The door at the back was open, which it should not have been, but they had heard nothing. Perhaps Mrs Limpet had forgotten to lock it. Still, Mr Gruff should have noticed. Tyro went in. Jess felt distinctly frightened at the sight of Tyro disappearing. She tried to call "No!" but nothing seemed to come out.

Tyro was in the preparation room.

There were no animals there now, though there were empty cages which had presumably recently held them. At the back of the room she noticed another door, which was closed. She hadn't seen it in the dark. Turning on the light she looked on the wall for a key. But there was no key there. Perhaps the room was too important to leave the key out and visible, even though the pupils would never normally come into this room. This made her more curious.

She searched and searched, in boxes, under bottles, on shelves. Jess, who had followed, suggested they go back to the school and see if it was in the central key cupboard by the main door. Then she suggested Mr Gruff might have it, or more likely Mrs Limpet, who would surely carry it with her. Tyro kept looking. She turned to the desk beside the door. There was nothing in the drawer.

Without thinking Tyro put her hand in her pocket and took out the 'wishing key'. She tried the key. To her astonishment, the door opened. She replaced the key in her pocket. It was very dark inside, though she could just make out steps leading down into the dark hollow beneath. She turned to Jess, who was shaking her head. She turned back hesitating a moment. Then, without knowing why, she made a sign of the cross, as if it might help fight the shadows. She thought of the tiny bottle and the toy sword and checked her bag.

"You need your head testing!" said Jess. "No!"

But Tyro didn't answer. She put her foot on the first step, but Jess held her back.

"I thought I heard someone," she said.

"Jess, look at this!" Tyro helped Jess to the entrance of the stairs. "When you see a dark tunnel, what else can you do?" she said, with a slightly nervous laugh. "Perhaps that's where Mrs Limpet gets her rats. I'm going down."

"Going down! What are you talking about? You must be joking. I'm not, and I'm not going to let you."

Jess held tightly on to Tyro's top as she tried not to look below, for fear she might be tempted too. Tyro wriggled free.

"Remember Orpheus!"

Tyro changed her tone. "Must be a cellar of some sort. I knew she was up to something. Are you coming?"

"No."

But though Tyro had broken loose, she could not let her go alone.

The first steps are always tentative, especially in the dark, even for someone of Tyro's character. There was not much light, though a switch at the top of the steps, which she flicked on, revealed a set of stone slabs, curiously out of shape, leading down. There was a musty smell. Tyro started cautiously. She felt for her phone, and the bottle and toy sword in her bag. And, yes, for the 'wishing key' in her pocket. To her it was like a game, a story, and these things would protect her, as they had, in her imagination, as a child. She went further. Without looking back, and holding one hand against the banisters in the wall, she called to Jess.

"Come on Jess!"

Jess was out of earshot. She had gone back into Mrs Limpet's room to make sure that nobody was around. She was now in a heightened state of anxiety, bordering on anger, but also determined not to let Tyro down, or to let her go too far. She was also going to secure their escape.

She ensured that Mrs Limpet's room could not be locked behind them, and quickly checked the outer door, which was broken and therefore unlockable.

Returning to the preparation room, she made for the

stairway entrance. Here she put a piece of cardboard packaging that was lying on the floor firmly under the 'cellar' door, to stop it closing and to allow a little more light, and air.

"Tyro!" she called, "we're only going to the bottom and no further!"

Tyro could not hear her, as she reached the bottom, where there was another door. She wanted to go much further. There was something almost of Mrs Limpet's stare in her eyes, so determined was she. There was an energy which seemed to pull her on, an atmosphere that tempted her to follow.

"Tyro! Tyro! Wait! Look at me! I was calling you!" screamed Jess, closing the gap between them.

Tyro was peering through a misted pane in the top half of the door, which she was giving a push. The door didn't seem to want to open. She could see nothing the other side, the light reflecting back at her, like a mirror. For a moment she caught sight of herself and jumped.

"I thought there was someone there!"

"Tyro! Listen to me! Look at me!" Jess screamed again. "There is someone here! Me!" she continued, touching Tyro on the shoulder.

Tyro looked round.

"I know you're there. I thought I saw a face in the door, though it was mine." She calmed a little, before continuing. "Sorry Jess, I was getting excited!"

She tried the door again. There was quite a substantial lock and a bolt at the top and bottom. The bolts were open, but the lock had, it seems, been forced. There were scratch marks by the key hole, and a twisted catch.

"Tyro! Wait!"

This time, Jess hit her hard on the shoulder.

"Don't ignore me! We've gone far enough. I think we should go back. Now!" Jess could sense the pull too, but was trying to dismiss it.

It was too late. The door had opened, and Tyro was going

through it. It opened onto a dark tunnel. The little light showed other doors on both sides, leading further into the darkness. There was a strange smell, and the atmosphere was harder, more static, and more disturbed. For a moment, Tyro was pushed back and bumped into Jess behind her.

"What on earth?" whispered Jess in amazement, keeping her voice down.

"What is it?" asked Tyro.

"I don't like it, not at all," continued Jess.

"What is this tunnel?" said Tyro.

"Perhaps it's a bomb shelter. There are secrets about the school which nobody knows. It has a horrible atmosphere. Look at this."

From the ceiling hung a sign, greying and torn. It was possible to read the words:

No unauthorised persons beyond this point.

Danger of Death.

There seemed to be a notice against one of the doors, but its letters were difficult to read. On close inspection, the word "SECURITY" could be seen. An arrow next to it pointed forward, into the dark, which read, "Domed Chamber."

Jess moved forward slowly, as if compelled against her will, and by her own curiosity. Tyro was alongside.

"The place is used. Look at the floor!"

In the half-light, what appeared to be freshly made footprints could be distinguished in the dusty floor. Tyro noticed a switch on the wall which she flicked. Now the long corridor was lit with a dull light, from flickering tubes along the corner between the walls and the ceiling. The walls were a dull brown colour, with a dusty sheen. Further ahead, beyond the door marked 'SECURITY', were other doors, on either side, at regular intervals. In the obscure light, they could distinguish a set of doors at the end of the passage. Though drawn towards them, Jess was praying these would be shut, as if she knew she should not dare to go on. On the walls of the corridor were small loudspeakers.

"Some kind of underground research centre, or command centre," Jess said.

"These footprints, whose are they? And the loudspeakers? Doesn't look like anything to do with the school," said Tyro.

"As far as we know," Jess added.

"What are you suggesting, Jess?" Suddenly Tyro was pleased to have knowledgeable Jess alongside her.

"Perhaps there is a link we don't know about. There have been unusual comings and goings recently, don't you remember? These prints suggest activity. And the speakers are connected. Look!" Jess pointed to the wires sticking out from the walls and newly sealed into the speakers. "These footprints could be Mrs Limpet's," she added, bending down.

"They look too big," replied Tyro.

There had been one or two unusual visits to the school in recent months, officials in dark cars had come to the Headmaster's office, and one or two men even in uniform, but these had been months ago, and hadn't aroused much suspicion at the time.

Tyro was moving forward, even more confident with Jess's enthusiasm. Were there limits to the game, to the adventure which she had so clearly imagined? She remembered as a child acting out those stories that her father had told her. She was happy as long as she could return to the safety of her room. And now? She went forward. What she didn't want was that the adventure should become a frightening reality.

"What do you think the Domed Chamber is?" said Tyro.

"A meeting room. I don't like this vibration, or the stale air. Let's get out of here, Tyro, come back another time with Rick."

Tyro and Jess looked in at a door which they tried to push open. A small room, with a simple desk and rusted cupboards at the back. A bit of old black twisted wire lay on the floor leading to the desk. Half-torn maps hung down from the walls. One was of East Anglia. Another of the coast of

Mainland Europe across the North Sea. On the first were several faded man-made marks, rings and pin-marks. On the other lines across parts of countryside, they could see the letters BH in the centre of the first map. They looked at each other. Around the letters were a series of rings.

"That's us," said Tyro. "The school is more famous than I thought. Rather this than lessons."

"And more dangerous," added Jess, sensing that they had gone further than they ought. "I wish we hadn't come."

Tyro looked at her.

"Because by knowing a little, we're obliged to find out more. Better to know nothing."

"Don't be silly Jess, it's only an adventure. Nothing can come of it. The war was a long time ago. These footprints could be someone like us, who made a discovery."

Jess thought immediately of Rick. There was a pause, as they looked around the room.

"Old telephone wire," said Tyro. "I've seen it in films. 'Reporting for duty!'" was all Tyro could muster as she saluted the guard behind the desk, who had moved there and suddenly looked like Sergeant Jess. But it didn't really work.

"They didn't have girls in the army in those days," said Jess.

"Except as spies," said Tyro.

They moved on down the corridor past three other rooms, all of them empty. One was much larger, and had pipes against the back wall, and a very old and decayed basin attached to it. Another contained a broken lavatory. Tyro looked at Jess, and sniggered. Tyro went over to the chain which still hung down from a dry tank and pulled. The chain broke and fell to the ground. Tyro's hands were now covered in rust.

"I'll have to wait," she said.

The attempt at a joke made them feel better. Despite their fears, little here had been touched for a very long time. They walked on to the second door at the end of the corridor. The air felt denser as they went. On the door were marked the words:

No unauthorised persons beyond this point.
Extreme Danger.

This time, there was no window.

Tyro looked at Jess.

"Shall we?"

They pushed the second door to.

This time it didn't move. They pushed again. Nothing. They heard a curious clicking sound. It came from the speaker in the corner above them.

Tyro and Jess pushed the door again. Harder and harder they shoved. Gradually it opened onto a small rectangular area which was hospital clean. To their left and right another corridor led away. At the end to the left was a set of circular stairs which led upwards. These they could see while holding the door open. They peered round the door, not wishing to let it shut behind them. In the other direction, a set of stairs led downwards. In front of them were two sets of lifts. The air was fresher but there was a harsh vibration in the air. The energy field was very intense, making them wince. Against the wall beside the lift they could make out a floor plan though they could not read it. There were a set of monitors, flashing lights, green, red, yellow, as if the whole place were alive, and its pulse was being taken.

"Wow!" said Tyro.

"Perhaps the scruffy entrance is to put people off," said Jess. "Look how clean it all is. Like a laboratory. And those lights."

"What is it, Jess?"

"It's active, whatever it is. Holidays or no holidays, somebody comes down here regularly. Somebody is working on something important."

"It is up to us to find out," said Tyro.

But the door suddenly became heavier and gradually pushed them back. This made them shove harder, but the door continued to shut until it shut tight. There was another click, which was obviously a lock.

"This door is being controlled, by some force."

"It's like somebody wanted us to see, but not to enter," said Tyro.

Jess was trying to think what it all meant.

"Not yet, anyway, unless it was some*thing*," she said.

"What does that mean?" asked Tyro, turning back in the direction of the stairs.

"It means that something or somebody knows we are here, but only wants us to see certain things."

"Don't be ridiculous," said Tyro. "You think that door's alive?"

"Not exactly alive, but being used. By whoever or whatever is here. Somebody's here. Down those lifts. I think we'd better tell Dennis as soon as possible."

"It's our secret. We're not to tell anybody."

"We'll come back another time. With Rick, and Tom. I think it's better there are a few of us," Jess said.

They reached the first door at the front end of the corridor. It had swung shut. They pushed against it.

It was locked. They pushed again. It was locked tight.

"But the lock was broken," said Tyro.

"What have you done, Tyro? We're locked in. We can't get out. What do we do now?"

It all happened so suddenly. The doors at both ends of the corridor were locked. Then the lights in the corridor went out. There was a further click. Tyro felt for her mobile phone. It was switched off. Then a crackle over the loudspeakers. The growl of a dog, becoming louder and louder. Suddenly barking and panting and running. The door at the far end swung open. At the same time, the door against which they were leaning opened and they fell out. They ran in a panic up the stone steps, the dog behind them gaining all the time. At the top they shut the door, and rammed the old desk against it and ran out of the room. Out of Mrs Limpet's classroom, into the corridor, into the air. They ran and ran, the dog now closing behind them.

Tyro and Jess ran over the tarmac drive by the school entrance. Jess fell. Tyro stopped to help her. The dog was upon them. It was Titan. Its eyes livid with unearthly rage.

The girls ran on, Titan following.

Then Titan stopped.

The girls were now in the churchyard. Their terror was heightened by curiosity.

They turned and looked back over to the main building.

Was it something about the churchyard that made Titan stop?

"Must be Gruff who called him. Didn't you hear a voice over that loudspeaker?"

"No, only Titan barking," said Jess.

They did not see the cloaked figure in black standing in the shadows of the yews. It also wore a red cross.

Titan was now sitting, whimpering slightly. He seemed to want to move forward, but could not do so, as if a barrier had fallen in front of him. He tried but failed. He barked loudly, turned and barked again. Then sat down and began to wash his body. But before long he got up, and moved away, back towards the school. Looking after him once or twice, he went out of sight.

Tyro looked at Jess.

"Let's get out of here! Leave the bikes and go straight down to the river."

"And Gruff," asked Jess, "where is he? Where there's Titan, there's Gruff."

"I'm sure Gruff was behind us, somewhere in those tunnels. I heard a voice that sounded exactly like his. Gruff now knows we know."

"Where *is* he? He's never far behind Titan."

"Probably locking up those doors."

"That's another thing. Some of those doors didn't have

proper locks. I also kept them open with bits of cardboard. They shut just the same."

"I don't know, Jess. All I know is that something very strange is going on and I want to find out more. In our school. Let's go to the river. If Gruff comes, he comes. We can confront him. It's better we face him upfront, and not wait for him to accuse us at his convenience. Just check your mobile."

"It's on."

Tyro saw that her mobile was also on again. She decided to text a message to her mum. "Mm, brng R to pub. V weird things on walk. By the river. c u soon. T."

"I don't want to tell her that we're at school yet, she'll throw a wobbly. We'll have to return, especially after what you overheard Dennis say to Mum. Come on Jess. Let's go."

Jess said nothing. Tyro wasn't at all sure that she meant what she said. Her enthusiasm kept her going, but the remnants of her childhood were being subsumed.

They walked into the open ground beside the churchyard and headed towards the river. The still fresh evening sun made them feel better, as did the thought of a M. Le Petit special, not so far off. They loved M. Le Petit. He made them laugh, and gave them special cakes.

"Jess," said Tyro as they made their way over the cut grass, "what do you think it is?"

"My father said something about researching energies, or something."

The full moon stood high in the sky in front of them, in one of those magical moments when it can be seen with the lowering sun.

"I forgot the full moon."

They approached the old boathouse.

"Let's take a boat to the Arms," announced Tyro.

"Cool!" said Jess.

Within moments they were upon it.

What they found at the disused boathouse didn't encourage

any trips down river. To their surprise, someone had broken in. Probably boys - Tyro thought of Rick. There was a boat in the water, which seemed to be in very good condition. As if it had only recently been used.

"This is supposed to be a disused boathouse," said Jess. "This boat hasn't been here long."

There were footprints on the side, where there had been some kind of fight. Tyro followed them to the end of the boathouse where there was a door, cut into the wall, presumably some kind of link to the school. A house that old was bound to have a link to the river. Tyro pulled the door open.

It was completely dark inside. The prints were certainly deep.

Tyro tried for a switch but found nothing. The wall seemed no more than cut out of the earth.

"Hello!" shouted Tyro nervously, in her deepest voice. Her voice resonated with the very slight lapping of the water against the boathouse edge. She could not have guessed how close they were.

Jess looked at the prints, and thought she could see faint marks in the now dry mud.

"What are these?" asked Jess.

Tyro joined her. She stared down at them. They followed the drops back to the door.

"I think you know, don't you Jess?"

"Someone has either been in a fight here, or someone has arrived by boat, by this boat, injured." said Jess.

"Which?" asked Tyro.

"Perhaps it's murder," whispered Jess.

The thought that they were at the site of a crime, now possibly murder, made Tyro shudder. Yet she also thought of the stories she could tell next term! She was not in the slightest bit concerned for her safety. The summertime visit to school was taking on a more dark, and in some ways attractive tone.

This was not something that she wanted to admit to. She could not have known that she was, without knowing it, just beginning to fall prey to the very powers that she was hoping to overcome.

"It's certainly recent. Tyro, what are we up against? Secret tunnels, doors that open and shut themselves, now blood."

"Looks like it. Whose?"

Tyro was looking inside the boat.

"And look here. A key." Jess pointed to a small key sunken in the mud. "Whoever has been here, dropped it."

"Yes, but whether they did it deliberately or not is another matter."

"What do you mean?"

"Supposing one person had the key, but didn't want the other person to know."

"I'd throw it in the river."

"And suppose you couldn't reach the river?"

"I'd throw it as far as I could. Or drop it and let it sink in the mud."

"Precisely, Tyro. I think we'd better get going. This needs adults," said Jess, picking up the key.

"Looks old, Jess. Might be interesting. Let's take the boat." She took the key out of her pocket. It looked similar.

The two girls got in, and untied the rope. They pushed it out of the boathouse and into the river.

The river welcomed them, as only water can. The boat drifted in the middle, whilst Tyro tried to fit the oars into place. Jess sat in the prow.

Once the oars were in place, Tyro began to row.

"We should go straight there."

"And the bikes?"

"Dennis can pick them up later," said Tyro. "Have a close look inside the boat, Jess, while I row. There must be some clues as to who's been using it, perhaps even if there's been a fight."

The water slopped playfully, leaving trailing and broken rings over the surface as Tyro rowed. Jess bent down to examine the ribbed hull and the holds in the prow.

The river flowed gently on, the water was clear enough to be free of weed, except near the banks where tufts of grass and the occasional reed formed the centre of a miniature world of its own. The call of the moorhen and the hasty retreat of a bird from one of these suggested a nest, and the clicking calls of another adult suggested the possibility of a brood nearby. An occasional swallow flew across the school field and skimmed along the surface. It seemed to touch the water, and was gone.

In the near distance, Burnchester Hall seemed as if it too had a life of its own, or was coming to life again.

"Only an oilskin, here," said Jess, looking into the hold. "Otherwise nothing."

The boat was moving steadily towards the boundary of the school. To the right, on the ridge, the Folly stood watch. Soon they would be in unknown territory, past the ancient wood and Shelter Field, before making their final assault on the Burnchester Arms. Tyro felt safer mid-stream.

She thought of what had happened, convinced that there was more to come, from the mask to the blood-stained earth. She knew, at heart, that they were onto something much bigger than they could handle alone, and, despite her pride, was now beginning to see the need to involve her mother and Dennis.

The thought that a man had been injured or killed hovered like a nightmare in that region where imagination and reality meet, with a silent but terrifying resonance. Yet still, it was of the order of myth, perhaps enough to protect them from the haunting truth that was being revealed in the unfolding story.

Jess stood at the prow, watching, less sure, and more frightened.

In the distance, a cloaked figure stood on top of the church tower.

A shout from the woods on the other side. Another.

"Get out of there! That's not your boat! Get out I tell you!"

Tyro rowing hard to the bank. Twigs breaking, a dog barking, a man standing on the far bank carrying a gun.

"Get out, or I'll shoot!"

Jess held on to the branches of the willow as Tyro got out. She tied the boat up, got out too. They both ran on, barely glimpsing the man who was walking along the other side shouting, holding a gun aloft.

"I'll get you for this! Mr Gruff will be the first to know. And don't think I don't know you, I do. Miss Wander. Trouble, that's what you are! I've heard all about you. And your friend is no better."

At this Tyro turned to see Mr Pinchet, Mr Strangelblood's keeper, on the far bank.

"There's a man dying of horrible wounds, and a wild dog is on the loose and someone's broken into the school and all you can do is shout at us! I'm ashamed of you Mr, Mr, Mr...."

"Pinchet. Mr Pinchet," said Mr Pinchet, calming a little, and all ears. "Dying? What are you talking about?"

But Tyro and Jess had run on. She wished she hadn't said anything. She wasn't going to tell him anymore. He wasn't to be trusted, she had been told. She wished she had held her tongue.

But it was too late.

The girls ran until they could see the Burnchester Arms, people outside enjoying the summer air, and there was her mother with Dennis, and Jess's mum and dad, Clare and John.

They ran up to them, panting furiously.

"What on earth....?" the adults said, simultaneously.

Rompy was all over them.

# 9

By the time M. Le Petit was bringing in their meal, Tyro and Jess had told most of their story to Abby, Dennis, Clare and John. Tyro gave the general outline, Jess added the details. Before the girls had got very far Dennis began formulating a plan, and had gone into the bar to fetch PC Relish (who was off-duty), as he had earlier told Dennis about the strange case of Mr Gruff. PC Relish had called Mrs Boot the previous evening to say that there had been no reports of Mr Gruff but that he might have gone on a detour and would, he hoped, be with her that day. She should therefore not worry unduly. Privately he remained very concerned, particularly after the visit to his house and the church. Mrs Boot was angry at his suggestion, but she agreed reluctantly that it was too early for a search-party, and promised to take no further action for twenty-four hours, when she would call again to confirm whether or not he had arrived, or for further news. In the circumstances PC Relish was praying for a miracle. Going 'walkabout', or absent without leave, could happen to anyone, particularly under stress. The delay gave PC Relish a little time.

Tyro was describing the exit to the tunnels and the arrival of ghostly Titan when PC Relish and Dennis returned. Whilst Abby and Clare were both proud of their daughters' nerve, Abby was also a bit angry with Tyro, especially as she'd told her not to go back to Burnchester. John listened carefully but as yet said nothing. The existence of the tunnels did not provoke especial interest, such was the known (or rumoured) history of the school (though confirmation was interesting). The details of doors locking and unlocking and sounds over the microphones were intriguing to say the least, even allowing for children's elaboration. They didn't express any doubts they may have had about the basic facts, nor did they reprimand the children. If that was to come it would come later. However, everyone was struck by Titan's inexplicable behaviour. More so by what he was doing alone.

Dennis had been on the alert since his sighting of the stranger at Warblersbay. The girls' story further aroused his suspicions. He felt sure they were connected. Equally, PC Relish felt that these events linked with the break-in and strange activities at St Mary Magdalen, something which was also of particular interest to Abby, who had reported to the Reverend John an incident that had occurred at All Saints Church the day before. PC Relish had been informed.

As they reached the climax of their story and the discovery of dried blood, an unwelcome intruder appeared on the scene, in the form of Mr Pinchet. He stormed in, in a rage at the girls for stealing the boat and for ignoring him, probably the more serious crime. They should be arrested, he said. "What was all this rubbish about a man dying?" he added.

With this the mood changed. Dennis immediately demanded details from the girls and from Mr Pinchet. It was with some relief to Dennis that Mr Pinchet had not gone looking for evidence before anyone else. However, the need for action became immediate, though he wanted to get as much in place before going in search. He also wanted Mr Pinchet on their side.

PC Relish took Mr Pinchet inside and consoled him with a few compliments and gratitude for being so alert and for taking such an interest in Burnchester, along with a large whisky chaser. This calmed him for a while. When Mr Gatherin appeared, Dennis discreetly asked him if he would keep an eye on Mr Pinchet, in case any details emerged that might be of interest. Dennis didn't quite trust Mr Pinchet. A second large whisky, and a further compliment, settled Mr Pinchet at the bar, and allowed him to hold forth to Mr Gatherin, though Mr Gatherin was continuing to serve and observe in equal measure, sometimes in doubles.

PC Relish and Dennis spoke briefly, in private, before leaving the bar.

Meanwhile, during these anxious manoeuvrings inside, as if momentarily to offset the growing mystery, M. Le Petit was doing due justice to his lunar character, dancing a little on the grass whilst holding a meringue pie with ice cream topped with strawberries as an added flourish, in his hand. He placed the pie on the table, and himself on Dennis's vacant chair, with the words, "I 'ave it on good au'tority" (meaning his own) "zat ze pie is of ze 'ighest calibre." With that he lifted one of Abby's hands and kissed it with a wink at the incredulous Tyro (who was thinking how fortunate it was that her mother was not an apple crumble), and returned to his duties out of sight, which meant putting his feet up. For him cooking was not only a creative activity and he an artist, but a mystery, like crime, filled to the brim with the most wonderful ingredients, and possibilities.

Dennis and PC Relish had walked towards the river for consultation. The first priority was to hurry to the boathouse and check the blood stains. It would then be necessary to make a thorough search of the grounds. Titan on the loose added to their conviction that the girls had been telling the truth and that Mr Gruff had been attacked. It was not clear who or what (PC Relish mentioned the Rev Sandal's remark in the church, to Dennis's interest) was controlling Titan, or why he should have escaped. At this the sight of the stranger's cold eyes appeared before Dennis's imagination. Dennis felt a striking pain, as if his heart was being pierced by a spear.

The possibility of needing further support occurred to both men. PC Relish put through a call to Wyemarket, to prepare the ground for backup should it be needed. With the sun beginning to set - they only had an hour or so of daylight left - their searches and activities could be seriously restricted without help, which, in view of the circumstances, seemed likely to be needed. Nevertheless, PC Relish did not want assistance at this stage. This was partly his own pride at wanting to deal with events on his own beat, but also because he knew that it was sometimes better to employ fewer people carefully, and he preferred to keep it in-house at this stage.

Having made arrangements with the others, Dennis and PC Relish set off on foot along the river bank in the direction of the school. By Dennis's reckoning they should be there within fifteen minutes if they walked briskly.

Dennis's mind was working overtime. So much was churning in his head, and the walk helped him through it. The break-in at All Saints, similar to that at St Mary Magdalen - seemingly, nothing had been taken, but a lot of mess had been made - added to the need for investigation. Desecration of the house of God was clearly not an issue for the perpetrators of the crime, which was beginning to have supernatural, or suprahuman, overtones. Climbing-irons similar to those seen at St Mary Magdalen made the connection virtually absolute. The attack was now on at least two fronts. The fact that this was so close to home was a further worry. How many people were involved, in the activities of this evening and recent evenings? Who were they? What exactly were they after? Why now? Dennis's mind returned to the stranger, and he thought of the Priory and the search for the missing fragment, believing that the full moon could not be ignored, both for the light it gave and the energy it released. That the events were connected to the history of the Hall, before it had become a school, seemed certain. Dennis's knowledge of these activities was by no means comprehensive, but he knew that the training of the spies (and presumably others) had included initiation into the mystery of certain mental arts, including energy and mind control for the purposes of engaging, counteracting and - it was hoped - influencing enemy thinking, in a desperate conflict, the outcome of which had determined the future of Western Europe, perhaps the world. The stakes then had been high. They would be again. The potency of the secrets that the Hall still contained became greater, the situation more threatening, as it emerged over the dark horizon, like a shadow over the sun. That the school and the church were also situated on or near places of ancient power, far older than the church itself, added to this mix, furthered by the mysteries connected with the Priory, the more shadowy Order of the Magdalene and the picture that stood on watch silently there. Somewhere hidden, perhaps nearby, lay the Spearhead itself. Once again, Dennis felt a piercing in his heart.

Dennis and PC Relish passed below Folly Ridge.

Dennis needed to know more. Mr Rummage was the obvious starting point. He would do what he could to find a contact for him, though "holidays are holidays, even for Headmasters," was Abby's view. He had asked if Abby would try to find out how he could be reached. Mr Rummage would be angry if he were not informed. More importantly Mr Rummage would know rather more about the background to these events, and their likely cause, as well as possible consequences. Time was of the essence.

PC Relish and Dennis began to run.

However, Abby being a nurse, her presence might be necessary immediately should they find Mr Gruff. So she decided to follow Dennis and PC Relish, suggesting that Clare and John took Tyro and Jess home and try to contact Mr Rummage. Tyro pointed out that she and Jess had left their bikes at the church; that as they had been at the centre of events so far, it was only reasonable that they should be allowed to be present. Besides they needed someone to show them the blood-stains.

So it was decided that Clare and Jess, much to Jess's annoyance, would go home to try to contact Mr Rummage, while Abby, Tyro and John went on to the Hall.

There were two further elements that needed to be taken into consideration. First, the stranger. Assuming his involvement, was he party to what was happening or an 'agent' of some power in the background? Who and where was he? And what should be done with Mr Pinchet, who had been given the task (albeit informally) of looking over things in Mr Gruff's absence, though he was suspect? And he had a gun. Dennis had sought Mr Gatherin's advice, out of Mr Pinchet's earshot.

Dennis managed to catch him between two servings, and briefed him as much as he could without interrupting the flow of customers. Mr Gatherin's face began to turn a shade of purple. Then it added the tinge of a smile.

The smile of one who had been sitting idly by for a long time in the expectation of some action. Age could not wither him, and certainly not his great comrade M. Le Petit! It was as if, after all these years, old comrades, Mr Gatherin and, yes, M. Le Petit (he would have to be told - "Don't fret, Dennis. He's not all that he appears") were being resurrected from a kind of death, though all Dennis was doing at this stage was asking them to keep an eye out for anything untoward and be ready to be called when necessary.

He briefly told Mr Gatherin what was happening at the school and his suspicions about Mr Gruff's fate. Mr Gatherin felt that they were being asked to take part in a mission that could, put dramatically, save their country. His eyes lit up, (what would they do to M. Le Petit's?)

"As for Pinchet," said Mr Gatherin by way of conclusion, "leave him to me. Better to have him involved. Best way to keep an eye on him. I'll tell him that he might have some shooting to do. That'll keep him awake."

PC Relish and Dennis passed Shelter field. Dennis had a quick glimpse inside the shelter, just as Tyro had done, and found nothing - though there were fresh depressions in the earth, as if someone had hidden or rested there. He was certain that the river formed the key link in the appearance and disappearance of the stranger and would be the conduit for any other intruders involved. The high water level, surely a function of the moon, added to his belief that it would be the ideal way of entering the school grounds, day or night. This could be done from a myriad number of points anywhere between here and the sea. Indeed it was possible to have made the route in its entirety from the sea itself.

They could hear the bark of deer as they passed the old wood, and the shriek of a barn owl somewhere towards an old ash on the far bank - perhaps the very tree from which Dennis had seen a bird the other evening on his watch. The bird appeared and flew across the river to the far bank.

They entered the school field, both men studying the ground as they went for signs of footmarks other than those of the children. They knew that Mr Gruff had probably taken this route himself, and would easily tell his prints by his old military boots.

Inside the boathouse PC Relish got to work immediately. A quick look at the earth floor revealed fresh marks - Tyro and Jess's, which hid other marks indicating that there had been a fight.

There were the stains in the earth, just as Tyro and Jess had described. Nearby, against the dark water's edge, to their surprise, they could see the boat was back. Hadn't the girls said that they had left it somewhere on their way to the Arms?

"These stains are definitely recent," Dennis said, as he bent down to touch them. "Perhaps there is still time."

The blotches of blood-soaked earth were hard.

PC Relish went forward into the back of the hut, where, hidden in the shadows at the back, was a door. The door was open.

Dennis joined him and together they hurried through it and looked around in the half-dark. The room was surprisingly dry, though a cold damp hung in the air. He scanned the room with the torch that he had brought from the car. At the back what looked like a tunnel led into the earth, presumably in the direction of the school, descending slowly. Where the dark and light became fused, between the room and the tunnel entrance, a shape lay on the ground. It was a body. Dennis and PC Relish ran and knelt down. There lay Mr Gruff, the guardian of the school's security, terroriser of the children, the keeper of keys. Mr Gruff's face, pale, his eyes staring upwards, his hands by his side. His clothes were ruffled but not torn. The tie round his neck had gone. He was in exactly the same clothes that he had been wearing two evenings before.

Dennis turned Mr Gruff's head upright. The eyes were nearly silent, and badly glazed. He quickly searched for a cut or injury but found none. Was his heart still beating? He bent down to listen and began to press his chest hard. He put his lips to Mr Gruff's and began to blow air into his lungs. PC Relish put his hands on Mr Gruff's chest and pushed hard to help the air circulate within.

Pausing, Dennis looked into Mr Gruff's face. Taught with fear, he was nevertheless in a kind of peace. Dennis tried again, muttering words under his breath, a vow to find the perpetrators, a plea to some authority outside himself for help. He wanted Mr Gruff to live. He would do everything he could to save him, even if the chances were slim. As he closed his eyes, to focus the direction of his breathing, again the eyes of the stranger came to his mind, like a shadow over him, like a shadow with no remorse, and with cold, driven eyes. The eyes were laughing. Perhaps they were looking at him now.

The two men paused. As they looked down, it seemed as if

there was a very slight movement in Mr Gruff's eyes, enough at least in their imaginations, to drive them on.

"How long has he been here, do you think?" asked PC Relish. He looked up and took in the rest of the room and the shadows of the tunnel. Both seemed to be empty, though a fear crept over him, as if they were not alone.

"Abby should be here by now," Dennis said distractedly. PC Relish ran out onto the grass. The car had just parked, from which Abby, John, and Tyro got out. All three ran down to the boathouse.

"In there," said PC Relish. "I've called an ambulance. We're not sure if he's alive. Been lying there some time, by the looks of it."

Abby rushed in.

PC Relish looked momentarily at John and then at Tyro. In that split second, John seemed about to try to persuade her not to follow her mother, but it was too late. Tyro ran in and stood beside her. Abby was on her knees feeling Mr Gruff's pulse, staring into his face, now trying to resuscitate him. Dennis stood with Tyro for a moment, then bent down too and asked Abby if he might live.

"He might make it, but I doubt it," said Abby. "If he's not technically dead now, he probably will be on arrival at hospital. He's been here too long, and will have been weakened by the loss of blood. Best not to move him, until the ambulance arrives. I'll go with him."

Abby knelt beside Mr Gruff. His stern face, calm, perplexing. She checked his pockets, and found a phone. He had a string tied round his neck. Looked like for keys. But there were no keys there. There was, however, a shape cut in the earth beside him. Abby pointed it out. Dennis had not noticed it.

"I have seen this sign before. Whoever did this, wants us to know. It's been carved in a hurry but it is recognisable."

"Who would do that?" asked Abby.

"It is the insignia of the Priory."

Dennis covered Mr Gruff with his jacket. PC Relish went over to the body, as if to guard it. Dennis took Abby and Tyro by each arm and walked them out into the air. Tyro looked up towards the school. How different from the term, she thought. How different from a few hours ago. What was being unleashed? What use would her toy sword be now?

It was getting darker. John, who had been keeping a look out for the ambulance, came up to them.

"Will he make it?"

"I don't know," said Abby. "He's a tough, proud man, but judging from his eyes he's been very badly frightened. Even if he lives, he may not live as we know it. Let's hope. Pray, even."

Dennis didn't feel like it.

"And the tunnels? Do we continue the search?" asked John.

"We have to. After the ambulance."

"But it's getting dark," Abby said.

"Yes, but whoever or whatever has done this can't be far. The moon will not be full tomorrow, and the weather's worsening."

Dennis walked over towards John. "I think it's going to be a very long and dangerous night."

He rejoined Abby and Tyro.

John thought he caught a glimpse of someone up by the Folly, but wasn't sure.

"There!" he called, as he caught sight of the image a second time.

But the moment passed. Perhaps it was only his imagination.

Tyro had run back inside and was looking at Mr Gruff. She didn't see PC Relish in the background, keeping watch. Poor Mr Gruff. His face looked more approachable. Less hard. He was human like everyone else. The person who she feared, who shouted at them during school, who marched about the school grounds like a prison officer, lay like a helpless child. She looked at him. She didn't want him to die. She saw him alive again, hoping that he would make it. She bent down and gave Mr Gruff a kiss. She made the sign of the cross - something she did, without knowing why, whenever she felt afraid - and said a little prayer. As she did so, she held in her pocket the toy sword. For a moment she thought of her father. He had died, but she no longer felt jealous. She put her arms round her mother, who was now back beside Mr Gruff and again trying to revive him. She wished that her sword could be made of metal. She wanted the real thing. And yet metal swords can kill. But the adventure that she had sought, on a summer's day, full of excitement and anticipation, had become deadly reality. The cold truth was dawning on her. The game was coming home. But she was not afraid. She was determined she would pursue it, even at her young age, wherever it led.

The ambulance drew up alongside Dennis's car. Two ambulance men came out carrying a stretcher and ran towards them. The blue lights flashed against the brilliant red of the dying sun. The moon full, in her glory, stood sentinel.

"In there," said PC Relish.

Within a few moments the two men came out with Mr Gruff covered in a blanket on a stretcher, Abby alongside, and placed him in the ambulance. His face was visible, and shone in the light of the moon, as if from another world. Was there still hope? Perhaps he would glimpse it and come back, as, it was said, people did.

PC Relish confirmed to his HQ at Wyemarket the imminent departure of Mr Gruff and the ambulance. He asked one of his colleagues to go to the hospital and wait for developments there. PC Relish remained confident that the three men and two women could handle the situation, and would call back if help was needed. However, they should be ready.

Dennis reached the ambulance with Abby and Tyro.

"I'll call you as soon as I can. Call me if you need me."

"Look after Tyro," she said, a mixture of anxiety, pride and anger, as she gave her daughter a hug. She knew it was no use trying to stop her now. She had wanted Tyro to come too but Tyro had refused. In view of the circumstances Abby had no wish for a battle, and Mr Gruff might be dying. "Don't let anything happen to her," she said to Dennis.

Dennis looked at his sister. There was nothing that he would devote his energy to more. But she was concerned that there may be circumstances outside anyone's control.

Tyro gave her a kiss.

"Look after him, Mum. See you shortly. I'll pray."

Abby was about to say something, but the ambulance pulled away, so she closed the door upon herself and waved through the window. It was as if the ambulance was going into a dark tunnel of its own.

Tyro confirmed to Dennis, PC Relish and John that the boat in the boathouse was the same boat that they had taken out a few hours before.

"It shouldn't be here," she added.

Their next task was to check the entry to the tunnel where Mr Gruff had been found. PC Relish led the way into the interior, following the decline for some distance. Even with Dennis's torch it was not possible to see whether there were any footprints on the ground. There were no lights and the walls were of stone, far older than the boathouse. After a brief time, Tyro between the two men, the three of them feeling their way by the hint of light behind them, they came to an iron gate, which was half open, as if it had got stuck. Not wishing to risk it and in the absence of any lighting, they decided to turn back and concentrate on the tunnels that Jess and Tyro had visited.

"We'll bring forensic in tomorrow," said PC Relish, as they emerged from the boathouse.

"Where's John?" Tyro asked. Dennis told her that John had decided to take the boat out and was already on the water.

"To check out a theory. He thinks he saw a figure on the hill, and wouldn't wait. We should have gone with him."

*

John had rowed to the far bank with his eyes fixed on the Folly, as the other three had gone into the tunnel.

"John!" Dennis shouted. He could just see him standing in the boat.

John, rather the  shape standing, tried to indicate in a hushed whisper not to shout too loudly, knowing how voices carry in the night, and afraid of other ears.

"You three go on. I'm alright. I'll catch up with you."

Knowing that time was limited, and night was creeping up on them, they decided to proceed, though PC Relish first wanted to look around the main school building. There was no time for co-ordinated action. Dennis and Tyro would go to the science block together. They wanted to maximise the spread of their search even if it increased the dangers. Dennis remembered his words to Abby. They felt that they were sufficiently close together to raise the alarm if anyone else was injured. The sight of Mr Gruff came into the mind of each of them. It spurred them on.

Soon Dennis and Tyro were at the science block, where, at least, there would be light. PC Relish was at the main school building. There may have been a break-in. The words of the Reverend John Sandals came to mind: "someone or something". Strange choice of words for a priest. The main entrance to the school was open. He entered.

A cloaked figure in black, watching from the yew trees by the Church of St Mary Magdalen, moved across the now empty drive, and entered the school, behind PC Relish. The image of a red sword-cross on its back. It moved in complete silence, like a spirit over the hard surface of the drive.

On the other side, hidden in trees, stood a second figure, also hooded and cloaked, also bearing a sword-cross. Beside it stood Titan, silent, eyes glazed. The two appeared to be different limbs of the same entity.

The second figure moved towards the science block and waited momentarily by the open door where Tyro and Dennis had entered. They had already reached the first corridor at the bottom of the steps leading down from the back of Mrs Limpet's preparation room. Tyro led the way, saying little. Dennis sensed something of her father's spirit in her. Abby would have been there too, equally unafraid, but more cautious, had she had the chance. Both would be proud.

*

John scrambled up the bank and ran towards the Folly. He looked everywhere for signs of an entrance in the earth but found nothing. He shook his head in disbelief. He looked back at the wood, and saw nothing but the shapes of trees, and heard nothing but the call of an owl. He returned to the boat. Now he began to row upstream, only illuminated by the moon. Then there was a whistle. He felt sure of it. He continued to row. His instinct told him to go past the school playing fields and approach the school from the eastern side, some distance from the main block, beyond the changing rooms. He wanted to take as wide an arc as possible, so that he might see anything that moved across the landscape. He knew he wasn't alone.

*

Tyro pointed to the rooms on either side. She explained everything, pointing to the loudspeakers from where they had heard the dog barking and the voice. Dennis said nothing.

They reached the second door - the door which had 'pushed' them out - it was now open. Tyro's excitement grew. A new sense of self flowed through her, yet what she had seen then, not so many hours before, was not quite what she saw now. She saw real danger, but was prepared to face it. She felt a huge surge of energy. That was her strength and birthright.

They entered the bright hall that she had seen with Jess. She wished Jess were there. Dennis flicked on the lights. Marbled corridors to left and right, one staircase going up, the other down.

The door behind them closed.

At first Dennis seemed unconcerned. He walked towards the lifts and read the instruction panel beside them. There seemed to be four floors, but no identity as to what they were. One floor up, the floor they were on, and two down.

Dennis then walked back to the door from where they had come. It was locked. He was beginning to feel nervous.

"There are several ways out of here, it seems. Don't worry, Tyro. We'll be out soon enough."

Tyro was afraid.

*

Inside the main building PC Relish checked the doors. Those that were locked he left, others that were open he entered to see that everything was in order. No-one had tried to enter Mr Rummage's study. There were no signs of any other activity on this floor.

A brief walk along the corridor confirmed, so far as he could see, that no-one had been in that direction.

He returned to the main stairway and went up. He entered the library. Here he went towards the reserve stacks at the back, that were normally kept under lock and key.

The door to this had been forced. Inside a number of books and manuscripts had been left on the tables and on the empty shelves. Someone had been searching the older manuscripts.

For the first time he noticed another door. In all the visits he had made to the school to talk to the students, and teachers (sometimes parents), he had often used the library. He knew the reserve room well, but he had never before seen the door at the back, because it lay hidden behind a false set of shelves. These had been moved sideways to reveal the now open door behind.

He stared briefly. He had been brought up to believe that Burnchester Hall was a warren. There were supposed to be secret 'priest-holes'.

The door led to a stairway, downwards.

He went in. The steps that led below were of wood, in keeping with the wood-panelled library itself, musty and aged, dents in the stairs where, over the centuries, unknown feet had walked. The Cheesepeake family came to mind. What secrets had been stowed away below stairs? What secret exits and entrances could this doorway have witnessed? He heard a noise. He paused. He was sure something was nearby. He paused again and called out.

"Identify yourself!"

His words became nothing but an absorbed echo in the depth of the earth. He heard the noise again. A shuffling sound. The light got dimmer and dimmer, as he fumbled against the circular wall. He proceeded downwards.

He could hear voices, surely? The light was extinguished. The little that had flowed from the library went out. The door at the top of the stairs shut. He could hear the sound of the shelf sliding across. He was now shut in darkness. He called out again.

Then he heard a voice. An unearthly voice close by. A whisper. He stood absolutely still in the pitch black, afraid of touching something. He could not move. He listened as intensely as he could. His heart beat fast. He crouched. Then it came again. The whisper simply said, "Welcome to your nightmare, Mr Relish."

Then, against the side of his face, he felt a gloved hand move to clasp his throat. At once he turned, lurched at the figure behind him, and tried to hurl it over his back. There was a low breathing. The figure seemed mostly hollow. All he clasped was a cloak, inside of which were nothing but the hard touch of bones. Nevertheless it had a huge force, and was able to throw PC Relish over. He lost his grip and started falling. The stairs were too steep for him to find his feet. He desperately tried to cling on but there were no banisters. He fell further, rolling over, but still conscious. He came to a halt at a landing.

From below, a light came on. The sound of feet, running up another set of stairs, this time of marble, white marble. In the dim light PC Relish could see two figures appear at the top of the stairs. Dennis and Tyro.

"PC Relish!" called Dennis. "Are you alright?"

PC Relish tried to get up.

"I will be in a minute," he said. "Up there!"

Dennis ran up the stairs. The light gave him enough to see. He stopped in his track. Above him at the top of the stairs, stood the figure in black, like an angel of death. The door behind it opened. Dennis went forward, but as he approached the retreating figure, a force threw him back. He tried again, but he could not move.

The figure stood at the entrance to the closing doors. In a low twisted voice of evil, the figure spoke.

"Leave this place! Take your friends with you! Do not interfere! Otherwise you will all die! Your time is running out!"

Dennis looked into the unseen face, behind the cloak of darkness, trying to glimpse its features, but he could see nothing. He concentrated on the voice.

"Who are you?" Dennis asked. "We are not afraid! It is you who will perish! Because you live under the shadows, and are afraid to reveal your identity."

He stretched forward and upwards and grabbed the cloak and pulled hard, but the door began to close behind the figure once more until Dennis's hand was held fast as it shut. The pain forced him to pull it out. But not before he had ripped a piece of the material from the cloak that the figure wore.

He ran against the door and tried to open it. He ran

downstairs again and joined PC Relish, who was standing beside a shaking Tyro. He knew in his heart that neither he nor they could deal with this creature alone.

Leading off from them was another tunnel, still walled in old wood. Below, the staircase of white marble.

"We must get out of here as quickly as possible! We need support!"

"You've got something in your hand!" said PC Relish.

"This way," said Dennis. "The door above is locked, and the stairs below go further down. The one we came in by is also shut. This must lead out somewhere. I would judge down into the field."

The three went on, again into the growing dark. PC Relish used his torch, as they continued up a slight incline. They passed a closed door.

They moved on, gasping the fresh air that seemed to be coming their way. They came to a stop. The tunnel led into the old boathouse, but the iron bars were down. They could not get out.

PC Relish, Dennis and Tyro were trapped.

*

When Abby got to the hospital at Wyemarket, the doctor on duty, Dr Bartok, took one look at Mr Gruff and ordered that he should be taken immediately to intensive care. Ipswich was full. He would have to go to Cambridge. Had he thought that there was much chance of survival he would have alerted the helicopter ambulance, but, in the circumstances, felt that little was to be gained. He did not hold out much hope. He decided that he should travel with Mr Gruff. He thanked Abby who was free to leave.

She had tried in vain to phone Tyro to see if there was any news. She tried to make contact with Clare, to tell her she was on her way back. Luckily, she was still at home with Jess.

No, she hadn't heard from any of them, and would be making her way back to the school with Jess as soon as possible, Clare explained shortly afterwards.

She was having considerable difficulty getting hold of Mr Rummage.

The school lines had, for some inexplicable reason, gone dead. There was no way that the local operator in Scotland could identify which house Mr Rummage and his family were staying in without a bit more information.

She had tried every route possible, but got nowhere. It was only when Abby suggested, in the car, that Jess might have Julia's phone number, that she had any success, but that was not immediate. Jess said that she had, but that her phone book was in her bag which was at Abby's house. So it would be necessary to go back to the house and try Mr Rummage once more from there.

"Hi! Julia," said Jess, as soon as they got back to the house. "Is your dad there?"

Jess explained that she would love to speak but that her mum's friend - she didn't like mentioning Abby, knowing what enemies Julia and Tyro were - wanted to have a word with him. It was quite important. "Yes, she was reading a good book, but things were better in the real world for a change," she thought, "if a little scary!"

"What does that mean? See you!" said Julia.

Mr Rummage really did not like being disturbed while on holiday. Added to this that he was just beginning to feel relaxed, aided by a swim in the sea and a brisk walk along the beach, his mood was not very receptive. At first he had pretended not to be there. However, when Abby took hold of the phone and explained to Julia that it was very important, Mr Rummage came to the phone, with the uninspired words,

"Mrs Wander, is something the matter? Can I help?"

Even Mr Rummage felt a little embarrassed at his lack of courtesy and soon listened carefully, but with a sinking feeling. What Abby told him wasn't a total surprise. What he heard was consistent with his own doubts and with a discovery that he had made that very day, on the hills at the back of the house. As a result, he was more anxious.

He listened without interrupting at all. He questioned Abby, then Jess (who was very embarrassed), on as much detail as both could give. The picture that emerged - Mr Gruff's discovery, following the bloodstains and the experience in the tunnels - horrified him. (Jess had said they were returning to get some books for the holiday project that Mrs Limpet had asked them to do, and became distracted by noises from the back room). Apart from Mr Gruff, what interested him most were two things. One was the details of the events at both churches - the attempted break-ins. And secondly, the discovery of the mask. There was a change of tone in his voice. He wanted a full description.

For a while he was silent. When he had heard as much as they could tell him, and he had asked as many questions as possible, and understood who knew of these events and who was present at the school, he asked for Abby's and Clare's telephone numbers and any phone numbers that might be useful to him.

"I will call you back as soon as I have something to offer," he said firmly, if apologetically. "I can't tell you how grateful I am to you, Mrs Wander, for tracking me down, and for taking so much care  of the school. I think you may have saved us a great deal more trouble, though we're not out of it yet. I know you won't mind my telling you that it may only just be beginning. Let us pray for Mr Gruff. Be very careful. We are dealing with dark forces. The enemy is stirring."

With that he put down the phone. Abby looked at Clare and Jess.

She went over to Jess, and gave her a hug.

"I'm proud of you. And Tyro. But we must be very careful."

She knew of course that Tyro might just have been the

energy behind this daring adventure but would not say so in front of either Jess or Clare. She wasn't sure if this was a good thing or not, especially as events were turning very sinister, though she had no doubt that the two girls were being brought closer together, and in that growing friendship, their differences would be their strength. Her immediate concern was that Tyro, Dennis and PC Relish might be in severe danger, so she urged an immediate return to the school, "to help in whatever way we can. It's going to be a long night."

Clare only then asked Abby to tell her and Jess what she had discovered at All Saints church. Abby did so, in the car, after she ensured that the house was properly locked up. She had been shaken more deeply than she was letting on, though she would not show it to either of the girls. A break-in so close to their home.

*

Mr Rummage was doing his best to relax. He was looking out to the other islands from the window of their house by the sea. There were seals in the water. Birds were calling. The sun, here, was still up. But it would not be for long. Jenny knew not to force him to tell her anything. She would learn soon enough. Julia was reading. Simon was playing football.

What was concerning Mr Rummage was something to do with the mask that the girls had found.

If he could fit one face to the image drawn verbally by Jess - a girl with a great gift for language and accuracy - it would have been that of Jane Fellows. Mr Rummage shuddered.

# 10

Dennis threw his full weight against the steel frame. PC Relish and Tyro added theirs, but they made no impression.

Dennis shouted as loudly as possible, hoping that John would hear. However, John had rowed upstream and was now circling the outer woods at the far end of the school grounds and making his way across the fields towards the science block.

PC Relish tried his phone to ask for assistance but the line was dead, as was Tyro's. The light of the moon, having given a glow to the landscape only an hour or so earlier, now revealed mist unwinding over the river valley.

"We must go back," Dennis said.

"I'll wait here, while you go with Tyro to find another way out," said PC Relish.

Reluctantly, Dennis agreed. It was their best chance.

Dennis and Tyro retreated into the tunnel. PC Relish scrawled a note on his pad in the dim light and wedged the end under one of the steel bars, then waited. He had given his torch to Dennis as Dennis's battery had run down. His mind was alert but the pain of his fall began to have an effect where he had struck his head, forcing him to close his eyes. But he fought every inch, determined not to let go of consciousness, and opened them again and again.

Dennis and Tyro walked side by side.

"We'll be alright," he said. "Think how many people know we're here! Mum should be back soon. There's John, Mr Pinchet, the police at Wyemarket."

"And Jess."

The events of the last half-hour had become confused in Tyro's mind with her earlier entry into the first tunnel, and she was unable to separate the past from the present. She was reminded of the terrible dreams that she had had after her father had died.

Yet while Tyro struggled to concentrate, her father seemed to be guiding her. It was as if his words were trying to reach her, and tell her what to do. She could feel them, in the background, emerging from some other place, as she could sense his face before her, just as he had been, reading to her as child. What she did not know was whether this was mere fancy or some deeper perception and ability to track other worlds. Nor could she tell whether those other worlds were part of her own.

The energy that had struck them on their first entry into the tunnel came and went in waves, sometimes submerging her, sometimes giving her what seemed an alien life force. It was as if she was being manipulated.

They made their way back towards the place where they had found PC Relish, at the landing between the wooden stairs and the marble steps from below. As they passed a closed door, Tyro thought she could sense something the other side. After they had passed, the door opened, and a cloaked figure emerged.

Dennis and Tyro halted at the landing, unaware of what had followed them.

"We must go further down. The ways out we know are blocked," said Dennis.

Dennis led them on, into the lit marbled hall between the tunnel back to the science block and the unexplored region below. And then they turned. There in front of them stood the cloaked figure, with no face. Beside it stood Titan held by a metal chain, sitting still. At first it looked in the direction of the two people, without any intention, it seemed, of moving.

Dennis moved Tyro to his side, and came forward a little.

The figure lent back and let out a huge hollow laugh. Something in its tone seemed familiar to Dennis.

"Soon the world shall be ours! Soon the power that was lost, shall be found, and shall be ours too!" He held out a document. "Courtesy of Burnchester Library. A map of the world below. Soon we shall find all the proof that we need that will give us power we seek. Lead on down!"

The figure seemed as much to look at Tyro as Dennis.

"Who are you? What riddles are these?" shouted Dennis, with disdain, whilst watching every movement, every ripple in the figure's dark robes. He could not see its face beneath the hood, but its voice, he was now certain, had a familiar ring, like the stranger's. Was it the same figure as before? He tried to see if there was a piece of cloak missing, but could see nothing. Nor could he see whether there was a sword-cross on the figure's back.

"Show yourself! How dare you hide beneath an empty mask! Creatures afraid of their own emptiness, afraid that they are nothing without the life given to them by others! Show yourself! You foul empty hollow!"

The thing moved forwards. Then it released Titan. Titan hurled himself forward, fangs wide, ready to strike. Tyro, drawn to his livid eyes, held hers firm. She tried to call his name, but could not. Dennis stuck out an arm. In his hand he still had a piece of the cloth from the other figure's cloak. At this Titan stopped, unable to go forward, but barking and baring his teeth. The figure struck out furiously to grab the cloth but Dennis swiftly drew back his arm.

"Get back, you foul creature! Get back!"

Dennis held firm, Tyro stood still next to him. One of her hands was moving inside the bag on her shoulder. Dennis faced the figure, and began to edge himself towards it. The figure was unable to move forward. It turned at the sight of the cloth, as if Dennis held the stigma of its own blood. Tyro clasped the tiny sword in her bag. To her astonishment, it cut her hand. She managed to find the hilt and gripped it tight.

"Attack!" the figure screamed at Titan. Titan tried again to move forward but could not.

"How dare you, children of this world!" screamed the figure. "You shall pay for this! You will all pay!"

He struck out at Titan with a bony claw. The dog whimpered but became more angry. Still it was unable to move.

The energy that was driving the dog forward was being countered by their own. They felt a surge of power, equal to the enemy they faced.

Neither would give in.

Then, as quickly as it had arrived, the figure turned.

"You are locked in here and will die."

With that it glided up the stairs towards the library, its hollow laugh vibrating back down in an echo. Titan followed.

Dennis raced in pursuit, but it was too late. When he arrived, the door was locked. They were trapped again.

He came down to find Tyro now in tears, and PC Relish trying to comfort her.

"What happened?" asked PC Relish, kneeling beside Tyro.

Dennis came up to Tyro too.

"It's nothing," Tyro said, bravely. Dennis looked at her in the eyes, seeing his sister there, and his friend, Jack.

"Just that I think I recognise this place. From somewhere. I don't know," was all Tyro could say.

"We have no choice but to go down," said Dennis, after Tyro had calmed. "The other ways out are closed. This is our only chance."

"Who are these figures?" Tyro asked.

Having left the boat upstream, John had circled the perimeter of the school guided by the light of the moon. He cut back towards the main buildings after a search on the far bank and in the woods.

He felt sure he had seen something at the folly, but had found no trace of anything or anyone there. When he heard what sounded like a muffled cry he became even more convinced. Whatever it was might have gone back in the direction of Mr Strangelblood's land, into the woods where the Iron Age fort stood.

He was confident in PC Relish and Dennis's ability to search the tunnel but was surprised to find that they had not re-appeared. He had expected to see them from the other side of the fields and now, as he walked back over open ground, even to bump into them. Surely Clare and Jess would be back soon.

He approached the back of the school, when he saw a cloaked figure come out of the main building. The figure's empty faceless shape gave John a start. He was both afraid and riveted. For a moment it seemed like a monk, as if one of the many who had lived in these grounds, no doubt, centuries ago, one of the many who inhabited the religious houses in medieval England, had come to life. Yet it crept over the ground like a treacherous spirit, waiting to prey on innocence for its own revival. He was afraid for the others. He concentrated and watched carefully. Had it been inside the school? Had it been seen by the others? Confront or follow?

John was beginning to feel the pull, especially now that what he thought he had only imagined, walked before him, like his own fate. But in this moment's pause and reflection, he didn't see another figure behind him, standing in the shadows, with a dog.

John watched the first figure go towards the church, where it seemed to disappear. Whether it was a spirit or a human in disguise he did not know. He walked up the line of trees towards the school entrance, with a view to crossing into the churchyard area to confront the apparition.

As he entered the churchyard, the second figure with Titan, walking silently and obediently, came out of the shadows. Titan, normally proud and aggressive, was beaten for the slightest disobedience. The whimperings were muffled, as if the sounds he gave out could no longer be heard by humanity.

John was now in the churchyard, by the west door of the church. He could see the door was open, and a soft glow came from inside. He bent down behind a gravestone and waited.

The second cloaked figure was now halfway across the drive, lit by the moon. It was walking purposefully towards the church, a cowed Titan by its side.

At that moment two broad full beams of light swung into the school drive and lit up the second figure. The figure turned and with a hollow stare, looked into the lights.

Inside the car, Abby was driving, Clare by her side. Jess was in the back seat visible between them. Rompy was with her. Rompy had been agitated as soon as they got in the car. Now he began to bark.

When she saw what was ahead of them, Abby was at first confused, not trusting her eyes. She saw a figure and a dog, recognised Titan and had assumed that it was Mr Gruff with it. But it could not be.

Clare was pointing and shouting something.

"Watch out! Watch out!"

Jess was staring ahead, screaming.

The figure thrust out an arm, accompanied by a command. Titan lept towards the oncoming car.

Abby, in her panic, instead of breaking, put her foot on the accelerator. The car sped forward.

John had heard the car. But the very same moment, something was coming out of the church, and he could not avert his gaze. The cloaked figure, followed by two others.

They moved in line as if floating across the grass and graves. They moved quickly towards the second figure just as Titan was in mid-air, leaping towards the car.

At first the car seemed to stall, but then it accelerated and swerved at full speed. It struck Titan, and the figure.

In her confusion and fear, Abby tried to slam on the brakes. She screamed, and jumped out, afraid of what she had seen and of what she might have done. She might have killed whatever it was. Her instinct was to help, in spite of her blind panic. At the same time she screamed out,

"Jess, don't get out of the car!"

But it was too late. Clare had jumped out of the other side, Jess behind her, and Rompy leapt in the direction of the other figures which were half-way across the drive, moving in their direction.

Abby bent down at the fallen figure, as the others closed upon her. Titan lay motionless beside it. The figure seemed nothing but a shadow on the ground, but for the sword-cross on its back.

"Abby, Clare, Jess, look out!" screamed John.

John hurled himself at one of the figures. He slid off its back. He scrambled up and tried again, just as the figure turned, revealing no face but making a hollow laugh.

Abby, stood up and faced the other cloaked figures.

"Get back you vile creatures! Who or what are you?"

The figures closed in further. John's arms now gripped the figure from the back, and he tried to drag it to the ground. Rompy flew at the others, but in vain. All three figures stopped in front of the Abby, Clare and Jess.

John was thrown to the ground. But he got up.

"Don't you dare!" he screamed.

One of the figures looked round.

"You have made a grave mistake," it said, looking at all of them seemingly at once, and then at Jess. "We tried to warn you, to frighten you, to keep you away. But you and your friends have been too curious. This one in particular and her friend. They do not know when they are playing with destiny. These are not the games of children."

It pointed at Jess who stood defiantly next to her mother.

"And where is my friend?" she asked. "And my friend's uncle?"

"And PC Relish?" added Abby.

"And who are you? What do you want? Why are you here?" said Clare.

The one who had spoken, who seemed in charge, said nothing for a few moments. He looked at the others.

"It will do no harm. Whether we kill you or leave you, it makes no difference. We are close to finding what we are looking for. We know it is here, and nothing will stop us. Nothing can stop us! We work for the Priory. We worked for the Priory hundreds of years ago, and we will do so in the future. We cannot die, for we are already dead. But we can and will be brought back to life, and can take human form. Nothing can destroy us. Nothing can stop us from living again!"

With that the three figures raised themselves up, as if they had been given new energy.

"This place has been a place of power to our order for generations. You and your kind have kept us out. But we will never surrender, until we have become lords of everything we claim."

The figure on the ground lay a lifeless heap of rags, not unlike those that Dennis had seen a day ago, by the entrance to the school. Then it emerged slowly from the earth like a resurrecting spirit, now reaching its full height. It held in its hand, or what would have been its bony hand, a book, which it had hidden in its robes.

"You have stolen that from the library. Return it at once, lest the curse fall upon you!" John shouted.

"Never!" screamed the other.

John tried to rush forward, but he was held back.

"And where are the others?" asked John.

There was another pause. The mist from the river had seemed to retreat leaving a wide view of the ground beyond, where the school fields lay, in the distance now, once more shining in the moon's light.

In this light, as if a cloud had retreated and revealed a true knight, John's strength grew. He approached them, as the tall figure answered,

"The others are below, in the tunnels of the earth. They are tampering with our power, though they are ignorant of it yet. They will meet other members of our order. They are shut in, and will not easily get out. Once they go below and enter the warren beneath, they may never be found, let alone come out of their own accord. But we do not care. None of you has the power that we need. We have found one of the things that we have been looking for."

So spoke the risen figure, the same which had left Dennis, PC Relish and Tyro underground.

Rompy was whining, but unable to move.

As the moon's power lessened, the figures seemed to shorten, bend, become smaller, until they were the size of the others. They seemed momentarily agitated, confused. They looked around them, into the distance, at the school, the earth.

"What's happening?" one of them said.

A shot rang out. John rushed towards the figures.

Then the four figures, as if under a command, moved towards the river, the rest following. They moved away from the school to the water's edge, towards the ancient wood. John tried to catch them, but he was repulsed as soon as he got close to them. It was as if their energy was fading, but they still had enough power to prevent him from attacking them. Yet all of them were drawn on, almost against their will.

"Who fired?" screamed Abby.

At the river's edge, the figures retreated into the night, now mere shapes, now nothing but shadows. They seemed to mix with other shadows by the river, one of them bent low, and then moved on. The three adults and Jess stood as if time and their memories were suspended. The power that Tyro and Jess had felt under the ground had now permeated the air.

"What is it?" said Jess.

They turned, and John tried to lead them towards the boathouse entrance.

"This is where I last saw Tyro, PC Relish and Dennis."

He found PC Relish's note.

"They're inside the tunnels!" Jess shouted. "We must help them at once!"

"We'll have to alert the others, before we go looking," said John. "We should call Mr Gatherin, to tell him to notify the police."

"First we find Tyro, Dennis and PC Relish!" said Abby. "And the figures? Do they just go into the dark, waiting for some mysterious future return?" she continued.

They tried their phones, but once more the power was dead. They could not make contact with anyone.

"We can't all go," John said,

"And who do you propose to leave behind?" asked Abby. "We're all in this together. Sink or swim."

With that John led the way along the river. His intention now was to try the tunnel entrance in Mrs Limpet's room, though he suspected that he might find something else. He therefore decided to take the long way round.

As they walked a terrible anxiety hung over them, compounded by beating hearts. The shock and bewilderment of what they had just witnessed, intensely real and yet somewhere beyond reality, and the horrifying obscure truths that had been spoken, kept them all transfixed in mind as they walked. Clare, Abby, Jess, and John, with Rompy, with his nose to the ground. Rompy had tried to follow the figures towards the wood without success. He had reached so far and could go no further.

They were anxious to find the others, but recognised that they themselves might fall prey to the same force and become victims too. And yet what force it was they did not know. Being trapped together might give a sense of solidarity, but if they were all to perish - Heaven forbid - what use would it be? Yet they had no other desire, and for this march they seemed to walk with one spirit and intent.

They had all heard the shot, but their concern lay elsewhere. What questions they might have would have to wait. Now, in the moonlight and lengthening night - it was past midnight - in the silence of an eerie moon with light and shade playing on all their senses, demons lurking in the shadows, false saviours in the rays of the divine, and obscure half-beings of every shade came at them from all directions while they went forward.

As they approached the east side of the school buildings, having swung round the far playing fields and now come back towards the science block, where they were to enter below, John, leading, saw a shadow to his right. It seemed to lie beneath a tree, itself a part of the hedge that followed the line down to the river and the playing fields.

He stopped and pointed. Rompy had already run in its direction. They approached and found a gap in the hedge. John went forward into it, and found they were in the thickest part, the width of two hedges and more, where was a small opening, like a cavern enclosed by bramble and thorn. The tree added great dignity and age to the space. It was clearly known to the children as the ground was well worn, and there was also a hut used by the groundsman, close to the boundary of the playing fields as they were.

"Look here," called Jess, who was looking at the base of the tree. "There's some kind of entrance."

"A fox," suggested Abby who came alongside, followed by Clare and John.

"I'm not so sure," added Jess, "foxes' earths normally smell, don't they?"

"It could be disused, of course. You're right," added Clare, bending down to ground level and examining the entrance, "there's something human about this. Look," she added pointing.

"The hole is open but I think there's some sort of door."

She felt inside. There was a rough piece of wood which she drew out and pulled out into the moonlight.

"We should move on," said John and Abby simultaneously. "We must find the others."

But in a moment they were all stupefied by a low sounding whistle coming from the tree. It was repeated.

Abby led Rompy to the hole. He went in.

Abby followed, having to push herself hard through the narrow  gap. She called back to the others.

"There's a tunnel in here. I'm going down."

One by one the four of them entered beneath the ancient tree, and stood inside its cavernous arms, before going down into this mysterious place.

*

Dennis, PC Relish and Tyro had reached the bottom of the marble steps to the floor below. Here they continued along the passageway, past the lift and continued on into the earth, another floor down. Already they had descended over one hundred steps (Tyro had counted them), far more than would normally separate the two floors of even the grandest building. Not wishing to go further unnecessarily, they proceeded along the passage which was lit by a glow permeating the walls at even intervals. There were no other chambers leading off. This made them feel more trapped.

They were intensely afraid.

At the end of the passageway, they came to a door which opened onto another passage which went off to left and right. Both of these were curved, as if they followed the shape of a large circular domed room. Doors opened into this space. The energy that was emitted from the chamber was intense.

Dennis brought them all close together. Keeping his voice low, he said,

"We have reached the upper gallery of the Domed Chamber. Whatever is behind these doors, be on your guard. Judging by the energy that we are now sensing, we may need to stick particularly closely together, and to engage with our strongest will. We have already met with figures who wish us to believe they are from some other world - though I have my doubts. If we show resolve we can meet whatever challenge is put in front of us. But we must keep our wits about us. Stay alert, and watch.

"I will lead, Tyro will stick behind me, PC Relish will follow. However difficult, do not be afraid. Do not give in."

# II

The trudge over the heather hillside had been long and hard. Clumps and divots, erratically interspersed, made worse by soft spongy ground, into which it was possible to sink, made walking slow and tentative, even though, by day, they knew the ground well. Patches of peat bog made a slip hazardous, though a visible track occasionally emerged from the otherwise unmarked moorland to guide them intermittently towards the summit that they now saw ahead. The beauty of the night lightened their load, and though it was not easy to combine looking at the sky with a careful tread over the ground, the late summer light gave the couple a springlike movement, suggestive of urgency, and animation, which made their progress seem swifter than it was. The wind, now that they were approaching the top, freshened their faces. The scenery all around them was beautiful, empty, and silent. Their inner concerns became secondary to the greater experience of the space around them.

In the near distance, now that they had reached the top, between the great slabs of upright stone, lay the sea, dark grey, shining under a glistening moon, the tops of waves lighting the surface with moving streaks, like shooting stars across an empty sky. Occasionally a bird would fly above the headland beyond, where the cliffs sank fast into the western sea (towards the bottom of 'the monstrous world'); then others, and with these, their cries, the urgent cries of adults with young to feed, night and day while the day lasts. For the winter here is long and dark and the birds will have flown far to the south to feed in more tranquil waters, and where the rocks are less old. For here are some of the oldest rocks in the world. Almost old enough to be not of this earth at all.

The stone shapes grew in stature as the couple approached. Against these upright pillars of granite, Mr Rummage and his wife Jenny stood small and fragile, and as temporary as the relative calm over which the stones presided. The brief arrival of man, who after all, had erected these monoliths, merely confirmed that the relationship had long been an unequal one, except that only one had the capacity to transmute the power of the other, which only the other had the power to give, for the good, perhaps, of humankind.

The children had been left at home, Julia absorbed in a book, Simon, filling in his football scrap book, while their father and mother had left, after supper, to go for a walk on the hill. The house was not visible from the tops, but Mr McCleod, the fisherman, who lived next door - that is to say a couple of hundred metres away - ensured that they would be safe. They were always safe up here. There was a faith and a community and a code which guaranteed that.

After the call from Abby, Mr Rummage had spent a quiet half hour finishing the meal that both he and Jenny had prepared. The pretended ease with which he chatted about the day with Jenny and the children (a term used by the egalitarian Mr Rummage, when the responsibilities of his world could not be equated with the partial experience of theirs), belied the unease, and the pressure that he knew was accumulating within, and helped him to focus on the key elements in what was a potentially devastating situation. Jenny could sense some of this tension, and did her utmost to help orchestrate his energies, implicitly guiding them in synchrony with her own, so finely attuned were they to one another, and so perceptive was she of the currents within him.

The attack on the school and the church (albeit less obtrusive), the curious discovery of the mask, and, most seriously, the savage attack on Mr Gruff, confirmed the convergence of dark forces, which he had long been aware of and which had been so forcefully hinted at in Cambridge only a couple of days before. That the Priory, or some such group, were involved seemed clear. But there was something more. The daring of the attempted break-ins, and the supra-human quality (was this a further attempt to mislead?), suggested a desperate and dangerous combination of forces and interests beyond a particular group, as if the aim was understood but the means were emergent but not yet clear.

The attack on Mr Gruff made things far worse, though he would be as well looked after as he could be. He would pray for him, as best he could, and try to contact Mrs Boot, whom he knew of, though had never met. That PC Relish was present gave him some confidence. That the Reverend Sandals was involved, and Dennis, who was aware of the training that he himself had undergone, gave him a little more and reduced his feeling that he would need to return immediately. The mask made him apprehensive, in view of the doubts already expressed by Mr Baxter over the role of Jane Fellows in their business. He had asked Mr Baxter to "check her out, again."

What else might be stirring in the normally tranquil grounds of the school, he could not know. That there would be much more to consider and try to counter than he had so far learned he was sure. Whether there had been any breach into the deeper subterranean regions beneath the school, not all of which he was himself familiar with, so extensive were they and as yet only partially re-activated, he did not know. Many were still dangerous, others presumed secret even from himself. He felt sure that at least some search would be made, both by the Priory and other forces that might have engaged and which had caused the damage so far. And also by Dennis and others in their attempts to prevent further abuses of the power that would probably have been needed even to have got this far. It was on this power that he must concentrate. If hidden power was a key source of the night's activities, it was his responsibility to do what he could, from where he was, with his knowledge and ability to try to counter it, though its potential was devastating, and its control uncertain. He would have to do what he could to generate and direct the positive energy needed to counter the dark forces that had somehow been released. Without returning immediately, which he did not think necessary at this stage, he could only do one thing. Activate the source from here, overlooking the western sea, by the Ring of Loth, an ancient site of great power, one of the many that interconnected across Scotland, the rest of the United Kingdom and further over the world. Here on the windswept summer moonlit night, alone with Jenny he would do his utmost to propel and cast out the demons that had crept from beneath the earth and sea, and strike them down.

There were grave dangers, including to himself. It was not always possible to control the energy once released, and focusing it would be difficult, without the appropriate receptors properly engaged at Burnchester, which were themselves decayed from lack of use. That he could release the energy at all, he was not sure, so erratic were activities of this kind. If he failed he might need to invoke and obtain the help of other forces, not something that he relished the thought of. The energy that he might release and direct could even be diverted and re-used by the very forces he was trying to suppress. The presence of the Wanders and others near receptors could harm them. But he had no choice. The possibility that the power might be lost altogether, even temporarily, to the forces of the other side, with the devastation that could ensue, meant that he would have to try. He thought momentarily of his research into particle physics, and wondered at how little he knew.

Mr Rummage made two calls. One to Mr Baxter, and the other to Doonwreath, the secret research station in the northern Highlands.

During supper, after Abby's call, he had asked Jenny if she would like to accompany him on a walk, couching it, for the children's sake, in terms of the need to work off his excess food, and to make the most of the light of the moon. He did not discourage his children from coming, but they declined.

The stones stood sentinel to oblivion, ancient effigies of pre-ordained power, the death of prehistory, the emergence of a kind of civilisation. Nowhere but in these empty spaces, once points of collective activity and symbolic pilgrimage, could such lifeless objects evince such potency in their stillness, such power in their silence. Crafted on sites of the most ancient worship, ritual, and arcane prediction, yes, of sacrifice, they underlie the arrival of other deities, and the later blossoming of the more humane religions, here, of Christianity, and its intellectual counterpart, secular humanism, which both irrevocably destroyed the stones their rites, perhaps to our partial cost, that even the stones could only feebly see. For their fate lay also in our hands, as they had in the hands of their creators. Thus creator and created stem from the same source, are made by mutual endorsement, if in failed recognition.

Here, as elsewhere, the stones were placed in an ellipse, reflecting the magical image of the heavens, to whom they now paid ironic homage. On this star-dimmed night, shaded by the potency of the moon, manicured by the wind and the vibrant sea, they seemed to look heavenward as if in some distant time, beyond time, in a far distant place, beyond anywhere we have so far travelled, from distant imaginings, in the minds of other civilisations, where they had been extracted, created, shaped and sent, for their eternity on our small earth, for our, and their, submission.

The diameter of the circle was large, each stone set many

metres apart, of varied height, each individual, unkempt, with lines and lichens, unbroken by storm, unbent by gale, only sometimes bowed by the frailty of their patch of earth. A few had fallen. Remnants of others lay elsewhere. The heather moor, on this high dry point, covered the gentle slope where they lay like a huge eye, set in ground, looking outwards to eternity. Had they been able to blink, they too would have disappeared into the memory of lost time. Their tears had long been shed, their stories told, their meaning lost. Only now, in the dawning of our new era, at the edge of a cycle whose meaning and purpose we can but glimpse, were we wondering again, learning from them again, as something more than just curiosity from a patronised past, an age merely of barbarism and dark. Now, the pagan rites that they helped shape, to which they bore witness, were seeking retribution for their dissolution. Their questionable divinity needed access to our own. Their gnostic message, integrated with the sophistication of our own religious myths.

How would this reconciliation be made flesh? "Who is that coming to the sacrifice?"

Mr Rummage had placed himself against his favourite stone which was at the highest point of the slightly sloping heather moor. Jenny stood opposite him on the far side of the ring, beside her own. Mr Rummage had stood for minutes, perhaps even hours, letting the wind blow in his hair, following the lines and faces in the rock, by the moon's light, the channels where the rain water could flow, the sharp indents where pieces had broken off. He waved at Jenny, who waved back, two children out of civilisation's reach, touched by a mystery beyond them yet of themselves. The shades of grey and black, infinite in their subtlety, more beguiling than any colour, more permanent than death, symbols of primal creation.

At first he looked across the stones. Had he imagined that each had bowed in some strange act of recognition? Or was it he who had bowed in deference to their age? The muddy patches of earth at their feet and the criss-cross of paths across the land between bore witness to the few visitors, shepherds, wanderers, who came to look, seek shelter, and redeem. And to the sheep, who left nothing but droppings.

Jenny was bemused, smiling, her world active and magical too, seeking more resonance in the realities of family (were the children alright?), the practicalities of home. She had the wisdom, as it was hoped he did in reverse, to understand enough of her husband's gifts to let them flourish beside the ancient hedgerow. In her discreet scepticism, the fact remained that her powers were as relevant and exact.

In that curious way in which ideas emerge from the least likely source, creations come from the remnants of decay, the lifeblood pulse runs through the veins of oblivion, and the Phoenix rises from its own ashes, Mr Rummage, in his unravelled mind, began to find the focus which he sought. The practised seeker knows that the path which flows and which leads us on ('which led by tracts that pleased us well'), both comes and does not come from the effort of discipline, the prescription of method, the alchemy of concentration. The blinding light which opens our minds to eternity, and to other worlds, and more, comes with practice, and yet also without practice, at random, like gifts from God, that seem distilled according to His will, conjoined with something that is only ours.

Mr Rummage looked forward. There in front of each stone a light shone, like an angel in the dark, against which each stone seemed but a dark shadow. These shadows tried to move, as if seeking to extinguish the light, but in their agitation they could not, were constrained by their own willfulness. The light, nothing more than a glow, remained there, as Jenny did, lit by the fragile space in which she stood.

Mr Rummage stared at the sky and saw the multitude of stars, the ancient Gods, sculpted in myth, beside warriors, by distant regions to which one day man would perhaps return.

This impulse made him shudder. It was in the clarity of the dark between the stars that he began to filter out the dead from the living, the dying from the newly born. He saw Mr Gruff's face, now his eyes had closed, still, calm, peaceful, ambiguous. He saw the shapes of Burnchester in a flood of light, every minute shape exact, more intense than at any time he had experienced while there. Every discolouration of brick and stone, every crack or dent in the wall was so confident, so exact, that it was as if he was more than there, and had created them himself. He could see the river, the Folly, the fields beyond. He could see the teaching block, the playing fields. He could see the woods surrounding Mr Gruff's house, and the woods beyond the river, towards the Burnchester Arms, now visible, beneath the trees. He could see the landscape of East Anglia, the United Kingdom, the sea, and the continent beyond. The world. And then in the penetrating glow the eye, the inner eye, destined to reveal the cracks in the earth that would take him in. The tunnels began to appear, now clear, now obscure, not fully formed, partially unshaped. One in use, another in poor repair. All this while, unseen, his face was touched by the wind from the sea. The birds calling.

He saw the cloaked figures move across the school, and the car arrive, and the figures drift across the empty space. He knew them for what they were. The sword-crosses, hollow images, like the false cloaks themselves. The Priory. He could even follow Dennis, Tyro and PC Relish under the earth, from here, high above it, going down. He could sense something darker still. He could see inside the school library, the beloved library, broken into. He could read, yes read, the manuscripts that lay about, one on the table, another beside the books lying on the shelves. On one he could make out the jumbled letters: *muchbuhijushin*. He could even sense the missing key.

He glanced across to the church, inside which the candles were lit and the picture rested in oblique tranquillity, the tower's stronghold broken into. The boathouse. Somewhere, in his mind's eye, projected onto the area around the school, he tried to find the Spearhead.

He began to shake. He could see the prostrate figure of Jenny on the ground, and tried to move towards her. She seemed in a lifeless pose, her clothes blowing in the wind.

The earth began to shake, the sky and stars moved, becoming a blur of light over the stricken dark. Mr Rummage tried to fix his eyes on a point in the centre of the circle, but could not. He tried any point. He could not do this either. He tried again to move, but was transfixed. So incomplete was his skill, so half-rehearsed, that he could only submit to the power that broke from the ground around the ancient stones and from within him. Streaks of light, pinpointed and racing at an extraordinary speed, arose from the black rocks. In a confusion of lines, like spears hurled in some ancient war at an unknown enemy high above, the intermingling beams fought and battled against each other with ferocious intensity, while fire-covered sparks flew in all directions, for a place in the story, until, high above the earth, somewhere between the heavens and the moor, they became one huge beam of light striking out into the emptiness above, lighting up the heavens and the earth, like a vast white bow into eternity.

His body gave way. His mind tormented, he sank to the ground, an afterthought against the massive stones. Nothing but an empty mask against the dark land.

*

Far beneath the ground at Burnchester, PC Relish, Dennis and Tyro stood transfixed in the circular chamber against the rail of a balcony that circumvented the huge dome. Like the shaded grandeur of an unlit cathedral, the empty grey space in front of them was saved from hollowness by a central wire that fell from the apex at the summit.

Beneath, on the ground, stood a circle of stones, twelve in

all. In front of each was a carved wooden seat, like a small throne. In front of six of these were the static figures of Abby, Jess, Clare, John, Rick and Tom. In the space at the centre, beneath the base of the wire which hung mid-way beneath the floor and the ceiling, stood, on a carved stone obelisk, a ball of pure crystal. Behind each rock stood a shadowy figure, a hooded spectre, a dark angel, waiting for the call, unformed but emerging into a ghastly shape, appearing like the figures that had followed the others above. But these had no sword-crosses on their backs. These were primordial. Neither solid, nor wholly spirit, somewhere between dying and death these shapes began to stir. The stones shook, the room echoed an empty boom, a hollow cry from the pain of history. From the stones a dark mist rose, like serpent's breath, above each rock, ill-defined until, above the obelisk and ball, beneath the end of the suspended wire, a shape appeared, was in the process of becoming, a haunting figure with eyes of damnation and the vapour of death.

At its emergence, the earth shook, and the ethereal figures bowed in terror.

Those still unshaped figures behind the rocks seemed to chant a haunted psalm, adding to the background murmur of a distant echo, a crescendo of demented ecstasy, only to fall and to begin again. Each burst of sound gave further energy to the central shape, until it reached its own point of completion.

Dennis, PC Relish and Tyro, unable to move, unable to speak, unable to shed tears, stood fixed in an unconscious trance, looking below. Their postures had been caught, each in its final gasp of movement, perhaps for ever. Dennis flailing with all his might in vain, alongside the fighting Relish. Tyro stood composed, as if prepared for this transformation into another domain. Yet, from within her unconscious transfixed eyes, she saw, or thought she saw, something other than that hideous shape below. Some rays of hope, contained within the frozen bodies of their relatives and friends.

They too were transfixed, their eyes raised towards the hideous figure that was forming, as if required to do homage. But only apparently so. In this falsified gaze, Tyro thought she caught the eyes of one of these figures looking up, that of her mother Abby, and then next to her, Jess, Clare, John, all bound by an indefinable force in resolute opposition to submission. Next to John, Rick and Tom. In those eyes that Tyro saw, she caught the unconscious struggle that was being fought. Those eyes, her mother's eyes, and the eyes of all of them, fought desperately against the dark energy that held them against their will. It was as if their bodies were effectively dead, their life-force was being drained into the shadows behind the rocks, but their spirits would not be controlled. Some angelic hope gave them respite, gave them a sense of the possibility of joy. Yet each was tied to the shadow behind his or her respective stone. Each except Tom, from whom a silent, soft light emerged, unhampered by the dark figure at his back.

The figure of incarnated death stood high above the glass ball, in the dark clouded mist. Its eyes, deeper than all time, as if raised before the birth of the world. Every layer of lie in those eyes held secrets, deceptions, foul conjoined efforts to rule. Now, almost formed, it was prepared to speak. The chanting reached a peak. As it did so, the figure stood high and erect.

The chanting stopped. The figures behind the rocks were now fully formed. The human shapes in front, seemingly entirely lifeless, stood. The pulse of dormant light secretly kept faith beneath their faces. Except in the glowing hue of Tom, who stood in wait for the wrath that would come his way.

It was at this moment that Mr Rummage had fallen. And the beam of light had been hurled upwards into the sky, like the spears of that ancient war, seeking its enemy.

*

The evil figure pointed to the gallery above.

"I command you to come down."

With this, it raised a crumpled finger up, and the frozen shapes of PC Relish, Dennis and Tyro were lifted up into the air, and as it dropped its arm, they were left against a stone on the floor beneath him, alongside the others. There were now nine of them.

"I....I...." the evil figure continued, uncurling its snake-tongue, as if no word of truth could ever come from it, and nothing but darkness and death could be touched by its sickly saliva, in the denial of all life, in the fallacy of corruption, in the stench of its ancient unreconciled, unarguable evil power.

It raised its arm as if in triumph, and lifted its neck and head up, and gave out a tumultuous laugh, as the executioner does for the benefit of his axe, and laughed again until the Domed Chamber shook. It seemed like a demented beast.

"Stop!" It screamed. "In the name of death, I will have silence. Hear me speak!"

Its audience was the world.

"In the beginning was me. The world was without form. The world was chaos. The world was without life. And then my brother, incarnate out of my side, stole my fire, and seizing power, brought order to the world, and life to the spheres. And hope of eternal life. I was cast out into the wilderness of death. But in that realm of death in which I walk, I have always sought to be restored to my kingdom, which will have no end. Now, as my death-souls have helped me seek the life-blood I need to be restored, I will again have victory. I will go forward again into the world, and restore worship, and obedience to me. In the end there will, as in the beginning, be only me."

It raised an arm and looked up to the summit of the chamber, as if in search of recognition, into space.

It looked down at the figures - the death-souls - below. The dark figures had now come forward leaving the still humans behind, and bowed, low, their faceless heads touching the ground.

All except one. One figure had not moved. The figure behind Tom.

"And what is that doing in this sacred place?!" screamed the Dark Master, for a moment losing control, and sensing betrayal.

The figure behind Tom bent down in shame. Tom's form remained intact, and kept its glow as before.

"I do not know, Master," said the figure.

"Do not know! What answer is that? You should know!"

"Yes, Master."

"Go, you have failed. You are condemned to everlasting torment. That figure cannot be destroyed. It is but spirit. Go!"

"No, Master!"

But the shaded figure fell away to nothing. Not a trace of energy remained, not a sign of its garments, not a hint of power. Only Tom remained, quiet, and unable to fall.

The Dark Master came forward, and came down to floor level, the centre of his troupe of death-souls, the stealers of all life.

He turned to the subtly glowing figure of Tom, and spat his wrath in his direction.

"Get thee hence!" he cried. "No-one, but no-one will defy me!"

The light in Tom began to fade. Slowly, slowly, diminishing, until it was nothing but the smallest pulse of energy and light, a small single candle in the dark dome. Just as it reached its point of extinction, it held its ground, like the last glimmer of hope.

The earth began to tremble, the ground shake. Each stone, poised in silent acquiescence, vibrated from side to side. The air was electric, the sound of galloping hooves rumbling over a vast plain, hordes of fighters, armies of the light, galloping, galloping, over the earth, in the sky, led by the beam, over the night land.

The Dark Master raised its head.

The sound continued. The ground shook more. The dust, which had accumulated over the dome's rocks, dispersed, creating a putrid mist, a contaminated air. The sound grew and grew, breaking forth from every corner of the dark, as if the whole world was being reborn, in this Domed Chamber. The cavernous regions below, the arteries of tunnels, shafts and vaults, half-hidden, unexplored, partially decayed, echoed to the terrible cry. Echoed with a form of laughter, like the laughter of fallen angels.

And then, in one stupendous blinding flash, highlighted from the wire that fell from the apex of the roof, a furious flame of enormous force and energy filled the tired air. This was followed with pulse and wave after wave of light, flooding the room, now an ancient chamber, gilt with gold, adorned with the magnificence of a noble past, where kings had sat in wise council, a chamber where knights had planned their paths to victory, where soldiers had prepared for the final battle, and now again, a chamber wrought of stone. And on the stone, the curious jumbled letters shone: *muchbuhijushin*. And then for a moment only, the Spearhead. It was gone.

Where there had been putrid air, the air was clean. Where there had been shadows, there was now light, chasing, chasing the death-souls out of the chamber, as they fled or tried to flee from their entrapment, back into the bowels of the earth, into the shadows of their own making. They tried to fight but in vain. For a second moment, for a moment only, there it stood, the Spearhead.

The Dark Master looked up in a hideous stare, awed, and in an explosion of dust, disintegrated into nothing. As strangely as it had arisen, it was gone.

Rats ran across the floor, and fled into unseen holes.

The human figures, held suspended, remained still.

*

High on the moors of the Island, the other human figures of Mr Rummage and Jenny were conjoined in the centre of the stone circle. The sky was clear. The earth still. A host of spirit shapes strove busily around them, pursuing their daily ritual tasks. The empty hill was now awake, but for one night. There seemed to be dancing. None of these were visible to Mr Rummage and Jenny, who were drained, tears falling from their eyes, of joy, and of peace, of ecstasy, however temporary.

They rested and looked over the empty sea to the west. The birds were calling, high in the summer sky, seeking food, out of the night waters, in their eternal search.

Jenny and Mr Rummage turned and began to walk down the slope, leaving the old grey lifeless things to a patch of windswept moor. Rocks. Nothing but rocks.

The spongy earth and the dry heather combined to make their path difficult. Jenny fell, Mr Rummage fell, trying to help her up.

It did not matter.

They walked on, somewhere in the back of their minds a residual memory, unfocused but real, of the events that had taken place. Of their tumultuous inability to strive against the power around the stones. Of the necessity of their presence to awaken them.

They felt the burning point of a spear across their hearts.

When they reached home Julia and Simon were asleep, a half-finished game of scrabble on the table. A finished packet of biscuits was scrumpled on the floor, beside two half-empty cups of juice.

On the table a message read, in hurried writing, 'Dad, someone called. Twice. Couldn't get name exactly - sorry. Think it might be Baxter, end of message.' Then, in another hand, Simon's, the words, 'Mum, Dad, where are you? Goodnight.' A few scratched kisses had been added beneath the scrawl. Jenny's training had done some good, after all.

Tired and drained as they were, neither wished to go to bed. It was one of those bewitching times, that can be achieved on holiday, when only the heart leads the will.

Jenny put the kettle on for tea. She went to the cupboard and brought out a cake which she had made that morning, with Julia and Simon's help. It was a chocolate cake, everybody's favourite. She cut two slices and put them on plates, beside the two armchairs in the comfortable, if sparse drawing room, with a window overlooking a slope that led down towards the sea. They were high enough never to be threatened with flooding, and low enough always to be in easy reach of its call.

"Didn't you see them, John?" Jenny asked.

"Is it too late?"

"Too late for what?"

"To phone back. See what, Jenny?"

"The figures, dancing on the moor."

"Figures? Dancing? I thought that was us."

Jenny smiled. "Never mind. I don't know. I don't know how important it is."

Jenny said this without a hint of criticism, but it was enough to get the response she needed.

"Sorry. I'll tell you now. It's important. Then you can tell me if it's too late to phone. And whether we - or perhaps I - should go back tomorrow."

Jenny's face was sad. Nothing could have induced her to return the next day, so soon after they had arrived; for her children, for herself, for her husband, she wanted nothing more than to have a proper 'break'. But she would say nothing until she had heard about the phone call that he had received earlier (though she had been close by), and some explanation of their walk to the Ring of Loth. She would like to have got angry, but knew that there was little point except for her own pride. She was part of a mystery that didn't allow her, or any of her family, the independence and freedom that many people, as she, longed for, but did not have.

John began. He explained the discovery of Mr Gruff, Tyro and Jess's search beneath the ground, the break-ins at the church. He also told her about the mask. This led to his meeting in Cambridge of a couple of days ago, and the outcomes of that. His shortened account was enough to give Jenny what she needed to know, though she couldn't but help ask, "Were there any tunnels that had not been searched or were not known?"

"Both," he replied. "So much has been in disuse for so long, that there are many passages, of which we know, but cannot access at the moment. Some, we do not know of."

"And the other?" she asked again, innocently.

"The house is so old, the foundations so ancient and the site so rich that there will certainly be many things as yet hidden beneath the ground, of which we have no current knowledge. Leaving aside the fragment of the picture."

"Which is why you and others are indexing the library manuscripts."

"In part, yes."

"And the Priory? How dangerous are they?"

"They have caused enough trouble so far. There may be others. It is by no means over."

"And the Spearhead?"

"We do not know. Perhaps we never will."

Shortly after this they went to bed, more exhausted yet more alive than either had ever known. Clearly what power they had encountered, and channelled, was not theirs alone. They knew that. Jenny, her mind on the dancing figures on the moor, suspected that John would have to return sooner than both wished.

# 12

M. Le Petit had had an unusually successful night, even for him. The miraculous strawberry pudding that he had made (with "ze crème from ze cow", a sacred one at that), had been more inspirational than even he would have thought possible, from any other chef. Not only could this be confirmed by the ecstatic reaction of the customers, but also because he had been so bold as to test it, in the most unlikely event of there being any irregularities of texture or tone.

After the Wander party had left - they had been generous with a tip (a practice which he deplored but felt it unfair to stifle) - one or two other customers had come in, including the man known by Dennis as the stranger.

Mr Gatherin had also noticed his arrival. He asked M. Le Petit to serve him with special care but without arousing suspicion, in an attempt to find out a little about him. M. Le Petit preferred to comment on his own work rather than to enquire into other people's, and found this difficult, but could be relied on to find out whether he was in a hurry or not, on the basis of the size of his order. Mr Gatherin was informed that the stranger was not apparently in a hurry, but was given no more information. He decided to try to contact Dennis by phone, but the phones were not answering. Nevertheless he was able to leave a message.

When the stranger had come in, there were a few people at

the bar, including students from Motley Fall, who had been out that day on a trip to the Theatre Royal in Norwich. M. Le Petit had hoped for a rest, but, as is the case with professionals of his stature, he put his best boot forward, and prepared for work. Mr Gatherin had briefed him a little earlier in the evening, enough to say those magic words, "Recalled to Life", words used by another master, in another context, all those years ago, as cryptic confirmation that something serious was going on, and that they should be on full alert. This worked wonders for the lunar M. Le Petit, and he worked on the stranger's meal with intense energy, as if he were preparing the last of this life, or for another.

Mr Gatherin had previously spoken to the dubious Mr Pinchet, who had been sufficiently informed and plied with drink to think that he was a necessary part of any group defence. He still wanted an explanation of Jess and Tyro's activities in the boat (as well as an apology), but Mr Pinchet, being a proud man, and a good shot (capable of hitting a rabbit on the run at 650 metres, according to him), rose to the occasion, and swallowed his beer. He prepared to take action. He would walk the woods above the river, with enough of a view of the Burnchester side, but out of sight, to see if he could find anything out. He could not get it out of his mind that it was the girls, and nobody else, who had been up to no good. Children, in his opinion, were normally the cause of trouble, even when there wasn't any. As with so many behaviours, however, Mr Pinchet's had a darker foundation. It wasn't just that he carried with him the obscurity of an employer whose reputation was as doubtful as his absence was general. Whatever the truth, people were suspicious of Mr Strangelblood because of his refusal to live in his grand mansion, and - the worse sin - to allow anybody onto his land, bar a very few employees, who guarded their privilege with pride.

Mr Pinchet's reputation may also have been influenced by

some of his own activities, which he was not altogether in a hurry to advertise. The fact that the stranger, it could have been argued, may or may not have accessed the school, at an earlier time, may or may not have been connected with his sweet-talking Mr Pinchet with compliments as to his achievements as a keeper, lubricated with whisky, to ensure that he would invite him onto the land to show him round, and cross the river. This had happened some months before, and had been unobserved by everyone but Mr Pinchet. It would have given the stranger the opportunity to observe the Hall, and Mr Gruff.

In this state of contradiction, Mr Pinchet left the Burnchester Arms shortly after closing time. Mr Gatherin, for the first time in many years, had not called last orders. Mr Pinchet thought it might be an oversight, but was too immersed in his own business, and whisky.

*

But it had not been an oversight. Mr Gatherin was acting tactically. He was spreading a little bit of confusion, so as to encourage the stranger into one more drink, hoping for Dennis's return. But he had failed. The stranger, as before, at another pub, had left, apparently to return, but had not done so. He had left a little bit of beer in the bottom of his glass, to suggest that he was savouring it and would be back for more. Mr Gatherin was not one normally to be fooled, but he had got it wrong on this occasion. Normally, he could assess his customer by various measures: the nature of the purchase; the table the person chose to sit at (inside or out); whether the customer would risk carrying both glass and bottle in one hand, or leave one and come back for the other; by his or her attitude to picking up the change - starting with the smallest values first and working upwards, or grabbing at random and shoving the whole lot higgledy-piggledy all at once into his trouser pocket or her purse. By these means and others, such as whether the customer was left-handed and how much of a pull he took on the first taste, he added to the evidence from which many things could be deduced, not least whether the customer might be here for the duration or here for a swift half and then exit, pursued by a bear.

In the case of the stranger, despite having studied his face, as he said to M. Le Petit, shortly after the stranger had left, in the privacy of M. Le Petit's cuisine, he had "blown it".

"Ce n'est rien," observed his mystical chef. "I 'ave it on good authorité, namely the gentleman 'imselve, that 'e was 'ere to listen for nightingales. This 'e told me when I asked 'im if 'e would like some more, to which 'e had replied, "yes", but that 'e could not stop. The conditions were perfect - there would be no better time. Ever."

"Ever?" enquired Mr Gatherin, returning to the bar, with emphasis.

"That is what 'e said," replied his friend with finality. "Did you check ze money?" he added.

"Of course, I did, my friend," said Mr Gatherin.

"I think you will find zat the money is false. I think we 'ad better send out a search party, mon vieux," added the Frenchman relapsing into the vernacular.

"False!" shouted the normally immovable barman, "False! I don't bloody believe it!" he added in his rich Suffolk accent.

With that he rolled back to the bar, checked the till and held a note up to the light. Sure enough, the thin metallic line which was normally woven into the fabric was missing. Amongst the change were some dubious looking coins.

With a swift and controlled look at the bar, to check who was in and who had left, he went to the back and made another call. This time to PC Relish. Finding nothing but an answer machine at his office, he tried the local police at Wyemarket, where he left a message, describing what had happened.

"Unfortunately, PC Relish is unavailable. Can anyone else help, Mr Gatherin?"

Mr Gatherin felt that they could not, so replaced the handset and went back to M. Le Petit, who was cleaning his cuisine utensils, in readiness for the next day. Only the students were left in the bar. They noticed that Mr Gatherin had left more empty glasses than usual on the table. This change in behaviour reflected his irritation and the new focus of his wounded pride. He was determined now, more than ever, to find out who this man was, what he was up to, and to get reparation.

Night had fallen over an hour ago, though the strength of the moon gave the impression of it being tenuous, as if the day was on edge, and struggling to breathe. The cloak of night, like the cloaks elsewhere, lurking in the mists and shadows, had not yet crushed the final breath of day, whilst the moon in her ambiguous glory managed still to retain her grip on the spirits and others who rose to pay her homage.

Mr Gatherin was now in stern mood.

"My friend," he said, to M. Le Petit, "my friend of many, many years."

Mr Gatherin had already spoken more words in one breath than he ever had in all the years that he had been barman, except on the occasion of his wife's wedding.

"We must send out a search party, or go ourselves. I will not be betrayed by a skunk who smiles so sweetly, and gives me false notes. I will go for him myself. You can come with me, though it may be better for you to wait here and keep watch."

"What about getting ze help of zose drama students? M. Dennis and PC Relish cannot be reached. I do not know where zey are, though it must be up at ze school. As for ze others, perhaps zey are in trouble too!"

"I do not know."

Then Mr Gatherin added, with all the weight at his disposal, which was considerable.

"I will go alone! You, M. Le Petit, will look after the bar for me."

"I will keep watch 'ere and be ready to, in Inspecteur Le Relish's words, tuer les bastardes!"

Staying behind was more conducive to the level of activity to which M. Le Petit had grown accustomed, and he had no idea who the bahstuds were, any more no doubt than the Relish.

"Keep the bar open, all night if necessary, only to friends, M. Le Petit, until we come back. These are exceptional circumstances."

M. Le Petit, donning his cap as guardian of the faith, was already in a state of near full alert and ready with his couteau for anything.

"I shall watch ze river," he said.

With a flourish he flew out of the back door, which led to the river bank. This is where M. Le Petit had his fishing lines, first for the pike from which he made the most delicious pike paté, and second for the slippery eels, which, though less common, still lurked snakelike in the murky water, which was quite deep here. He looked into the water, and imagined a monster swimming through the obscure reeds towards its prey, like a dark cloud, over the light of the sun.

Mr Gatherin left, taking his mobile. "Waste o' time," he thought, the thing being dead to the world, like most sensible people at this time.

He strode out into the moonlight.

Mr Gatherin was really not as swift on his feet as he would have wished, but he was fuelled by outrage and fury. Never in all his time as a barman, through all the troublesome times, years ago, during the war, when he was genuinely young, and the various blips in local social history since then, had he ever been given a false note. There had been trouble locally in the past, several attempted break-ins at Burnchester Hall, and at least one at the Lodge, the home of Mr Strangelblood, but apart from a few fights, not a single incident of this kind under his charge. He took it as a personal affront, and as such it was his duty personally to find the culprit.

What he lacked in youth he said to himself, as he searched the car park in vain for any sign of a car, he would would make up for in cunning. In this respect Mr Gatherin and the Relish, were of the same stock.

He dismissed the idea of driving. Although the roads were narrow and there were relatively few of them, he felt certain that he would be somewhere in the vicinity. This made it more difficult, but there were others on the ground, including Mr Pinchet, and, he hoped, Dennis and the others, who, between them would somehow ensnare him. What the stranger might be doing concerned him less than to right the wrong which had been done to him. It was his pride that had been hurt, though he was also an enemy who needed to be caught.

Mr Gatherin went back down to the river and started along the bank sniffing as he went, like an old dog, looking for a bone that he had left somewhere, without remembering where.

*

Mr Pinchet had been true to his word in keeping an eye on the place. He had walked along for a quarter of a mile or so, high enough above the water to be hidden from anyone walking along it on the other side. This was his territory and he felt at home. He wasn't sure what was expected of him, but he presumed that he should double his efforts to find out who might be in the woods, or on the grounds opposite. The slight intoxication that he felt made him more ready for the enemy than he would otherwise have been, though it also meant that his eyes were not quite as focused. He held his gun, open but loaded.

Mr Pinchet knew his ground well. He normally felt comfortable in the shadows of these ancient trees, even though the wood itself, being ancient in origin, and the host of the remains of the iron-age fort, high on the bank above the river some few hundred metres on, might, to a more imaginative mind, have been a source of mystery and fear as much as comfort. Had he been more sensitive, he would have been aware of kingdom's living alongside him, of animals and spirits and other life forms of the forest, who had dwelt here, as they have elsewhere, for longer than human history. He might have imagined the earliest residents of the fort during their lives. He might even have seen figures gliding past along the different lines of their history. His ignorance of these things was to a small extent beneficial. He could not in any way interfere with their activities, and they continued to exist and operate under his otherwise observant eye, that could have benefited from being observant also in mind. He missed much more than he saw, a condition not uncommon in people generally.

One of his duties as keeper of the Strangelblood estate was controller of vermin. This curious phrase meant that certain creatures (generally small) suffered terrible losses and were in constant fear of their lives. The fight was unequal, the balance of power weighted in favour of Mr Pinchet's weapons, and the results often cruel and gruesome. The carcasses of stoats, weasels and crows would dangle from the barbed wire that edged parts of the estate, and especially the hatcheries deep inside the forest, where against all the rules of God's kingdom, and the law, he used to set traps for owls. The vermin, being ruthless themselves, but part of a different order, did their best to exact retribution from time to time, either alone, or with the aid of non-vermin, who in other circumstances they ate - such is the imbalance of power even in the land of animals.

The confidence that comes from carrying a loaded gun, and being ruler of his unequal domain, led Mr Pinchet to believe that he could handle any comers: the poachers who came onto his land from time to time, sometimes without his knowledge; the antics of the children from Burnchester, when playing truant from their cross-country runs and hiding up amongst the summer leaves while the rest struggled on over the ground to home; courting couples and, worst of all, archaeologists. All these he could handle with both disrespect and disdain. Occasionally local boys came along the river and tried to camp or light fires. He normally tolerated them, if they caused no trouble, and did not stray too far into the woods, where they might interfere with his hatcheries. Mr Strangelblood, though not often in residence himself, made a strict rule to allow no-one near his house, and as few as possible on his ground at all, even where there were ancient rights of way.

Tonight was different. A different feeling pervaded the wood. Insensitive as he was, Mr Pinchet could feel a different energy. He did not, for the first time in his life, feel completely at ease. For the first time Mr Pinchet felt the need for his gun, as opposed to the support of it. For the first time ever he kept the barrel loaded, and now primed shut.

He watched and listened carefully as he walked slowly through the trees. Then he paused, sat down, and waited. He began to drowse. Experience had told him that silence and stillness are the greatest friends of the night. Enemies have to move. They do not have the luxury of lying low, especially enemies with little time.

It must have been around midnight and he had begun to doze, his head falling forwards, his knees coming at him like clenched fists, in the blur of half-closed eyes. But he forced himself awake and kept looking up.

He saw a movement along the river bank. It seemed to be a shadow, a human shape. There were others. He could not count. They seemed not to be walking, but drifting. Was this a dream? He shook himself awake, angry with himself. They were still there.

He crouched low, though he doubted that he could be seen from below in the trees above the river. As the figures moved on, he began to follow at his higher level, and then, finding one of the deer tracks that led down to the water's edge he made his way towards the river and the figures to get a closer look. He could not be sure of his prey, and he held his gun closer. For the first time Mr Pinchet was afraid. Occasionally he heard a stick crack underfoot, making his heart leap, and his anger rise, now mixed with terrible and growing anxiety.

The figures were on the very boat that Tyro and Jess had used earlier that evening. They were going the other way, back in the direction of the school. The profile of their faces remained hidden beneath their hoods, as they moved silently through the  flickering light of the riverside alders, like wanderers out of the underworld, into which he seemed to be being drawn. All except for one face. He looked again, creeping forward closer to the bank. A pang of recognition punctured his heart, which started to beat furiously. It was the face of the stranger, the man in the Burnchester Arms, the man, who, all those months ago, had paid him to take him onto his land. Guilt and agitation shook him, as he tried to grip the gun he held. The face turned. It was indeed the same man.

In that tiny moment, Mr Pinchet's eyes were impaled by recognition, and though the stranger's stare was impassive, they were enough to destroy. Without thinking, Mr Pinchet began to raise his gun. The stranger turned dismissively, as if to say "You cannot touch me! Traitor!" and tapped the shoulders of one of his crew. This now turned and looked, like a puppet. It had the face of a woman, a face that he had seen before. Mr Pinchet could not believe his eyes.

Mr Pinchet knew he had been seen. His first inclination was to shout a warning. Such a group would be violent and would not heed his pleas. That they were on a terrible errand, from some other place, he knew, despite his blind intolerance. It was as if he was having to face the consequences of his lack of imagination. His authority was limited to the innocent, and his cries might be as futile as the tears of the damned.

He followed the boat along, as if drawn. Now they were

adjacent to the ditch that led off the river, back onto his land, towards the fort, which lay inside the forest under a mound of grass and trees. This was nothing but a mass of rubble covered over, difficult to walk across, unfertile except for the occasional birch on the top.

The boat moved on.

Mr Pinchet heard a commotion. He saw lights far ahead. There were shouts across the water, towards the school, people and lights somewhere between the trees in the distance, on the school grounds. He tried to get a better view but saw nothing but shapes criss-crossed by the lights of what was now clearly a car, near the Hall itself. He wanted to shout out, but could not, as if he had been gagged. He felt breathless, imagined hands now tied around his throat. He wanted to scream, to attract the figures on the river, the iron stare of the stranger, now close to him, and now in sight of what was happening far ahead. He wanted to regain control.

The boat stopped against the far bank.

Mr Pinchet raised his gun and pointed it in the direction of the boat. He took aim and fired. He then lifted the sights a little and saw the figures far ahead, whose faces briefly turned. He saw several that he knew.

Immediately, he crouched in the shadows. He moved silently out of sight over the back of the fort, and towards the valley that led back up to Folly hill. Which way to turn? He did not know whether to stay to help the others, to stand his ground and attack further or return. He was confused, fearful of the consequences of his action, knowing that he had scored a hit.

As he regained his breath, he decided that he must find out what these figures were doing on the school grounds. Even he had noticed the sword-crosses on their backs. Why were they here? He had not been told what the others knew or guessed. He must also find help, get back across the river, which he could not swim. Among them was the man who had paid him handsomely, he kept saying to himself, for permission to look over his terrain. He wanted to get his revenge for being double-crossed. He hoped he had drawn blood.

Then a thought occurred to him, rose up in his mind against his will. A thought that he must suppress. Was Mr Strangelblood aware of what was happening, in some way connected? He cast the thought from his mind, shuddering at the guilt of his own suspicions, but they would not entirely go away.

But a greater guilt arose in his mind. He had broken one of the cardinal rules of his trade. Bluster and shout as much as you like, but never fire. But he had done so. He had taken aim at the man who had broken his word. He was pleased.

One of the shapes in the boat sank down, a thin trail of blood emerging on the black material of his shoulder, staining the sword-cross on his back, mocking the illusion. One helped the wounded figure, who now clutched his side. The other shapes, in temporary confusion, also sank low into the boat, while the other figures crossed the school grounds, as if in response to a call for help, slowly coming their way. The moon was now clear in the sky above, and beyond, the other figures were clearly visible, as were the people he had recognised.

The figures approached the boat. They stood for a moment, as if in consultation. Then they proceeded along the bank.

From a distance on the far bank Mr Pinchet stared through the sights of his rifle. He could now see two women he recognised, Mrs Wander and her friend, a man (he knew the face but not the name) and Jess. They had moved on to the boathouse and were now near the eastern end of the school. The figures in the boat, despite their setback, perhaps because of it, had cast the boat off again, and were moving in the direction of the people. The figures seemed intent on cutting the people off, and preventing them from discovering too much. They hoped to entrap and silence them, as their brethren had failed to do, but their power was unreliable, and seemed intermittent. And yet they were compelled on. For all their power, they were still only in the process of being reborn. For these were also human, flesh but not flesh, living in the shadow-land, striving for their own master.

The figures in the boat drew up to the bank and got out by the boathouse, disappearing immediately. The stranger, though wounded, was the most determined, leading from the front. He took a key from his pocket and opened the iron gate that had fallen shut so dramatically over Dennis, PC Relish and Tyro. This had been the key taken from Mr Gruff. They continued through the tunnel until they reached a door and entered.

Here they continued on to another room, which had a lift. They called for the lift and got in. Shortly afterwards they emerged into another corridor at the back of the huge Domed Chamber where Dennis, PC Relish and Tyro were overlooking the balcony, looking below to ground level.

At that same moment, at the woodland edge in the grounds of the Hall, near the exit of the trees that led up to the Folly, Mr Pinchet was struck to the ground. The four figures who had earlier passed the stranger's group stood over him. His eyes stared upward in terror. The normally proud, self-important and pompous Mr Pinchet was now reduced to a dazed vermin, the gun at his feet, barrel empty and twisted. The figures, without visible faces, stood above him, exuding a putrid breath. In moments his eyes glazed over, unconscious, near their shadow-land. He too was a betrayer.

One of the four took out from inside his cloak what looked like a pouch, which moved from side to side, as if it were alive. With skeletal hands, he opened the pouch and drew out a rat. The rat tried to drive its teeth into the bony hand, but to no avail. The figure seemed to laugh and placed the rat next to the neck of the fallen Pinchet. Here the beast, in a moment of ecstasy, drank deep from the swollen veins in the neck of the unconscious man.

The rat was replaced, Pinchet was left on the ground at the edge of the wood, and the figures from the Priory moved back into the shadows. Here, they disappeared.

Beneath the ground, by the Domed Chamber entrance, the stranger and his group appeared through a door at the base of the dome, behind the twelve stones and human figures who had been placed in front of them. The people were dazed, the dark shadowy shapes  behind the stones, like their own shadows, waiting to be called, yet chanting for their master to appear.

The stranger and his group were just in time. The energy was at its height and the chanting increasing, while the terrible figure of the Dark Master appeared in front of the ring, and brought down the others from the balcony. Protected from its power, and knowing that some other energy had been released to counter it, the stranger watched, without entering, seeing what he could gain from this tumultuous moment. His own soul had long since perished, and he was no longer prey to the powers of light and dark. That struggle had long since gone. He had made his choice and was already ensnared by the figure whose will he had accepted, and the path he had been given. He had been received during the last reincarnation of the Dark Master, and had been given his orders then. Now he could witness the re-emergence, with a pride, yet fear, in case his soul might be snatched again, for some other purpose than the one that he now wanted for himself.

The stranger watched the ceremony and the lowering of Dennis, PC Relish and Tyro. He had felt the tremors and retreated into the cavernous background, out of sight of this huge force that would devour him also if he were to come into its orb. He shook in fear, praying for his own survival. His task was of this world. And when the descent came, and the shadows became rats and the Dark Master disintegrated, he waited, relieved, in the shadows of the hall, for the captive people to return to consciousness. He was confident that his own power, and their condition, would make them easy prey. He could not kill them, they were too valuable. He needed to be able to return, he needed to infect them with his own code. Besides, he needed help to find the Spearhead. The Spearhead above all would give him earthly control. The Dark Lord could be master of his world, but he would be master of this.

# 13

The ordeal had been intense. But in a state of unconsciousness, their knowledge of events was as in a dark dream, where there is no light, no escape, no possibility of time. They had been spared the worst, by being not wholly in this world - yet frightened of what they had experienced in the dark recesses of their minds - somewhere half-conjoined with the powers that had temporarily seduced them. Had they arrived a little later, they would have been spared, on account of the ecstasy that had been revealed; had they arrived before the evil shapes had begun their soulless incantation, they might have been subsumed into eternal dark. But they had come too late to ensure their being taken, and, fortunately, not too late to be saved, by the mysterious, overwhelming light that had reduced the Dark Master and the spirit figures to nothing.

Tyro, Dennis, PC Relish and all the others had each experienced events in their own way, according to their own personalities and powers, but not in a conscious state. The two groups had been brought together by a separate route, but shared an experience that would unite them together, uniquely.

John, Clare, Abby and Jess had been tempted down the tunnel under the old oak, by the whistle that Jess had recognised and at John's insistence that he had seen figures near the Folly, which must have come from somewhere. Following his intuition had proved right. Below ground, in some rough hewn tunnel, freshly made and crudely structured, they had indeed encountered figures, but not those that they expected - rather Rick and Tom, who, in the midst of these other activities, had been doing their own exploration. That they should be burrowing underground, in the dark, in the middle of the holidays, was itself extraordinary and needed explanation. At first John was angry that they were here, in the cold damp, in extreme danger, and gave them a brisk 'telling off'. But seeing that it was to no purpose he asked what they thought they were doing? The thought that the tunnel might collapse  gave added urgency to his concern while Abby and Clare tried, in vain, to show them some motherly sympathy. At their approach, Tom cowered away, though Rick was more forthright, telling them to go away and to leave them alone.

"Promise not to tell anyone about our tunnel," Rick had snapped. "This is our secret."

It was Jess who saved the situation. She explained how Rick and Tom had helped them find Rompy when she and Tyro had visited the school. Jess laid it on thick, and looking shyly at Rick, pressed him to answer and to confirm her story by adding "Remember?"

Rick looked briefly at her, and nodded, and a slow warm smile appeared to broaden on his otherwise wary face.

There was no time for further anger. A brief explanation showed that Rick and Tom had been digging the tunnel for some time, for a reason they would not give. They knew it led somewhere. They had already explored other tunnels, one of which Tyro and Jess had entered earlier that evening, as had Tyro and Dennis. Rick had implied, evasively, that Tom was acting as a kind of guide, for it was he who seemed most familiar, and most at ease, in this dark place. Tom remained silent in the background. Abby felt some sympathy for him, and determined to give him more credit and observe his behaviour more closely from now on.

Once John's anger had subsided, it became clear that Rick and Tom would be useful in the search for Dennis, Tyro and PC Relish. John therefore changed his tone and asked them to explain what they knew, perhaps a little angry at himself.

The tunnel that Rick and Tom had made, slowly dug out of difficult soil, broken with patches of sand, and upheld by stakes and sheets of metal and strips of wood (pinched from wherever they could, including Mr Greene, the school gardener's, sheds) had reached the end of its journey that very evening.

Only a short while earlier they had found that their tunnel broke into another which had already been excavated. This joined one of the main long-established channels of the complex web that lay below the school. It had been their intention to find the 'treasure' that they believed existed (one of the many rumours), and were disappointed to reach an empty hollow, but were also proud that they had made their own unique way into the system. Jess now realised why Rick had looked so sheepish when she had asked him why he was so muddy, the other day.

Rick and Tom had seen figures elsewhere in the grounds of the Hall that evening, but had observed similar activity many times, over several weeks, knowing that, whoever these people were, they were preparing for something important. They had been careful to keep out of their sight, and through careful observation and patience knew enough of their movements to know how to avoid them, just as they had known about the movements of Mr Gruff, and could avoid being discovered by him. They wanted to keep the information to themselves, until now, when they were forced to disclose what they had been doing, and what they knew.

"Where does this lead?" asked Jess of Rick, touching his arm, as they entered the older tunnel.

Jess had been given the task of leading with Rick, on Clare's advice. Rick would reveal more, through her, and be less brittle, than if he had been quizzed by an adult.

They had followed the tunnel, in the direction of the vibration and the incantation, desperate to find the others. The air was putrid and stifling, as if they had entered an active catacomb, but they had to find the others, come what may.

Abby's fear for Tyro and her anxiety about Dennis made her call out, in vain, against the dull interior and the oncoming sounds, which seemed like a dull hypnotic chant. She wanted to scream at God, so trapped were they in their total loss of control. The attacks from the figures outside became confused in her memory and her desire to find her daughter.

"Supposing," she said aloud to herself, "supposing something has happened to them?"

"Suppose nothing," said Clare, trying, against her real feelings, to be rational. "It doesn't do any good. Let's only deal in facts. They may be safe. As we are."

But Abby could not forget what had happened outside, the hooded figures, and the violence, and the words that they had spoken - that the others were trapped - nor the power that had prevented them from attacking, and the 'barrier' that had saved them from attack. In the back of her mind the shadows of these figures seemed to follow them. She hoped that the figures would not again materialise and that they would not be here ensnared. She fought the illusions, but they knocked again, against her conscious mind.

Jess left marks along the wall of the tunnel as she went, in the event that they would have to retrace their steps.

As the group had walked forward stumbling in the dark, the sound of chanting grew, beckoning downwards like a seductive spell. They had no choice but to follow, if they wanted to be redeemed.

They approached the entrance at the base of the dome, walking carefully, following the glimmer of light ahead of them. John went to the front. The incantation was increasing. The air grew fouler, and he began to choke. They proceeded into the chamber, and saw the huge grey dome above them. They saw the crystal ball at the top of the plinth, and above that, wire that fell from the apex of the roof. They saw the stone slabs in a circle around the outer perimeter of the room, and they saw the carved chair in front of each stone, and a shadow behind each, as if waiting.

The energy had drawn them in. It was now so strong that they could not have turned back, had they wished to. It was at this point that their minds began to lose control, each fighting breathlessly as if drowning. Clare clutched Jess and Rick to her, Abby tried to hold Tom, but he stood aside, the only one untouched. Tears fell down Abby's face at this strange rejection. She could not do the job she was best at, the nurse, for this child who was a damaged mystery. She was without her daughter, and without her brother (and her husband), and felt more alone than all the others except this boy, who she could not help. And yet it was in his silent, lonely strength that she regained some control, enough to survive the death that she thought would be her fate. How many had suffered like Tom, and much worse, throughout history. Here was a boy, alone, and yet the strongest of them all, for reasons that she could not understand, as if he had been her son.

The noise was now deafening. The glow from the crystal ball was intense and the vibration in the air almost too much to bear. They held their hands up to their ears. John desperately called to them to retreat, trying to drive them back into the tunnel from where they had come.

But as he tried, the line of dark figures emerged from behind the stones. They had no sword-crosses on their backs, and seemed darker embodiments of evil.

John shouted. Every sinew in his body drove him against these phantom shapes, but in vain.

"Get back!" he screamed, fighting, fighting, fighting, against the debilitating emptiness that seemed to swallow him up as he tried to push his way forward. They had appeared from behind the stones, as out of nothing, yet the sound of the chanting seemed to come from them also. And now they began to move.

Clare screamed at John as she and Jess ran to the other side of the room, followed by Abby and Rick.

But Tom would not move. He stood impassive and still, as if he had the power to prevent the figures touching him at all, and yet was in the presence of some other power that enabled him to hold his ground. For now other dark figures appeared behind Clare.

"Mum, behind you!" screamed Jess.

Clare raised her arm against the figure as it caught her and led her struggling to one of the chairs in front of one of the standing stones of granite. Jess was next. Then Rick.

Tom had now moved to a position in front of another stone. Two figures had tried to catch him, but their attempts were useless. Their arms flailed as if at nothing. He stood firm, looking into a middle distance, with a smile of cold inertia on his peaceful, curious face. Their inability to touch him, and his smile, added to their fury, which they were compelled to vent on the others.

John continued to fight. He was now on his knees, desperately seeking strength as best he could, whilst fighting off the bony fingers that pushed him down. Two of them had hold of him and dragged him to one of the stones. Strange mysteries of sacrifice passed across his mind, as he screamed. These were truly evil.

"Do not give in! Do not...."

This gave Clare strength. She reached out to touch his head as he passed her by, but she could not reach it.

Abby had tried to pacify the figures, but it had not worked. She was led - their laughter mocking her gentleness - with Rick, to her place along the line of people, each standing in front of a stone, each with a figure behind, like their own shadows, doomed and inexorably linked.

Only Tom's shadow-figure seemed unconnected. Yet Tom was not attempting to escape.

*

In that moment between waking and unconsciousness (like that, perhaps, between sleep and death), Jess saw, or thought she saw, her friend Tyro above. But she could not move. Only her eyes showed a dim recognition, and a life-hope that Tyro could sense. For it was her.

As the chanting reached a crescendo, and the Dark Master had appeared, there seemed a counter-force at work in their minds, and yet from somewhere else, holding them on this side, preventing them from crossing over, suspended in an empty space between activity and choice.

After Tyro, Dennis and PC Relish had been transported down, Dennis and PC Relish had tried in vain to reach out, to come forward to join the others. Their efforts were nearly crushed by the hold that the Dark Power had over them, fixing them into a death-like trance. Yet they too had been touched by the counter-force which had been unleashed from outside.

In that moment of near ecstasy, flowing with the mesmerising energy from above, when the chamber became one with its past and glowed in riches of gold, its drapes of noble banners, where knights had prepared for the final battle, the still human figures had seemed cloaked in royal garments. Not of royal blood, but of the nobility that comes from the struggle, an infinitely more pervasive and sustaining force.

How at an unconscious level, this devouring mix of dark and light, of the enchantment of myth and the stabbing pain of actuality, of mystery with enlightenment, of the eternal quest; how, exactly, these contradictions, tempered by personality and age, affected their subjects, these people here, or anywhere

- for they are not exclusive to the stories of men - will in part be seen in the events to come.

That Tyro and Jess will have been touched, in no small way, to the core of their souls, or will have had those elements within activated by dim recognition, is certain. Two girls, exploring their school in summer, could not, have never, perhaps, been subject, or been privileged, before their time, to the sights that they had seen and the feelings encountered. Many have encountered death, the loss of a mother, of a father, been subjected to the cruelties known to the world, but few have encountered directly the beguiling emptiness of the bottomless and endless night of the source of all these ills, the Dark Master. Except perhaps, occasionally in their dreams.

And the others? Abby, Dennis, Clare, PC Relish and John, will have interpreted differently these encounters, these dark energies. Their focus, different. The end, the same: how never to allow a repeat of this near-tragic failure, and guarantee, for ever, the supremacy of light over the dark? A task which they had already enjoined, open to all men, at all times in history, in all places of the world, but only chosen, or forced upon a few, whose destiny has so decreed, in the context of their wills, and of the will that shapes their end, "rough hew them as we will." The only person who could not be touched was Tom. His destiny was as clear as the light that shone from him. His journey had already been made.

After the moment of partial victory, the light and air became filled with the music of birds in song, and gave them all a vital glow. For a moment they remained still, like unborn images of the day. For a moment, a glorious light shone over everything. Even the stranger's dark, sub-human crew, standing apart, watching in the wings, were unable to return into the chamber, though he wanted to capture the human figures. The light was more powerful than the dark tempting incarnation of the Dark Master, to whom he was no longer a simple vassal.

And then the human figures began to move, the life-blood

regenerated, as if waking from a night's unrest. The dull light of the chamber returned as they opened their eyes, though the air was clear.

The present dawned, and their smiles were reclaimed by the anxieties of their entrapment, and the fear of what was yet to come. And yet, being now all together gave them a strength and a will that the stranger and his crew could not have foreseen.

Tyro ran to her mother, tears rolling down her face. John and Clare took Jess by the hand and danced around the dormant stones, who, it might have appeared to some, gave a rather sombre bow. A similar dance occurred inside an ancient circle of stones in the Northern Highlands. PC Relish went to shake the hand of Dennis, who was trying to hug his sister and his niece. Immediately he began to think of where the bahstuds had gone. Rick and Tom turned to each other in amazement, and looked up. They began to edge away.

The stranger, with his own dark, if lesser, powers, untouched by the sordid energy of his ancient Lord, The Dark Master, was ready to ensnare them. He had placed his now substantial crew in a circle around them whilst they enjoyed a moment of joy. But he had not bargained for the new collective force that he would encounter, and as swiftly as he wished to strike, he would decide to flee.

He called from one of the dark corners of the chamber. They turned. The rope was thrown, like a living snake, but it was repulsed. They saw his shape, they saw his face, out of the shadows.

"You!" shouted Dennis. "Now you will pay for what you have done!" Dennis leapt forward, his strength and will combined into a furious and dangerous power of his own.

The stranger stood his ground.

"You cannot escape. All the exits are closed, all the doors are sealed - only we have the power to leave. Do not be deceived by a moment's joy, the childish ring of ecstasy, I will have my due and nothing will stop me from getting it. I demand to know where you have hidden the Spearhead!"

Two of the Priory reached out as Dennis struck at the stranger. In the same moment, PC Relish, John, Abby and Clare spread out instinctively, and circled round them.

Tyro reached into her bag. She could feel the bottle and the silent sword. She drew the latter out. Amidst the passion and confusion, the moment of terror and joy entwined - at that very turning point - she could see that what she held, though she had felt its sharp edge before, was no longer the toy sword of her childhood, the symbol of her wish to play, to emulate, but a real sword, that shone in the dull light. Its edge was razor sharp, and yet her hand had not been touched. She looked at it spellbound, as if it was part of herself, and yet a separate companion, in the darkness, brilliantly hewn from the forge of the ancient smithy, perhaps the self-same from the myths of which she had heard. She could feel at once its power, though its size was compact, and despite its razor edge, it held no danger for her. It could carve mysteries out of rock, separate illusions from the sea of doubt, cut deep into the heart of matter, and rest there where it touched the source. She was almost ashamed, as if the gift was not yet to be shared, as if those around her would not be able to see, let alone believe, even though to her it shone untouchable in the darkness. She was not afraid of its power, even its power of death.

She pointed the sword at the stranger. In a moment he was repulsed, and the figures trying to hold Dennis were repulsed.

The stranger glared, sensing futility. Some truth had been held up to him that he could not absorb, some energy beyond his powers, ancient, from the smelting of the old rocks before time, when the sun and the earth were still compacted in one tumultuous ball of irredeemable fire. He could not even look at it, knowing his powers were not enough. It seemed the others could not see. He turned to flee. The other figures held their ground before turning, giving their master a moment to escape.

The stranger stood beside the tunnel opening.

"We will return! You can never escape! We will get there first. We will have what we need, and then you shall all perish! Be warned!"

The stranger looked up at the crystal shape from where the Dark Master's form had arisen, blood dripping once more from his wounded shoulder - it was as if Tyro's sword had touched it and drawn blood - and ran out of the dome and up the marble stairs. He was followed by two of his tribe.

PC Relish, Dennis and John fought off the remaining figures, and struck one to the ground, the others fleeing in aid of their master. The struck figure let out a cry. PC Relish turned him over. He seemed to recognise the face as one who had been caught in the grounds of Mr Strangelblood, three months ago. But the face was almost unrecognisable, as if some demonic ritual had erased its human shine, a pallid torpor reflected in his eyes. PC Relish and John held him fast. There was no way he was going to escape now.

"Bring him up," called Dennis as he made his way in pursuit of the stranger, "and hold him fast. I'm going after the others. PC Relish and John can follow with their captive but the children remain with Abby and Clare."

Everyone believed that they held the upper hand. Then Abby said, "We can't be separated again. We must stick together, at least follow you, all of us, even if we can't keep up."

But Tyro, Jess, Rick and Tom turned and rushed out, in the other direction.

Tyro just had time to turn and call to her mother, "This way, Mum! Tom has a plan!"

The four of them went back the way they had come, back along the joining tunnel, back towards the tunnel that the boys had built, following all the way the marks that Jess had made. It was something that Tom had indicated by the look in his eyes and the pointing of his finger that made them do it, and believe that he knew something that they did not. He was at ease in this subterranean Kingdom. And to prove it, he didn't go in the direction that the girls had imagined. They were conscious of fear, yet were able to overcome it. And still adventure called, though the sword's edge was now sharp, belonging to a new reality. Tyro had repulsed the stranger, but she did not know the power she held. Thus they hovered between the two worlds.

Abby screamed after the children, but in vain. She tried to call Dennis back, but he had gone, and PC Relish and John were taking their prisoner up. She took hold of Clare's arm and followed as quickly as the could.

At the place where the boys' hand-crafted tunnel joined one of the main arteries, Tom stalled. But instead of going back up, he continued on, into the nether region. Jess tried to call out, but in vain, and they went on into the gloom, only lit by the light of the boy himself.

They ran on.

"Where is he taking us?" asked Tyro of Rick. Tom was ahead.

"Don't worry," said Rick. "He knows this place like the back of his hand. He knows what he's doing. He's trying to find a quicker way out to forestall the figures."

"What is this place?"

"It's part of the old cellars of the Hall itself," said Rick. "You go ahead of me, Jess!" He held out his hand.

They continued on until they reached an old brick chamber, like a cellar. Here they went down some steps at the bottom of which was what seemed like a huge track dug out of the earth in an arched tunnel. It was as if they were in another age, for here, at the entrance to the track, there appeared not just the light of the moon, but waiting for them, a carriage and four horses and a driver, ready to drive them off.

"Which way, Master Tom?" asked the driver, with a slight bow and surprising courtesy.

"Into the forest," said Tom. "To the old fort."

"Yes, Master."

And with that the four children got up into the carriage, in what was now a moonlit night, and instead of being surrounded by the dark walls of a musty tunnel, they galloped in the open air, over a high hill, towards the wood that seemed to come at them.

Tyro looked at Jess in amazement, yet taking it as natural. Rick was looking backwards while Tom was saying something to the driver, who they could not see.

Rick, next to Jess, pointed to the Hall below, their school, in the valley, bathed in light.

They saw the three figures (the stranger clutching his shoulder) cross the open expanse of fields towards the river, and pause at the water's edge before climbing into the boat.

They saw three men, Dennis, PC Relish and John, follow, and leap into the water, swimming out, by the light of the moon. The three figures in the boat fought them off until the boat turned over, but not before it had reached the other side, and the three figures ran into the wood, the same wood that led towards the old fort.

They continued to gallop. They saw the three drenched men get out of the water and continue, following as best they could. And then the trees obscured them. The beautiful moonlight-painted leaves over them brought a peace that was quite new. The carriage slowed, as they trotted along a well-worn track in the wood itself.

"Where are we?" asked Tyro of Tom.

"This is my home," said Tom, who got down off the carriage. It was the first time he had spoken to her directly. "Wait there."

Then they came to an enormous house, the same, she thought, as where Mr Strangelblood lived. It seemed older than Burnchester. But she couldn't be sure.

While they waited Tom went to the door, which was opened by a man dressed in Elizabethan clothes, and the man bowed and went back into the house while the boy was waiting. The man returned and gave the boy something, and following him, a dog. This was a huge mastiff bitch, powerful but immaculately trained. Tom returned with the dog, and told the others to descend.

"Please wait here," he said to the driver.

The four children went on down the slope, into the forest again, Tyro and Jess turning to look back at the house, about which they knew but which they had never seen, and took each other by the arm, as if seeking comfort from each other.

Tyro's eyes said it all. Never had such a mixture of bewilderment and excitement flared from them. Yet there was a tinge of sadness too.

"How come," she said in a whisper, careful not to attract Tom's attention. "How come we've never seen this house before?"

Jess stared ahead of her, and then said, "Whose is it?" And then, with a curious emphasis, "and who is Tom?"

"This makes up for the figures, and the fear," said Tyro without answering, "and," here she struck a very delicate note, for her, "and Mr Gruff. This is beyond imagining."

There was no time for further talk. As they went on into the wood, an owl appeared at the top of the tree under which they walked. It seemed to look at them for a moment, moving its head from side to side. Then it called. Tom looked up and raised his hand. Other animals appeared along the track, in seeming co-ordination, and followed them as they went further in. There were rabbits, and stoats and weasels, and hedgehogs, and a badger, and mice, and a hare (who lived in the wood at night), and voles. They seemed to have come to watch. Despite the fact that it was summer, there was a scent of spring in the air.

They came upon the place where the old fort stood. Where there had been grass tufts, over a ruin of uneven ground, there was a beautifully carved stone fort open to the sky.

In front of the fort, on the ground, lay the figure of Mr Pinchet.

The fort door was open. They went in. Inside there were figures, sitting around, morose and lifeless, in simple white robes, from another age. There were no crosses on their backs. They were unafraid.

*

When Abby and Clare reached the junction where the children had gone straight on, under Tom's guidance, they became confused. Their anger returned, and they decided to go back up the tunnel which they had descended earlier. Slowly, they climbed up into the fresh earth towards the ancient tree, calling in the muffled hollow as they went. They could not know that the children had gone another way.

When they reached the open air, and saw the light of the moon above, the children were nowhere to be seen.

"They must have gone on, instead of up. What do we do now?" asked Clare, Abby now almost in tears.

"We either go back down or try to find Dennis."

"If we try go back down we might get more lost."

"But we can't leave them."

As they turned to descend again, they caught sight of three shapes running across the open ground some distance ahead. One was bent and clutching its shoulder, and then, close by, they recognised Dennis, PC Relish and John, after them.

"Dennis!" screamed out Abby.

She shouted again. Then they both tried, but they were too far away and the three figures seemed to be drawing away.

Abby and Clare descended again into the earth, more confident, but still afraid, calling again, their voices absorbed into the emptiness. They reached the bottom of the freshly dug tunnel more quickly, and now the confidence gave way to panic.

"Tyro! Jess! Boys!!" shouted Abby, feeling her way in the darkness. "Answer me!"

"Jess," Clare called. "Girls! Boys! Are you there?! Please answer us!"

But the calls died in the hollow interior.

"We must continue. I am never going to lose sight of Tyro, or Jess for that matter, again. Damn Tyro, it's all because of her impulsive and bullish character!"

"You love her," said Clare sympathetically, "and you wouldn't have it any other way."

Abby calmed down a little.

"I suppose not," said Abby with a sigh. "She's not unlike her father in certain respects. Or me!"

"Which way now?" Clare said.

They had gone some way along the unknown passage when Abby shouted out. As if in answer to a prayer, light flooded the interior of the hall, for that is what it was. They found themselves in a wood-panelled room, close to a stone staircase.

"Where are we?" asked Clare.

"In the Hall itself, somewhere in the kitchen area, I can smell it. The tunnel we have come down must be a link of some sort."

There was a door at the far side of the room, which seemed to lead to a backroom, perhaps an exit. A larger door stood at the left-hand side of the room, which also led to a passage.

"This must be part of the original building," Clare said. "It's very old."

Abby and Clare crossed the room and left by the smaller doorway. There they found another door, which led outside. They pushed it open, and stood in the open air. They saw below them the river and the woods beyond, bathed in moonlight. But now there was no sign of anything moving.

Abby let out a piercing cry, "Where are you?"

There was a pause. And there was silence, except the sound of their tears.

In the confusion and uncertainty, PC Relish and John at first decided not to take their prisoner with them. Dennis would need help. They had to make a split-second decision, whether a live human captive, who might give them the information they needed, was more important than the possibility of catching the stranger, who had others with him and against whom Dennis would be no match. PC Relish, unhappy at missing an opportunity to catch the other 'bahstuds', took out his handcuffs and handcuffed the wounded man.

"Do not leave me alone, in this dark! Do not leave me! This place is terrible. Did you not see?" the man shouted, trying to shroud his eyes and pointing - in the air - to the imagined crystal ball and the plinth. "I shall die."

This made PC Relish smile, partly because he didn't believe it for one moment (criminals were both actors and liars), partly because he knew that his handcuffs were made of the latest and most unbreakable of all materials, and that if he were to do so it would be on account of these, not any dark forces.

"If it is haunted," said PC Relish, "You should be in good company, whoever these 'figures' are. Tell us about it when we return. A little solitude will do you the world of good."

"But you cannot escape! The doors are locked and you will get lost in the vast caverns that make up this dark region."

"In which case," said John, "we will be in good company."

"But only I can show you the way out," added the man, with an element of honesty, though his knowledge, being low down in the order, was limited.

PC Relish was getting angry at the delay, but was persuaded by John that this might be true. So he handcuffed the man to himself, and the three followed up the stairway as quickly as possible. He uncuffed him by the exit of the main hall, and left him facing the river, restless and helpless, fixed to a metal bar.

By the time Dennis had leapt into the Dean after the wounded stranger and the other figures, John and PC Relish had caught up with him and followed him into the cold water.

Dennis was a powerful swimmer, and reached the other side within a few moments of the stranger's exit. Dennis did his best to twist around the trees at the water's edge, though the stranger continued to increase his lead. Nothing would stop Dennis now. Even though the two other figures threw objects in Dennis's way, he jumped and turned as well as any wing three-quarter slicing through the opposition. PC Relish and John were dripping wet too, and together they climbed the hill, following the figures, towards the fort, keeping to the water side.

They saw Mr Pinchet, nursing a wound to the head with one hand, a repaired gun, open, in the other (his unearthly attackers intending he would use it for their ends). PC Relish, thinking that he had deliberately failed to challenge the figures, screamed out, "What the hell are you doing, Pinchet, letting the bahstuds go without stopping them?"

This seemed to have a galvanising effect on the keeper, and yet his reaction was slow, and his movements cumbersome. Nevertheless he turned and pursued the fleeing group, keeping the gun uncocked at his side, but it was not the Pinchet who they had known, and PC Relish could now see that he was wounded.

As the stranger passed the fort he glanced upwards. He saw a child, standing above him. The child stood perfectly still, watching. It was Tom. He was holding back the mastiff, while Rick, Tyro and Jess, wanted to join in the pursuit. But there were other figures behind them, the shapes from the old fort, who would not touch them. These white-robed figures were aroused by the shouts of the stranger, as he passed.

"Take them all!" cried the stranger.

"We cannot! We will not! You are not our Master!" one of them shouted back.

"Will not! Who are you to deny me?!"

The stranger looked at the child again.

"You!" he cried. For an imperceptible moment, it seemed as if the stranger paused, in what seemed a passing tremor of recognition. Could it be that he was afraid?

Tom looked expressionless, still, cautious. As if, somewhere in the past, he had learnt something against this evil semi-human. As if, somewhere in that waste, this man had played a role in the devastation of his earthly life, which had yet led him to a kind of salvation. This something seemed to give him power over the stranger, but also put him in greater danger.

In that same moment, almost imperceptibly, the stranger slightly lost his concentration and looked about him, and saw that a stillness had overcome the group, as if the stare that arose in his eyes, the darkness that he projected, enveloped the whole group in a trance. But it was the child who held him still.

"I!" said Tom.

The moment could have been the end for the stranger. Dennis was now within inches of him. He hurled himself at him with all the force of a demon. The impact was so powerful that the stranger could not but fall heavily to the ground, twisting in pain. This was no spirit.

Dennis tried to grab him by the neck, but his hands were caught in the pleats of the cloak that hung about him. The stranger wriggled and twisted, like a snake, until, as if by dark magic, he managed to slither free. The children were seemingly held back and could do nothing, though Tyro felt the sharp edge of the sword at her side and tried to point it. It did not work. PC Relish and John's path was blocked by the figures from the fort, now afraid of the stranger's power. Nevertheless, they seemed only half-willing, and PC Relish struck one of them down.

The stranger ran. He ran with the swiftness of a panther. Such was his fleet of foot, in human body, draped in inhuman robes, that he fled through the forest. Dennis, in the struggle to hold him down and from the force of his impact, had twisted his ankle and could only stumble, though he would not stop. Some other power drove him on, like a residual blessing. He pursued the stranger, swearing under his breath, fighting his pain.

A shot rang out. The stranger continued. Mr Pinchet had missed. PC Relish could not believe it. Nor could Dennis. Had it been deliberate?

Though still bleeding from the earlier wound, the stranger's need to escape was greater than the loss of blood.

But everywhere that he went, other living creatures tried to block his path. Those who had suffered from Pinchet's traps and bullets took their chance. But they were too small to be of help.

The figure who PC Relish had felled was now in combat with him.

The figures above the fort now spread out into the wood, but left the children untouched. They formed a wide arc and drifted across the wood towards the northern boundary where the stranger and Dennis were fleeing. They stood like a regiment of souls outside the woodland edge, on the adjacent field, ahead of the stranger. The stranger approached them, followed by Dennis. They let the stranger through, and closed to capture his pursuer, but they could not. As Dennis reached the line, they let him through. A sound could be heard from the wood. Galloping hooves. Out of the wood came four horses, followed by a carriage with the children inside. They charged at the white figures. The force and the still light of Tom caused havoc in their ranks, as if they were no match. The figures fled in the direction of the wood, some seeming to dissolve into the air.

Dennis leapt onto the passing carriage, which seemed to ride above the field.

The stranger was now some way ahead. He turned and

laughed, his face now a contortion of demented lines.

Two of the Priory figures moved towards their master. They carried the cloak that had been discarded, which he needed to transform. But the horses were too swift, and Dennis passed the figures who had returned to give back the cloak, only to have it snatched by Dennis himself.

But the cloak would not be held. It was itself alive and wrapped itself around the struggling Dennis, until he could not see.

Tom touched the cloak, and it fell to the ground, nothing but a pile of rags.

The stranger hurried on, now the other side of the field, fox-like, cutting back towards the river. The horses were not swift enough to turn.

The stranger continued until he reached the river and saw the boat crewed by two of his troupe.

He screamed in anger, and leapt aboard.

The carriage had now turned along the hedge against which the stranger had turned.

Tom explained that the horses could go no further. This was the limit of their domain. Beyond, they would become nothing.

"Take us to the river then, Tom," said Dennis, "and leave me there, to continue. You must return to find the others and tell them what has happened. I think Abby will know where to go. You must all go with her. Tell her 'crabs'."

At the river, Dennis saw the boat in the distance some hundred metres off, followed by two men, who he took to be John and PC Relish.

Dennis got down, and continued, thinking that he could not catch up, but calling as he went. The pain in his ankle was acute and he was exhausted. But he would not stop. He would not stop until he fell.

Tom took Rick, Tyro and Jess back to the fort. Tyro was determined to find Abby and Clare to give them the message.

The four children seemed almost to be part of one family now.

Tyro felt in her bag and found the bottle that her father had given her. It was her wishing potion. The sword this time had not worked.

Could this be the one time to use its magic? What future might require other needs? But she could not think. With the sword in one hand she broke open the bottle and drank.

At first nothing happened, much to Tyro's disappointment. But suddenly all changed. Her head became clear, the surrounding wood and trees were showered in brilliant white light, the fort seemed newly made, Jess and Rick took on a glow, and in Tom light seemed to be radiating outwards. For the first time she saw him as a real person, and for the first time she saw her friends' inner light.

"What's the matter?" asked Jess, "you don't look normal!"

"Oh I'm normal, Jess, it's you who look different!"

So the potion gives you insight, thought Tyro to herself. "Dad!" she called.

"What did you say, Tyro?" asked Jess.

"We have to find Mum and Clare!" said Tyro, "and then we have to cut off the others."

"If they follow the river, that will be easy," said Jess, logically. "All we need is a map and a car."

"If only we could catch up with them!" said Rick.

Tom said nothing. He was standing by the carriage, stroking one of the horses. Tyro turned to him.

"What do you think, Tom?"

Tom at first said nothing. It was very unusual for Tyro, or Jess, or any of the girls, in fact most of the boys for that matter, to talk to him at all, except to say something horrid. This was the second time that Tyro had ever spoken to him directly.

Tom continued to stroke the horse. She felt as if she and Tom were connected in some way, and he could feel it, but was too shy, or uncertain about how to respond. They seemed to be on the same wavelength, in same world. Most of the time they were not, Tyro had always thought. It was never good even to be seen in the same room as him, never mind be close enough to speak.

Now it was different, and she did not know why.

"One wish," said Tom, to Tyro, in an almost silent whisper, that to the others, seemed no more than a whistle, or a sigh. Even Rick felt momentarily left out, though it didn't seem to bother him, perhaps because he was talking to Jess.

Tyro was bewildered. How did he know about the potion, let alone what her father's instructions had been? She was dumbfounded, but being Tyro, was not going to let it show.

"Yes," she said. "Not much, is it?"

"Depends," said Tom, "depends on the wish," he continued, "and how effective it is."

"What would you wish?" asked Tyro, suddenly interested in what Tom might have to say, rather than in her own opinions.

Tom searched for an answer, from the inner realm of his curious history. There seemed a moment's understanding, mixed with a timeless sadness. Tom would have said that he would wish to be loved, and to love, which for him were part of the same thing. He continued to stroke the horse.

One allowed the flowering of the other. But he was not confident enough yet, and perhaps not sure enough about it, and his feelings were there in a jumble, as they always were.

"I think," he said quietly, like the rustling of the leaves in a wood, "I would wish to have the ability and opportunity to use all my faculties to the full."

This sounded like his father, from another time. It could not have been his own words, but what were? The words seemed to echo for Tyro too.

Then he added with a strange certainty, "I think you should ask to be able to fly."

Tyro loved the idea, but thought it rather childish, not something for a girl of very nearly twelve, who was now facing the world in a new way, whose imaginings were becoming a reality. She tried to touch Tom, then turned away, as if the time was not now. Seeing the others watching, she was brought back to earth.

"We must find the others, and help Dennis catch the stranger!" she shouted.

"Let's go and find Mum and call the police!"

"We can also get help from the Burnchester Arms," said Rick.

"We can all go together."

In the background they began to hear a sound. Like a purr. A hum, over the ridge in the distance.

"I will take the horses back, and join you later," said Tom. "They cannot go any further today."

Tyro looked at him as if she was sorry for something.

"Why not?" asked Jess.

But there was no answer.

Tom had begun to move off. However, before doing so he had looked up at the sky, and said to Tyro in a whisper.

"You can fly in many ways," he said, "and you can sometimes take others with you, if they are willing. And are prepared to make the sacrifice."

With that he looked down and walked off into the wood leading his favourite horse. The mastiff followed behind.

The other three stood a moment. They said nothing.

"Shall we go?" said Rick.

"Yes!" said Tyro. "Follow me."

And with that she closed her eyes, thought for a moment with all the will at her disposal, as if she was staring deep into some unknown, but friendly eyes, and opened them again. She looked about her, bent her knees a little and moved her arms forward, finding her balance. "Now," she thought.

Her feet left the ground a little, and she wobbled, trying to keep balance, but that made things worse. So she tried to go back down again, but she couldn't do that either. She wobbled more and more as she rose into the air, so much so, that by the time she was above the ground she was almost horizontal, with her eyes looking skywards and her feet kicking, as if she were swimming on her back, which in a way she was. At the same time she was screaming and laughing, in a panicky sort of way. Then she relaxed, and within moments she had righted herself, though she was now several feet above ground, and rising.

Jess and Rick stood and stared. They couldn't believe their eyes. Jess tried to catch hold of Tyro's disappearing legs, but they were almost out of reach and she just caught them before she had to let go. Tyro went up higher. Jess was getting angry as well as frightened. She was almost beside herself with not knowing what to do, so she shouted out, "Tyro! Come back down at once! What do you think you are doing?"

"Come on, Jess! Follow me!" said Tyro, doing a twist in the air so that she was now looking back down at her friends.

Jess realised she had sounded like her mother, so she calmed a little and began to plead, then to giggle. Soon she was laughing joyously!

Rick was already laughing, whilst trying to jump off the ground, but he kept falling back down.

"Come on," Tyro said, "this is best!"

"But we can't, Tyro!" said Jess.

"Try," said Tyro. "Concentrate, but don't think too hard! Imagine with it! Try, Rick!"

And try they did. To Jess's amazement, in a few seconds she also rose into the air, and so did Rick, who was now alongside her, and who had a huge smile on his face. They too did a little tumble and turned (Jess hated this), but soon righted themselves.

"Just think what my aunt would say!" screamed Rick.

"What would they say at school?" asked Jess, now feeling the cool night air on her face like the glow of early sunlight.

"Think what our parents will say!" Tyro added.

And with that they rose into the air high above the wood, and with a wonderful view of the whole landscape could see below, lit by the moon's rays, and the rays from elsewhere, whose source was as yet unknown, and they saw Abby and Clare, standing beside the car.

Tyro called out, "Mum, Clare! Look!" and they flew on towards them.

The two mothers, practical by nature and experience, were tired and desperate. They heard a call, and by chance looked up. They nearly died in their shoes! Three children, (two of their own, their very own) were flying towards them, almost as if they were angels (they knew they weren't), in the moonlight! Flying!

# 14

So strange and stressful had the night's events been, so tired were Abby and Clare, that the sight of three children flying in the air, two of their own no less, high above them, seemed quite consistent with hallucination, out of exhaustion. Even after reality dawned, and after the initial shock, they took it almost for granted - "We'll have to talk about this later," Abby said in an undertone to Tyro (who could not hear), looking up at her hovering there, whilst looking at Clare.

"Come down at once!" called Clare to them all, in a fit of panic.

"I don't know how to!" shouted Tyro, echoing the thoughts of all three, though Rick had gone off for a spin on his own, before coming back to hover by the two girls.

"Perhaps we just have to think about it hard," said Jess. And with that they closed their eyes, and thought about it hard, and within moments they were falling onto the tarmacked driveway beside Abby and Clare.

"Must have thought about it too hard," said Rick with unusual accuracy. "My feet hurt."

"What on earth do you think you are doing?" Clare said to Jess after she had landed. Abby looked askance at Tyro as if she was up to something, and hadn't quite fully registered what she had seen. Tyro let it ride, guiltily excited in her own confusion but with a clear sense of having done something that they could not.

Abby decided it best to ignore the impossibility of what was going on. There were more important matters to think about. Besides, dark figures that floated over the ground were, perhaps, no less inexplicable, so she moved on.

"Where's Dennis?" asked Abby, "and John and PC Relish?"

"Some distance downstream, trying to catch three of the figures. We must help them, or try to catch up, but I don't think we will. The figures are too quick, even though one of them is injured. Besides, Dennis, John and Mr Relish are getting tired." Tyro paused. "What are these figures, Mum?" she added.

"There's no time for that now," said Abby, more aggressively than she intended. "Did Dennis give any instructions to you Tyro, before you left them?" she asked.

"All he said was to tell you what had happened, and that you would know where to go. He mentioned crabs."

"What does that mean?" asked Clare.

"I think he means Warblersbay, where Dennis first saw the stranger," answered Abby.

"But why there? It's a long way off," asked Jess.

"He's always going on about the river, Mum, and how it links to the sea eventually - a bit like our geography teacher," said Tyro.

"And the underground streams."

"But it's an awful long way and there are a lot of streams to cross and ditches to follow before you reach the estuary."

"Besides, the figures are in a boat, and Dad and the others are on foot," said Jess.

Abby was trying to make a connection between the figures who seemed to glide and be powered by something outside them, and the flying children. The look on Tyro's face seemed to suggest a similar thought, but she turned away.

"Then I don't hold out much hope of catching them," said Abby. "This is what we'll do. Clare and I will head for the coast by car, keeping as close to the boat as possible, and, where the road crosses the river at Boxford, we'll wait and pick up

Dennis, John and PC Relish (assuming they come that way), and take them on. If we don't see them, we'll go to Warblersbay anyway. You three can come with us too. It's probably safer."

Abby knew that this was unlikely to persuade her daughter, who could, it seems, now fly, but she had to put on a brave face, against which she couldn't hide a half-smile.

In fact, this provoked an immediate reaction, but from Jess.

"We'll act as a link between Dad and the others and you, seeing as the sky is clear, and we'll be up there," she said brazenly.

Before Clare had time to reply, Abby had already spoken.

"OK, but don't go flying out of control. We'll get going."

For a moment she and Clare waited, watching the children, as if they might learn something they could later copy - though they would never have dreamed of trying anything in front of them. But seeing their embarrassment, Clare, whose attitude had also changed, pulled Abby aside and back towards the car.

In doing so, she whispered something in Abby's ear.

Left alone, the three children tried to fly again, but their feet remained firmly on the ground. Tyro closed her eyes, and concentrated hard, while the other two watched, but nothing happened. Then Jess and Rick tried too, but again nothing happened. Tyro was frustrated. Jess looked thoughtful, but did no better. Rick just kept trying.

"What now?" Tyro said, bitterly disappointed, as if Tom had let them down, and was teasing them.

"Perhaps we should...."

But before Jess had finished speaking, each felt a lightening of their toes, and then their feet, and then their legs, and then their bodies, and finally right up to the hair on their heads. It felt like a rush of wave energy, a cleansing through the whole of their body that lifted each part as it went. Their faces relaxed, and against their will they closed their eyes.

They stopped thinking hard. And then it happened again.

That strange sensation of being close to the ground but not quite touching it, safe but floating. The gap grew, and they began to wobble, and their arms began to move as if trying to hold on to something, but failing miserably. They went higher, and their arms steadied despite the tendency of their feet to fly forward and upward in a reverse summersault. At least the girls' did. Rick was in such a hurry to be off and beat them, that he seemed to be trying to ski with his arms up the imaginary slope into the sky, and he bent his knees as if he might gain advantage with an additional push. His eyes were wide open, but he went no faster. Now too the girls looked about them, in awe, fear (the second time carries with it more responsibilities), terror! But what could they do?! Then, as their bodies steadied, and their arms calmed, and they lost conscious control, they laughed. Such a beam of light from each face!

With that they were up and free and soon they were high in the air. They saw Abby and Clare waving at them from out of the car window as they sped out of the drive of Burnchester Hall. Not only could they fly, it seemed, but they could zoom, with their eyes, to look more closely at things below. None dared to ask the source of this questionable skill. None would have known the answer, then. Perhaps they never would, though Tyro had a feeling deep within her.

At first, after the initial rush, before her eyes could settle, and her body hold steady against the night air, high above the ground, Tyro's head was full of confusion. What would their friends think, when they told them that they could fly? It dawned on her that they would not be able to, without proving it, and then they would become jealous or angry, so it might be best not to tell them at all. How long would it last? What happened if they lost control, or fell from a great height and broke their bones? She thought of Icarus and his going too close to the sun and his wings melting and falling into the sea. But this was the moon, and they had no wings (that she could see anyway), yet they were flying, like good witches of old, by some hand that wanted them to know.

The exhilaration and anxiety of the flight itself very quickly took over.

Once they were up, they had to keep control of their bodies, though it seemed to come naturally to Tyro, who took the lead in keeping the right way up. She seemed just to do it, without understanding, but with intense concentration, and respect for the wind, and her imaginary wings. She was worried that the power might disappear as quickly as it had come. Jess got into difficulties because she thought too hard. It was only when she began to lose control that she seemed to steady. Rick was like a newly sprung dog, racing with all his might for a fake hare, which went round and round in circles. But he soon got the hang of it, and he steadied. Probably because he took it for granted, without understanding it at all.

They had to learn to change direction, though this seemed to follow their thoughts. This was made easier by the full moon which allowed them to see the landscape, though there were fewer stars to navigate by. Perhaps they needed a full moon and a clear sky. What would happen if there were clouds? After that they had to control their height, which seemed to follow the same pattern. So it was that they were travelling at different heights and at first at different speeds. Rick made a quick sortie over the wood and then flew back again, Tyro and Jess unintentionally flew over the school, and stared down in amazement at the roof, pointing to a helicopter landing pad there, hidden behind the tower. Tyro tried to shout to Jess, but the wind made it impossible. She had to point instead.

It seemed that they could only travel independently a certain distance, as if they needed to have a common goal or thought to focus their energies, and it was only together that they had enough to allow them to fly at all. But all this was speculation, and most of it done after they landed some time later. At this point they didn't know and probably didn't care.

They were together again, high and free. They loved every moment, even Jess, who had been so afraid!

The wind blew through their hair, tightening their clothes about their bodies. It was cold, but bearable. The hardest part was keeping their eyes open against the wind, but by holding them half-closed, they could see clearly enough. The landscape glowed beneath them, the school, the fields, roads, the river winding towards the sea (Tyro thought of the two sticks) and the woods. Wasn't that Mr Gardner's house, tucked away behind that hedge? They peered down in search of Mr Strangelblood's mansion, and Tom, and the horses, and the carriage. But it must have been obscured by the trees, for it was not visible. They forgot the figures, which they could not see either. It was hard to imagine the earlier event in the Chamber.

Tyro caught a glimpse of a small boy walking a horse into a stable and gave him a shout from afar, of course in vain. But she pointed and the others noticed him too, and tried to add theirs, and then he was obscured, until another gap appeared.

There he was again, looking up, and he waved a solitary hand, especially it seemed at Tyro.

They wanted to fly over the fields and villages and to visit the local town and to swoop down and try all sorts of daring manoeuvres that they had seen in films. In fact Rick was doing just that, but not getting very far with it. They thought of flying to London (if only they knew the way), or Scotland (even more difficult, though they all knew the Northern Star), even to visit their homes (though the thought of Aunt Patrolia's reaction - they would have to pass Rick's house - seemed to unite them against the idea). Besides, they had a task in hand and Tyro felt a responsibility, not only to Dennis and John and Mr Relish, but also to the gifts that she had been given by both her father and Tom (she assumed), and that made her concentrate. She would never have implied, of course, that Jess didn't feel any responsibilities also. Nobody was going to control Rick.

The river seemed to pass below them very quickly, Shelter

Field, Folly Ridge long left behind, the Burnchester Arms, and the fields beyond. They flew on, surprised at the distance that the figures had gone. Occasionally a car on a road below would be seen to crawl along at this very early hour, and one or two people stirring on farms, now that the harvest was getting under way. There were sheep, and cattle, and odd-looking birds, which must have been chickens scratching for dawn worms. They began to feel a little nervous once they had left the countryside that they knew, but were exhilarated enough, and awed by its beauty, to forget their fears.

The landscape reflected the moon's rays, in radiant silver beams. And yet from time to time, beneath the surface of the earth shadows lay, shapes indistinct, half-hidden, unfinished, hinted at, some like ancient figures carved deep beneath the surface, from other ages. The school itself had seemed like that, it seemed to be the armour of a shape whose body lay prostrate beneath the ground. There were other shapes, along the river shallows, under the summer fields, where the crops had been cut: the ruins of old monasteries, adjacent to houses in villages. And then they saw the three figures of the Priory, moving along the water in their boat, the red sword-crosses against the black cloaks in the silver sheen, oblivious it seemed to those above, and the three men, struggling in pursuit. They thought harder and tried to increase their speed.

It seemed as if they could only control their flight so far, and were guided by some other energy, which was outside their knowledge or power.

The other anxiety, and a fearful one, was that it must be nearing dawn and that they would lose their powers with the oncoming light. The silver moonlight was just at moments augmented by the glow of a distant golden light, as if a hand from over the horizon - a hand extended on an arm of light - was trying to touch the moon's rays and be hauled up by them. Thus the sun sought help from the moon for its resurrection and the life.

Tyro tried to point to the emerging dawn, but a cloud would pass and they were safe again.

"Supposing we're seen?" said Jess to Tyro as she flew close by her. "My hands are cold!"

"I guess we have to cross that bridge when we come to it," Tyro replied, not quite appreciating the effect that seeing three figures flying high in the air, like witches, might have.

"I'm more worried about the dawn and falling to earth with a crash," she said, but added (Rick was out of earshot) "I guess we have to be discreet about it in future and only fly when nobody's looking!"

"Look! There! Down there, just by that bridge!" shouted Rick.

They looked down and saw three men still running beside the bank, but struggling here in the weedy soggy earth. A heron shot up into the air as one of them passed. They were all exhausted and dripping with sweat.

Some way ahead, the boat skimmed along the water, now on a wider stretch of river, beyond the bridge, which linked to another smaller ditch, forming a short cut to the main river leading to the sea.

"If they take the ditch route," said Jess, "there's no way Mum and Abby can catch them. We could, but what can we do?"

"If they follow by the main stream, they have a chance."

"I wonder if they can see us?" said Tyro. "I mean the stranger and his crew." She assumed that Dennis, John and PC Relish would be able to, just as their mothers had. The idea of Mr Relish, looking up at them as they descended to earth, made her laugh.

The idea that the figures might not see them got Jess thinking, but she kept the thoughts to herself for another time. The figures would not see them, she felt sure.

"I'm going on," said Rick. "You two go down."

Without a further word, Tyro and Jess began to descend.

As they did, a car passed on the road, and stopped on the

bridge. There was a shouting, and screaming as Abby pointed skywards. The three tired men looked round, and saw two shapes coming out of the sky at the same time.

"Not more of the bahstuds!" said PC Relish, thinking it was more hooded figures.

"Tyro! Is that you? What on earth.... I mean, in Heaven, I mean in sky, are you two doing up there?" said Dennis, almost lost for words.

He was too tired to say any more.

"How are you doing, I mean getting... I mean did you get up there?" added the stuttering John, "Jess?"

John then simply looked at the girls and said, "Jess! Is that really you?"

There was no time for explanations.

"Get in quick, if we're to catch up with them!" shouted Abby as she leapt out of the car and tried to push the three men into the back, all three sodden and tired but still willing.

"Explanations later!" she added.

"See you later, Dad!" called Jess rather shyly, and nearly falling over herself in an airborne somersault.

With that, long before reaching the ground, the two girls rose up again and continued on, though they kept lower this time, close to the tops of the trees.

They pointed at Rick up ahead.

The sight of PC Relish staring out of the window of the car into the open summer sky, completely drained, made them all laugh. Not more than he did himself. For there was magic in the air that was suppressing the dark powers and had transformed everything, even though the figures might escape and darkness had been revealed. Where had it come from? For the moment they felt confident that it could be handled.

Inside the car which Abby was driving, PC Relish reminded his fellow passengers that he had alerted his colleagues, who would no doubt be taking action now, not having heard from him for some hours. He could not anticipate the response but he suspected it would be thorough.

In the background the hum grew and grew into a steady sound. Then a second, not dissimilar sound joined it, and the two became fused into a sort of nocturnal growl.

"To the sea!" said Dennis, barely able to keep himself awake, now that his body could rest, though his energy began to return with the help that had come to hand. He looked at Abby and Clare, and said, while giving her a gentle pat on the shoulder,

"What took you so long?"

"Why were you so slow?" retorted Abby.

"We'll hear everything about everything later," he continued. "Thanks for making it just in time, I don't know how much longer I could have run. It was these guys who helped me."

He turned to his friends, "Keep our eyes open. John, you that side; Mr Relish (it was Mr Relish now), out of the back. I'll keep an eye out this side."

"We have to be careful they don't double back, or turn sideways," John said. "If they abandon the boat, or go up one of the many creeks, we'll never find them. They could disappear altogether."

"I don't think they'll do that," said Dennis, "I think they're going to head for the beach, but you're right, we have to be careful. They came from nowhere, and they may well return to a place unknown to any of us. The forces of the dark tend to disappear at the sight of dawn, or change shape."

"I don't think they've got a choice," added Abby, "now that we have airborne assistance!"

"Airborne assistance can't see through trees, or underground. The river is surrounded by reeds and old tracks and shacks left by farmers in the past. They could disappear very easily. The area is spread with bunkers, even bomb shelters, where they could hide, or go to ground. There are many underground links that remain unknown."

As the car sped along, all eyes were on the fields and ditches on either side of the road. At times what seemed like shadows shifted in the undergrowth as they looked, but nothing substantial enough to make them pause. Abby held her foot as hard as she could on the accelerator. Occasionally a pair of eyes would look up, and then look down again, as if they were not quite prepared to accept what they had seen. What would you do? They all wanted to ask the same question, but it seemed inappropriate in view of their race against time, and the hooded crew who must be stopped. But then curiosity got the better of one of them.

"How on earth, dare I ask, are they able to," John could barely speak the word, it seemed so extraordinary, "fly?"

It seemed as if each person was about to react, whilst looking out into the growing dawn light. But each held his breath, not quite certain what to say. Dennis had wanted to comment from his experience of mental training, but it didn't quite seem the same, allowing your mind the freedom to roam, directed if you were an adept, even for your spirit, if you believed in it, to leave your body, and journey across the spheres. But physically to fly was quite beyond him. It was almost as if he was being tricked into belief, despite apparent substantiation. This reminded him of something, but he said nothing about that! He knew there might be a connection, but he was not ready for it, and focused on the search for the figures, who were out of sight. It was Clare who responded to her husband, touching his hand with some uncertainty, as if the idea might taint.

"Later," she said gently, "we've got a job in hand." And then she added, "I don't know how to believe it either."

"How dangerous are these figures?" asked Clare, bewildered and angry, at the cause of robbery, violence and possible death.

"It depends who is responsible for the events of tonight, most importantly the attack on Mr Gruff," Dennis said. "There seem to be different groups, working under the same overall Master, unless that too is a figure of our imagination. But some may be independent, using the dark as a cover for their own designs. I believe that is the case of the group we're following, which I take to be the Priory. That is why we must catch them, though I don't hold out much hope. Without direct contact with the leader - who we call the stranger - despite our captive back at the Hall, we will remain as ignorant as if they hadn't appeared at all. I am sure it is they who attacked Mr Gruff."

Dennis continued.

"They are dangerous because of their violence, their allegiance, and because of their powers, but with the coming dawn, and the number of people aware of their presence" - to this, PC Relish nodded - "they can't afford to get too engaged with us, until they have found what they are looking for, the Spearhead. Our main concern is that they disappear altogether. Though how they abandon their bodies is beyond me. They are supposedly human after all!"

"Leave their bodies?" asked Clare, "what do you mean?"

"They're human, but also possessed by evil, and in order to disappear, the dark spirit must leave the human body to which it has become attached."

"And then they die? The human body I mean?" asked Abby.

This was all too much for PC Relish.

"I could do with a good breakfast," he said. "Got to keep body and soul together."

The others glanced at each other.

The change of subject focused their minds on the job in hand.

Abby continued to race along the small roads which led towards the sea, following as closely as possible the line or presumed line of the stream. When she came to the main road to the sea, she put her foot down hard.

The moonlit landscape flew past, farms, meadows, barley fields, mixed woods and hedges, and now a few scattered houses as they passed through a village. To keep the men awake, the windows were wide open, the night air filling the space immaculately. The sky seemed like the dome of a great cathedral.

Behind them appeared the flashing of a blue light, the car racing up to them at full speed. It was followed by two others.

As one of the police cars began to overtake Abby, with the window down, a police constable shouted a few words, in a friendly tone.

The two cars raced side by side on the open road, the wind howling between them, as each held steady, while Abby wound her window down too.

"Good evening, Ma'am," said the driver of the police car, probably doing about 75 miles per hour, "everything OK?"

"Perfectly," said Abby in disbelief (more so, even, than seeing flying children), keeping her eyes on the road. The thought of the flying children made her shudder. Supposing the policemen had seen them? They might have thought they had seen a UFO! But their eyes had clearly not strayed too far upward.

"PC Relish, here for your support," said the officer sitting in the passenger seat of the police car. "Full briefing required."

"Evening, Bob," said the Relish, quite content it seemed to continue the conversation in flight, so to speak. "No time for a full report, alas. Suggest you go on ahead and make for the coast road. Keep an eye out for the three men - figures I should say. They may go across the fields, though they are currently on the water. We expect them to head for the harbour at Southwold. Oh, yes. Be a bit careful, they have the ability to change shape and disappear."

PC Relish said this with a degree of subtlety to which he was not used, to make his colleagues know that they were not dealing with ordinary mortals, though the effect wasn't perhaps as anticipated.

"Like all criminals," said the man called Bob. "See you at the harbour. We'll be careful, don't worry. We're also armed and the army's on full alert too, expect some action on the beaches.

We'll get them!"

The capture of the figures was more significant than Abby or Clare had realised. Nobody had mentioned the military before. Nobody had mentioned guns.

Abby's car sped on, the three police vehicles overtaking them.

Rick, Tyro and Jess were now flying low over the fields adjacent to the estuary on the approach to Warblersbay church. They had kept the three figures in sight, but were finding difficulty keeping sufficiently low not to be seen, and sufficiently high to have a good view. It seemed as if their power was fading. This meant that from time to time they lost the figures. The landscape was sandy and bare, with the occasional belt of pines, and scattered farm buildings leading down to the water's edge. The tide was high.

As they approached the coast, the problem grew. At the first light of the rising sun, they seemed to stall, and begin their descent to earth. Then a cloud would pass and their powers would be restored, only to fail again as the cloud passed. They were going to have to land.

It was that magnificent time when the world begins its regular resurrection, and the blackbirds and thrushes begin their ritual chorus - against the mellower tones of the secretive nightingale.

The three figures had taken the short cut onto the main river, and had now moored beside a belt of trees on the estuarine flats that led to the harbour where the Neptune was waiting.

Tyro, Jess and Rick had managed to overtake the figures and land on an open patch of ground beyond the wood where they had stopped. They had run to the nearest ditch to watch.

The figures appeared. However, they did not take the path that led to the harbour, as was expected, but, it seemed, straight across farmland in the direction of the sea.

"Shall we follow them or warn the others?" whispered Tyro when she saw what was happening.

"You and Jess go and tell them, I'll follow the figures," said Rick.

"I think we should all follow," said Jess.

"But they have to be told," said Rick. "You two girls should stick together. I don't mind which, but we can't hang around. These figures might disappear from right under our eyes."

"OK, we'll follow them, and you go to the harbour, Rick, to meet Dennis and everyone," said Tyro, wanting to see the capture of these things first-hand.

Rick set off along the path that followed the estuary.

The girls ran over the rough heathery ground towards the sea. At first the going was easy, the low tufts of heather interspersed with open sand made for a clear run, but then the heather became thicker, and there were patches of gorse, which also blocked their view from time to time. They managed to keep in sight of the figures, one of whom, on occasion, turned around, apparently keeping watch in case anything followed.

Even though the net was closing in on them, and Dennis and the others were on their way, if not already at the harbour, the girls were still wary, not easily forgetting the events of the night, for all its dreamlike distance. The hideous realisation that they might have been locked underground and kept captive and perhaps even have died at the hands of these demonic figures - as Mr Gruff might do - made them doubly sure not to get too close. Even her newly metal sword, Tyro felt would not be enough. At the same time, Jess now urged Tyro on, to get as close as possible. This change didn't go unnoticed by Tyro. Nothing would prevent them from seeing the events to their conclusion. They felt sure that the figures would be captured. It was only a matter of time.

Their tiredness soon took over, and their feet became heavy, as they crossed the heath in the emerging light. Ahead the three figures were now out of sight, so they had to guess the general direction, hoping that the figures wouldn't suddenly turn, like foxes chased. The figures were now visible again, their black cloaks waving in the wind.

Intermingled with the sound of the crashing waves, and the wind, and the occasional cry of the gulls, another sound had grown up, the hum that had run in the background, now growing into a throb, like the rattle of an engine.

The girls crossed a road and onto more heather.

"There!" said Tyro, pointing ahead. The two girls looked at the belt of pine trees ahead of them, but could not make out for certain whether it was the trees or the figures which moved.

The throb grew louder. There was, as before, another hum in the distance. The throb became a rattling engine. The girls turned, and saw, to their amazement, something hurtling across at them from the road. It was a strange shape. A Vehicle. No! A tractor!!

"The General!" screamed Jess.

Both girls jumped for joy and danced around, hugging each other, even though they were a little older.

Sure enough the General was steaming over the heath, brushing aside the heather and gorse bushes, and moving towards them at speed. The girls watched in amazement as the General, thrusting fumes into the air, as if panting for breath (or coughing for lack of it), approached, with his lieutenant in the cockpit. The General came up and pulled up alongside, the noise almost deafening. There was Luke, jumping down to the ground,

"All aboard!"

"Luke," said Tyro, "what are *you* doing here?"

"Questions later," said Luke, "answers later still. Get up! Others've gone on."

The girls climbed aboard.

Luke put his foot down and the tractor leapt forward, throwing the girls almost out of the back.

"Hold on tight! The General, starving. Breakfast at dawn, I promised him! But not before the job is done!"

From this height they could see the land a long way ahead, even through the belt of trees which Luke was having to negotiate.

"You know the way!" shouted Tyro to Luke. "How come?"

The answer appeared in front of their eyes, if intermittently, leaping and bounding over the heather, and running like a furious ferret, as he had never run before. The three figures were in the distance, but the gap was closing, as he gave chase. Yes, Rompy, dear old Rompy, leaping like a salmon from water and rushing with all his might towards the salt-smelling sea. He turned and barked, as if to say "hello!", and went on again.

The girls leapt up! The General steamed forwards. Luke watched the land ahead for any ditches or dips, to make for the smoothest run possible.

They could see the sea ahead. They were approaching the cliffs at Dunemoor.

The three figures could be seen going over the edge, as the General closed the gap.

Once the tractor reached the edge of the cliff, Luke turned the General off, and there was the immediate sound of the wind, and the other hum emerging to the north.

Ahead they could see the water, and now it was below them as they reached the cliff edge. A small stretch of beach lay between the bottom of the cliff and the sea. The three cloaked figures were wading out in the water. There was the boat, some distance offshore, to which they were heading.

They could see a police car speeding along the sand from the north. In the sky, a huge object seemed to appear in the growing dawn. It hovered above the sand and then began its descent. The vibrating throb of the helicopter purred loud as the girls and Luke, led by Rompy, tried to descend the perilous steps cut into the side of the cliff-face to the beach. The sand blew into their faces as they approached the helicopter, whose door was now open, just as the police car arrived.

Out to sea the three figures had reached the Neptune.

The boat moved off at speed. A police launch appeared from the north, and gave chase.

From the police cars, Dennis, PC Relish, John, Abby and Clare came out, as well as three armed policemen who ran to the shore and took up position ready to fire at the boat as it sped away. Mr Gatherin was with them.

From the helicopter several people appeared, two dressed in army uniform, and five who Tyro recognised immediately. Mr Rummage, Mrs Rummage, Mr Baxter, Ms Peverell, and Rick! They made their way onto the beach, with the light of the sun coming up over the horizon ahead of them. The helicopter engine stopped, and again the wind called in the July morning.

Rick came over to the girls and gave them both a hug.

Along the beach stood all the players, Tyro now with Abby and Dennis, beside Clare, Jess, John and Rick. Mr Gatherin was next to PC Relish who was giving instructions to the other officers whilst looking through binoculars out to sea. Tyro thought of Tom.

Mr Rummage stood with Jenny, Mr Baxter, Ms Peverell and the two army personnel.

They watched the police launch circle and approach the Neptune.

Over the hailer, thrown by the easterly wind, they heard, in crackled tones, the words,

"Give yourselves up, or we will board!"

The figures could no longer be seen, and the Neptune sped on. The warning was given again, but to no avail. Finally after the third warning, the launch moved in.

The people on the beach watched.

The boat drew alongside in tumbling waves. Now they were tied up.

Now they would have them.

The group along the beach watched expectantly, in silence, for the prey to be apprehended at last.

They waited and waited. No sound from the police launch.

Silence.

And then, over the radio, they could hear the words,

"Nothing, Sir. Empty. The vessel is empty. There is nobody aboard."

The line of people stood for a moment looking out to sea, and then the light of the sun seemed to shake them into movement, and they turned to each other, all of them wondering where the figures had gone.

The Neptune clung to the police launch. An empty shell. The sun was now up. The figures had disappeared. The insignia of the Priory clear in the morning light.

# 15

Tyro held her breath, pushed her arms forwards, swung them back and kicked her legs. It was difficult to keep her body down, the air in her lungs and her natural buoyancy seemed to want to draw her up to the surface, just as she wanted to remain below. She scanned the sea bed, only a couple of metres beneath her, by moving her eyes from side to side, following the sand, but now, entering an area of rough, sponge-like rock, dotted with anemones, and, here and there, touched with coloured fish. Just occasionally it reminded her of flying, though that experience had not been repeated. She sometimes wondered whether it had happened at all. And yet she imagined it would be repeated, when the moment was right, and she was ready. Could she ever create it at will?

After a while, breath bursting from out of her, she allowed her body to rise to the surface, then lifted her head into the warm air, and let her feet and legs drop whilst she trod water (like squashing crushed grapes), throwing her head about, to shake out some of the drops, and to let her hair fall in the sun. She could hear the voices of other children (and adults), playing in the water, on the beach. Occasionally the purr of a motor boat would emerge and fall away, and from time to time, high in the air, a skydiver glided effortlessly on the warm upward currents that rose to the tops of the hills over the bay. Sometimes you would mistake them for birds.

From where she was she could see the house where they were staying not far away, a few metres from the beach, it moved up and down, and in front of it, a small group of people, who had settled in this tranquil bay, and beyond the small village, that led up the the foothills of what would become, step by step, the Pyrennees. The family had, after all, come to France.

Tyro's back was as brown as it was going to get - she was unhappy with that. Some distance off, further out to sea, towards a rocky promontory that protected the bay from the larger waves, Jess, dear Jess, was climbing out of the water, and making her way up the rock to a place some three or four metres above the water where there was a natural platform. Here she stood up, and got ready to dive. Next to her was a dog, with a wagging tail.

"Watch me, Tyro!" Jess screamed. Tyro waved.

And in Jess went, followed by Rompy. Having been here for nearly a week, Jess's bellyflops were now more graceful near-dives. She had worked the technique out, after drawing the way it should be done on a piece of paper. Tyro, a good swimmer, was better at diving, perhaps because she thought about it less. She had changed since the beginning of the holiday. She had grown to listen a bit more, and to be a better friend, giving more credit to Jess for her intelligence and knowledge than she had only a few weeks earlier, before the events at Burnchester Hall, to which, she couldn't believe, they would be returning in a couple of weeks, for the start of a new school year.

Her feelings were mixed. One the one hand she wanted to allow recent events to lie low in her mind, and gestate while she worked them through, as her mother would say. On the other, she was more determined than ever to continue the quest that had begun by following a scent; to continue to explore the different strands in the mystery that had emerged before and after that fateful night. Her experiences had galvanised in her something ill-defined but connected with the transformation of her sword, and the memories of her father. The sword had begun to remind her of a crucifix, so she had tried hanging it about her neck occasionally, but not visibly. Her rejection of religion, which she equated with going to church (her mother had tried on many occasions to get her to accompany her, mostly in vain), was tempered by an arcane respect for ancient symbols. Her logic was her own.

There were many elements in the story (for that is what it felt like), some she had become aware of and had answers to, others which were still hidden from her, and to which she did not. What was the underground domain beneath the school? She now had a better idea, but only a first glimpse. The Domed Chamber, for instance, was a place of ancient ritual, but with modern resonance, of ceremony, of power and magic. She felt a shudder as she thought of it. Some dark image walked into her mind, as if on cue, to remind her of the dragon she must finally destroy. A central instrument in the creation of energy, good or evil, a weapon in the delivery of war. How far did the domain stretch? She didn't know, but nor it seems did anybody, such were the ruined and unmapped caverns leading off from the known branches and paths. Who or what were the strange beings, and who was controlling them? There were many theories. You cannot fight mere shadows, and be hurt (as Mr Gruff had been, and Dennis in a smaller way), yet some seemed ethereal, ghostly, from other worlds, to which she felt even Tom seemed to belong, and yet from which he was protected. One group of figures had seemed to draw others, though they were not obviously connected. How had Mr Rummage countered the emergent Figure of Darkness (for though she was not conscious, such a figure of sorts inhabited her memory, and had arisen from its ancient open grave) from so distant a place - so she had learnt from her mother much later - on a lonely island, the Island, off the mainland of Scotland? That was a mystery of divine telling. What had happened to Mr Gruff - and Mrs Limpet, who, she was now aware, had been taken to hospital where she had been admitted for a 'rest'? What had happened to them all when they had been underground, in a trance-like state, under the spell of a terrible force, present, but not visible to her conscious mind? What was her role in this? What was that dark energy, and why was it that, even now, in the glorious respite of the sunshine and sea, did she feel compelled to meet it, as if drawn to some ancient sacrifice?

Such questions came to her from time to time, like waves breaking on a desert shore, calm, if confused, but inescapable. Sometimes they came in dreams, connected with images of her mother and father, who seemed to be trying to guide her away from that path. She had discussed the events with Jess and Rick and of course her mother and Dennis (and Clare and John), and they had all had a 'de-briefing' with Mr Rummage, who had explained some things. This had been held in a private room at the Burnchester Arms, out of hours, in the presence of Mr Gatherin and PC Relish, with the addition of three new faces - one from the Ministry of Defence, another from the police, a colleague of PC Relish's. Both had been on the beach at Dunemoor. Mr Baxter had been invited, recently back from his trip to France with Ms Peverell (she smiled at Jess and raised her eyebrows when she heard) along with a man called Mr Brock. The Reverend Sandals had not been there, though Tyro took it that he had been informed of everything that had happened, given the 'break-ins' at the churches.

There was a splash. It was Rick.

M. le Petit, on that day, had done everybody proud with coffee and tea and cake ("Incroyable!" he said of it himself as he entered from the kitchen on tiptoe holding the plate aloft, "a cake à l'anglaise"), but adding some petits fours of his own design, flavoured with fruits from the market at Sleepsake.

Mr Rummage had explained something of the history of the

underground 'kingdom' (he also called it 'queendom'), where spies and others had been initiated in certain techniques. The place was an ancient site of worship and divination, or some of it was, particularly the Domed Chamber. It was perhaps older than Stonehenge. Some of the rocks and the arched roof had been constructed from the oldest rocks in the world, transported thousands of years ago, from the north. One rock, indeed, had not been identified. The underground warren's extent had never been fully explored, so many tunnels and arteries having been blocked or having collapsed into dangerous disrepair. Others were not known about at all. The man from the Ministry of Defence had provided some maps, but they were incomplete.

The techniques developed concentrated on mental powers: how to tap the power within each of us and ally it to the entrapped primordial energy of the stones around the Dome, and elsewhere, in order to fuse the two, and focus them in the theatre of war. This ancient art was known to a few and had to be treated with enormous care and skill. In the wrong hands, and wrongly used, the power would be uncontrollable, and would result in the loss of civilisation to the power of dark. It would also result in the destruction of individuals who tampered with these forces, or became prey to them. The Spearhead, which was lost, gave vital meaning to this energy, and was the element most needed to complete the armoury. The time had come, they were told, to resurrect these ancient skills and begin training anew, for the power of dark was abroad once more, and in a quest for domination, nothing would stand in its way. It was essential to find the Spearhead.

There were those from the other side who knew the techniques, though the places where they could be learned or practised were still guarded, mostly, by the forces of good, of which the Dome beneath the Hall was one. The dark forces often had to operate in secret, underground, in small groups or societies, sometimes with a different purpose from the one they portrayed to the world. The forces of good needed also to be aware of and be able to utilise selectively even the dark power, in order to transmute it into light.

Tyro had heard all of these things from Mr Rummage, and Mr Baxter. The words were clear, but the meaning was often not. She had heard but not fully understood.

She remembered that the power could be used for good or evil. Evil forces sought to use power, of any sort, for their own ends, leading to despotism and death. There had been a time when evil seemed to be gaining the upper hand, but it had been eventually overcome, though the battle is never ending. Burnchester Hall (and the Domed Chamber) had provided some of the vital energy that made victory possible. Here, as elsewhere, they tried to counter it, by combating the Dark Lord, known as the Dark Master. They were told how this ancient battle was waged by the true Church, whose purpose was to reveal and confirm the triumph of light against the dark, in the message of the Gospels, through Jesus, but not only there. For there was a faith and a truth within each great religion which stood guard against the dark of all humanity. The Dark Master had tried to rule the world, and was always ready to exploit the weak, or chaos, so that the seeds of darkness could flourish in the attempt to prevail.

The ability to develop these powers was made easier by the use of symbols, as the history of religion showed, through its rich traditions of paintings, and sculpture, sometimes underscored by the older images from the pre-Christian era. For not all that had been known before was bad. So it was that the best of the so-called pagan was integrated into the Christian tradition. The Spearhead was one of the most powerful symbols. It was literally and symbolically capable of great force, in the story it invoked and the inspiration it generated. The combination was indestructible, and it was this that was constantly sought, just as it was this was was always in need of being defended.

The Priory and others, insignificant perhaps in themselves, would always try to exploit opportunities, and there were times, conjunctions, when the chances of triumph were more likely, and the outcomes potentially more devastating.

One of these was now. The Church had a great weakness. It had, at times in its history, become corrupted, in terms of the power it wielded and, some believed, in the message that it delivered, sometimes too removed for the needs of people, whose basic spirituality was never in doubt. The Church had also created many myths, and was vulnerable to the truth being exposed, to its own mask being revealed. Now, of course, people were aware of so much more than they had been in the past, and the threat of being undermined by some secret knowledge becoming public today, was less likely than it might have been in an earlier age. Though some people believed it would still lead to the Church's demise, and give new opportunity to those who sought power for their own ends, which could come about by the exploitation of any weakness.

Symbols had the ability to inspire and galvanise people into action beyond their normal selves. Symbols, allied to other capabilities, technical, psychological and personal, were still of huge importance. And these, though now weakened, were still recoverable, according to some.

The Spearhead of Destiny had been mentioned. This struck a deep chord in Tyro, though she had no knowledge why. It reverberated, as words sometimes do, touching some insight, some future possibility, some echo of meaning, in advance of its creation, in anticipation of its fulfilment. Why had her sword been transformed now? It also struck a chord in Rick who went out and bought (they had all been given a small reward for their work) a metal detector. He set off immediately, searching the grounds of the school by day and night, despite being warned off by Mr Rummage. He kept it in the tunnel which he and Tom had built.

The most important thing that Mr Rummage had said, as far as Tyro was concerned, was that they were now all in it together, and that he would ask them to be discreet, knowing that stories were slipping out, and would continue to do so, and that these would no doubt grow. Tyro, Jess, and Rick (with Tom, should he agree - he had gone away somewhere when they had discussed it), had thought of forming a club, by invitation only, sworn to secrecy, and to help each other. But they did not want to prevent anyone from joining for no good reason, so if they did, she hoped, it would be open to anyone who was willing and true. Tyro realised that this was a bit immature, but it was, in this sense only a disguise, a cover for the bigger task. Yet she knew that the game was also real, for she was drawn to the dark force, just as Mrs Limpet had been (as they were told), but would only admit this to herself. Her destiny was also connected with this fact, drawn forward by impulses beyond her, yet herself, some negative, from which she could grow and have the light revealed to her, and reveal the light to itself.

At the 'de-briefing', each had been asked to tell the assembled group what had happened in every detail. At first this had been fun, a chance to show their important part in the story, but they were asked to repeat it over and over again, and it had begun to get boring. Tyro became intolerant when she heard how some, even slight, details were recorded differently by others, including Jess, from her own. She wanted the telling and the events to be on her terms, not theirs. But it was for Mr Baxter's report, Mr Rummage had said (he would also write one of his own), and it was important to get everyone's perspective, as each might have something to offer that was unique and valuable. Certain details might only become important looking back, when others had been added to them, Mr Baxter had said, and when he reminded the girls that it was no different really from giving different opinions in class, Tyro relaxed a little. Mr Baxter was going to bring all the strands together, all the stories, so that they might read, look at the different bits to see whether a pattern would emerge, that could help them prepare for the next stage, for that there would be one, there was no doubt. And the stakes were increasing all the time.

During the periods of repeated questioning, Tyro started to imagine she could fly again. It was extraordinary that flying was the one thing they had said nothing about, neither she nor any of the adults who had observed it. This was so far outside the understanding (and fragile wariness) of those present to believe that it had actually happened. It was as if it was too unbelievable to discuss, and had to be kept in reserve, for another time. The girls felt guilty too. What made them able to fly and no-one else, apart from Rick? Did it make them witches? And Rick? No way, thought Tyro, unless it was perhaps good ones. Why were the adults so defensive?

For her part, Abby didn't like the fact that everything was being recorded, so Mr Rummage turned the tape off, and then they could all relax, and were free from the constraints of thinking they might say something stupid or wrong.

There had been even more questions, especially from the men from the Ministry and the police, but very few answers, and those not very satisfactory. Mr Rummage had informed them that there was to be an important increase in security at the school, though the details were still being worked out, and some would remain secret. He said that they were sure there would be other attacks, though when and in what form he had no idea. He felt - and here the man from the Ministry supported him - that it was important that the school be kept open (Tyro had not imagined otherwise, and looked at Jess as if to say, "What's he talking about?"), as long as the safety of the children remained paramount (more looks from Tyro) - here Abby's intervention was pre-empted. But he could not guarantee it, Mr Rummage continued, though he would do his utmost to do so. This led to a very considerable and heated debate, led by Abby, who was only reassured by virtue of the fact that Mr Rummage had two children at the school, and was as protective of them as she and other parents were of theirs. After this, the man from the Ministry of Defence gave them a brief history of the tunnels (under pressure, it should be added), and the training of the agents, though he was not as forthcoming as they had hoped. Mr Rummage finished by saying that the whole area would be thoroughly searched, by forensic as well as general police staff, particularly around points of major contact, most notably Mr Gruff's attack, and the church towers. He would do his best to seek Mr Strangelblood's co-operation (he was being contacted), with the police's authority, but as he was so often away, he wasn't hopeful, and his present whereabouts were not known. Mr Gruff's condition was being closely observed, and Mr Pinchet had agreed to be examined by the same medical team. His final remarks were affirmative and cautious, but also grateful. Lastly he asked Mr Baxter if he would reserve some details of his researches in France for a later date.

At this point the young people had left and the older people remained for a further hour, talking into the evening, while Tyro, Jess and Rick walked along the river bank with Rompy (who had been asleep by the fireplace in the main bar), to Shelter Field, where Tyro and Jess had sat earlier in the holiday after they had run from Mr Gruff and Titan, and seen their sticks in the water. When they reached the field, Jess wondered aloud - not something Jess did very often - whether the sticks had reached the sea.

The children were not afraid to revisit any of the places, thinking that they could not suffer from anything worse than they had survived and that, well, the holiday adventure had now turned into history, and could start afresh from a different point. The two girls and Rick were ready for anything. Anything at all. Besides, they were not really children anymore.

\*

Abby called from a deckchair by the water's edge.

"Tyro! Tyro! Come in now, you've been in too long! Come and lie in the sun! And call the others!"

Tyro woke from her reverie - how strange that thoughts seem not to have the same timescale as ordinary things and events, they could all be there together, lots of them and make sense at once, like the stars in the sky, unlike most school work which was often so confusing, though supposedly logical. She didn't believe much in logic, though Jess was doing her best to change her mind. Abby reminded her of the school holiday project she had not done. "Oh no!" Tyro sighed, and then thought of the reading she was supposed to do. Things didn't have order, until there had been chaos first, she thought. That's it. Too many ordered things hadn't been allowed to be chaotic first which is why they didn't work. No system could be imposed before its time, nor yet be recognised before it had emerged. No system was sufficient. Yet chaos could not be allowed to rule. Was this true also of belief? Then she wondered whether ideas lived, beside normal things like eating and swimming, and whether, if you had several ideas at once, they lived altogether, in different places, both separate but interconnected, if only you could find the link. And did this apply to time? If she thought something, it seemed to fill space, as Blake had said. It was one of Mr Baxter's favourite phrases. She had remembered that.

Tyro shouted, "Jess! Rick! We've got to go in! Rompy!"

And with that she dived again and made towards the others, her goggles glued to the marvellous world below, so like the stars and the galaxy, as she imagined them.

And as she watched, an octopus wriggled from under a rock. Other thoughts came to her. She addressed them to the octopus, in her mind.

How would she cope with the new term? How much would

the rumour-mill of school, already potent with tales from the Unusual Cheesepeakes and ghosts and dark deeds, discover and distort, and how would she suffer or be mythologised by it? So many people had been involved, so many strands of the local community, with connections beyond it, that stories had already begun to circulate, strictly though Mr Rummage, and the police, and even the Ministry of Defence, had given instructions to play things down. But unexplained church break-ins; wounded and terrified staff (Mr Gruff had made a recovery, though how full was yet to be seen; Mrs Limpet had had a breakdown and was still in hospital; strangers, and cloaked figures, some wraithlike, others 'real'; break-ins at the library and the experiences in underground caverns; all these things had, in some form or other, been translated into stories of the demonic, sometimes the miraculous, against which the forces of good, in the forms of Mr Rummage and them of course, had prevailed. She became angry.

The octopus continued to wriggle.

*

Before the party had set off for France, Mr Baxter, in Cambridge, had sat at his desk. Beside him two masks, one of Anger, the other, a new one, of Laughter. In front of him, a report, which he had recently completed and was about to send out to Mr Rummage, and to all those who had been at the Arms meeting.

He had not written 'strictly confidential' on the top, as that was obvious, and would draw attention to itself. But he was pleased enough to offer himself a glass of beer, before putting the copies in the post. On second thoughts he decided to deliver them himself. He did not want them to fall into the wrong hands, especially as some of it was only speculation. He had called the report: 'Background to and a summary of the evidence concerning events at and around Burnchester Hall, on the evening and night of the .....July: Full Moon.' Yes, he would leave 'Full Moon', and laughed. He would follow with the report about France.

*

The rumour-mill. Fact and fiction. Masks. That Mr Pinchet, who was believed by himself to have made a full recovery from the bite that he had suffered, should be the instigator of such tales, in the summer evenings at the bar of the Burnchester Arms by the river Dean, may have accounted for their dubious accuracy, but the fact that Mr Gatherin (still smarting over the fake money) and M. Le Petit ignored, denied or acknowledged elements of his stories, only when absolutely necessary, in front of paying customers, confirmed that in essence, something very strange had been happening at the Hall (as well as their growing doubt about Mr Pinchet), for which the Reverend John Sandals was preparing a service of thanksgiving, and PC Relish a comprehensive review of security (with Mr Rummage), not least in preparation for the next year's grand celebrations. And the press had begun to dig. They loved to dig. Like Rompy, like Rick, like Tyro. One of the press headlines read: "Dark deeds at Mystery School". Another, "Burnchester mystery leaves locals aghost".

No-one had been able to contact Mr Strangelblood.

*

Tyro was trying to catch further glimpses of a star fish that Rick had found (Rick was in the water below Jess, urging her to go higher and really take a leap, as he had done). Rick was full of confidence now, and nearly talked as much as the girls, and from time to time did his best to irritate them, with great success. Tom's absence had made Tyro sad, as he had been so helpful to her, and touched her with his kindness. She felt his

269

presence, though she might not admit to it.

"Jess, I'll race you in! Come on Rompy!"

Tyro had caught up with the others. The girls raced as fast as they could, doing their best to avoid the other swimmers, with Rompy between them, head proud and fur stretched back. Rick went to climb the rock for another dive. This time higher than he had been before. He was quite fearless, which frightened Abby, though Dennis admired him for it.

"Well done, Rick!" he shouted at the top of his voice.

Rick's face bobbed up from the surface of the water. He looked in Dennis's direction.

"Time I went back in," Dennis said, and made his way to the water.

The girls had just climbed out and grabbed towels from the beach.

Rompy shook himself wildly.

"Rompy!" cried Abby, "not here!"

"I thought you were going to do some sunbathing," said Clare who was an adept. John was reading a book. He wore a large hat, to the consternation of the children, but not the locals, and of course not the other English or other nationals, because that is what they expected from "Les Anglais!" (They are all mad there).

Tyro watched Dennis swim over to Rick. Together they went back to the rock and got out again, for another dive. Rick followed Dennis to another, even higher point. Dennis dived. Moments later, Rick, jumped, with a huge yell!

John looked up from his book.

*

Some hours later, Abby sat on the veranda, overlooking the same sea. They had just finished supper. Tyro, Jess and Rick were doing the washing up - they certainly had changed. John was making coffee in the kitchen, and doing his best to

270

encourage the children, who were making a mess. Dennis sat next to Abby, ready for a last swim before the sun set, though he enjoyed swimming at night too. Clare had decided to go for a walk along the beach, with Rompy.

"Penny for your thoughts," said Dennis, looking at his sister.

Abby put down the report she was reading and looked at him briefly.

"I was thinking about the Old Hall. Whether it was alright."

"I'm sure it will be. Your friends are very reliable. And there's Bill."

"Not just that. There's Biscuit. He'll miss us. And there's the church next door, full of unresolved mystery."

"I think that was just desperation," said Dennis. "They didn't know where to look or what to look for, so they chose as many places as possible."

"Two places," said Abby. "Have you read the report?"

"Yes, but while I'm on holiday, I am going to do my best to forget it. There's a lot to think about. And a lot to do," he said.

John came out with the coffee, placed it on the table and went to the edge of the veranda. He saw Clare with Rompy and walked out onto the beach to join them. There was laughter from the kitchen.

"Mine's black, no sugar," a voice called.

"OK, Clare."

"Can I read you some bits? Not the whole thing, just bits that interest me. I won't ask you to comment. I want you to know what my interests are."

"Go on," said Dennis.

"Let's see."

Abby picked up the report (it was Mr Baxter's) and flicked through the pages.

"Here. This is what he says, rather what the evidence is, about the church break-ins. 'The two break-ins at St Mary Magdalen and All Saints remain a mystery. Nothing was stolen, except two cloaks. Damage was minor as the attempts had been careful. It is presumed that the Priory or whoever was responsible entered in the hope of finding something that they didn't, presumably connected to the Spearhead, for their own dark purposes (though they claim to have taken something significant from the library at Burnchester Hall). Perhaps they were disturbed before they could complete their search. Apart from the picture itself, which is heavily alarmed and indeed attached to the altar wall, the church wardens and the Reverend John Sandals confirm that nothing of value is kept in either church. We do not believe that the picture was of interest to them.

" 'The climbing spikes on the church towers are particularly curious. They seem to have been fixed into the wall without any breakage to the stonework. What the figures might have wanted from the tower, could only, in our view (that is, the committee's) have been access into the church, or, less likely, a commanding view over the country, as a look-out. Nobody has come up with a  satisfactory explanation for this. The irons remain fixed to the walls of the church, though the attachments have been taken for examination. It seems that the metal itself is also highly unusual. Certainly it is outside our experience.' "

"Perhaps the tower represented some form of conduit for energy," said Dennis.

"What do you mean?" asked Abby.

"We know that the power of the enemy is dependent on secret knowledge and the capacity to develop great energy. Not dissimilar to the energy that seems to have saved us in the Domed Chamber. It's just a phrase that PC Relish mentioned to me. The Reverend Sandals mentioned it to him. He said "some-one or some*thing*" had tried to break into the church."

"But what's that got to do with climbing-irons on the church tower?" asked Abby, sceptically.

Dennis remained quiet, unable to answer. There was a pause before Abby continued. It was as if she was trying to cover up for their inability to come to terms with what might have had happened.

"About Mrs Limpet. This is an extract from the Doctor's report - I know Dr Bartok well. 'Mrs Limpet (of Burnchester Hall) had been referred to us by her GP, as suffering from depression. Following an examination, and extensive interviews (she had been in therapy for some months) she was diagnosed as suffering from a form of hyper-anxiety, in part the outcome of a generally nervous disposition, increased by the recent death of her husband following their divorce, and was placed under observation. She was prescribed powerful tranquilisers. She later admitted herself to us on 26th of July suffering from a form of delayed shock and amnesia, and was retained until the 30th. She has been sent to her mother's house to recover before we can recommend that she returns to work. She has a sister, but she seems not to have seen her for some years. One of the most interesting features of her case is her belief that she was also somebody else, whose name she has not given. She even talks of multiple identities. And experiments on rats.'

"Do you remember what Mr Baxter had said about her? The mask that Tyro and Jess found in the churchyard looked like Jane Fellows, of the Courtly Institute. Ms Fellows had been helping Mr Rummage and Professor Southgate. She is an expert on medieval art, in particular on the triptych at St Mary Magdalen. It turns out that, on enquiring at the Courtly, Mr Baxter was told that they had no-one of that name there. Mr Baxter suggests that the mask they found may have been worn by Mrs Limpet, and that she had been acting as Ms Fellows. They had been beaten at their own game. Other masks were found in her flat."

"You'll be telling us next she was a witch. Have we found the broomstick yet?" Dennis burst out. This was too much even for him. "How can Mrs Limpet have acted as a young attractive researcher, whilst in reality being a frail, middle-aged, and rather plain, nervy teacher, suffering from depression?"

"It does seem unlikely! I feel sorry for her," Abby said. "She is supposed to be a good teacher, when she's well."

"That would explain, or could explain, her double identity. But why?" said Dennis, now curious.

"Suppose she was acting as an agent for the forces that wanted the information about the Spearhead and access to the library. Suppose she had made some sort of pact with them, and had been in contact with them through the tunnels? After all it's her classroom which links to the tunnels, and she was well known for her experiments."

"That might also explain her behaviour to the girls that day. And if she had a breakdown before finally succumbing to those forces, that would have saved her a more terrible fate. It might have acted as a kind of warning."

"Precisely. Her disposition was her weakness and a strength. But why lock up Tyro?

"Let me go on," Abby said. " 'Following the boarding of the Neptune, the boat was found to be completely empty. It was towed back to Southwold and kept under the observation of the coastguard and harbourmaster, who had already given evidence about the man he believed owned the boat. But he could not pin anything on him, except that his movements were unconventional. He was generally courteous. He had no other information. We have found no trace of a person by the name he originally gave - Borlick. How the boat continued for some minutes to power itself is not known, minutes that is after the three figures had still been seen on board from the helicopter. It is speculated that this again has to do with the energy that they were in some way able to release and use, though we do not know how.' - Here is the most interesting bit. - 'Frogmen were sent beneath the vessel to examine the boat, whilst at sea. They found no evidence of an exit or of any method by which they could have left the boat through the hull, though they could have gone overboard. However, we are aware that the boat was some hundred feet above part of the now submerged city of Dunemoor at the time they disappeared. We simply ask whether, far-fetched as it may seem, there is a connection and recommend further research into this possibility. We know Dunemoor was a great religious centre during its heyday in the Middle Ages. Dunemoor is known as the city beneath the sea. It also, incidentally, had a church dedicated to the Knights Templar, with whom the Priory claims a connection.

" 'It has been suggested that the cloaks that the Priory wear are to give the impression of being a genuine religious order (with sword-crosses on their backs). But what other importance the cloaks might have, is not clear. There were other figures. Were any of these orders in league with dark forces?' "

"Given the intolerance of the Church at times in history - that may answer itself. The Inquisition is an example, the religious wars of the sixteenth century another. Go on, Abby," Dennis said.

By this time, John and Clare had returned with Rompy who was now in the kitchen demanding a biscuit. The children had returned and gone out again to the beach. John and Clare sat down, and drank their coffee.

"Stay in sight!" shouted Dennis to the girls and Rick.

Tyro, Jess and Rick, all turned.

"We're only going to look at the water," said Tyro. "Might even read my book!"

She held up a book high. They went on the few metres to the water's edge.

"Tyro's changed," said Abby. "All the children have. We all have." She paused. " 'And the figures themselves. We cannot presume to know what happened in the Domed Chamber, as all interviewees (that's us!) were not conscious, though they were aware of horrendous nightmarish energies and images during this state. Some manifestation of evil is presumed, though other figures seem also to have been involved at least in a secondary capacity (the stranger and the Priory), as well as some of those at the site of the Old Fort on Mr Strangelblood's land, though these may have been spectral and insubstantial. We are concerned as to the after-effects and longer-term effects of these experiences especially on the children, but also on the adults. We wait the evidence of Tom to help us here, though he has not been available yet.' "

"Tom's not like the other children, not being at school very much and with, shall we say, unusual habits," Dennis said. "There's something very odd about that house, which we know so little about. I shall make a point of finding out more as well about Mr Strangelblood. Tom is a mystery. Has anyone been to Mr Strangelblood's house?" he asked.

There was silence.

"Tom's great. He's my son, so to speak," said Abby, "and Tyro loves him," she added. "Besides, there's something pretty odd about Burnchester Hall, in fact the whole place! Let me go on."

She continued to read. " 'What we do know is that energies present in the chamber were of a huge magnitude. The dangers inherent in the situation remain critical. If the enemy/ies are able to return and develop it, especially if they have other help, such as from the power of the Spearhead, or what they claim to have taken already from the library, we may be doomed. For our knowledge is also limited, though it is greater than theirs for now. Evil is at work, though, in our opinion, there is some human involvement also - that of the Priory - and both have been temporarily defeated, or suppressed, or frightened off. But in view of other conjunctions, they are likely to return. For these reasons, we have made significant recommendations for the protection of the school, its children and staff, the building and the resources within its boundaries, not least the secrets still to be found.' "

"I think I'll have some more coffee," said John. "Anyone else?"

Everyone needed more, and so he filled their cups as they watched the children by the water. Rompy was asleep at Abby's feet.

"Let's have a break," said Clare. "We've had enough of all this, haven't we?"

"I guess so," said Abby. "But I'd just like to read what it says about Mr Gruff and then read a bit from Mr Rummage's report."

"Two minutes and then I'm swimming!" said Dennis.

"OK," said Abby. "For the last time then.....for the last time this holidays. Before we go and pack...."

"Have you seen the sunset?" said Clare, reminding them there was another world out there to be explored.

They all looked out over the sea. The sun was indeed just beginning to set over the sea, the tip of its orb just catching the waves, which momentarily held it up, it seemed, before inviting it below. The moment reminded them of the greater world beyond their own, and yet it was, for the moment at least, only with their own that they could deal.

" 'The case of Mr Gruff,' " Abby began. " 'Following admission to  hospital - the report was written by Dr Bartok - on the 13th July, Mr Gruff was placed in intensive care. The severity of his condition suggested that recovery was improbable. Two factors seem to have been involved. Weakness from loss of blood, resulting from an incision in his neck made by a small weapon, we think, though we are not sure. The second, the result of a blow to the head, which was likely to reduce the chance of a return to consciousness. Judging by the initial immobility of his eyes, it is clear that he had suffered from a terrible shock, as well as one or more physical blow and cut.

" 'His sister was informed, but advised that she would be unable to speak to him normally, and that she should only visit in the knowledge that he may not recover fully. This information made her distraught, and she was unable to make the journey, though she phoned almost on an hourly basis, generally in tears. Unfortunately, though understandably, this took up valuable time.

" 'Mr Gruff remained still for several days, during which time, we expected to see his passing.

" 'On the seventh day, there was a slight movement of the eyes, and brain activity increased. That night he moved and began to mutter in his sleep, albeit short incomprehensible phrases. The following day he remained unconscious though his eyes began to move more frequently, as did his body, in starts. By the night some semblance of life was returning. Nurses close to him saw that he had wanted to speak - he seemed to be trying to speak someone's name .... before falling back.'

"I'll shorten it," continued Abby. "He did recover, though it took two weeks, and then it became clear that he had a complete memory loss about the incidents leading up to his 'accident'. He knew that he was due to go on holiday and spoke as if it were imminent. He recalled a walk by the stream, and even a call on his mobile, but not until night-time, during a dream, did he repeat some of the phrases that he heard, which led to his terrible ordeal. On waking, he remembered nothing. It was during his period of dreaming that Dr Bartok recorded his brain activity, and the dreams, using what he calls the Dream Notation Chamber.

" 'After recovery it was decided that he should be sent directly to his sister, which Mr Rummage arranged. Following discussions, Mr Rummage has agreed, assuming he is fit enough, to allow him to return to work, on the condition that he is kept under observation, and that he be given assistance and much fuller support, given the general security situation, until it is clear as to whether he makes a full recovery, though it is felt that he will effectively be retired. Mr Gruff's main concern was for his dog Titan, which seems to have disappeared. He only spoke one word during his unconsciousness: "Master", presumably Headmaster.' "

Tyro imagined Mr Gruff's face in front of her, as it was while he lay, barely alive, on the dark earth.

"Poor Mr Gruff," said Clare. "I hope he will be alright."

"Such things normally have a far greater effect than at first it seems," said John. "We will have to keep a close eye on him."

"I'm concerned about this cut. Who or what made it?" said Dennis.

"Now it's you, Dennis, saying who or what." said John with a little impatience. "How can it be *what*? Our enemies are not things!"

Dennis said nothing. There was another brief pause.

"And now for Mr Rummage's report. As you can imagine, he tries to bring together the elements not covered by Mr Baxter, some of which we know, and place them in the context of the Hall's history and the threats to it and now to all of us. He confirms that nothing of any value was stolen from the library, despite the claims of the cloaked figures, suggesting that the most important documents had been removed to another location - he doesn't mention where - though he also confirms that documents of considerable importance do exist, regarding the training techniques, alchemical texts from which they arise, and those relating to the history of the Church in general and of the tryptych in particular. There could of course be texts of interest within the library still, but these are outside his knowledge, and he would be surprised if the Priory should know about any, unless they had prior information, or indeed help from the inside. He confirms not knowing the whereabouts of the missing fragment, though he believes it is in the grounds of the school. This he, and others, are still researching from the archives in the library and elsewhere.

"As for the Spearhead, all he will say is that myths of this type are likely to be based on fact, but he says nothing about its possible whereabouts, presumably because he doesn't know, which is why the fragment of the picture is so important. The underground systems have barely begun to release their secrets. He also confirms that the MOD has undertaken to help him map the underground systems in full, and that some areas have been used more recently, including the Domed Chamber itself. There have been occasions when threats to national and global security have been extreme, and at these times, all resources have been made available to the authorities in the fight against them. This explains the condition some of it is in, and the lights. He says that he has not made up his mind how best to accommodate developments in the context of school activities, or what impact events and their outcomes will have on the running of the school. All he will say at this stage is that the threat has increased and he will do everything in his power (everything is underlined) to prevent a repeat or a similar event occurring, though he adds, these things are partly outside our control and the signs are not encouraging. They are many people, many groups, irrespective of the Priory (this may only be a smokescreen, he notes) only too willing to serve their own ends. He does not speculate as to the exact nature of the threats - we have had hints - except to add that the powers of darkness can appear anywhere, and we should be vigilant and strong. Regarding the hooded figures who caused such terror during the night in question, he only says that in his view some may be apparitions, others people posing as belonging to a religious order (the Priory), some even perhaps figments of our imagination. Fear, he says, creates images and symbols that arise out of them, which we take to be real. He does say that the so-called stranger, one of the three who escaped by boat, was a manifestation of the real, and took physical form. We also have the captive who was first imprisoned in the Domed Chamber and is now under police guard, being questioned. So far he has provided no information, though we believe it will only be a matter of time before he does. We are dealing with dark psychology and demonic powers, which have the capacity to destroy us, if we let them take hold, as well as to take different forms.

" 'I will have more to say about how we combat these at another time. In passing, I will add that my wife Jenny played a vital role in this on the night of the full moon, with her own powers. That these techniques should be more widely known, I can see now, and I will make it my duty to initiate others into some of them, though such techniques carry great dangers and responsibilities. I will keep you all informed of developments, and hope that you will do the same. Needless to say, all this is confidential to the recipients of the report, which should be destroyed, or returned to me as soon as it has been assimilated.' He then signs his name, and adds a note of thanks to each of us. There is a final note underneath. 'Two pieces of information have recently come to my attention. Our Naval Defence has notified me that during the escape of the Neptune, and at about the time of the disappearance of the figures, a small underwater object was registered close by, by our sonar systems, thought to have been on the seabed, though it was too small to have been at first thought significant. However, it may turn out to be. They have no knowledge of any unfriendly vessel being in the vicinity at the time. The second is that a local farmer, Mr Granger, who I think we all know (if not his son, Luke) found during post-harvest ploughing - how early they start these days - an object, in fact a small casket, of interest, in fields adjacent to the school. He has kept it, and awaits our advice. Please ignore the press reports. There will be more. Another nightmare to be managed I'm afraid, unless we can turn their interest to our advantage. Their imaginations have certainly been working overtime.' "

"It seems like the beginning, rather the end of the beginning," said Clare, with a sigh. "Come on, let's make the most of our last few hours on holiday, and all go for a swim!"

They all looked at her in surprise, but without any question.

Within minutes all of them were in the water, splashing about like children, to the consternation of the young adults.

"OK, if we can't beat them at their own game, we'll beat them at ours," said Tyro. "Attack!"

And attack they did. Four adults, and three young adults, and a dog swimming in the warmth of the evening sun, and enjoying every minute.

*

Biscuit was asleep on Tyro's bed when he heard a familiar scrunching noise on the drive below. Though there had been other people in the house (friends of the family) whilst they had been away, he knew the special sound of that particular car.

He got up and walked along the corridor, and made his way down. He might persuade someone to feed him, again.

Bill was at the back of the house taking cuttings down to the bonfire, which would not be lit until the autumn. He also heard the car, but continued working, as it was familiar. He was pleased that the family were back, bringing a certain chaos - that of family life - to lighten up his steady routine. The summer had been a good one, with the usual amount of rain but with rather more sun, and he had made good progress, tackling some of the larger jobs, like mending the fence in the field at the back of the house. He had had some help, though he generally preferred to work at his own pace.

When the car pulled up, sagging with the weight of all the occupants and the luggage which was on the roof, Abby looked out of the window, to assess how far the familiar sight of home had changed, or had remained the same. The ivy on the wall had been trimmed, but was still sufficiently abundant to be recognisably the house's own. The wysteria was over. Roses were out along the front of the house. A flycatcher clung to the telephone wire that led to the road.

Two other sets of eyes looked out from the back, as a cat appeared through the flap in the side door. With that the girls jumped out and Tyro grabbed Biscuit and gave him a huge hug.

Dennis got out of the driver's seat and opened the door at the back for Clare to get out first, followed by John, and Jess, who had been sitting on both of them in turn on their way back from the airport.

John and Clare stretched and began to unload the luggage from the roof. Dennis helped them and took their pieces to their car which was parked under the trees in front of the house. Rompy galloped off round the garden.

Abby opened the door. She sniffed the air in the kitchen, as if to check it was still friendly, put the kettle on and food into the cat bowl, then went through into the hall to examine the post - most of it bills no doubt. The thought that she would have to sell the house came to her again, though it seemed less important now and she fought it off, just as she fought off the thought of returning to work. She thought of her late husband Jack. A tear ran down her face. She continued to look round. Flowers had been placed everywhere and there was a note from Jane, her friend who had brought her family to stay to look after the place whilst they had been away. There were chocolates.

"How lucky you are to have this house," it said. "We loved it. You deserve it, but it is a lot of work for you. Never get rid of it. Thank you. Love Jane, David, Sam and Emily. PS Hope you had a wonderful time. XXXX. I'll call soon. There are bits of news to tell you, like the arrival of reporters at the door. I soon sent them off, though there were some creeping around the church and, well, I've left all the press cuttings on your desk. Love to Dennis, and of course Tyro. Stay calm. I'll call soon."

John and Clare's car was packed. Abby was outside again, hugging them goodbye. They wanted to get back home, of course.

"It's not as though we're far away," Clare said, as she gave Dennis and Abby a hug and a special hug to Tyro. Then Jess hugged them all with a special hug for Tyro - "It's all your fault," she said in a whisper.

John said goodbye and they were off. Rick had been dropped off to a predictable tirade from Aunt Patrolia, but incredibly happy that he'd been invited. He had had a wonderful time. He blocked out his aunt's pleasantries with plans for his next search, with Tom (and Jess and Tyro). Uncle John had shaken his hand. He was now as determined as anybody.

Dennis said hello to Bill, as he came round to the front of the house, and Abby joined them. After a brief conversation they all went in for tea.

Tyro was with Rompy in the garden.

"Rabbits," she said.

Soon she was in her room. She lay on the bed, in a dream world, not knowing where she really was, yet feeling at home, half-wanting to go away again. She got up as Biscuit entered and jumped onto the bed and purred.

Tyro took a box from under the bed and opened it up. She returned the empty bottle, and the wishing key. How important they had been! The little metal cross-sword she kept about her neck. She took it off and examined it. For the first time she noticed that the handle was jewelled, shining in the warm light. Within the jewels, which were of a wonderful array of colours, she could make out something else. Letters seemed to appear, in a jumble. Almost like a clue. But before she had time to read them they were gone. She put the cross-sword back around her neck. She closed the box not knowing when she would open it again. She felt a little older, more thoughtful, sorry for her selfishness, but also a little angry. She looked at the diary that she had left in full flow before they went away. She put the book which she had been reading on her bed. She stroked Biscuit and then she went downstairs. He mind was full, yet empty too. She knew that this was just the beginning. A new year loomed. Her project!

In the kitchen, everything was back to normal already. Tea

was on the table. The phone rang. It was Jess saying she was back.

"I've got some good news," said Abby.

"My project, Mum! I've got to do my project!"

"Dennis, Uncle Dennis is going to be staying for a while. He's going away for a few days soon but will be back."

"Brill! I like Uncle Dennis, but it's you I love, Mum," she said.

"Can you help me with my project, or can I ask Jess over and we'll do it together?"

Abby gave her a huge hug and said, "I love you too, Tyro, more than anything. I'm going to do everything I can to try to make you happy."

"And by the way Mum, my room's tidy, all the jobs are done. Can I phone Jess and go for a bike ride then? I'll do the project tomorrow, as well as the washing-up."

"I think, for once, darling, I'm going to say no!"

For further details about
DM Productions books please contact:

DM Productions PO Box 218
IP22 1QY
UK

Fax: +44 (0)1359 251092
email: burnchesterhall@yahoo.co.uk

Books can be ordered from any bookshop